THE QUEEN
OF RAIDERS

ALSO BY SARAH KOZLOFF

A Queen in Hiding

THE QUEEN OF RAIDERS

Sarah Kozloff

A Tom Doherty Associates Book

New York

THE QUEEN OF RAIDERS

Copyright © 2020 by Sarah Kozloff

Excerpt from *A Broken Queen* copyright © 2020 by Sarah Kozloff

Edited by Jen Gunnels

A Tor Book
Published by Tom Doherty Associates
120 Broadway
New York, NY 10271

www.tor-forge.com

Tor® is a registered trademark of Macmillan Publishing Group, LLC.

Library of Congress Cataloging-in-Publication Data

Names: Kozloff, Sarah, author.
Title: The queen of raiders / Sarah Kozloff.
Description: First Edition. | New York : A Tom Doherty Associates
    Book, 2020. | Series: The nine realms; 2 | "A Tor Book"—Title page verso.
Identifiers: LCCN 2019042698 (print) | LCCN 2019042699 (ebook) |
    ISBN 9781250168566 (trade paperback) | ISBN 9781250168559 (ebook)
Subjects: GSAFD: Fantasy fiction.
Classification: LCC PS3611.O85 Q46 2020 (print) | LCC PS3611.O85 (ebook) |
    DDC 813/.6—dc23
LC record available at https://lccn.loc.gov/2019042698
LC ebook record available at https://lccn.loc.gov/2019042699

Our books may be purchased in bulk for promotional, educational, or business use. Please contact your local bookseller or the Macmillan Corporate and Premium Sales Department at 1-800-221-7945, extension 5442, or by email at MacmillanSpecialMarkets@macmillan.com.

First Edition: February 2020

Printed in the United States of America

0 9 8 7 6 5 4 3 2 1

To Dawn,
who believed in this the most

Combining Talents

Alone, who firm of feet can stand
'Gainst tugging tide or greedy gale?
Yet braced and plaited hand in hand
Companions can survive travail.

PART
ONE

⁓

Reign of Regent Matwyck,
Year 12–13

Autumn and Winter

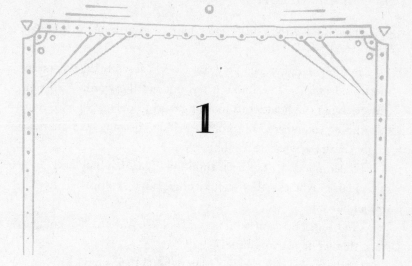

1

Yosta, The Free States

Thalen's Tally Book: 4 Men

Codek tipped his glass upside down to reach the clinging drops of wine while Wareth sucked on a chicken leg, getting the last shreds of meat and flavor. Thalen himself scarfed down the bread crust that Tristo had left behind on his plate. Meanwhile, the fire reached some pockets of sap in the burning logs, causing loud pops.

They had supped in silence in this small sitting room normally saved for visitors too genteel for the common room, and easiest for the innkeep to heat in these empty hours before dawn. A moth-eaten rug held court to a jar of withered flowers, but the diners found even these details homey; they were starved for food and comfort after their desperate trip hiding in the dark, leaky hold of a small fishing vessel, fleeing from now-occupied Sutterdam to the seacoast city of Yosta on the other side of the Free States.

The fire lifted curdles of briny steam from their damp clothes. Faintly, the men heard the clang of the fog bell guiding ships to harbor.

Thalen broke the quiet. "How long do you think we'll be safe here?"

"Best not to dally," said Sergeant Codek, absently tugging on his bushy sideburns. "The innkeep has put out the word. We'll start interviewing candidates this morning, and I doubt we'll have trouble finding volunteers. Our problem will be choosing the right men. Light cavalry is what we're looking for."

Thalen nodded. "I've been thinking. They not only have to be formidable fighters—they should offer extra skills. We'll need a healer, for sure."

"And someone good with horses," added Wareth. "I'm going to miss that white mare of mine."

"And a cook," said Codek. "Men fight on their stomachs."

They all contemplated the carcass of the cold chicken they'd just devoured.

"You know we can't take him with us," Sergeant Codek said as he nodded toward Tristo. After leading them to the Three Coins Inn, cajoling the owner into heating them up a late-night supper, and shoveling in enough to fill his own empty belly, the youth had curled up on a short bench in front of the fire and fallen asleep. With his dirty, small face relaxed on his cushioning hands, Tristo looked even younger than the fifteen summers he claimed.

Wareth, the Vígat cavalry scout, resettled his broken arm in its sling. "Ach. You can't leave him behind. You'd crush him."

"But we're putting together a troop of skilled fighters," Codek argued. "Tristo can't ride and can't shoot; fuck, he's never held a real sword. He'd just be an encumbrance. And it would be murder."

Both Codek and Wareth looked to Thalen for a ruling.

This is how it's going to be, from now on. A thousand decisions: from trivial things to matters of life and death. I didn't ask for this role.

Nevertheless, Thalen found himself the leader of this small group, a group he thought of as "the original survivors." Thalen was the one who had hatched the plan of invading Oromondo with a tiny strike force to terrorize their enemy's native land, in hopes that such an incursion would lift the occupation of the Free States. So he turned his blue eyes on the sleeping street urchin he'd known for about three weeks, since they met amongst the corpses after the battle. Tristo's collarbone had healed quickly, and the lad had not complained once during their voyage.

"We are all taking a suicidal gamble," Thalen said slowly. "Tristo has as much of a right to make his life count as the rest of us. As to what he'd contribute . . . he offers something just as valuable as fighting skills—we've all seen how resourceful he is. If he wants to come, I want him with us."

It might have been a quirk of the fire shadows, but Thalen thought he saw the sleeping boy's mouth twitch up at the corners.

Free Staters had lost many kin in the battle they now self-derisively called "the Rout," and in the days thereafter Oro soldiers had rampaged farther east, burning, looting, enslaving, and raping. The friends Thalen had left behind in Sutterdam had fanned rumors of Thalen's plans. Men who escaped followed these murmurs about Thalen's gamble to Yosta. Free Staters' humiliation, desire for revenge, and willingness to do anything to rid their countries of these conquerors led to a crowd of men jostling outside the Three Coins Inn the next morning.

The first person in line turned out to be the Three Coins' own man-of-all-work.

"I wanna go with ya," he said.

"We need to engage professional soldiers," said Codek. "Have much experience in that line?"

"A bit. Give us a chance, won't ya?"

The four original survivors exchanged glances.

"Just a chance," urged the man. "It's only fair."

"Auditions in the yard out back?" Thalen asked his comrades.

"All right," agreed Codek. He turned to the applicant. "We'll test your fencing and archery."

Thalen watched from a back window. Tristo ran about drawing a rough target on the woodshed wall. In the meantime, Wareth, who couldn't fight with his broken arm, offered the candidate his own sword.

Codek pushed his sleeves out of his way, pulled on the gauntlet tucked through his belt, and slashed the air a few times to warm up. Then he turned to the inn employee.

"Whenever you're ready."

The man grabbed Wareth's sword too tightly. He raised it over his head two-handed—treating it as if it were an axe—and rushed at Codek, yelling, "Aargh!"

Codek stepped forward, his sword blocking the overhead blow at a diagonal. He pushed outward in such a way that his attacker's own momentum carried his sword wildly to the outside, while Codek deftly circled his point to the man's throat. The inn worker scowled with embarrassment.

Tristo broke the uncomfortable moment, coming forward to put his hand on the applicant's sleeve. "It's not fair, you know. Only soldiers like this sergeant get fencing lessons, and they practice for years. You, you've got something more special—you've got guts.

"Maybe you'd do us a service? I need paint for this target here; you're just the person who could help me find some. Where should we look for it?"

Soon the survivors developed a ritual. Thalen and Wareth would conduct an initial interview, and then Tristo would escort the man to the backyard. If he passed Codek's audition, Tristo would then escort the applicant into the kitchen for something to drink. Growing up as a street orphan in Yosta, the boy, with his cropped hair and stunted growth, had developed a disarming facility in getting strangers to confide in him. Within moments they would be telling Tristo their darkest secrets. The "Mead Test," once institutionalized, washed out blackguards and troublemakers. While Thalen wasn't looking for under schoolteachers, he couldn't sign up anyone so difficult he would disrupt their troop.

After a few hours Codek grew bored humiliating farmers and dockworkers. He varied his audition routine by ambushing candidates in the inn's shabby hallways: Wareth would escort them toward the sitting room where Thalen waited at a little table while Codek stood, dagger drawn, hiding in a recess.

On that first afternoon, a muscled bald man wearing a silver earbob in his left ear smelled the ambush from six paces' distance. He drew back with lowered brows and a suspicious smile.

"What are you playing at?" he asked.

Codek stepped out of hiding and held out his hand. "Who might you be?"

"I'm Kambey," said the stranger. "I've been the weapons master of Yosta's Upper Academy for twenty years."

"And why do you want to join up with us?" asked Thalen.

"I just told you," Kambey growled in a gravelly voice. "I've taught hundreds of Yosta's youths. How many did I send to the Rout? How many were slaughtered?"

The original survivors exchanged looks. "Glad to have you with us, Kambey," said Thalen. "Your skills will be invaluable. Could you confer with Sergeant Codek about our arms and equipment? We have no time or money to fashion armor—can we buy it secondhand from Yostamen?"

"I doubt if there's a breastplate left in town," said Kambey. "But we could get gambesons or leathers fashioned. We'll set Tailors Row to work."

In the morning of the second day they found their healer, a middle-aged man named Cerf who had lost his sons in the Rout and his grief-addled wife to suicide. And the original survivors were also gratified by the arrival of three trained Vígat cavalrymen—Fedak, Latof, and Jothile—who had escaped the chaos of the Rout as a group.

These three worried that Thalen would think them cowards for fleeing the battlefield.

"Set your minds at rest," said Thalen. "I was *there*. I cursed the generals for not falling back to regroup. Retreating would have been far wiser and more effective."

"Besides." Codek pointed to the grimy neck drape wrapping about Fedak's throat and Latof's bandaged foot and crutch. "Your scars show you engaged before you fled the field."

"Men, understand this," Thalen said, "I won't ask you to charge the whole Oro army—that's not tactics, that's folly. But we will be setting off to gain Oro attention and pull them back from the Free States, possibly at the cost of our lives. Nobody should harbor hopes of coming home. If you want to rethink volunteering, do it now."

The cavalrymen's faces turned somber, but none of them backed out.

Wareth asked to examine how well their horses had weathered the stress of the battle and the long journey. "Healthy, trained cavalry chargers are almost more valuable than men to us," he reminded them all.

In the afternoon, Kambey, the weapons master, who had taken over the tryouts, reported that a bodyguard to a rich Jutterdam merchant had a powerful arm. Moreover, his father had skill as a swordsmith. Though Tristo warned Thalen that this applicant, a stocky man named Kran, had a hot temper, Thalen decided that his skills made him worth the risk.

After a break, Thalen, returning to the sitting room, was surprised to discover a stranger perched on the edge of his table, carefully cleaning caked dirt off the bottoms of his fine leather boots with the tip of his dagger.

"How did you get in here?" Thalen asked. They had their newest recruits monitoring the line outside.

The interloper was slender, with coiled muscles; he wore a neck drape and beret of shimmering black velvet, with his chestnut hair hanging in a long tail down his back. He motioned upward with his knife. "I jumped from the store next door onto the roof and then came down the stairs."

Wareth overheard this as he entered and emitted a low whistle of appreciation. "Huh. Nimble, I take it. And stealthy."

"I'd prefer to say I'm quiet," said the stranger. "I'm the best scout in the Free States."

"Why didn't you wait in line with the others?" asked Thalen.

"Because," said Kambey in his guttural tones, scowling, "folk might have recognized him."

Thalen turned to Kambey. "You know this man?"

"Well, we haven't spoken before, but I can guess who he is. Gentlemen, may I present Adair, the leader of the Wígat Waylayers."

"At your service," said Adair, with a graceful bow.

"No shit?" said Tristo. "The Waylayers are the most fearsome band in Wígat!"

"In the Free States," Adair corrected him mildly. "We're respected because we always get our haul."

"Modest too, I see," said Thalen.

"I don't see the point of modesty or of waiting in lines," said Adair. "I have certain"—he waved his dagger in a graceful circle—"talents. And I'd like to offer them to your team." He turned to face Thalen, intuiting who made the final decisions.

"But how could we trust you?" asked Kambey.

"I doubt there's much to steal where we're going," said Adair with a dazzling smile.

"No, of course not. But we could be double-crossed," said Thalen.

"Double-crossing is too much trouble. I relieve travelers of their goods because I'm lazy. I make it a point not to injure them—much—because riling up the law causes too much trouble. Besides, consider: if I wanted to turn you in to the Oros, I could tell them you're gathering here."

"I'd run you through!" Kambey growled.

"You could try," Adair replied, with that same smile.

"How about we spar a bit in the yard so I can test your skill with that fancy piece of steel you're carting round your waist?" Kambey challenged him.

When they left the room, Thalen turned to Tristo. "Forget about the mead. This one's too poised. But bring him back to me after the fencing."

"You already know he'll pass the audition?" asked Tristo.

"Without a doubt. No one's that cocky without reason," Thalen replied.

To the clang of metal and the roar of Kambey's curses, Thalen gently turned away an archer with a hacking cough whom Cerf, the healer, had vetoed, saying he doubted the man would survive the winter. Thalen then updated his notebook tally of the list of volunteers, considering their strengths and skills. As of now Wareth was their only trained scout.

Tristo escorted Adair to Thalen with an admiring light in his eyes.

Thalen expected Adair to swagger, but the man who sat in front of him grew serious as he met Thalen's gaze. He kept his body still—he didn't fidget or show nervousness—but Thalen sensed that he could spring into action any second.

"Tell me, *why* do you want to enlist?"

"Just because a man's a thief doesn't mean he can't be a patriot."

"Well, let's think about that," said Thalen. "Patriotism implies caring about your fellow countrymen, while stealing from them implies the opposite."

"Maybe a man wants a second chance?"

"A second chance at what? Be specific," said Thalen.

Adair paused a moment. "Freedom," he answered. "I'd rather be dead than an Oro slave."

Thalen held his glance, wondering if he dared trust him.

"And I have more to offer," said the highwayman. "Do you have a cobbler? You're going to need one. Men travel and fight on their feet, and boots can make all the difference. Before I joined my current 'trade,' I apprenticed to a cobbler." He thrust his feet forward, showing off his elegant boots.

"I hadn't thought about that; you have a point. But how do I know you made these? After all, you could afford to buy the best boots available—or you could have stolen those."

"I sign each pair with my mark." Adair turned down the leather on his calf; Thalen saw the carving of an intricate "A" floating on a sword.

Perhaps the whimsy and conceitedness amused Thalen, or perhaps he felt drawn to someone with artisanal skill. He decided.

"Be sure you gather all the shoemaking tools you need."

Adair stood up, his cocky smile back in place. "'Gather' as in 'purchase,' or 'gather' as in 'collect'?"

"Purchase," Thalen said firmly, and he reached in the box on the table for some coin Hake had already sent.

"Save your money," said Adair. "Come to think of it—catch!" He tossed Thalen a coin purse.

"Ill-gotten gains?" Thalen asked, hefting the weighty leather bag.

"Too proud to use it?" Adair asked.

"Maybe once," Thalen admitted, "but I left a lot of pride on a field outside of Sutterdam."

Adair stopped at the doorway. "By the way, one of the men queuing outside goes by the name Slown. You might be tempted not to take him because he has a hitch in his stride. That would be a mistake. Slown's got the best aim I've ever seen. He can hit a sparrow midflight."

"I'll keep that in mind," said Thalen.

Although the people who lived in Yosta were busy trying to prepare for the upcoming Oro invasion, Yostamen who had been turned down for the expedition still wanted to contribute to their venture. Thalen gratefully accepted their help: he asked volunteers to obtain supplies and to find them a ship. For both the town's safety and his own purposes, he also sent men and women out to relay stations, watching the roads for any sign of Oro approach. Each additional day they remained they gathered essential fighters and supplies, but these preparations would all go for naught if Oros arrived en masse and captured them.

A tailor was pinning a quilted, deep brown gambeson around Thalen when Tristo burst into the shabby sitting room grinning from ear to ear. "One of me mates has shown up!" The boy's infectious delight pulled the other three survivors to the long kitchen table, where his ravenous friend now sat catching up on missed meals.

Thalen managed to turn his gasp into a cough: Tristo's "mate" turned out to be a woman of about thirty summers. She wore men's clothes, including a leather weskit, and wore her hair cut above her ears. She was in the midst of scarfing down cubes of venison on the point of a wicked-looking dagger with a thick hand grasp. She nodded but kept chewing.

Codek said to Tristo, "Lad, I am happy you're reunited with a mate from happier times. That'll be important to all of us. We're pleased to meet your friend. But we can't take any women on this expedition. She wouldn't be strong enough. No offense, ma'am."

Tristo chortled. The woman swallowed her mouthful and wiped her lips on the back of her hand. She stood up; Thalen could see her muscled shoulders and thighs. She walked over to Wareth, who was younger and taller than Codek, holding out a rough hand.

Wareth smiled his broad smile, which lit up his whole friendly face, and held out his hand too. "Ma'am, pleased to make—" In a blink she threw Wareth down to the ground on his back, though she took care not to jostle his splinted arm. Her dagger glittered at his throat.

"My pleasure, horse soldier," she rasped. "Name's Ooma." She threw the knife in the air so that it twirled end over end, and then she snatched it out of the air by its handle. She held her hand out to Wareth to pull him up. As he regained his feet, she pivoted to face Codek; before he could react her dagger had snagged a patch of his bushy sideburn.

Tristo, grinning, said, "Ooma's awful clever with her knives."

"What about swords or bows?" asked Wareth.

"Haven't had much use for them in the back alleys of Yosta," she said. "Now, my knives . . ." She advanced toward Thalen.

Thalen held his hands in front of himself. "Peace, Ooma. You have proved your point. I am such a poor fighter that besting me would be no sport."

"What good are *you* to the expedition then?" she asked. "I recognize the military man's experience and straight talk, and this tall fella's got the bowlegs of cavalry. Why should *we* take *you*?"

"Good question, Ooma. I ask myself that five times a day."

"And what do you answer yourself?" she asked in her raspy voice, not rudely, but not backing down.

"I thought up this plan, and I am going to make it succeed."

Codek put in sternly, "Thalen is our commander."

"Huh!" she answered, reserving judgment, and sat back to her meat and bread.

Tristo said to his new comrades, "Ooma led our gang here. She kept us all alive. Taught us all everything we know. Ooma, how many Oros did you gut in the Rout?"

"Didn't gut a one, lad. Had to go for arteries in the leg or neck 'cause of that rat-fuckin' armor. Bloody work."

With more respect in his tone, Codek persisted. "Still, having a woman around could bring all kinds of trouble."

Ooma grinned. "I don't lie with men, old fella. Men around me usually catch on. And if they stay mule-stupid, my dagger teaches a lesson."

So Ooma joined the group. And despite Codek's reservations,

she was not going to be the only woman after all. They chose a husband and wife, Moorvale and Maribel, as their cooks after asking them to prepare a midmeal out of restricted supplies for the partially assembled troop.

"The grub is great," said Codek through a mouthful of food. "But ma'am, I wonder if you're strong enough for the rigors of this venture."

"Call me 'Cookie,'" she said. "Let me show you something." Much to their horror this middle-aged woman put her foot on the bench on the side of the kitchen table and started to pull up her skirt. "Hey, handsome," she said to Adair, "squeeze them muscles in my legs."

"Rock solid, Madam Cookie," Adair pronounced.

"I'd like to see *you* lot work on your feet from morning to dusk and cart bags of flour and buckets of water." She grew angrier as she spoke. "*Strong enough!* I'll show you *strong enough!* Wait till you see my muscles!" And she started to unlace her tapestry bodice.

"No, no," said Thalen hastily. "We'll take your word for it."

But Cookie's dander kept rising. "Strong enough! Why're *you pups* doubting me? *He's* the one"—she pointed to her husband—"who complains he needs to sit! He's the one you should be misgiving!"

"Calm down, will ya," said Moorvale. "True, I have my aches and pains. Sometimes in the middle of the day I sit for a spell and work on my sideline trade—a trade I wager might interest you." He crossed to the side of the kitchen, where he had parked a large, lumpy burlap bag before they started to cook. He brought it to Kambey.

The instant Kambey grabbed the covered-up contents he said, "A crossbow. Quarrels."

"Let's see," said Codek.

Kambey drew out the items and passed them around. Slown whistled over the workmanship as Kran sampled the pull of the bow.

"An atilliator!" said Thalen. "Were we really so idiotic as to think to set off without one! Moorvale, I want to talk to you about the repeating crossbows from the Rout. I've been wondering if we enlarged the feed slot—"

"I won't go without my wife," Moorvale interrupted. "Not only does she bake a mean biscuit, but she's a crack shot."

"And I won't go without my lardwit of a husband," said Cookie. "Gonna take death's dirty breath to part us."

Codek, stubborn, looked at Thalen. Thalen grinned and held up his hands in mock helplessness.

"Well then," said Cookie. "Now that's settled, who's for more biscuits and gravy?"

Many people raised up their plates.

Gathering sufficient healthy horses trained for fighting became Thalen's biggest concern. In this, the group was aided by the Oros' brutality. The stable master of one of Fígat's cavalry stations, a man named Gentain, had had daughters of eleven and twelve summers. When Oros molested his girls and then slashed their throats, Gentain vowed they would not lay their hands on the last thing left to him of value—the horses still in his stable. In the dregs of night he snuck up behind each Oro guard and strangled him with his daughter's shawl. His twelve well-trained coursers became the backbone of their string.

On the fifth morning, the original survivors chose four more cavalrymen (friends from a Jígat regiment), an archer, and a man who—though slow-witted—wielded a six-foot quarterstaff of red oak with fluid strength.

Rumor reached them that the Oros had moved en masse into Jutterdam. The Three Coins innkeep told his female servants to pack up and flee.

On the afternoon of their sixth day Wareth interrupted Thalen's intense study of maps with a little whistle. "Here's a gentleman says he knows you from before."

Quinith, Thalen's close friend from the Scoláiríum, entered the sitting room. Soiled bandages festooned his head, and his cream silk coat hung stiff with mud and sweat.

"Quinith!" Thalen embraced his friend. "What happened to you? Sit, sit. Drink a glass of wine."

"Here's to freedom." Quinith raised the glass, then drank it down without stopping to breathe. "Ah, Thalen! I'm so glad to see you. I was so afraid I'd miss you, I rode like a madman."

"Have another drink. Do you know anything about the Oros' movements?"

"No, I skirted towns and came overland.

"As to what happened . . ." Quinith set down his glass. "Well, from the Scoláiríum, I traveled to my family's manse. I helped my mother and my young sisters hide with a woodsman's family and then returned to guard the estate with my father. A small squad of Oros showed up after two weeks. We would have stood by if they'd just pillaged food or horses, but they bludgeoned our butler and my father intervened, which meant I had to jump in too. In the scuffle the Oros went down, but my father did as well."

"I'm sorry, Quinith," said Thalen. "And that's when you took that blow on your head? Were you knocked cold? We have a healer—let's get Cerf to look at it and change the bandage."

Quinith waved away Thalen's concern for his health. "Everyone has lost kin, and in truth, I did not harbor much love for my sire," he said with somewhat elaborate casualness. "I came as soon as whispers reached me where you were."

Thalen felt torn. "Quinith, you are a feast for my eyes, yet we can't take you with us. We have as many fighters as we can engage. Food and supplies keep me awake at night."

"You mistake me, Thalen. I know I am not fit to join your band. Aye, at the Scoláiríum I taught you basic fencing, but I'm hardly a warrior. After my little engagement I puked and shook for days. Obviously, I am not cut out to be a fighter; I belong at the Scoláiríum singing about real heroes. But I came to offer the talents I do have—you know I'm a terrific manager. Tell me how I can help."

So, over the sounds of Kambey drilling the recruits in the inn's cobbled courtyard, Thalen and Quinith conferred all afternoon about sneaking into Melladrin, setting up a long supply chain, and communicating from the field to suppliers. Quinith advised creating a quartermaster base in the Green Isles out of the reach of the Oros; Thalen begged Quinith to find a way to smuggle Hake to that base to make use of Sutterdam Pottery's contacts (and to get his injured brother out of the occupied city).

As the shadows lengthened, Thalen inquired, "What tidings of Gustie?"

Quinith looked away at the mention of his lover from the Scoláiríum. "Ill rumors, but naught confirmed." He changed the subject by asking, "What do you call your group?"

"I hadn't given it a thought."

"You need to have a name."

Thalen mused aloud, "Well, let's think about that. We're not 'soldiers,' really; but I don't plan to plunder, like highwaymen. 'Trespassers'? 'Invaders'?"

"Hmmm. 'Raiders,'" said Quinith definitively.

"Fine. But why?"

"Two syllables always works better in songs," said Quinith.

Thalen shook his head, bemused that even under these circumstances Quinith fell back on his expertise.

Quinith continued, "Do you have a good sword for this venture?"

"Good steel is wasted on me."

Quinith drew his own weapon out of a leather scabbard embellished with gold and silver: the rapier had gold-and-silver filigree on the pommel and intricate handguard, and the blade glistened. He offered it to Thalen with formal grace, the handle resting across his waist-high hands.

"If you will take my grandfather's sword, then I will feel part of the vengeance."

Thalen tried to refuse, but Quinith wouldn't listen.

He spoke over Thalen's protestations. "And I have another weapon I insist you accept. Follow me." Quinith led Thalen out to the street. There, next to his mud-splashed palfrey, lay an even dirtier wolfhound, with amber eyes and a lolling tongue.

"This hound belonged to my father. When we fought the Oros, he chalked up more kills than either of us. He's invaluable."

"No, Quinith, thank you, but no. I don't want to take a dog." Thalen was peeved. "If he's that vicious, how can I control him?"

Quinith would not accept his refusal. He claimed that if Thalen became the one who fed the dog, the wolfhound would transfer its loyalty to him. When Sergeant Codek joined the argument he—traitorously—agreed with Quinith. "Them wolfhounds are worth gold in a scrap; we'd be muckwits not to take him."

Thalen stared at the wiry gray dog with annoyance and tried to marshal another argument.

Quinith said, "The dog answers to 'Maki'; the sword, my grandfather named—"

But at that moment two Yostamen came galloping down the street, their horses foaming and trembling.

"A company of Oros approaches!" one shouted.

"Where are they?" Thalen shouted back.

"On the Coast Road traveling north from Jutterdam. When we first spotted 'em, they was maybe two days away; but it's taken us relays at least half a day to get here."

Thalen took a breath, raised the glistening rapier in the air to capture everyone's attention, and began issuing orders.

Some hours before dawn, the wolfhound, Maki, trotted alongside Thalen's Raiders as they hastily loaded their ship. Thalen had twenty-six horses and twenty-two men.

We've got two scouts, Adair and Wareth; three dedicated archers,

Slown, Cookie, and Yislan; two pros at hand-to-hand, Weddle and Ooma. Swordsmen aplenty. Kambey and Kran may be the strongest, but Britmank and Jothile are the swiftest.

Divide the troop another way—I've got two cooks, a healer, a horse master, a cobbler, an atilliator, a swordsmith, a weapons master, and a sergeant. And a brace of quartermasters.

What I don't have is a wisp of a plan of getting these Raiders into Oromondo to let loose the kind of havoc we need to raise.

The Oros are just about to set upon Yosta to ransack, murder, and rape. It feels wrong to flee . . . unless this wild gamble is the only way of saving my country.

Tally: 4 Original Survivors + 18 Recruits = 22 Raiders

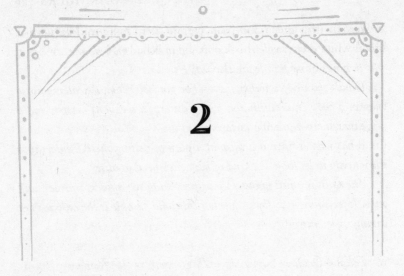

2

Slagos, The Green Isles

Gardener was dividing ferns in a shaded bed in the rear of his plot when he sensed the Nargis heir arrive. Laboriously, he pushed himself off the ground, leaving his tools half-buried in the dirt. He stood still a long moment, checking that he had not made a mistake, observing her disembark with his inner vision.

He washed his hands in a nearby bucket of rainwater and then strode to the bed of blue orchids, hearing the bees buzzing around the open blooms. With practiced motions he harvested a large armful of blooms with long stems; these he strung together to make a lei. He walked to the Spirit's statue in the courtyard and hung the offering around its neck. Then he said a prayer of thanksgiving. He had hoped this might come to pass, but Mìngyùn's threads swirled without order during these troubled times.

When he finished his prayer he returned to his work, concentrating on tidying the garden and the courtyard. Sometime soon she would visit, and he wanted to show the grounds off to their fullest advantage.

. . .

A woman in a green-and-pink caftan tied at the middle with a broad white waist sash whistled as she polished tables.

"A good morn to you, darlin'," she said to Wren.

"And to you. I've hardly eaten for weeks. What do you recommend?"

The round-faced, big-chested woman wore her wavy brown hair untidily piled on top of her head. She paused to regard Wren with measuring eyes.

"First voyage, eh? You do look peaked. Perch yourself hereabouts and I'll set you to rights in a tick." She called words Wren couldn't distinguish to figures working behind her in the kitchen area.

Wren sat at the long, wooden counter in the low-ceilinged, whitewashed room. The woman poured her a mug of a cocoa-cinnamon-chili tisane and gave her a basket of bread made from grains Wren had never tasted before; as the server moved about, her loose sleeves showed that she had a green vine tattooed around her wrist. Wren drank thirstily and enjoyed the sun slanting in through the windows, warming her kinked shoulders and making the morning dust motes shimmer.

She had been ill throughout her voyage to Slagos from Gulltown: her throat and head pained her, she developed a cough, and her stomach heaved. Her roommates in the women's stateroom made themselves a nuisance with their chatter and whining. She caught one of the children pawing through her belongings and prying about her hair tonic. Or perhaps her fellow passengers got on her nerves because she felt so sickly? But worst of all her troubles aboard the ship, she discovered that when she went out on deck to breathe clean air and get away from her roommates, the sailors peppered her with rude comments. When she sought out the shipmaster to complain, he pinched her bottom and laughed at her.

The brazen idiot! When I'm queen I'll—I'll do something unpleasant to him.

Wren keenly felt the loss of all the safety and care she had taken for granted in Wyndton, rustic as that village might be. There, under Stahlia and Wilim's protection, she had been sheltered from want, rudeness, strangers, or loneliness. On the *Island Flyer*, abruptly thrust into a rougher environment alone, she felt baffled, then frightened, then furious.

Disembarking in Slagos came as a welcome relief. As soon as her feet hit solid soil her empty stomach growled, but she walked through the island city awhile, looking at the whitewashed buildings of clay brick, each festooned with flower boxes that, though it was winter, overflowed from every window in this moderate climate. Pale yellow butterflies flew in singles, doubles, or swarms.

Then she chose a tavern, the Blue Parrot, several streets away from the wharf. It had a cage outside filled with parrots (though none were blue). They squawked loudly upon seeing her; Wren heard, "*Majesty, Majesty, Majesty.*" And two friendly terriers darted out from a shadowed passageway to wag their tails and get acquainted.

The tavernkeep broke in on her thoughts as she poured Wren more hot, spicy liquid. "Getting you some eggs first, and then soup, little darlin'."

Wren had felt so low that this stranger taking care of her soothed her as much as the food.

"What's your name?" Wren said.

The woman stopped her work and leaned on her arms across the counter. "I'm Zillie."

"Is this your place?"

"Aye. I bought it from the previous owner eight years ago. Islanders don't like to boast, but I serve up the best meals in Slagos. Darlin', you aren't traveling on your lonesome, are you?"

"Aye." Wren couldn't help but reach out to this kindly stranger. "May I ask you a question?"

"How can I help you?"

"When a woman travels alone," said Wren, "how does she keep

men from bothering her? I have a knife and know how to use it, but I judge that would lead to trouble."

"Aye, keep your knife hidden unless a man lays his hands on you. But you have another sharp weapon—your tongue. When I first opened this place, didn't I have a time! But I've learned when to laugh at a man, when to cuss him out, when to bring him down, and when to pretend he ain't in the room at all. Just takes a bit of practice."

The owner straightened up. "Your eggs must be ready, darlin'; let me fetch them."

Wren ate the eggs and herbs, savoring their warm, soft texture. The Blue Parrot started to fill up for the midday meal. The tavern-keep next brought her a steaming bowl of soup made with shellfish. Wren scarfed it down with more bread and started to feel much stronger. As she paid for her fare she asked Zillie, "Do you know where I can get lodgings?"

"Head up the street a few more blocks away from the harbor," she said, gesturing with her chin because her hands were full of trenchers. "When you come to the Garden of Vertia, turn left. A number of clean, respectable houses back that way rent to travelers. Good fortune, darlin'."

Wren thanked her and followed her instructions. She was not sure she would recognize a Garden of Vertia, but no one could mistake it. Small stones arranged in elaborate, swirling patterns marked the approach to an open gateway. In the middle of the walled courtyard stood a figure taller than the tallest person. It was wrought from green marble, vines, and moss so cunningly inter-mixed that one would be hard-pressed to point to exactly where the living material left off and the stone began. The figure had no legs, or at least the leg portion of its body had been replaced by twisting vines. Its gender was indecipherable because it had male attributes from the waist down, but female from the waist up. It held a basket of stone and living fruit pressed against its torso, and the other hand offered a cupful of liquid. The long hair was either marble carved to look like or actually made up of greenery. A necklace of interlaced orchids hung around its neck.

Wren gazed at the courtyard with wonder for a few moments and then reluctantly pulled herself away to journey farther down the road, surveying the houses. Several posted hand-lettered signs reading "Lodgings." She chose a house that appealed to her and knocked on the door. The elderly householders offered her three different rooms; the cheapest, which she selected, was situated in the back of the building.

The landlords asked for the first week's payment in advance; Wren fished out the coins she had brought from Wyndton. Like Zillie, the landlords were practiced in the exchange of foreign silvers and coppers against their own currency. They left her in possession of her tiny but private room.

Wren opened the window shutters onto a small garden, not at all disappointed to discover that she had no view of the sea. She placed her bag on the only stool and hung her cloak and hat on the only hooks. A waist-high shelf held a ewer and a basin. The bed was an unfamiliar design to her: the frame sat only a hand's length above the floor, with the cross lashes made out of a springy reed. The mattress material was white linen; whatever was stuffed inside smelled sweet. She lay down on the bed to try its comfort and—full of good food and feeling safe for the first time in weeks—fell asleep.

In the midafternoon when she awoke, Wren took stock of her situation. Wilim's purse had gotten lighter; she needed to find a way of earning her keep and saving money. If she was to buy passage to Liddlecup, the capital of Lortherrod, where she had distant kin, she needed to find work.

After freshening up, she gathered her bravery to leave her sanctuary for a further look at the harbor city. The afternoon had waned, as had the sun's ferocity. Wren noticed that most of the citizens, men and women, wore loose gowns like Zillie's; the men tied theirs with a broad green sash at the middle, which held a knife scabbard, but no one strolled around armed with swords. Everyone also wore hats of braided straw they called "toppies" against the glare. Wren located an apothecary shop for when she ran out of the hair tonic that turned her blue hair a dull and lifeless brown. She also spied a market of open-air vendors selling secondhand clothes and fabrics; she walked the aisles, coveting the unpatched stockings, and wondered if she would ever be able to buy changes.

As she strolled the streets she paused to read all the tacked-up broadsheets she could find. Since Slagos was a major port, it received news from many lands. The Oros had solidified their hold over all of the Free States. King Rikil of Lortherrod had called for an alliance of Powers against Oromondo, but Weirandale had remained unaccountably silent to this plea.

Wren grew hungry again but needed to avoid the expense of a tavern. In a cobbled triangle between buildings she saw a stand selling skewers of roasted meat that, judging by the number of sailors clustered around, offered good quality and fair prices.

She started back to her tiny room to eat, but ended up pausing once more at the gate of Vertia's Courtyard. With tall trees dappling the fading light, the statue's grace created an air of serenity.

As the island sunset colored the wide sky with pinks and oranges, an older man with a heavily seamed, coffee-brown face, wearing a simple green robe and a broken straw hat, came to sweep the courtyard and remove the now-withered floral necklace. He nodded and smiled at Wren.

"I am a visitor, not a worshipper. Do I intrude?" she asked.

"The Garden of Vertia welcomes all. Will you be staying in Slagos a spell?"

"I don't really know. I'm not eager to get back on board a ship!"

A yellow-and-green parrot perched nearby repeated with perfect mimicry: "Board a ship. *Squawk!* Board a ship."

"The sailing life doesn't suit everyone. I too prefer my feet on steady ground. Islanders are clever with our boats, but unlike the Lorthers we do not worship the sea. We worship the Spirit of Growth, who gives us food, wine, beauty, wood, thatch, and shade. But more than these gifts—Vertia is the Spirit of the Life Force, of the desire to live and multiply."

"How long have you tended this garden?" Wren asked.

"Oh, many years. Come. I should like my orchids to meet you."

Wren followed him through a stone portico. A flight of nine wide stone stairs led down to a large walled garden of artfully arranged and meticulously maintained fruit trees and flowers.

"How do you keep it so perfect?" Wren asked.

"I treat it with the best food for the soil," he chuckled. "A gardener's sweat."

"This is truly a tribute to Vertia," marveled Wren. Her new acquaintance beamed at her praise. It was only as he reached up to pick some ripe fruit for her fastbreak and she saw him feeling about on the branch that she realized his milky gray eyes were sightless.

"Thank you for this. Pray, what should I call you?"

"'Gardener' is the name I prefer now."

Wren gathered a little more courage. "Gardener, might you have counsel for me? I need to find work here, but I can't imagine what kind of job would suit me or what I'd be fit for."

"Gardeners love being asked for advice, for we grow very sage." He smiled at his own pun. "Come, come. A young woman such as you must have many skills."

"I do have a knack with animals," Wren admitted.

"There," he said, with satisfaction. "Many Slagos businesses use horse carts to get their wares down to the docks. Perchance a concern needs help with its horses?"

"Would anyone take me, a stranger, on without a vouchsafe?"

"I will vouch for you," said he.

"How could you do that? You hardly know me! You don't even know my name."

"*Squawk!* Know my name. Know my name."

"Ah, 'tis not true. I see you clearly. As for names, well, they are easily adopted and just as easily shed when they no longer fit. I myself have worn several in my thyme." He paused to make sure she had heard the pun. "Tell anyone that Gardener will vouch for you. I think that will assuage any doubts."

"I am indeed in your debt." For her "Wren" persona in Wyndton she had adopted a meek, high voice; this evening she sounded older and more confident.

"No. If you feel indebted, 'tis to Vertia. The Spirit drew you here. I am just its Gardener. Feel free, my dear, to come back anytime. The peacefulness or the fruit or any help I can provide: all are yours for the taking.

"But let me offer you a word of caution: whatever you do, stay away from the Green Isles Bank. As anyone would tell you, Slagos attracts a number of people who are paid to further the interests of other lands. Some of these people might be watching for a foreign young woman such as yourself."

"*Squawk!* Stay away, stay away, stay away. *Squawk.*"

Wren felt a chill to learn that this island teemed with spies as eager to find her out as her pursuers back in Androvale.

Gardener continued, "Rumor even reached me that the bank director is in the pay of the Lord Regent of Weirandale, and I don't trust his people either. They seek a young woman with special Talents."

And the old man winked at her, confirming Wren's guess that somehow he recognized her.

In the morning, Wren ate her unfamiliar piece of tropical fruit (she liked the taste but struggled with the seeds) with the bread and a cup of tisane offered by her generous landlady. Then she allowed her nose to lead her to a nearby concentration of horses, which turned out to be Dock Street Haulers and Livery, a large stable of cart horses fronted by a manure-strewn yard that at the moment presented a tangle of wagons, drays, chaos, and shouting.

A short, rotund man in silk breeches and pointed shoes and gartered stockings much too fine for his surroundings provided most of the shouting: "What!? Ain't you got those beasts hitched yet? What's the matter with you!? Those ships won't wait on you muckwits!"

And the workers rushed around cursing and yanking at the horses, who balked at the noise and tense atmosphere.

"Here, let me help," Wren said to the stable lads. "You've got the wrong one on the wrong side." And she moved the gray horse to the left side and the dappled one to the right, which is where they felt more comfortable. Then they stood still and allowed the boy to collar and harness them up. Meanwhile, Wren got two other teams sorted out: the workers had been trying to hitch together two horses who chafed one another, so she swapped the two mares and told all the horses to settle down and cooperate. She promised the white-socked gelding plagued by a skin rash that she would doctor him when he returned, but he needed to bear up for a little while. More teams trundled off. Then she got the last horses out of their stalls and held their heads while the lads collared and harnessed them and the final teams rolled away. Wren grabbed a pitchfork and started to muck out the none-too-clean stalls.

Stillness settled over the yard. The red-faced owner who had been doing most of the shouting studied Wren with his mouth open. "You there! Come here."

Wren walked up the steps to the office porch where the man stood. "What do you mean, coming in here and shifting all the horses around?"

The quiet, retiring personality she had put on for many years was not going to help her now. Actually, she realized, it had not been working since she left Wyndton.

"Your workers do not know their own stock. If you want the

horses to perform well for you, you have to treat them better and understand them. And all your carrying on is just making the yard more troubled."

The owner glared at her. "You've got a lot of sass, coming in here—"

"And showing you how a competent stable manager could help you make your deliveries on time. I'm looking for a job. If you don't hire me, I'll wager I could find a competitor down the road, and with my help his stable will win away all the customers who are fed up with your tardiness and excuses."

Wren boldly turned her back and started to walk away. "Hey you, wait!" shouted the owner. "You're hired. Starting now. We have another group of deliveries for the next tide."

"How much do you pay your current stable manager?"

"A silver grape a week."

Wren knew nothing about Green Isles currency, but on instinct she snorted and again started to walk away.

"Hey you! Wait!" shouted the owner.

"You'll pay me double that to start and triple after you see how much money I save you. Tell your lads I'm the stable manager and they have to follow my instructions."

"They aren't going to like taking orders from a wisp of a gal dressed so strange."

"That's why you have to tell them. You can shout loudly enough. I've heard your lungs."

He glared at her again but turned his attention to his workers. "Listen up, lackwits. This here is your new stable master. Jocko, you mud rump, you're fired. Every one of you is to take orders from her. Hey you, what's your name?"

"Kestrel," she answered.

3

Wyndton

When she received her mother's message about Wren running off with a sailor lover, Percia left Gulltown and returned to the Wyndton cottage. Her family needed her, and Percia felt too unsettled to dance. Although the dancing master complained about her leaving the troupe in the lurch, the Gulltown Dancers would just have to handle their performances to celebrate Harvest Fest and Winter Solstice Fest without her. Truth be told, Percia had grown tired of the master's demands, tired of constantly being sore, and very tired of the other girls' backbiting and jealousy about her featured roles. So in some regards, this summons home arrived at an opportune time.

In Wyndton, Percia's anger warred with worry and grief. No one had had an inkling that Wren had been sneaking off with a sailor; Percia wracked her memory but could not piece together even the slightest hints or clues. Percia felt betrayed: why wouldn't her sister have confided in her? Tilim acted fretful; her mother moved around in a distracted daze.

Yet for all their agitation, it was her father who concerned Percia the most. Papa kept running his hands through his hair, and often he paused midstride, as if forgetting what he had been about to do. Sometimes he refused to talk about Wren at all and forbade any family discussion about her abandonment, and other times he spouted rubbish such as, "She had to fulfill her destiny."

Over the course of a few weeks her mother and Tilim outwardly adjusted to Wren's desertion. Mother went back to her tapestry because she couldn't afford to lose time; Tilim tried to concentrate on his schooling. Percia took over the daily chores Wren used to handle. In the evenings she tried to cheer up her family by performing simple jigs with Tilim while her mother sang familiar tunes.

But Papa's state of mind grew more worrisome instead of better. He pushed away his plate at mealtimes. In the middle of the night Percia heard him pacing back and forth downstairs muttering to himself. Whenever he did ride out on his circuits, his first words on his arrival were to ask if anything untoward had happened during the day. Percia wondered if he expected Wren to return as mysteriously as she had disappeared.

Once he frightened Percia by mumbling, "What if you can't trust your own memories? Your own mind?" Another night he grabbed her mother by the upper arms and asked her hoarsely, "How much danger stalks us still?"

"Wilim, Wilim," her mother had answered, "what do you fear? What's gotten into you? This can't just be about Wren leaving us."

But Papa had nothing to say in reply; he merely hugged her so tightly she had to struggle to disentangle herself.

Percia and her mother tried to talk to him about what ailed him, but he wouldn't respond. They took him to see Sister Nellsapeta (who shook her head sadly), and even the healer, Goddard, who also could do nothing for Wilim but who charged them a silver tear regardless. "Something's broken in his mind," Goddard said, stating the obvious. "Feed him beef broth, keep him busy, and hope that time will cure him."

One day Duke Naven sent word that he wanted Wilim to

attend him at the manor house. Her father embraced each of them and rode off on Syrup. When suppertime came he had not returned, but this had happened before; occasionally roads or bridges were washed out or the duke kept him late or sent him on a commission. Percia and her mother waited up for him, but after moonrise Mother said they should go to bed; Papa must have spent the night at the duke's estate.

The next morn, when Percia came down to wake up the fire, she saw Syrup standing alone in the yard still saddled and bridled. His reins were tightly wrapped around a length of broken-off tree branch that he dragged about like an unwanted companion.

"Mother!" Percia shrieked in alarm.

Stahlia came running, and they both went outside to look at Syrup.

Mother could no longer keep her anxiety hidden. "When your papa gets home I think I will take that famous hazel switch to him for fretting us this way. You see to Syrup; I think I'm gonna ride by Sergeant Rooks's on Barley and see if he can find Wilim."

Percia wished her mother had allotted the tasks the other way round, but she groomed and fed Syrup, made fastbreak, and then walked Tilim part of the way to school, just so as not to be alone with her thoughts.

Of course Papa'll be back when I get home. I've been gone so long.

But the house sat still and empty, with only the stupid chickens clucking about.

I'll do the washing up and start heating the water for the laundry; Papa'll come walking in with a long story, and later we'll all laugh about this.

Yet Percia had gotten the clothes washed and run them through the mangle before she heard hoofbeats. And then it was only her mother returning. She looked hopefully at Percia, and Percia had to shake her head.

Mother said, "Sergeant Rooks is going to try to follow his tracks toward the duke's manor and back again. Just in case of highway-men or such. . . . Baki, you should have gone with him yesterday." Baki, the ugly mutt Wren had insisted on adopting, blinked at the note of reproach in her voice and nibbled an imaginary itch on his back hip.

Percia laid out several cold boiled potatoes, and they sat at the scrubbed table for a quick midmeal. At first they tried to think of innocent explanations for why Papa had been gone this long, had not sent word, and Syrup had broken away home; these stories be-came so improbable that they moved on to suppositions about Wilim being a little bit hurt, say, from a fall that broke his ankle. Rooks would find him, fetch him home, and someday they would laugh over all this worry.

Percia went out to hang up the wash in the autumn wind, which made the clothes dance. She kept thinking she heard a noise and would run down to the end of their lane to see if anyone approached, but the road offered only the scrape of crispy leaves. Eventually mid-afternoon crept up; Tilim would be on his way home.

"Take Barley," Mother said, "and ride Tilim over to his friend Kipper's farm—ask the missus if she'll keep Tilim till this is settled. I'm sure she'll agree."

Percia grabbed the activity gratefully. On the way back she slipped into the Church of the Waters and said prayers for her father and her family.

He'll be home by now!

But the only person at their house was Mother, and her face when she came running out at the sound of Barley's clomp smote Percia's heart.

As daylight slipped away, Mother and Percia sat in the creeping darkness, holding each other's hands across the table. Her mother grabbed so tightly that it hurt, but Percia would not complain.

Finally, Baki barked and they heard the sound of a horse's hooves striking the packed dirt of their yard. Mother threw open the door as Percia picked up the lantern from the table. In the lantern's flicker they saw Rooks ride into the yard with a form wrapped in a blanket tied on the back of his horse. Stahlia tried to rush out to it, but Percia grabbed her around the waist. Rooks came in the cottage door. He took off his cap and held it awkwardly in his hands.

Then he took hold of both of Mother's hands, his cap—now forgotten—falling on the floor. "He's gone, missus." She nodded but did not speak. "I found him in Anders Wood." She nodded again.

"Highwaymen?" Percia asked as the lantern trembled in her grasp, sending unruly shadows around the walls.

Rooks shook his head, and Mama, staring in his eyes, mirrored his action, shaking hers. "A rope," Rooks replied.

"I don't understand," Percia whispered.

Rooks's gaze remained locked on Stahlia's eyes. "I'm awful sorry, missus. He hung himself. I had to cut him down." Her mother uttered a cry and slipped to her knees. Percia threw herself to the floor, hugging her mother to her.

"My Lem is on his way," Rooks mumbled. "He's gone to fetch the villagers." Though tears streamed down her face, Percia nodded her head to show that she had heard him, and she rubbed her mother's back while Stahlia rocked back and forth on her knees, her knuckles stuffed in her mouth to muffle her screams. Baki started to howl. Rooks grabbed the lantern off the floor and banged around the larder, coming up with a bottle of Papa's whiskey. He made Percia drink, but the two of them together couldn't get any into Stahlia; she just made huge gasping noises as if she could not get air into her chest, let alone swallow.

Finally, Lem appeared in the doorway. With soothing words and gentle tugs he managed to get both Stahlia and Percia up off the floor, found handkerchiefs to blow their clogged noses, and wiped their faces with cool, wet towels.

Then the small cottage started overfilling with Wyndton friends, many still wearing nightcaps or night-robes under their cloaks. Percia found herself passed from one embrace to another, sleeping draughts raised to her lips, and Dewva and Nettie tucking her into bed like a child. In her drugged doze she heard her neighbors downstairs talking drunkenly or weeping.

In the morning, Percia looked in her mother's bedroom. She lay still, just staring, wide-eyed, at the eave. "Mama?" Percia asked.

"Fetch Tilim home, lamb. We should all be together."

Percia went downstairs, finding that Lemle sat awkwardly at the table with Sister Nellsapeta. She told them of her mother's wish.

"Rooks is hanging around outside," said Lem, "wanting he could do something useful. I'll send him."

Nellsapeta rose and hugged Percia close. Percia murmured, "We were just beginning to get over Wren, and now this—" and the tears welled up all over again. "Why did he? How could he? Didn't he know how much this would devastate us?"

"My child, we can't know what Wilim wished or feared or wanted," Nellsapeta said. "We can only know that he must have been in anguish. And we know that pain is over now; he has joined the Water's Flow. We can do naught for him. Our job is to find solace for you, your mother, and brother. When I lost my family, a Brother of Sorrow told me, 'Grief is the price we pay for love.' 'Tis a heavy price, but we have had life's sweetest fruit—now we must swallow the bitter."

The Sister toasted some bread and encouraged Percia to eat what she could. Then Mother came down; she had changed her clothes and replaited her hair. Nellsapeta offered her the traditional circlet of grief, a stiff headband that gripped the bereaved's forehead, holding a short gray veil that fell from the hairline to the top of the eyebrows. Mother settled it on her head as if girding herself for battle.

"When Tilim gets home, I want to be the one to tell him," she said.

Stahlia watched by the window, holding a cup of holly tisane she neglected to drink. Percia looked around the rooms for dishes to wash from last night, but the neighbors had left the cabin spotless. When Tilim rode up, sitting with a proud but wary grin up front of Sergeant Rooks, her mother went outside. Percia buried her head in Lem's chest so she would not have to see the change in her little brother's face.

During that endless, awful day, Percia realized she had never asked Lem how much *he* had suffered over Wren's disappearance.

"Did you know about her lover?" she asked him when they were alone fetching firewood.

"There's no sailor," he said with conviction. "And no matter what folk say, I know she's not with child."

"What? Then why did she leave us?"

"Percia, you knew her best," Lem answered. "I just always got the sense she didn't really belong here." Percia gaped at him in confusion.

As the day wore on, neighbors crowded in with food and with talk about the burial. Her mother wanted Papa buried beside her parents in the back pasture, and all at once she wanted it done immediately. With difficulty they persuaded her to wait; Duke Naven and his people planned to attend the service, and they would arrive tomorrow in the forenoon. So Mother went out to the stable, where the townsfolk had laid out Papa's body. She wrapped a scarf around the horrid chafing on his neck and placed a kerchief over his discolored, swollen face, and sat with him until the stars and moons came out. Then she ordered Baki to stand watch over him the rest of the night.

The next day the sun shone around scattered clouds with a brightness Percia resented. The duke and duchess and their party—including people from all around the ward—arrived. All of Wyndton gathered in their fest clothes first at the Church of the Waters and later in the pasture behind their cottage. Many people spoke earnestly about Wilim: about his calm and patience, his funny jokes, his helping hands, what a fine strong man he was, such a good husband and father, so deft at keeping the peace, and so loyal to Weirandale.

When it was Mama's turn to speak, she said simply, "He was my harbor, my hearth, my home, my heart."

Duke Naven pressed Stahlia's hand and made her vow to come to him if their family ever had need.

"What did you want to see him about the other day?" she asked him.

The duke made a noise of disgust. "Some political nonsense from Cascada. Regent Matwyck has got us all chasing our tails. I have decided to put a stop to it. 'Twas of no matter whatsoever and unrelated to this tragedy."

Sister Nellsapeta sprinkled a carafe of water from the fountain in Wyndton's church on the burial mound. When they sang the traditional "Sleep of the Blest," Percia could hardly get sound out of her closed throat, but her mother put her intensity into the song, and her strong voice carried them all through. As they had no flowers, Percia, Dewva, Nettie, and Lem scattered pine cones and seed heads on the grave.

Later, after scores of villagers had offered to help them with everything from patching the roof thatch to digging a new well, everyone went home. Percia sighed with relief. She knew she would want the support of her neighbors in the days ahead, but this evening she craved just her mother, her brother, and privacy.

They sat at the big table, now such a small group. Oddly, their stomachs hummed with hunger, so they indulged themselves by taking little tastes from many of the dishes left for them. After they were sated, Mother had them hold hands.

"We shall not want," she said firmly. "We have a little saved; my weaving can support us; and we have many friends to help us should need arise. Baki is a fierce guard dog, so we will be safe with him here, even without a man in the house.

"It is just we three now. Promise me you will never leave. Or no—I don't really mean that. Just promise me you will never leave without telling me, without saying goodbye. *That* I could not bear again."

"I promise, Mama," said Tilim solemnly. "I'll watch over you and Percia. I'm not Papa, but I'll keep you safe—I vow. And I'll learn to patch the roof so you don't have to ask anyone for help. I know that would hurt your pride."

"Of course, Mother," said Percia. "We must stay together."

"Aye," said Mother. "We three will stay together."

"Papa is truly gone," said Tilim with a catch in his voice. "We buried him. But Wren is only missing. You'll see—one day Wren will come home, and she'll never disappear on us again."

4

Melladrin

Tally: 22 Raiders

As the skiff pulled into the cove, Thalen watched the shore anxiously. The night's gloom smothered all the features of the land, and the crash of the waves covered all sounds. When he jumped out, the thigh-deep seawater shocked him with its cold bite, but no alarms rang out and no arrows thrummed through the black night. Slipping a bit on rocks, slapped by waves coming behind and tugged by the current as it receded, he waded cautiously toward the shore.

Maki the wolfhound leapt clumsily out of the skiff to join Thalen, hitting the water with a splash. His height allowed his nose to stretch above the surface just as he stood; he sniffed the new smells yet showed no particular concern as he paddled alongside. Together, they led the first eight men to the pebbled shore. Thalen dispatched Wareth and Adair to scout; then he sat on a rock to empty the water out of his boots as Maki shook himself dry. The skiff fetched another ten men. Thalen wrung out his wet stockings and retied the hair that had come loose from his hair leather.

Since the cove proved to be deserted, the sailors and the last squad of Raiders risked the noise of hoisting their horses from the hold and lowering each into the water to swim ashore. The skiff made two more trips back to the Yosta ship for their supplies. The sailors called, "May your Spirits be with you!" or "Freedom forever!" then returned to their vessel, which used its long oars to back out to sea.

On the sandy beach Maki shook the water off his coat again and raised his leg on a piece of driftwood. Thalen interpreted his nonchalance as a good sign.

The scouts returned with the all clear, so Codek ordered the loads of supplies distributed onto the horses and had the troop mount up. The sharp-sighted amongst the Raiders could just make out a path in the scrubby grass climbing from the beach up to a cliff. A short ways from the cove they came on Metos, the dot on the map Thalen had aimed for. The Raiders searched the six thatched huts; all stood deserted and still, the only sound the crash of the waves on the cliff front. Undisturbed sand drifts indicated that these dwellings had been abandoned for many moons. Sergeant Codek assigned watches.

So far, so fine. I have not gotten us all killed yet.

In their cramped shipboard cabin during the last weeks, Codek would grow angry if Thalen said such things out loud. His square jaw set more grimly, and his twice-broken nose looked sharper.

"Look, you want to have doubts—have doubts. It's good for commanders not to strut so cock-of-the-walk. But in front of the men—and the blasted women!—you act like you know what you're doin'. The first rule of command is to inspire confidence in your men. If I see you're muckin' up, I'll tell you quiet-like. Swordsmen and cavalrymen we could find; people who come up with strategy and hold maps in their heads are in short fuckin' supply."

Thalen lay down on his blanket on the straw bedding, his hands interlaced around the back of his head, reviewing everything he had ever read about Melladrin. The Melladrini no longer worshipped any of the traditional Spirits of Ennea Món, preferring to pay homage to the Lattice of Stars that guided them at night.

The Melladrini gave the constellations their own names: the Field Mouse, the Tiger, the Boar, the Bow, and the Herder. In fact, the oldest legend about the Causeway of Stones claimed that those enormous stones linking Melladrin and the Free States came when the Herder dropped her girdle from the heavens. Thalen pondered a snatch of a rhyme: "Through starlit centuries untold, a bridge betwixt the plum and the gold."

Eight hundred years ago this had been a thriving, populous nation, though never one based around industry. The Melladrini grazed enormous herds of a singular breed of antelope on their grass seas; they used these beasts for meat, hides, and bone. During the winter they gathered in great temporary cities such as Drintoolia on the east coast, Marchat in the middle of the country, and Melgellia in the west. During this season they lived in modest dwellings with thatched roofs and penned their herds in enormous corrals. The women bartered stags and does in the service of a sophisticated breeding program, designed to enhance the qualities of all the herds. The sophistication of these winter compounds, their markets full of valuable goods (including a rare, soft textile the men wove out of flax fiber), and the good food and fellowship offered in their eating places impressed all travelers and drew traders from throughout the lands of Ennea Món.

But one trading ship inadvertently caused doom by bringing rat pox to Drintoolia. Mellies had no defenses against this plague. In three years their population shriveled to mere handfuls of shocked survivors. Although the port of Drintoolia remained active—mostly because the Oros, lacking an east coast port of their own, used it—the other two cities died. Then a series of harsh winters and the cessation of the painstaking interbreeding programs decimated the herds of antelope.

This history led the Melladrini to disavow Ghibli, the Spirit of the

Wind, which had not helped them in their hour of need. It also left the Melladrini wary of outsiders and committed to a nomadic life-style. The books Thalen had read weren't sure if the antelope species still roamed the inland seas of dry grasses, or whether—unprotected by herders—they had all fallen prey to the fierce Drinian tigers.

In the morning light the Raiders searched the hamlet thoroughly. They found several spinning wheels and wooden battens used in the process of converting raw flax to thread. They also saw signs of battle, including the bones of an aurochs and bits of broken crockery. A well stood in the center of the town, but they couldn't draw water from it because it stunk with the odor of decay.

"Why would anyone—even Oros—foul a well?" asked Weddle, the quarterstaffer, who tended to be slow on the uptake.

Thalen reasoned it through. "Well, let's think about that. Oros want to kill off as many Mellies as they can. Mellies disperse when overwhelmed and then regroup to ambush later. Depriving them of easy water would be a way to make their lives harder."

They rested the horses for a day after the stress of the long voyage and cold swim. The next day Thalen felt eager to press on at a good pace to make up for the lost time. The weather was cool but here (next to the coastline) not frigidly cold, and they saw no sign of Mellies or Oros as they headed southwest across empty grassland under a vast sky of unbroken gray that made them keenly aware of their insignificance.

Thalen was calculating distances in his head when trouble arose from the most unexpected quarter—the heretofore mild-mannered horse master, Gentain. Gentain insisted on dividing the troop into three groups and putting each of them through their paces. Thalen figured out that Gentain based these groups on riding ability: caval-rymen dominated group one, their breastplates shining in the winter light, automatically arranging themselves in a neat double file. Group two—where he had been placed—had a more motley appearance; Cookie's skirt billowed when she galloped, and some men wore boiled leather tunics, while others wore padded gambeson doublets whose top, canvas layer had been fabricated out of whatever color fabric the Yosta tailors had had at hand. Group three—the archers Yislan and Slown; Tristo and his friend Ooma; Cook, Weddle, the quarterstaffer, and Cerf, the healer—came on so slowly that Thalen had time to notice not only that their gambesons ran from black (Cook) to deep green (Yislan), but that their head coverings ranged from the neck drapes Ooma and Tristo had tied on to warm their ears to Cerf's incongruous, high-crowned beaver hat, which he had flattened and tied under his chin with a strap to keep it from blowing off.

Self-consciously, Thalen reached up to touch the broad-brimmed hat he currently wore. Adair had casually skimmed it across the table at him two nights before they left Yosta. Thalen had wanted to take off the ostentatious white feathers, but Codek had forestalled him, arguing that they made it easier for the men to recognize him at a distance.

After watching group three trot to the horse master's satisfaction, Thalen rode up to his sergeant to confer. "Is this man playing with me? Can't he make his changes at midmeal or tonight?"

"Gentain had precious little time to study the men on the horses in the yard of the Three Coins," Codek explained. "We've got some shaky riders with us—that Ooma's grabbing her saddle like to break her fingers. Even with the more experienced cavalry, believe me, getting the right person on the right horse will more than make up for today's fits and starts. And save a mess of trouble all in all. Just bear with this."

Gentain changed Thalen himself out twice. "Gander's got a high step, sir, and you can't find a good seat," he explained. And some hours later, "Your seat is fine, sir, but your touch on her reins is too gentle. That Acorn, she's got a hard mouth and she can't feel your commands."

"Who's this one now?" Thalen warily eyed the horse Gentain

pulled behind him. It was dirty white, with rather unattractive pink nostrils and gray blotches on its back haunches. It stood tall and rangy, and its scraggly mane and tail added nothing dignified to its looks.

"Let me fix the cinch, sir. This here is one of my own; I always called him Dishwater. He don't look like much, I'll grant you, but he's a keeper. Course, we could change the name to something more suitable for a commander."

"No, 'Dishwater' suits him." Thalen patted the horse's neck. "Hey, boy."

"Sir," Gentain interrupted his attempt to get acquainted. "We should halt for the night soon. The horses aren't hardly at their full mettle."

"Nor the men neither," put in Kambey, the weapons master, who rode on Thalen's left.

"Right," said Thalen, who already felt worn out, but who would have died rather than admit it. "Have the scouts found a likely place ahead?"

"The sergeant sent Adair forward," said Kambey.

Maki, the wolfhound, materialized at Thalen's side when he dismounted for the day at the camp the Raiders had established. Thalen groomed Dishwater with care and hobbled him so he could graze. "Horses first, or you'll end up walking" was Gentain's creed, and Thalen intended to set an example for the men.

"Who's got my pipe?" Yislan, the archer, called out, cranky-voiced as usual.

"What's in this saddlebag? I'm holding this crap ransom for my bedroll," called Literoy, the talkative Fígat cavalryman, who was a big tease, and very popular among the men.

"Should the camp be this noisy?" Thalen asked Codek while he was attacking the supper that Cookie finally ladled up. "Aren't we giving away our location?"

"Commander, anyone or anything with ears has heard us all day

long. We ain't been a bit stealthy-like. First nights, everyone's kinda
nervous and stumble-foot. Hot food should have been ready when
we finished picketing the horses, but the cooks couldn't locate the
right pots. Give me a week, and I'll have 'em setting up and breaking down camp smooth as a peg in a groove."

"Been a long time since I had my peg in a groove," commented
Adair with a bawdy wink.

Thalen had just taken a bite of dry ship biscuit. Laughing, he
simultaneously choked and sprayed wet crumbs everywhere, which
everyone nearby found doubly hilarious. Maki swept up the crumbs
in the dirt.

Codek stood up, trying to turn his grin into disapproval. "I'll go
set the watch."

Tristo approached to tell Thalen that his tent was ready for him.
The Raiders had lugged with them only two tents: one for command and one as an infirmary. Inside, Thalen relished the break
from the cold wind, lying on a slatted bed frame that got him off
the freezing ground, and having the cheer of his own fire heating a
small brazier, but he missed the fellowship of the rest of the group.
He had never slept out-of-doors before, much less on a desolate
steppe under an impassive rain of starlight, and he found the experience unsettling. Briefly, he considered offering the tent to the
two women of the party, but he abandoned the idea as ill-advised
because if he gave up the tent to Ooma and Cookie, Codek would
use it as an argument that they shouldn't have brought them along.

As Thalen had discovered, the wolfhound was too long and stiff
to curl his body; Maki settled near the brazier with a contented sigh,
and his rhythmic breathing provided a companionable note. Thalen
stretched his lower back and rubbed his inner thighs, cataloguing
the soreness that would set in tomorrow.

The next day, although Gentain switched out other Raiders, he
nodded with satisfaction when Thalen cantered by. Thalen soon relaxed on Dishwater, whose gait seemed to match the rhythm of his

own body and who responded to the slightest pressure of rein or leg as if anticipating Thalen's wishes.

"That horse was meant for you," Wareth commented. Thalen grinned at him, pleased with the affirmation. When he needed advice he sought out Codek or Kambey; when he needed the support of a friend, he looked for Wareth's easy smile.

"Maybe we don't look grand, fella," Thalen whispered to the horse. "But you take care of me and I'll take care of you. We'll be a team."

He resumed his mental calculations about leagues per day to the base of the mountains ahead. Then, thinking of Dishwater, he double-checked the adequacy of their store of oats.

5

Cascada

Matwyck hated resorting to brutality. Truly, he did. Violence was too coarse, too messy. Yurgn seemed to have a taste for it, but not him. Resorting to violence signified that his schemes had not succeeded as well as they should.

But in this case what else remained? Lady Tenny had eaten up so much time combing the three Eastern Duchies, questioning young women, midwives, and peacekeepers. He had instructed his carefully chosen guards to keep their eyes on her.

Yet when the guards and Tenny finally returned to Cascada, claiming the princella had probably never hidden in the Eastern Duchies, of course he had to test this assertion against the Rortherrod Truth Stone. When he asked for it back, she handed him a stone that was similar in shape but a fraud: he knew this instantly because its gritty texture differed from the real stone's smoothness. He'd made his soldiers search her belongings and they'd found the real item. And when he held Tenny's hand to the Stone, lo and behold, she admitted that many moons ago she had paid Naven's little housemaid to find her a river stone of equal size. Then, she had interrogated the princella and let her escape! She had slipped a fake onto the table right in front of the guards' fool noses! Incompetence such as theirs could not be allowed to go unpunished—Matwyck had had his soldiers beheaded that night.

His best chance to track down the heir had been lost due to Lady Tenny's perfidy.

He should have known better than to send her. She had double-crossed Queen Cressa; she would have no scruples at double-crossing *him*. He had miscalculated. Tenny, though, would have to pay the price, because leaving her alive would be a daily reminder of his error.

Withdrawing a key from around his neck, Matwyck unlocked the guest bedchamber where she had been his captive since yesterday. He locked the door again behind himself, turning into the finely appointed room.

Dressed in a fancy brown velvet gown and one of her endless store of patterned, foreign turbans, Tenny sat motionless, staring out a window toward Nargis Mountain. She had pulled one of the side armchairs to face out; Matwyck carried a chair next to her.

They sat together, not speaking, for long moments, almost as if they were companionable old friends. Matwyck wondered what his life would have been like if he had married a woman such as Tenny, rather than Tirinella. When he was merely an ambitious merchant would she have accepted him? Probably not—her quick mind would have resisted his blandishments.

Oh, he felt not the slightest lust toward her angular body (well, that could have been satisfied in other ways), but he admired her ability to deceive her guards and to put her thumb down and change the shape of the future. She might even be as clever as he was: what a relief it would be to have an equal as a companion! Sitting there, he felt that perchance she understood him best of all the people he knew. And he realized that with a woman of her mettle by his side, there would have been no limit as to what he could accomplish. Mayhap he wouldn't now be needing to spend a fortune to keep the gentry in line and to build up his private guard. Marcot would have inherited her boldness, rather than Tirinella's scruples.

Well, he should soon be rid of Tirinella's disapproving looks and sighs. And her influence on Marcot.

What is Tenny thinking, sitting here with me so long? Is she scared of death? Does she appreciate that I am solicitously keeping her company?

Finally, Matwyck sighed and reached in his pocket for the vial of hemlock. Stabbing, strangling, beheading—such procedures would not be fitting for a lady of the realm.

He placed the vial on the windowsill in front of her gaze.

She spoke, not looking at him. "I have a boon to ask, Lord Regent."

He said nothing, just held his templed fingers to his chin.

"I would much prefer SeaWidow Cliff," she said, her voice steady.

Ah, well if it is just the method of execution—that's another matter. The cliff. Well, why not? And with the cliff, the body would be taken care of; no need to sneak it out of the palace.

Matwyck repocketed the vial. "Very well. I will send your escort within the hour so that you don't have to wait. Farewell, Lady Tenny. It has been a pleasure knowing you." He kissed her hand.

A rather gallant gesture, and I executed it so gracefully.

He was unlocking the door when she got in the last word.

"Matwyck, I suggest that you take your family and flee. Retribution is coming."

He slammed the door closed more violently than he meant to.

She said that to unsettle me. Should I change my mind and have her kilt some another way? Stoned to death? Ah, but that would show weakness and reveal that her parting thrust had hit home.

Tenny sagged with relief when Matwyck finally left her in peace.

Ever since she had reluctantly thrown in with the plot to overthrow Queen Cressa she had felt tortured. Finally, by recognizing and shielding Cerúlia in Gulltown, she had found her chance to make amends.

She had no close family who would grieve her death. She had taken care to update her will, pay her servants a year's severance, and mail some goodbye letters before Twitch and Stare insisted she report to the Lord Regent. She hoped that Belcazar, her erstwhile colleague as Queen Cressa's councilor, received the farewell note she sent. *He* had stayed loyal; he deserved to be the one to live to see Cerúlia's return.

She prayed she wouldn't disgrace herself by succumbing to terror on the cliffside. She had felt absurdly calm all night. She had savored the fine fresh linens on the bed, the pitcher of cool clean water, and the sight of the sunshine glittering on snowcapped Nargis Mountain. On the mantel she had found two painted, ceramic figurines of catamounts: one sleeping in a curl and one on guard, with eyes wide and tail held high. Though not an animal lover—nor a fan of decorative knickknacks—she'd laid them next to her pillow as she slept.

When she heard the tramp of several feet outside the door, despite her resolution her pulse jumped.

6

Jutterdam, the Free States

One of the oldest cities in the Free States, Jutterdam sat on a spit of land that extended out into a bay. It was further fortified by high stone walls around the outskirts. Even during the current Occupation, the Central Market in Jutterdam still operated, though the wares on offer were sparse and of low quality. Gustie wandered through the half-deserted stalls desultorily looking at the vegetables and cuts of meat.

When she bought some wizened beets, an elderly woman she had never met before said to the vendor, "I'll give this lady her change." And with the coins, she pressed a note into her palm. Gustie hid the note in her belt—better to look at it where privacy was assured.

"The Crones" had become the heart of the Free States' Defiance Movement. The young men had been killed or fled into exile; the Oros kept the older men and grown children as slaves, shackled and locked up. The young women were either in hiding or, like Gustie, kept as comfort women of Oro officers. Only the oldest women and littlest children managed to move through the streets with relative freedom. So far the Oros gave no sign of suspecting organized opposition.

Gustie had been captured six days after the Rout. She should have squirreled herself away in remote hills or forests, as meeker, more sensible young women had done, hoping to escape rape at the hands of the conquerors. But she had been too headstrong and eager to fight; she had lent her skill with a bow to a rearguard platoon in Jígat. The battle she fought against some twenty Oro Protectors was doomed before the first arrows flew. Soon all her Free States comrades lay dying or dead and she found herself surrounded.

Their sharp-tongued prize with her chin in the air impressed her Oro captors. They tied her hands and brought her as a trophy to Jutterdam. Her captors dragged her to the formal Council Hall, where, along with other comely women, she stood on display in the center of a large, wood-paneled room decorated with dark oil paintings of long-ago Iga royalty. Starting with the highest-ranking officer present, Oros selected women to serve as their bed warmers.

Gustie realized that refusal or struggle meant immediate death. Gustie watched a girl of perhaps fourteen summers plead for freedom and, when her entreaties did not avail, pound her fists against the white-haired officer who chose her. He took out his dagger, cut her throat on the spot, threw her body down, and selected another candidate.

Still staring in shock at the crumpled child in a slick of blood, Gustie had hardly noticed that a stocky man with six flames tattooed above his left brow had strode into the room, received salutes from all the Oros present, and begun to walk around her as if she were a prize heifer.

Weeks later, despite her disgust, Gustie felt perverse pride that her Oro held the rank of sixth-flamer. He had requisitioned a nobleman's stone house of three stories near the center of town. The sixth-flamer's status lent Gustie status; she ate better than the women of lower-ranked soldiers, and she did not wash or cook for him. As was required of all comfort women, Gustie wore a bright red bodice at all times, but her skirts and chemises were fashioned of silk and velvet.

Umrat actually paid scant attention to Gustie; he regarded her as a prestige object to parade about to impress underlings and as a body for his intermittent pleasure. Fortunately, his sexual taste involved normal intercourse and his grunting and pounding lasted only a few moments. She could pour wine for him, grace his table, fetch his boots, soap his back, and generally serve as an attractive, subservient ornament . . . as long as she could keep her focus on the day when she would empty a quiver of arrows into his broad, self-satisfied chest.

She repeatedly imagined these arrows, one after another, vibrating. She pictured his stupid, ugly face contorted with pain and shock.

Today she hurried back to the sixth-flamer's requisitioned manor. During the daylight hours Umrat kept busy at the docks, organizing food shipments to Oromondo. His orderlies and adjutants working in the public rooms smirked at her, but none dared touch or even insult her. The brigadier's emblem she wore around her neck served both as a slave chain and a protective ward.

Gustie passed into the privacy of the second-floor bedchamber.

Urgent need for Driscoll's treatise The Obsidian Mountains: Legends and Truth, last seen in S Library. Can you obtain? Bring to jam vendor.

Gustie lit a candle, burned the note in its flame, and sat down on a small couch to consider the message. Like many in the Defiance she had heard the whisper that Thalen of Sutterdam was leading a team of Raiders into Oromondo. Only Thalen would want a book from the library. Who in Jutterdam knew that she had also studied at the Scoláiríum? Who knew that she was eager to contribute something substantial to the cause? How could she find a single book amongst the thousands of volumes hastily stashed in the caves?

Never mind the caves. How could she get Umrat to allow her to leave Jutterdam?

Gustie grabbed her string shopping bag and went out once more. This time she walked to the dim apothecary shop a few blocks away. She toyed with looking at the sparse display of bottles until the shop emptied of other customers. Then she approached the elderly woman who struggled to keep the shop prosperous.

"I need your help," Gustie said. "I need a potion that will make me break out in an unsightly rash for a few days."

The woman looked at her sharply over her spectacles. "I don't have anything that would do such a thing. And whyever would you want one?"

"I need a man to leave me alone for a while."

The woman glanced at her brigadier collar. Then she moved quickly amongst her bottles. "Here. This is syrup of apricot pits; we use it to purge the body of suspected poisons. It will induce vomiting ten minutes after taking. Yet you'd recover quickly and without ill effects."

The apothecary would not accept money for the vial, pressing it into Gustie's palm and closing her fingers around it. But as cover for her trip, and to be certain the woman saw some profit from her kindness, Gustie bought a bottle of jasmine-scented hair oil.

That night at supper in the formal dining room, Gustie kept the vial up her sleeve during the first course at the large table that now seated only two. She complained of feeling unwell, but Umrat just grunted at her and continued reading his reports and sucking on marrowbones. Gustie got up to refill their glasses with wine and surreptitiously poured the vial into her own. If the syrup had any taste, the wine masked it. She sipped her wine at first and then drank it down. By the time the orderly brought the sweet, her stomach roiled.

"Brigadier, I am afraid you will have to excuse me. I am quite ill," Gustie said, standing up a little feebly. Her timing was perfect—the moment she moved, she spewed all over the floor.

Umrat leapt away from her. "By the Fires, woman! You disgust me! Get out of my sight!"

"Yes, Brigadier. I think I need to lie undisturbed for a while."

"Don't come back to my rooms until you are cured," he barked, his face curdled in revulsion. "Orderly, clean up this mess! Get her out of here!"

One of the adjutants took her elbow; Gustie puked a second time in the anteroom. He led her down into the cellar, away from the rest of the house, to what had probably been the servants' quarters in the time when a Jutterdam noble owned this mansion. Gustie broke from the man's arm to vomit a third time in a corner.

The adjutant fetched some water and a cloth. Gustie cleaned herself up as best she could.

"I'm so sick!" she said faintly. "Take me to a healing center, I beg you."

The adjutant looked indecisive. Gustie moved as if she would brush past him, but having grown wobbly in the knees, she grabbed on to him for support. She pressed her body against his, hoping to arouse his lusts, or remind him of why Umrat kept her, or make him worry about contagion—anything that would stir him to action. The soldier hesitated, holding her up awkwardly; then he sat her down on a bench and ordered out the brigadier's carriage. When they traversed the streets Gustie's now-empty stomach stopped heaving, but she kept up a steady stream of moans and fluttered her lashes.

A Free States healer, a woman with a slumped stance and smudged hollows under her eyes, greeted the carriage outside of a rambling set of wooden buildings. She listened to the officer's account of Gustie's sudden attack. When she knelt to place her head on the patient's chest to hear her heartbeat Gustie pulled her head to her lips as if she were too weak to speak above a whisper.

"Put me in a solitary room and draw the guards away. For the Defiance."

The healer stared at her a moment and then called to the stretcher-bearers.

"She could just have a stomach grippe, but there's also a chance this might be the black tide plague. Take her to the isolation room in the rear and leave her be. Pull the guards away just as a precaution—the black tide is wickedly contagious. I'll keep watch on her myself."

"That's awful good of you, Healer Dwinny," said one of the stretcher-bearers. "Black tide! Creeps! Don't touch her now." The stretcher-bearers carried her to the room and dumped her onto the bed so as not to touch her.

Gustie rested on the barely cushioned plank, beside which stood a pitcher of water and a pile of clean cloths. The heaving had subsided, though she felt a bit wobbly.

She dozed on the bed for an hour or two until the building quieted. Then she tiptoed out of her room and down an empty hallway. She found a back door close at hand—to her wonderment the lock had been prevented from latching in place by a piece of catgut that neatly held its prong up. This allowed her to creep out into a backyard full of debris and then into the lightless city streets.

Gustie had to locate a horse. Stealing one of the horses the Oros had commandeered was out of the question—that would raise alarms and a search. So, a citizen's horse.

With everyone struggling to survive under the yoke of their conquerors, she felt bad about this. Walking quickly, keeping to shadows, with eyes peeled for Oro guards, she snuck through the deserted streets, heading vaguely toward the commercial part of the city.

Eventually, she heard the clip-clop of hooves striking the cobblestones. Was it an Oro patrol? Even her brigadier collar wouldn't save her, for there could be no legitimate reason for a comfort woman to be walking the town in the wee hours of the night. Gustie pulled herself into a recessed doorway, but it didn't provide much cover. Coming down the street lit by a few oil streetlamps she saw a milk cart pulled by a knobby-kneed horse rendered even more unappealing by rain rot. An ancient woman held the reins; a boy of no more than six ferried the bottles to doorsteps.

Gustie took the gamble. She ran out from her hiding place toward the cart.

The woman pulled up, and the boy ran to her side, as if to protect her from Gustie.

"I need a horse on urgent business for the Defiance," said Gustie with her natural imperiousness. "Could I take yours for two days? I swear if I'm alive I will return him."

The woman stared at her slack-mouthed. The boy was quicker-witted. "Gram, she wants Creamy for two days."

"So I heard. Not deaf yet. Help me down." She clambered down slowly, afflicted by rheumatism. She went over to the cart stays and began laboriously unfastening them; the boy sprang to help her unharness.

"We have no proper bridle or saddle," the milk woman apologized.

"I'll have to manage with just his halter and your reins," Gustie said. "Where's your stable? Where should I return him?"

"Lowlands Dairy, off of Market Street."

"How will you get on without him?" said Gustie.

"We'll pull the cart ourselves. Done it before."

Gustie had qualms: this withered lady and that little boy pulling the heavy milk jugs? Maybe she could find another horse. The old woman saw the indecision on her face. "The sooner you're off, milady, the sooner you and Creamy return."

The boy led the horse to the steps to a closed shop; Gustie used the steps as a mounting block.

"We've had him my whole life," said the boy. "He's a good horse. You'll bring him home?"

"I vow," said Gustie.

"May your Spirit bless you and keep you," said the dairywoman.

"And yours," replied Gustie.

She grabbed Creamy's mane and nudged him with her knees. As they trotted off, she looked behind herself; she saw the woman grab one of the cart's stays and the boy put the other on his shoulder.

Gustie rode to Electors Gate. She pulled her chin down to cover the glint of her collar and hid from view on the far side of an empty hay wagon, unnoticed by bored and sleepy guards.

She directed Creamy over Electors Bridge and out into the chilly night, letting the horse find the well-contoured road in the pitch dark, hiding in the cover of the copper beach forest whenever she heard another rider approaching. She would have to find a saddle and proper bridle in Latham. And she was freezing in her dinner gown; she had not thought to smuggle out a cloak or boots. Actually, she hadn't *planned* this mission at all—she'd just launched into it. Quinith had always chided her for impetuousness.

Pushing Creamy hard, she made it to the small hamlet of Latham around midday. She knew the town well from her years at the Scoláiríum, so she was able to slip in through side streets. Villagers saw her, then looked away, but she was lucky enough not to run into any authorities. She rode into the stable of the Humility Tavern and knocked softly at the kitchen door.

The innkeep, Wrillier, a man who knew her from happier times, opened the door.

"Why, is it Mam Gustie? I am glad to see you alive. What are you doing here?"

"And it makes my heart glad to see you. You and your family—?"

"We've escaped harm thus far." He shook his heavy head. "But don't ask about other villagers."

"Wrillier, I put a horse in your stable. You will care for it? And find me a saddle, bridle, and cloak?"

"That I can do, mam." He had catalogued her red bodice and her neck chain. "But I can't invite you inside the inn. The Oros use it as their headquarters. . . . There are three Oro officers jawing upstairs this minute."

"Not to fret, Wrillier. But I need something to eat and someone to lead me to the tutors' hideaway. I must meet with them."

"We smuggle them foodstuffs when we can. But I'd be missed if I took you. My Winka, my daughter's gal, will show the way. Wait in the stable while I roust her from wherever she's hiding from chores."

Gustie slipped in with the horses. She washed the road dust off in the trough and stole a horse blanket for warmth (though she crinkled her nose when she wrapped it around herself). Winka, a sturdy girl of around seven, with big front teeth, joined her in a few moments. She carried a jug of hot mead for Gustie and handed her a slice of ham between two pieces of bread. Ravenous after her ordeal, Gustie polished off the food in big bites. Winka held her finger to her lips and led the way out of town through backyards and alleyways. A few dogs barked, but Winka shushed them. Gustie gathered that Winka used this route often.

When they reached the woodlands outside of town, Gustie tried to ask Winka questions about where they were going and how far, but the girl just put her finger on her lips. This made Gustie worry about the nearness of Oro patrols. If she was caught she would be executed on the spot, and she'd be responsible for the child's death too.

After climbing a forest trail for an hour they stopped for a rest. Gustie's house shoes—open at the toe—were not up to this hike, and she kept getting dirt clods and twigs caught under her hose. Winka waited impatiently while she cleared her shoes yet again. Then Winka risked a whisper: "Not far now."

They ascended into a thick stand of spruces. Winka gave a low whistle and received one in return. A very grubby little boy with clothes covered in sap clambered down out of the tree. "No one behind you, Winka. Did you bring any food?"

"Not this time. I just brung her," she jerked her thumb toward Gustie. "She needs to see the tutors. Where are they?"

"In their cave up the hill," said the boy.

"Could you keep your eyes open?" Winka asked. "Next time I'll bring a special treat just for you."

"Meat pie? Even bread and butter would be swell," said the lad, and started climbing back up.

Winka led Gustie to the cave. The young woman heard the inhabitants before she saw them: the wooded glade echoed with coughs. The cave yawned large enough to shelter two dozen people from the elements but offered only dank, hard rock. A group of ragged, dirty, and thin women and children, most afflicted with a catarrh, milled about outside and inside. Listlessness hung about them like a shroud, as if hiding idle in the forest for moons had taken its toll on their spirits.

One of the women looked up at their approach. "Is it—is it Gustie?" she asked. Gustie had trouble recognizing her. "Tutor Irinia?"

"Gustie, is it really you?" Tutor Irinia, whom Gustie barely knew, threw her arms around her. One after another the Scoláirium faculty and servants gathered her in their arms until she ended up in the embrace of Rector Meakey. Gustie would never have recognized her, because she looked so emaciated: her black-brown ringlets had lost their bounce, and her eyes had lost their sparkle.

"We are starved for news. Tell us what you know," her former headmaster insisted. So Gustie sat down on a log and told them how she was living with a sixth-flamer; how she'd heard that Quinith had escaped to the Green Isles; how Thalen was leading an expedition; how "the Crones" were organizing the Defiance; and why she came to be searching for them in their woodland hideout.

She asked them in return, "Tell me what you know about the Scoláirium. Did the Oros invade? Did they burn the library?"

"No," said Rector Meakey. "They rampaged through the grounds one day, but Granilton accosted them. He convinced them that our Spirits would consider their presence on the campus a sacrilege and if they did any damage they would be hexed with pestilence."

"Crafty of Granilton," murmured Gustie. "So is he still watching over the property?"

"No," said Tutor Andreata. "He convinced them that the grounds were sacrosanct, but he said nothing about himself. So they grabbed him, tied him to a stake, and burned him as a sacrificial offering to their Pozhar."

Winka added solemnly, "His bones are hanging still, outside the gate. They clink in the wind."

Gustie put her face in her hands, trying to shut out the image. She shook herself a little, realizing that she couldn't indulge in horror or grief. "Tutor Irinia, I have come all this way to find a book Thalen needs. Do you know in which cave the Earth and Water books ended up? I have to search for Triscoll's *Obsidian Mountains: Truth and Legend*."

Irinia automatically corrected her, "Driscoll's *Obsidian Mountains: Legends and Truth*."

"Impossible to find a single book in the storage caves, simply impossible. Out of the question," said the rector, speaking on top of her colleague.

"Yes, the rector's correct. The caves would be totally impossible. However"—Irinia paused, holding up her index finger—"I had my own copy in my personal chambers when we evacuated. I remember I had been reading it because I wanted to know more about the mountain range."

"Can we just walk through the estate and into Scholars' House?" asked Gustie.

"Maybe at night," Winka contributed. "Maybe with a ruckus drawing attention on the other side of town."

"Winka, my dear! You are as smart as a dolphin! I mean it," said Meakey, with a bit of her former enthusiasm. "Now, you head back to your grandpapa's and see if he can organize any sort of distraction for after sunset. A tiny fire, or just a wee drunken tavern brawl."

Meakey ordered, "Gustie, you need to lie down for a while. You were up all night riding here, and we hope you'll be up all night riding back.

"Irinia and I will plan the raid on Scholars' House. Oh, this is going to be such fun—to take action rather than just sit here useless!" A hint of sparkle had returned to the rector's eyes.

Gustie lay down on a bed of leaves covered by her stolen horse blanket deep in the back of the dim cave. Even though tattered and dirty children came to stare at her with curiosity, Gustie fell asleep.

Shortly before sunset Tutor Andreata, her former mentor in Ancient Languages, shook her awake. She sat for a moment next to Gustie on the pallet of leaves.

"For what it is worth, my dear, I believe you made the right choices. As long as your brigadier does not beat you. Hiding keeps one safe, but one feels so useless spending one's days cowering like a twitching rabbit. I am proud of your sacrifice. You must hold your head up high and never feel shamed."

"I'm not ashamed." Gustie thought this was true. "I'm not bedding the brigadier of my own volition."

"Do you want to escape? Stay with us?" Tutor Andreata asked. "We could find some other way to get the book to Jutterdam."

"No, that's not necessary," said Gustie. "I don't want to hide. I want to be in the center of events, and with Umrat I am well-placed to aid the Defiance."

Rector Meakey appeared. She brought Gustie a mug of water and shards of a tasteless, broken cake made out of acorn meal.

Gustie said her farewells, and Meakey, Irinia, and she trekked out of camp on a trail different from the one she had walked in on. It was not full night yet, but by the time they reached the Scoláiríum the clouded sky blanketed out any starlight. Blundering, feeling their way, they snuck into the once-manicured grounds through a back entrance and made their way toward Scholars' House.

Inside the familiar marble halls of the two-story building, Gustie heard the scurry of mice or other small rodents fleeing from their intrusion. Rector Meakey led the way toward her own chambers near the entrance and by touch and curses located candlesticks and flint. She held her hands over the flames to shade them, but if anyone watched the building, the sudden blossom of light announced their presence.

Tutor Irinia's personal study lay down the right-hand hallway. She rummaged through the books for long moments while Meakey held the candelabra up and Gustie strained her eyes and ears at the doorway.

"Ah-ha! I found it!" she announced, triumphant. She handed the book to Gustie. "But I think I'll grab a few more to better pass the time in the forest."

"What a marvelous idea!" said Meakey. "Let's fetch one book from each of the tutors' studies to raise her spirits. But no heavy encyclopedias. Mind me now: small volumes." Gustie and Tutor Irinia ran into one office after another, Irinia taking the first floor and Gustie the second, grabbing the first slender book that came to hand in the darkness. Even with the stairs, Gustie finished her round a little quicker than the older woman; she returned to Meakey's candles to inspect her haul. The book her hand had chanced upon in Tutor Andreata's chamber was in Ancient Orlundian. Gustie knew just enough to translate the title, *Pozhar, The Fire Spirit of the Obsidian Mountains*. She opened it, shivering when she saw the pages of ancient maps. This might also help Thalen.

Tutor Irinia caught up with them, panting. She had her allotment of books tied up in a bundle in her ragged apron. Meakey was taking Gustie's books out of her arms when they heard the front door bang open. They froze in terror.

"Who's there?" quavered the voice of an elderly man.

Gustie's heart sped up, but Meakey chuckled. "It's only our old porter," meaning the man who had fetched Gustie for her first appointment with the rector. He came creeping down the hallway holding a stick of firewood over his head as a weapon.

"We are here, Hyllidore," Meakey called softly. Hyllidore came into her candlelight, dragging his huge shadow behind him. He had sustained injuries; he limped on his right leg, wore a patch over his left eye, and unhealed whip lashes ran down the left side of his face.

"I'm happy to see you, Rector! It's been right lonely." His lips quivered, and his good eye watered. "I've been hiding in closets and cellars. I've been watching out for the place."

"And you have done an excellent job, Hyllidore. Most excellent! I am so delighted you found us tonight. I need a bit of sacking for these books, see, and you are the only one who could find some quickly." While Hyllidore limped off to find her bag, Meakey turned to Gustie. "You must go now, child. Hurry."

"Send all our love and prayers to Thalen," Irinia added.

"Farewell," Gustie said hurriedly, though she longed to linger with these older women who gave her comfort. She crossed the courtyard and passed through the entrance gate. If Tutor Granilton's bones were still hanging nearby, the darkness hid them and the windless night kept them silent.

By the feel of the ground under her thin shoes she was certain she followed the road to Latham. She hurried as fast as she could, depressed by the cold and the thought of the lonely journey ahead. She drew closer to the town proper and was trying to recall the best back alley path to the Humility Tavern when she heard a stirring to the left. A horse nickered softly.

"Is that you, mam?" came Wrillier's soft voice.

"Aye," replied Gustie, much relieved.

He came closer, a blacker shadow in the night, although Creamy's light coat caught whatever light was available. Wrillier bent down to give her a leg up. Creamy now boasted a proper saddle and bridle.

"I put a bite to eat in a package behind the saddle, Mam Gustie," said Wrillier, "and I borrowed a warm coat for you. I've gotta get back. There's a fire in the Quill and Ink, and I'll be needed."

"Thank you for everything, Wrillier."

"Just get these white-haired pigs out of my country!" he called after her in a low tone.

Gustie backtracked to Jutterdam, recognizing how lucky she was that Creamy was accustomed to making his way in the dark. As she rode she puzzled over how best to use her placement to help the Defiance. She realized that being placed with a sixth-flamer brought her special opportunities.

Umrat barks at me like a dog or a servant. What if he actually cared for me? What if he told me the Oros' plans? How could I get into his confidence?

Rattling noises—the clink of metal and the tread of horses—signaled an Oro patrol coming close. Creamy and she rested behind some bushes. Later, she hid from some wagons going the opposite direction. Other passersby were few in this war-torn land at night.

At Electors Gate her luck ran out: the guards yanked aside the coat she held closed in one hand to reveal her chain and bodice.

"Why were *you* outside the city?" the guard asked suspiciously. "Where have you been?"

"Brigadier Umrat allowed me to visit my sick mother," she said. "I am returning, as promised."

"Umrat? Umrat wouldn't allow such a thing," said another guard with a disbelieving huff.

"Are you saying that *Brig-a-dier* Umrat is callous or unkind?" she berated the guards. "I am his woman. Shall I tell him what the gate guards think of him? We often discuss his underlings. Give me your names; I already see your flames."

The guards backed down in the face of her imperious anger.

"Aww, get on with you. Ain't none of our business."

Gustie rode straight into town and found Lowlands Dairy

without much trouble. The establishment sat deserted, so she concluded the woman and boy must already be out on their rounds. She left Creamy alone with some sleepy dairy cows in a tumbledown wooden barn that reeked. She knew she should groom him, but she decided the new tack was payment enough for their trouble. Reluctantly, she also left the heavy coat Wrillier had given her.

The dairy lay closer to Umrat's than the healing center. Walking through the streets in the midmorning light was the hardest part of the journey. She had to move slowly and not draw suspicion, even though everything about her called for investigation. Her hose were torn, her dress a mess; she was filthy and exhausted when she slipped into the rear of the mansion's yard, snuck through the back door, and retreated into the small servant's room.

She hid the books inside the mattress ticking. She kicked off her dirty clothing and shoes and wadded them into a ball in the corner of the room. Then, naked, she crept into bed.

A couple of hours later the adjutant who had escorted her down here almost two days ago woke her up.

"When did they release you?"

"A few hours ago."

"You don't have anything contagious?"

"No, just a stomach grippe. But they told me to get my rest."

"How did you get here? Why didn't they put you in a carriage?"

Gustie mumbled, "I don't answer for the healing center. Go away. I need my sleep."

"Answer me!" he ordered, jostling the bed with his boot.

"Go away! The sickness has finally passed."

"I don't understand why—" the officer said.

Gustie sat up angrily, letting the cover slip down. The adjutant stared at her naked breasts. "Look you," she spat at him. "I'm here, aren't I? Returned to duty like a proper slave. I don't know what you're playing at. Get out of this room right now and leave me be or

I'll tell Umrat you've been pawing at me. Maybe he'll let you choose the penalty: ears, nose, or fingers."

"Oh, shut up, you heathen bitch." The adjutant left the room and slammed the door.

Gustie slept until midafternoon. Then she wrapped herself in a blanket, found the orderlies, and demanded that they heat her a bath and bring her food. She tossed away the stockings she had been wearing and threw her clothes in a laundry tub as if to soak the smell of vomit out of them, but actually erasing the traces of forest sap and road dust.

She brushed her hair until it shined and dressed in a clean gown with an apron that boasted large pockets. She laced her red bodice on tightly so that her waist looked tiny and her bosom strained at the top. Then she took her string bag out to the markets to look for a delicacy that would please her "special" brigadier.

Mickleberry jam would do nicely.

7

Sutterdam

"I hear footsteps!" Hartling warned. The other men and boys crammed into the brick cellar of the guild hall sprang into action, sorting themselves out according to a practiced method. The more grizzled and less attractive men moved to the front of the room, hiding from easy sight the stripling boys and their ailing fellows resting on rags.

Their Oro captors had proven too apt to grab a comely boy for a night of gang rape. One lad had died of his internal injuries, and Samil, the younger brother of one of Harthen's chums, had committed suicide a week after his mistreatment by hanging himself from a hook.

Something broke in Hartling the morning he saw the purpled and distorted face of a boy he had known since his own sons were little.

The sick were in danger for different reasons: the Oros prized strength above all, and anyone infirm became a target of their scorn. Moreover, since they valued their captives only as beasts of labor, they might decide that an unhealthy man wasn't worth feeding and dispatch him, as they had already killed one of Hartling's long-time kiln stokers. So though the front of the cellar offered drier and fresher air than the damp rear wall, whenever an Oro approached, the Sutterdam men quickly rearranged themselves to block potential victims from sight. It was one of the only gestures of resistance left to them.

The lock on the large doors rattled. Four captors had brought their fastbreak. "Two lines, double quick," a jailer ordered, and the prisoners obediently queued up, each with his bowl. The porridge that they were fed morning and night tasted awful, but it provided (barely) enough fuel for their daily exertion. Once a week they were given a lemon each, to prevent scurvy.

Four captors made a tempting target for the sixty desperate captives, but no one had attempted a breakout since the first week. A gang of stevedores had jumped their guards, throttling them or knocking them down, and rushed out into the yard, where the Oro company had promptly captured them. The rest of the slaves had been marched out to watch while two of the Sutterdam stevedores had been thrown to their deaths off the rooftop, two flayed, and two burned alive. These object lessons, and the shackles that now enclosed their wrists and ankles, put an end to escape attempts.

"Line up," shouted their captors, and the men moved into two lines for the march to the docks. Unless some other, more pressing task presented itself, they spent their days loading cargo vessels taking Free States foodstuffs to Oromondo.

The walk through the fresh air to the docks was Hartling's favorite part of the day because he got to see his city. Citizens had learned which routes the Oros favored, and often they'd paste signs inside windows. These could offer general cheer, "Stay strong, Sutter men," or personal messages, "Alcott, your wife safely delivered. A healthy boy!" The Oros ripped the signs down, but new ones always sprang up overnight, and eventually the occupiers ignored them.

Hartling scanned the signs. Today he saw nothing for him, but weeks ago he'd spotted the message, "Hake and Thalen live!" That Harthen's name wasn't listed hadn't surprised him; he'd always known the boy would come to grief. Sometimes as he marched, his steps echoed an eight-beat chant, "Harthen, my lost and foolish boy. Harthen, my loved and foolish boy."

Looking down a side street, the potter and his fellows saw a flash of colored skirts indicating that a line of female slaves was being escorted to their own work duty, packing fruit or sewing grain bags or whatever their Oro masters set them to. A man behind him started screaming, "Ekisha! Ekisha! Ekisha!"

The Oro guard slapped him with the flat of his sword to shut him up.

Dully, Hartling wondered if the man had really seen his daughter or if he raved.

At the docks, the workers split into teams: those carrying crates aboard and those packing the holds. Hartling, who had a good sense of space, usually was ordered into the hulls of the ship. This kept him out of the weather and saved him some steps, but the holds were airless and stifling.

At midday, the Oros offered no food to their slaves, but they permitted a short rest quayside.

Hartling collapsed on the wharf, leaning his aching back against a piling. A water girl approached him with a skipper of water, which he drank gratefully. The water boys and girls were Free States children who waited by work sites all day for the chance to succor their enslaved fathers and brothers. They all carried heavy water buckets; some had rags you could use to wipe the sweat and grime off your face, and a few brought bandages for the inevitable cuts and scrapes.

The really brave ones also carried messages. If an Oro guard saw a child slip a message to a slave the child would be whipped with a metal-tipped cat of nine tails that gouged their skin—that made the children more careful, but it didn't deter them.

"Water?" A boy not more than five summers approached Hartling with his bucket. Since Hartling had already drunk, he almost waved the child away toward a worker who needed it more, but he recognized him as the son of his neighbor on Lantern Lane.

"Aye, more water," he said, and the boy approached. Hartling drank again.

"You need a bandage on your hand?" said the neighbor boy.

"Yeah. Thanks, son."

As the boy came close to tie a wrapping around Hartling's right hand, he whispered, "Mam Norling says, 'Don't give up hope. Things are happening.'"

"That's too loose, son. Tie it again," Hartling said out loud. As the boy came closer he whispered in his ear. "Have you seen my wife, Jerinda? Do you know what's happened to her?"

The boy shook his head decisively, but Hartling saw the truth in his frightened, gray eyes.

Hartling collapsed against the piling. He'd known since the Rout, but he'd fooled himself into holding on to a speck of hope. The boy's eyes had taken that away.

The boy moved on before the Oros got suspicious. Hartling started to take off the unnecessary bandage when he looked at it more closely. The white fabric had pink and gold flowers embroidered on it. He recognized the material as the tie of Jerinda's best apron, the one she wore on fest days. He'd bought this for her as a Solstice present when Hake was a baby. . . . He'd bought her a flowered hat when Thalen was born and a silver hairbrush for their youngest, Harthen. He'd loved to present her with gifts: Jerinda's face would flush with anticipation, and her eyes would shine. She always said that he chose with exquisite taste, and she treasured her few fancy possessions.

Closing his eyes, Hartling feasted on his memory of her face. He lost himself in memories of those days—days before they knew how blessed they really were.

Hartling smoothed the scrap of material and raised it to his lips. Maybe he should rejoice that she had died rather than live in mistreatment, but his jaw shook and he had to hold in sobs. Like a pot that had been dropped, he felt shattered.

"Rest's over. Back to work, you dogs," shouted an Oro, interrupting Hartling's reverie. The Free Staters slowly returned to their assigned tasks for the afternoon shift. The hold smelled of bilge water and sweat.

"Pick up the pace, you lazy curs!" yelled one of the guards. He took out his whip and hit the lash against the men's legs—just controlled little pops, but they hurt like blazes.

Hartling moved mechanically, his mind far away. An hour into this shift one of the slaves, a man who'd been unable to keep his rations down for several days, dropped a sack. It split open and grain scattered in the hold. The Oro monitor grew incensed; he grabbed the man by the collar and kicked him up the ladder. Hartling and the other men stopped their stacking in the hold and heard a splash.

"They've thrown him into the harbor," a man commented.

Their remaining guard smiled with satisfaction. "Who's holding the odds?" he called out. "Ten to one he don't rise."

They could hear their guards betting on the survival of their friend with loud calls and whoops of laughter. Apparently, the man drowned.

Hartling looked around, unable to recognize where he was or what he was doing. He stared at his own hands, confused.

A man with a cruel expression and a sword at his side struck him across the back with a leather whip. "You there, get back to work."

Hartling gazed around the dim hold, registering the activity. He imitated the other men in the hold who were, for some reason he couldn't remember right now, packing grain sacks.

"Hartling, are you all right?" hissed one of the other workers.

It took some long moments before he realized that "Hartling" was his own name.

8

Melladrin

Thalen lost his first man well before the Raiders ever engaged in battle.

Slown, the archer recommended by Adair, didn't chat or josh around; they heard from him only when his preternaturally sharp eyes picked out a bird on the wing. Riding by chance next to Thalen, he remarked, "Snow cock, over yonder." Later he said, "Black bulbul, see it?" Thalen couldn't spot it, but he pretended to.

Slown never griped, and he pulled his weight and a bit more; if he was no one's close friend, he also rubbed no one the wrong way. The Raiders learned to gather wood wherever available on this arid plain; Slown was always the first to see a grove of slender aspen trees or spy a broken, burnable limb in the grass. Since fire kept them alive, his eyesight was a valuable resource. Near a rivulet, Slown was also the first to see the print of a tiger foot. After that, the Raiders learned to camp a safe distance away from water sources.

That morning, a small groan escaped Slown's lips as he waited in line for fastbreak.

"What's the matter?" asked Tristo.

"Don't know."

"Sit down a moment. Your face's gone wrong."

Slown tried to sit with control, but his legs gave out on him, leaving him collapsed on the freezing ground. Thalen dropped his own plate and hollered for Cerf. They got to Slown simultaneously, Cerf yanking the layers of clothes to put his head to the collapsed man's chest and abdomen, Thalen placing his hands on either side of the archer's face and holding his gaze. Slown's eyes blinked twice and then froze, half-open.

"Damnation!" swore Cerf. "His blood sloshes about like a river. Must have blown an aneurism."

"What's that?" asked Cook.

"It's when a blood vessel swells up out of shape; then finally it swells too much and bursts and you bleed to death inside."

Jothile, one of the Vígat cavalrymen, young and graceful with a long, caramel-colored face, asked, "Did he have this any-ism because he's old or because he got injured once?"

"No one knows. People get them. It's just their awful luck," said Cerf. "Don't worry though, son, this isn't something other folk can catch."

In the shocked silence, Adair, who had known him the longest, pulled Slown's coat back in order and passed his hand over his face, closing his eyes.

"He didn't suffer," Thalen said to Adair. He stood up and looked around, weighing their options. "We can't bury him. The ground's too frozen."

Adair answered, "Right," still staring at the lifeless form.

Thalen surveyed the Raiders clustered around Slown's body. Most looked completely stricken, as if this were their first sight of death. Thalen knew this couldn't be true—all the soldiers had seen death in the Rout, and in their prewar lives everyone had routinely lost friends or relatives in their home villages. Thalen himself had held his brother Harthen's body, crawled over corpses, and picked up severed heads when he searched for Hake. . . . He could still feel Harthen's weight against his chest, the squishiness of soldiers' limbs under his knees, and the hard skulls in his hands. Slown's sightless eyes brought back memories he had tried hard to shut out of his mind, but he didn't think the other Raiders shared his gruesome visions.

Then, in a flash of insight, Thalen understood the expressions on the faces around him. It was one thing to sign up for a hopeless mission when your blood runs hot for vengeance. But in the last two moons, the Raiders had all gotten used to living. While this journey might be arduous, they were still alive, sharing food, camaraderie, and the austere grandeur of the prairie. Slown's sudden death reminded them of the likely end of their mission.

"A cairn?" offered Cook, breaking in on Thalen's train of thought.

"Can we find enough stones?" Thalen asked, and everyone glanced at the frozen turf covered by a skein of snow in which longer, brittle grasses jutted out like sparse hairs on an old man's chin.

"Not a lot of rocks about," said Gentain, ever alert to conditions that might affect the horses.

"Still, let's try," Cookie urged. "Poor soul. We can't just leave him like that."

And so they spent the next hour trying to gather rocks. The few lying on the surface were so small they didn't fill a palm. The frozen soil gave up half-buried, larger stones with stubborn reluctance. But the search gave Thalen a chance to get over this loss of his best archer and ponder what he needed to say to his troop.

After they had wasted all the time they could spare, he had Sergeant Codek call everyone together. He and Cerf wrapped Slown in a canvas tarp. Their meager pile of rocks didn't cover the tarp but did succeed in weighing it down against the wind's disrespect.

Thalen took off his hat. "Raider Slown," he said, choosing his words with care. "None of us knew you well. But we did know that you wanted freedom for our homeland. And you showed bravery—enough bravery to accompany us on this mission into strange climes. And that's more than sufficient for us to honor your memory.

"We will strive even harder so that your death—like that of our friends and family in the Free States—won't have been in vain. The soil of Melladrin here will always hold a memory of Yosta. The birds that fly these skies will watch over you.

"Those of you who worship a Spirit, say a prayer now." About half of the troop knelt and prayed, while the others stood still.

"Does anyone else have anything to say?" Thalen asked. He waited a long moment, but no one spoke. Then he took out the assorted feathers he had picked up among the grasses and laid them out in a fanlike pattern on Slown's chest. They didn't quite look enough, so Thalen pulled off one of his hat's showy white feathers and added it to the collection. Adair jumped to help him pin down the decoration with rocks.

"Slown. Comrade. Friend. Raider."

Literoy pulled out his fife to play a dirge, but Thalen shook his head, fearing the sound would carry too far. Then Thalen led the troop away from the burial site.

The steppes of Melladrin stretched to the horizon, desolate and seemingly endless but always subtly changing. As the Raiders progressed, they passed through areas chewed up by the passage of an enormous army of boots and hooves. They also rode through acres where all the grass had been burned down to the soil. As for people, they came across no inhabitants and only occasionally saw deserted thatched huts, which contained only discarded weaving tools.

In unspoiled areas they might spot a small herd of wary antelope grazing and watching for threats. Twice the scouts and cavalry succeeded in driving the animals into the range of their archers. Raiders feasted on the novel but welcome meat. Vatuxen, another cavalryman, whose family had worked leather, led them through the steps of drying, degreasing, and tanning the hides (which took much more time and effort than they anticipated). Thalen left the decision of what to do with the skins up to the men: he was pleased to see that the Raiders chose to allot the new resource to the least warmly dressed of their group and that they all worked together on cutting and fashioning. Tristo and Ooma gained leather hats, while Cookie and Yislan got shoulder wraps, and Adair stuffed everyone's boots with scraps of fur to hold more body warmth around their feet and ankles. The Raiders scrupulously rotated the largest hides amongst themselves as extra sleeping blankets.

Swaying with Dishwater's gait, Thalen mused how they could cross the border into Oromondo. Of course they couldn't take the direct route down the coastline: that way would lead straight into impassable mountains and Onecaster, a Magi watchtower city. He had also skirted the official pass, the Mouth of the Mountains, aiming for a section of the mountain range between Threecaster and Fourcaster, on the wisp of a hope that his scouts could find a way through. Past Fourcaster they would hit the impenetrable barrier of the canyon carved by the Protection River.

This venture's slim chances rested on circumstances he could not control. As commander, he knew he was a fraud.

Well, not a complete fraud. Codek and *A Leader's Duties* concurred that the most important part of being a leader of men was to have and convey a compelling objective. And he was the one who had gotten this expedition organized, hadn't he?

Thalen set himself to serve as an example in small ways. He followed Codek's instructions about how to stand watch, Gentain's rules about care of horses, and Kambey's strictures about caring for his rapier and dagger to the letter. He took a turn at all the mundane tasks, such as scrubbing pots or lugging water. Even on the coldest days, Thalen washed and shaved to keep up appearances.

In addition, he made a point of listening to any advice and offering praise for jobs done well.

But how do these small gestures make up for my lack of experience? Why should these men and women trust me—a raw Scoláiríum student—to make the best decisions in a pinch?

Codek argued that the trappings of command, such as calling Thalen "sir" and "Commander" and housing him in a private tent, would instill a habit of respect. Privately, Thalen wondered if such symbols would suffice, especially with those among the troop who were unaccustomed to military discipline.

Thalen had been expecting a challenge for the last few weeks. The euphoria of the new adventure had worn off, and though the riders did not encounter deep snow, Slown's death and the constant cold wind left everybody edgy. The deserted nature of the steppes made all the humans cluster close together, aiding Thalen's ability to pick up on subtle warning signs, such as Raiders falling silent when he walked by (obviously they had been talking about him); Kran making an unnecessary, elaborate bow when Thalen asked him to move out of Dishwater's way; an "Aye, sir," that came a little too slow or too fast to be comfortable.

The book that Granilton had pressed upon him, *A Leader's Duties,* warned Thalen that all men following a new superior will need to test his capabilities and dominance. This test would be especially salient on a mission with high stakes and deadly consequences. Thalen was younger than most of the Raiders, and not as skilled with weaponry nor as physically tough. He didn't have Adair's breezy swagger and storied history, nor Kambey's years of teaching. Sooner or later one of the Raiders would demand he prove his mettle.

Codek, Wareth, Kambey, and even the damn dog took to clustering around him, trying to ward off the trouble that tingled in the air.

But tonight Codek had been called to the horse pickets to confer with Gentain and Wareth over Wareth's mare, Custard, who had bruised her hoof. Thus, hunkering against the blowing spits of ice pellets over the dregs of their meal, Thalen reeled off the first names that came to mind for first, second, and third watch.

"I ain't taking second watch again; I had it just the other night," said Weddle, stamping his quarterstaff into the ground for emphasis.

The scholarly side of Thalen wanted to consider the merits of Weddle's complaint and set up a system of distribution of watches that everyone would acknowledge as perfectly balanced. But he sensed the sudden strain in the air and saw how everybody else stopped going about their business and watched out of the corner of their eyes to see how he would react to a confrontation.

Here it is. Perhaps Weddle always had to be the one; Yislan and Ooma show more smarts and caution. Tristo warned me about Kran's temper, but he's not directly involved. Weddle is just big enough, cocky enough, and just dumb enough. Though even he chose his moment well.

Time slowed down for Thalen. He saw Kambey's hand move to his sword pommel. Adair's body coiled even tighter. Maki, eating scraps that Cookie had saved for him, lifted his head from the dish and pulled his lips into a silent snarl.

Thalen forced himself to swirl his cup a moment and take another sip. Then he stood up to his full height. He stood more than a hand taller than Weddle.

"Raider," he said, his voice softer, not louder, looking Weddle directly in the eyes. "Perhaps you didn't hear. I gave you a direct order. Some other time we'll discuss the ethics of watch rotation."

Weddle glanced around, playing to the crowd, gesturing broadly. His voice got louder. "And all I'm saying is: that's not fair. Ask Sarge. I had second watch just the other night. He assigns watches—

you . . . do whatever it is you do." He looked around at his audience again for approval, a shit-eating grin on his face.

"Codek is dealing with a lame horse tonight. If we don't set Wareth's horse to rights the whole troop will suffer. Do you think your comrades would appreciate if we all had to take turns walking?" Thalen took another sip of his tisane, unhurried, unruffled, his eyes never leaving the Raider's face.

Weddle continued, "No, but, I mean, all *you* do is fuss with your papers and maps and such, *sir*."

"Aye, I do. That's why I was awake during second watch the other night, and took a turn around the perimeter, and saw you dozing at your post."

Weddle became abashed but also more truculent. "So you're giving me another second watch as punishment? That's not fair!"

"*Fair?*" said Thalen. "Let's think about that. Is it *fair* that Slown died? Is it *fair* that Britmank and Literoy have been suffering from a grippe for a week? Is it *fair* that Cookie's ears are frostbit? I haven't heard a one of them complain. Either you're willing to suck it up and work for the good of all, or you can turn around now and ride back to Metos. I'm sure the Drinian tigers would appreciate a solo rider."

Thalen watched emotions war on Weddle's face.

"I ain't riding back to Metos!" Weddle spat out sullenly.

"Glad to hear it. Then go get as much sleep as you can before second watch."

"But—" Weddle just couldn't concede. He looked around at the others grouped around them.

Once Thalen noticed Weddle glance at his fellows the first time he just waited for his chance. *Fuck it,* he thought. *I tried reason.* The tepid liquid in his cup was worthless, but the cup itself was made of tin. Thalen lunged forward and brought it down *smash* right on the bridge of Weddle's nose.

Weddle dropped like a stone to his knees on the frozen ground. He yodeled with pain while blood streamed out of his nostrils.

Thalen looked at the other Raiders, all of whom stared open-mouthed at their downed champion. Thalen forced himself to control his thudding heart. Deliberately, he brought the blood-backed cup to his lips as if he were taking another sip (though in actuality all the liquid had splashed out).

Forcing his voice to sound neutral, Thalen remarked, "I trust that in a battle Weddle can cope with a broken nose more stoically. Anyone else feel the need to complain about anything?"

Ooma smiled broadly. Latof, one of the Fígat cavalrymen, who tended to follow stronger personalities, shook his head vehemently.

Codek came running up. "What's going on?"

"Ah, Codek," said Thalen. "How is that horse doing?"

"The horse?" asked Codek, confused. "But what—"

Kambey, rising, interrupted him. "The commander just assigned watches. Where's Cerf? I might ask him to take a look at our friend here, though I'm not sure what a healer can do for a broken nose."

Something passed wordlessly between Kambey and Codek, leading Codek to catch on to the situation. "You do that. *Com-man-der*," he stressed the word. "Do you have any other instructions?"

"Just make sure that Weddle doesn't take advantage of this mishap to cut out on second watch tonight," said Thalen.

"Of course not, sir," replied Codek.

A Leader's Duties counseled, *"Once a reprimand has been delivered, move swiftly to normalize relations."*

"Here, Weddle," said Thalen, holding out his hand. "Let me give you a hand up." Weddle reached for him, and Thalen pulled him into a standing position. "Pain abating a bit? I'm sure Cerf will have you put to rights in a few days. Everybody knows you're one of our strongest fighters. I need you."

"It's not as if a broken nose will spoil Weddle's looks for the ladies," said Kran, publicly switching sides.

"None of you muckwits is worth a second glance," Codek grumbled. "Let's get this camp in order. Too noisy by half."

Tally: 22–1 (Slown)=21
Horses: 26

9

Slagos

Kestrel settled into a routine at Dock Street Haulers. Touching the horses as often as she did helped her connect with them, and she stretched her Talent by communicating with several at a time. On days no ships berthed, she delighted her charges by taking them out of their stuffy stalls and leading them up to a narrow, green valley where they could roll in the grass and run free. Boiled sweets were cheaper and more readily available in the Green Isles than in Wyndton; her other method of winning the horses' hearts was to treat them with bits of mint-flavored candy. She taught the horses what she needed from them so that in time she could open all the stalls and they would cooperatively pair themselves off and put their heads down for the workers to harness them up without a single command being spoken.

In Wyndton she had always hidden in the shadows. This position at Dock Street Haulers offered her a small realm to rule. Kestrel had more trouble with the people than the animals: after trying unsuccessfully to win them over, she had to fire several of the stable workers and drivers who were fresh with her, rough on the animals, or just resistant to change.

The owner supported her decisions because the horses' improved health and the end of the chaos in the yard meant that Dock Street could meet ships and pick up cargo from local businesses in a timely, calm, and professional manner. In a moon, he had received so many compliments and so many new commissions that he bought another team and raised Kestrel's pay without her even having to threaten.

With money filling her purse, Kestrel bought two changes of buff-colored broadcloth trousers, white canvas shirts, and an additional black corset at the secondhand market, in order to have enough to wash, hang to dry, and wear. This outfit was hardly typical garb for an Islander woman, but enough foreigners thronged the city that no one particularly cared about her choices.

Occasionally, she also treated herself to a supper at the Blue Parrot, both for the hot food and Zillie's company. In general, she spoke as little as possible in front of strangers, for fear her Weir accent would give her away. But in the weeks she had been living in Slagos she had become an accepted "regular" at the Parrot.

Zillie had certainly become a friend. Kestrel looked up to her, admiring her good cheer, stamina, and her ease with all sorts of people. Often she helped Zillie open or close up the tavern, just to have the chance to talk to her alone. And she studied how Zillie handled the men who came into the Blue Parrot. "How's my beauty today?" she accepted as a friendly remark. When a man asked, "Why didn't you warm my bed last night?" Zillie retorted, "*Your* bed? 'Tis full of fleas," which brought general laughter at the expense of the customer who had crossed a line.

When two men approached Kestrel one night saying, "Hey there, darlin', you need some company," and started to pull out the stools beside her, she spoke up loudly, "My own thoughts suit me more than your twaddle," which made the men back away with their hands up while the room broke out in laughter. Zillie winked at Wren.

Zillie knew how to disarm unwanted attention but she also amazed Kestrel in her bold relations with men who appealed to her. Kestrel learned that different countries had different customs regarding love affairs, with Weirandale tending toward the prudish. Zillie treated intimate relations casually; she invited to her bed those she fancied, kept lovers around while the enjoyment was mutual, and bid them goodbye without tears when they left on voyages or when the spark died out. She prevented pregnancy with an herb.

Once, on her way to the Blue Parrot for fastbreak, Kestrel saw Zillie passionately kissing a sailor in the slender alleyway between the tavern and the next shop. Kestrel quickly looked away and proceeded inside. In a few moments, Zillie entered, smiling.

"You should see your face!" Zillie teased. "Don't be so embarrassed, darlin'. Someday you'll realize that desire is one of the greatest gifts of life." She pulled her apron on, getting ready to start the morning. "Just be sure, darlin', that it's *your* desire and not just his."

Meanwhile, Kestrel managed to avoid any interaction with the Green Isles Bank; if the owner asked her to deposit money, she told him she was too busy running the stable. But she worried about spies constantly. How many people did Matwyck have on the payroll in Slagos? How could she be careful, if she didn't know whom to avoid? How could she determine who might be in the pay of a foreign realm?

Eventually she lit upon the parrots.

You understand me, don't you? she asked a red-throated parrot who had perched on her windowsill.

Indeedy, deedy, Your Majesty.

Do you understand other people? You repeat what they say.

These songs mean naught—they are just fun to sing.

Will you learn new human songs for me? Will you try to find particular ones?

Through repetition in her lodging's courtyard night after night, she taught a flock of five parrots to distinguish key sound patterns, including, "Mat-wyck," "Ma-gi," "Or-o-mon-do," "Weir," and "prin-cel-la."

In the evening, parrots flew onto the tree outside her window to repeat any possibly incriminating phrases. Often they caught the wrong "songs," such as phrases about "candlewicks" or "wine cel-lars." But when one parrot mimicked a male voice—"Mat-wyck's latest orders!"—she knew she had hit a seam of gold.

Once Kestrel determined that the assistant manager of the bank served as the Weir spymaster of Slagos, she had her parrots listen to and repeat all the conversations he engaged in. By tracing each encounter, eventually she unraveled a network: the harbormaster worked for Matwyck, as did one of the major ship outfitters. Scores of people (including one of the drivers she had already dismissed) were "on the lookout, on the lookout, for any lone young woman."

Accordingly, when she wasn't working or visiting with Zillie, Kestrel kept a low profile, often spending her free hours in Gardener's refuge.

He instructed her in herb lore, deepening the bits of knowledge she had gleaned from Rooks and Lem. She learned how to make poultices for wounds or infection and how to treat pain and fever. She enjoyed learning the unique properties of each herb—chamomile helped with sleep; lavender eased worries; and bergamot flavored a fine tisane (and her hair tonic).

As they ground herbs, Gardener waxed poetic about gardening, offering his years of wisdom. He told her that even when little change is visible to watchers, roots grow underground. He spoke about how some plants grow hardier after a stress such as a cold snap. Some plants need careful cosseting; others would take over if not held in check. The old man admitted that he had discovered that certain specimens were just unsuited for his garden and he'd had to give up on them.

"Kestrel, always keep in mind the garden maxim: first plants sleep, then they creep, and finally they leap."

A white parrot on a garden wall echoed, "Sleep, creep, leap."

"The reason we prepare the soil so well for new plants is to help healthy roots flourish. You have healthy roots."

"How does a person grow healthy roots?" Kestrel humored him.

Gardener crouched back on his heels with an enigmatic smile. "How do you think?"

Kestrel thought about how tenderly he handled young seedlings and how he gently watered and protected them. But the parallel with her parents and Nana caused her chest to ache.

Kestrel changed the subject. "What plants would be useful for coloring hair?"

"Henna will dye hair orange—though not as red as the Rorthers'. Chamomile will yield a yellow color, especially if mixed with honey or lemon juice; in Alpetar—which is more isolated than here—most folks' hair still shows yellow. Sorrel roots, grass, nettles, and spinach might make a tint to mimic Island Green, but the tint won't last."

"Yellow, yellow, yellow," echoed a parrot in exactly Gardener's tone of voice.

"Could anyone make a blue dye?"

"The indigo plant yields a deep blue. The shade is off."

"That's good to know," she answered, reassured, "even though Nargis would never allow an imposter."

During another visit, when Kestrel helped Gardener stake some shrubs, she asked him about loneliness. Being orphaned had scarred her, as had all the years of hiding her identity. And now she hid in a foreign land and she envied Zillie's love affairs.

"Gardener, are you lonely here in your courtyard?"

"Lonely? When I am surrounded by so many longtime companions?" He gestured toward the plants and trees.

"No, that's not what I mean. I'm thinking about romance. Have you ever been in love?"

"Of course, my dear. Three times. The first time was with a man who did not care for me and broke my heart. The second time was with my sweet wife."

"You were married once upon a time?" she blurted out, widening her eyes. "Where is your wife now?"

"Years ago I buried her in the southwest corner. Do you see those beautiful lilies? She nurtured them."

Kestrel wasn't sure whether she found using a loved one as fertilizer touching or disturbing.

"And the third time?"

"Ah," said Gardener. "The third time has been the most rapturous. Who would have known that in my elderly years I would find such tenderness and fulfillment? And know that I was beloved in turn."

Kestrel startled at this statement, for she had never seen a woman in the courtyard or Garden. Instinctively, she looked around to see if Gardener's paramour was hiding behind a tree. Glancing about, she saw the statue of Vertia, and the truth of his rapture dawned on her.

"How I envy you," sighed Kestrel, stretching her back. "To live beside your beloved. Mostly I miss particular people. But I have also journeyed so far from the Waters. Their sound and scent and touch seem like a distant fantasy. I'm so homesick, Gardener. And I often wonder if I have been forgotten or abandoned."

Gardener reached over to stroke her cheek. His rough skin felt like the softest blossom. "Never that, my dear, never that. I'm certain that your Waters long for you even more than you miss them. In the Garden of Time consolation grows."

One early evening Kestrel trudged in the direction of her lodging, worn out from two ship arrivals and three departures. She also felt cross because she'd had an altercation with a merchant who had held up the hauler's whole choreographed schedule by not having his shipment ready for loading.

Gardener met her at the entrance to the courtyard, his face scrunched with worry.

"Oh, at last! I need beg for your help."

"What's happened?"

"The Garden has been invaded! Plants destroyed."

Kestrel took a look at the damage in the waning light. Several beds had been eaten down to nubs, others nibbled, and still others just willfully trampled. She squatted to examine the tracks in the soil and teeth marks on leaves.

"Groundhogs," said the woman who grew up in rural Wyndton. "They tunneled under the wall over here . . . and over there." She pointed before she recalled that Gardener couldn't see her gestures.

"Vertia's Blessing should have kept them out," he said, tugging on the long sleeves of his green robe in distress. "Why now—"

"Well, it didn't. And since they've sampled your plants, they'll try again. We need to stand watch, armed with hoes. Especially in the mornings and the evenings."

"But I am an unsuitable sentry," said Gardener, "and you need to report to work. I could ask for help from other friends but I thought . . . can't you use your special Talents to keep them out?"

Kestrel didn't have the heart to tell Gardener that some pest animals, like the raccoons that raided the chickens in Wyndton, wouldn't obey her.

"Well, I can try," she sighed.

She exited the Garden and paced its perimeter, following the disturbed earth, but she lost the groundhogs' trail. Soon, however, she realized that just as Gardener needed to lean on her skills, she required the assistance of groundhog experts.

Two terriers lived in the shady passageway between the Blue Parrot and the Breaking Bread Bakery. Both Zillie and the baker swore they didn't want them there, but Kestrel had spotted the plates of food left out and had marked the dogs' plump bellies and sleek coats. Kestrel trudged to the dogs.

Terriers, she called. *You're skilled at dealing with varmints, aren't you?*

Of course, said the bigger one, standing up from the pile of rags someone had deliberately left him and stretching his front legs. *Why dost thou think these places have no rats?*

Will you help me track a family of groundhogs?

Let's at 'em, said the smaller terrier, twirling in excited circles. *Cheeky, smelly, nasties. Let's at 'em. Let's go! Where? Where?*

Once Kestrel put them on the scent, the dogs promptly cornered the groundhogs in their burrow. The terriers rushed, frantic to attack, but Kestrel held them off to give the invaders a warning.

Groundhogs! You can find plenty to eat on this fertile isle. Why did you dig into Vertia's Garden?

Tasty treats, replied the biggest groundhog.

But that space is special, sacred. Will you promise to stay out in the future?

Why should one?

Because I'm asking you to.

One does nay have to listen to strange human. Be gone!

Yes, you do. I COMMAND you to leave the Garden alone.

Go choke on scat! said the groundhog, using her hind paws to scratch a shower of dirt in Kestrel's general direction.

Obviously, Kestrel had not yet mastered commanding unfriendly beasts. She loosed the dogs. The air filled with growls and the groundhogs' shrieks, causing such a commotion that people in nearby houses came to their doorways to see what was afoot. In a trice, the terriers shook the dead rodents in front of the onlookers with pride. Kestrel checked that the dogs had taken no bites and thanked them for their help. Then she reported to Gardener that she had dealt with the problem.

Gardener's gratitude embarrassed Kestrel.

"Really, I did nothing, I just fetched the terriers."

"It may have been an easy service for you, my dear, but you saved the Garden." He sat down on his stone steps, exhausted from the loss and stress, murmuring to himself. "Now, we must consider: Vertia must have allowed this to happen for a reason. What is the Spirit teaching us?"

Kestrel snorted at Gardener's parable seeking. "I think it's simple. The lesson is: 'Everyone should have a dog.' I'm off to bed. I'll try to stop by tomorrow to help you replant and stake."

10

Melladrin

Wareth rode point, but he didn't range far ahead. Sergeant Codek had pulled all the scouts in close (just barely out of sight), because their path now wound through an area where long-ago water courses had cut the land into a maze of bluffs. Wareth agreed with Codek's placement. Most of the day, in addition to freezing, he had felt an itchy sensation on the back of his neck, as if the Raiders were being watched or followed.

The feeling of "presence" grew stronger, but no matter how quickly the scout whipped his head this way or that, he saw nothing but emptiness and heard only the constant whistle of the wind. He kept imagining a tiger was stalking him—at night the Raiders frightened one another with stories about their size and ferocity. *Well, fuck it,* he thought, he would just have to risk the men's joshing; he was going to ride back and give warning. He would turn around in this flat bit here—

He was surrounded. A second ago the tops of the bluffs stood empty; now twenty-odd brown- and plum-haired archers had arrows aimed straight at him.

Wareth raised his hands, hoping these people understood the gesture meant surrender. Apparently they did, because a man grabbed Custard's bridle and gestured for him to get down. No one spoke. Wareth slid off his mare, and several people grabbed his arms and pulled him forward two dozen paces to hide them from the main troop following.

Wareth looked around and realized his ambushers had chosen the perfect spot. The Raiders would ride into this treeless, dry wash and be surrounded by archers perched on high. And they were downwind here; even the wolfhound would not scent danger.

He pulled in a gasp to shout or whistle a warning, but before he could utter a sound, hands stuffed a rag in his mouth and iron grips closed down on his arms, holding him tight and quiet.

It only took a few minutes until the rest of the Free Staters rode right into the trap. Sergeant Codek looked around warily, but Thalen rode lost in thought, as he was wont to do. No one shouted or cried out when they spied the archers above them, though Britmank and Latof cursed softly.

Commander Thalen smiled broadly, as if he had been hoping for exactly this encounter.

"Melladrini, Star Followers, we salute you," he said, and he bowed his head low while holding his right hand on his chest, and his left hand palm upward to the sky.

One of the archers, a woman whose long plum-colored hair had only a few strands of light brown, stepped forward. "Stranger, how do you know our greeting?"

"I have studied your people for many years. I know, for instance, that the bracelets you wear mean you have two sons and three daughters."

"You're right. But other foreigners murdered one of my daughters and both of my sons. We have not even found the body of my second-born."

"I am grieved to hear this. Those foreigners, the Oromondos, also killed my brother and my mother."

"I am grieved to hear this."

"Some people say 'Talking of sorrow makes it lighter.' Could we confer?" asked Thalen.

"First, your soldiers must lay down their weapons."

Commander Thalen raised his voice to all. "Drop your swords, your daggers, your bows. All of it. On the ground. Now."

"But, sir," protested Ooma, "they could shoot us down."

"Raider, if they wanted us dead, we would have been crow meat weeks ago. Do as I say." The last words were spoken with a whip-crack of authority.

The Free Staters dropped their weapons.

"Now, dismount," Thalen ordered.

Thalen and the older woman walked a ways in front of everyone, talking. When they were about fifty paces in front, they sat in the grass, sheltered from the wind by tall hillocks, conversing animatedly.

Wareth's captors released him. He strode over to his sergeant, hanging his head.

"Are you hurt, Wareth?" Codek asked.

"Only my scout's pride. I led us straight into their ambush."

"No, lad, you led us straight into an important parley." Codek turned to the rest of the troop. "Smoke your pipes, stretch, whatever you wish. Just don't do nothing stupid. We are going to cool our heels here a while."

Wareth got a drink of water and wiped the fear sweat off his face.

Adair patted his shoulder. "I sensed them; but I never spotted them either. Never seen their like for walking without sound and moving without even throwing a shadow."

"Tristo!" Thalen called. "Bring me water, honey, and salt. And two cups."

Tristo gave Wareth and Adair a quizzical face and ran to do Thalen's bidding.

They watched Commander Thalen prepare two cups of salted water, one of which he offered to the old Mellie woman. She drank hers down; then he drank his. Thalen then poured more water, liberally stirring in honey. They drank their cups.

That seemed to conclude some ritual. The archers relaxed and lowered their arrows. Wareth looked closely at them for the first time and noticed the absence of young men.

Thalen called out, "Raiders, we move forward, at a walk. Load your weapons on your horses and lead them."

And he and the old woman strode ahead at Thalen's long-legged pace, continuing on the Free Staters' trajectory toward the snow-capped mountains of Oromondo now dominating the whole horizon.

After about an hour, Thalen called for Sergeant Codek to join the conversation, and the Mellie leader called in three of her people. Codek shook his head negatively, but from the looks of it, Thalen overruled him.

Codek returned to the men. "The commander has made an alliance with the Mellies; he has convinced them that we mean them no harm and we share a common foe. He has told them of our mission. They worry that if the Oros pull out of the Free States, they might march back through their country—which is exactly what they don't want. But the commander has persuaded them that the Oros will hurry by ship to the harbor city, Drintoolia.

"They have naught to gain by helping us, but they too thirst for revenge. This group is going to talk to others, and lead us to a mountain pass in between the Magi's watchtowers. They believe the Oros ignore this chasm because it's really narrow."

"What's the price of this assistance?" Kambey asked. "What's bothering you?"

Codek cleared his throat. "We have to let a small group of Mellies join with us."

"Where's the problem with that, Codek? They've proven they are superior trackers," said Adair.

"Two females—the leader's surviving daughters. And an old coot, her older brother."

Tristo laughed out loud. "Oh, for fuck's sake, Codek! We know that women can be great fighters. And you're an old coot yourself! Can I meet them?"

"Actually, that's a good idea. Run up to the commander before he agrees to this deal."

Wareth wondered whether Tristo's easy charm would work on Mellies without mead; he couldn't hear the conversation, but he watched their body language. Tristo talked to a sinewy older man with a close brown beard; now they both were laughing. The two young women wouldn't look Tristo directly in the face, but one of them gazed in the direction of the band of Raiders. In a flash she raised her unusual bow and loosed. The arrow flew straight through the crown of Codek's battered cavalry hat.

Everyone—Free Staters and Mellies—laughed at the look of total shock on their sergeant's face.

Wareth flicked Codek's hat. "I think we'll be lucky to have them. And I sure feel lucky, 'cause when chaps think back on this day, that arrow is what they'll recall, not my scouting!"

"You was always a piss-poor scout," said Codek. "Who lost his mare *the first moments* of the Rout?"

Laughing with the group, Wareth pretended to take the jibe in stride, but the sally hit his pride as smartly as the arrow had skewered the sergeant's hat. He couldn't help suspecting that Codek had taken his own humiliation out on the handiest target.

That night during supper, Wareth managed to sit beside Thalen. The elder Mellie spoke to their commander. "We've been watching out for you. These came from the Free States by kayak and runner. There's a bit of quiet trade (and a bit of smuggling) between our nations— at least there was before the Oros marched through." Out of his satchel he pulled a package wrapped in oilskin. Wareth wondered if it contained something special to eat. When Thalen unwrapped it, the scout was disappointed to discover it only contained two books.

Yet Thalen held the volumes tightly to his chest, his hands caressing the leather spines. "I never really expected to see these," he said. "How . . ."

The Mellie man smiled. "Ah! We have relatives across the Bridge of Fallen Stars: some of us have even intermarried. Have you ever met a woman named 'Rel-lia'? She is the daughter of my mother's cousin. I believe she holds an important position in your country."

Thalen obviously wanted to read the books that instant, but he recollected his manners. "Thank you. You have already done me an essential service. What is your name?"

"Tel-bein. My nieces are Eli-anna and Eldie. They will not speak to you because they observe a year of silent mourning for their lost sister. It takes great strength to keep the Silence of the Stars. They are made of sterner stuff than I am."

The graceful young women both wore their hair—light brown with slight strands of plum mixed in—in an elaborate plait curled on top of their heads like a crown. Like Tel-bein, their clothing, woven from some unfamiliar soft fiber, consisted of grass-colored long tunics reaching down to their ankles, slit in four places for movement, over formfitting, plum-colored trousers. And they wore open vests of antelope hide, fur side facing in and the hide side decorated with embossed patterns of constellations. Their hats and gloves were of rabbit fur. Even while eating they kept on their leather forearm shields and settled their bows next to their knees. The women looked so alike Wareth struggled to tell them apart: by surreptitious study, he eventually decided that Eli-anna was a touch taller, while Eldie had a scar on her chin.

"Where is the rest of your squad now?" asked the commander.

"They are spread around us in this formation," Tel-bein drew the shape in the soil. "They keep watch for other threats, and they will spread the news about your clan to other bands. They will leave us at the end of our range, and my grandmother's sister's band will take over guarding us."

"I am very grateful your people will meet the next boat bearing supplies and bring them to the pass."

"Each family will move those supplies forward through its range."

Wareth asked, "Will they be tempted to look at the things and even keep the food for themselves?"

"No," said Tel-bein; he sounded amused rather than offended. "What would we want with your food or arrows? Our own are better. Tomorrow or the next day, I can lead you to a ravine teeming with wild boars, and we can hunt for fresh meat. And I will show you warmer places to pitch camp, where the wind isn't so hungry." His voice got harder. "Besides, you say you need your things to kill Oros. We want vengeance. They burned our grasslands and slaughtered many of our people. My son died in our stand to hold the Mouth of the Mountains. So, if you need those supplies to help you, you shall have them."

"Good," said Thalen, and he clasped hands with the elderly man. "I have to admit—I was counting on some sort of assistance. We'd never make it without you."

As Wareth moved toward his bedroll, Codek intercepted him. "I noticed your eyes on the new additions, those Mellie females," he said. "You and all the others, you're to leave 'em alone. Do you hear? That's an order, Wareth."

"Sure, sure," Wareth responded peaceably, though he felt unjustly accused.

11

Pilagos, the Green Isles

Olet had literally opened his arms, his business, and his purse to Hake and Quinith when they had arrived a moon ago. The news of the deaths of Jerinda and Harthen had shaken Olet. Olet had no family of his own, and Hake realized that all these years he had looked to the Sutterdam clan as if it were an idealized surrogate version of his own life. Hake believed Olet when he vowed he would give his right arm to bring Jerinda back or to see Hake walk again. Olet set up one of his outbuildings to serve as combination living quarters, office, and warehouse for his visitors. He arranged for their meals to be delivered.

Hake started to adapt to his life without the use of his legs. The wheeled chair that Ikas had fashioned for him helped; he could now move from sleeping nook to business room and even roll short distances on a smooth outside surface without asking for assistance or being carried like a babe. In addition, he had built up enough strength in his arms and chest to do many things for himself, such as hoisting his body in and out of bed.

Even more curative, though, was the sense of purpose he gained from having a crucial task to perform. He and Quinith had become quartermasters to the Raiders.

Quinith had proven himself a resourceful and persistent partner; his privileged family background bequeathed him a confident approach to difficulties, as if it were unthinkable that the world could refuse his requests. For Quinith, tracking Hake down in Sutterdam, whisking him out of the occupied city, and hiring a boat to transport them to the Green Isles were challenges easy to surmount. However, it was Hake who had thought of making their destination Olet's Olive Oil in Pilagos. And it was Hake who had experience as a supply master and contacts with many merchants.

Together they calculated how soon Thalen's Raiders would need resupplying with food, clothing, and arms. Too much and their goods would be a burden for the troop to carry; too little and the Raiders might be in need. They had to count on Thalen setting up a supply route through Melladrin; their job centered on getting the provisions to the coastal hamlet Metos.

Thalen had asked them to send at least six replacement horses and fighters. The horses presented little difficulty; Olet knew a reputable stable yard, and he helped them buy a small string of mounts that were healthy and willing, even though they were not pretrained for battle.

Men, eager to join the fight, followed rumors and Olet's hints and sought them out. Some the quartermasters turned away as not suitable, no matter how thirsty for revenge. However, Quinith tested the skills of two young brothers and approved them; Hake suffered a pang at their enthusiasm, which reminded him of Harthen's. A Green Isles healer named Pemphis also convinced them of his abilities and resolve. But the other applicants turned out to be too old or not strong enough.

The day before the resupply ship, *Island Courier,* planned to set sail to Metos, a knock on the doorframe interrupted Quinith's and Hake's argument over how many water bags to pack.

"Excuse me," said a wiry man with short brown hair at the entrance. "We heard that you might be hiring men—fighting men."

"That's right," said Quinith. "Who are you?"

"Fighters." The man flashed a quick smile that revealed some missing teeth. His pal was a larger man with a barrel chest. Their good-quality coats and breeches showed hard wear. Both wore doublets of boiled leather.

"I see that. I'm Quinith and this here is Hake."

"Shyrwin," said the stranger, coming forward to shake hands.

"Nollo," said his companion, hanging back but touching his forehead in a casual salute.

"Yes, we're looking for men to join an expedition to help the Free States. Actually, we can't pay; we're looking for volunteers."

This set the men back; they recoiled and their noses wrinkled.

"You don't pay . . . anything?"

"Sorry, we can't," said Hake. "Pity you made the trip out here."

The two strangers retreated to the doorway and conferred in muted tones.

"We're still willing to go," said Shyrwin.

"Why?" asked Hake. "Are you Free Staters? You don't have the accent."

"Nah," said Shyrwin. "We're what some call 'travelers of the world.' As to why, we crave to be where the action is. We get restless-like, sitting around scratching our arses. These Isles are boring as shit."

Hake frowned. "Most of the Raiders have personal reasons for joining—reasons that make them willing to put up with danger and a hard slog."

"Oh, we're willing all right," said Shyrwin with a small smile. "And peril is our business. Where would you be sending us?"

"Eventually, into Oromondo," said Quinith.

"Ah, why didn't you say so! That land's just crawling with gemstones, right? Any problem with us gathering up a few while we're there, kind of along the way?"

"If you *live* and stumble across gems, you can help yourselves. But you've got to survive first. You look as if you might have had fighting experience," said Quinith, eyeing the swords and daggers that hung easily around their waists and the scars that snaked about on uncovered brown skin.

"Oh, that we have."

"Would you mind sparring a bit with me in the yard, just to show how you handle your weapons?"

The three left the room. Hake tuned out the sounds of their practice bouts as he took advantage of Quinith's absence to move all the leather water bags to the pile of supplies to be carried down to the wharf.

The three returned in a few minutes. Quinith panted while the newcomers looked as if they'd been picking berries.

"How's your archery?" Hake asked.

"Left our bows in town at our inn," said Nollo. "Thought it would look strange since no one here even walks around with a sword. Didn't want no city watch questioning us. You'll have to take our word for it."

"Are you fleeing the law?" Hake asked, trying to figure out what was "off" about these volunteers.

"Nope. We're on the right side with all the authorities." Shyrwin met Hake's glance without equivocation.

"Answer a question," Hake said. "Quinith and I disagree on how many water bags to send. He says they're heavy and in the way. I say, better to have than to want. Given your experience, what do you think?"

"Send all the water bags you can lay your hands on," said Shyrwin. "Cain't ever have enough water. Water is life."

"Would you fellows wait outside a moment while we discuss?" asked Hake.

The men nodded and left the building. Hake could see them through the open door. Nollo was whistling to the sky while Shyrwin fussed with his sword and scabbard.

"So?" Quinith asked Hake.

"I'm not as sure about them as I am about the others," Hake answered.

"Me neither," agreed Quinith. "We never considered mercenaries. But we're out of time and options. Thalen wanted us to send six, and without these we'd only have three. And they're really fearsome fighters. Much more versatile and experienced than those two brothers. Can we afford to leave the Raiders shorthanded until we find the perfect men?"

"No," said Hake, with some reluctance. "And this may be our only chance to send reinforcements."

Quinith walked to the doorway and called out, "We sail tomorrow—is that a problem for you?"

"Nope."

"You'll be joined by a few others we've already enlisted."

"Whatever."

"Do you need any money to buy personal gear today?" asked Hake.

"Nah, we're good as to gear," Shyrwin said. "But we'd take it kindly if you want to treat us to a last blowout at a tavern. . . ."

One of Olet's messenger girls ran into the room. "There's a carter and a seamaster in the yard. They say they're in an awful hurry."

"I must confer with them," said Quinith. He offered his hand again to the new men and passed them a silver grape. "Meet me at dawn at the *Island Courier*. She's berthed at the third pier."

"We'll be there," said Shyrwin as Quinith and Hake turned their attention to the last bundles of the supplies.

12

Needle Pass

Tally: 21+3 (Eli-anna, Eldie, and Tel-bein)=24

After three moons of hard riding through freezing wind, gradually climbing higher and higher in elevation, their lungs adjusting to the altitude, Thalen's Raiders reached the Obsidian Mountains. These hulking monsters filled their vision, gray and foreboding, with white caps that both knifed the daytime sky and loomed ominously into the nighttime heavens.

The Needle fell in a blind spot between two of the watchtowers of Oromondo, each the traditional holding of a Magi.

"Needle Pass" was the Mellie name, of course; to their knowledge the Oros had never named the thin break between the towering mountains, and Oros wouldn't, under any circumstances, consider it a pass. The Mouth of the Mountains stretched wide enough for two dozen aurochs to ride abreast. By contrast, the Needle was going to be a tight squeeze for the broader horses, and the mounts could carry no packages overhanging their sides. The stock of dried berries and thistle seed flour that the Mellies had gifted them plumped up their supplies, but balancing the sacks would be tricky.

The men were all thin enough, Thalen noted. These three moons had burnt off the last of the baby fat on Tristo's face; the cavalryman Rowe's paunch had disappeared; and though he did not see it himself, Thalen knew the sun and wind had weathered his skin, which previously had been sheltered in the dim recesses of the library.

Thalen had changed in less visible ways too. He had watched Kambey's and Codek's manner of giving orders, solving disputes, offering reassurance or a stern hand as required; just as he'd studied Gentain's ability to sit his saddle so lightly or Kran's effortless strokes while sharpening his sword. He scrutinized his companions as if they were books and learned them cover to cover.

At this point, he could read the Raiders' moods from the way they held their reins or adjusted their hats. By design, Thalen spoke little and never raised his voice nor joked around. He was chary with praise but even charier with rebuke; he conveyed his firmness by looking these men and women—nearly all of whom were older and more experienced than he—straight in the eye with an unwavering gaze. He constantly conveyed that their mission was deadly serious and of the utmost importance.

Fortunately, their horses appeared to be in good shape. Their string had weathered the rigors of their travel well, growing thick and shaggy coats as protection from the elements. Before attempting the Pass, Gentain suggested that the Raiders trim their hooves and reshoe them all. This had two advantages: the chore both prepared the horses and lightened their burden of spare horseshoes.

Driscoll's *Obsidian Mountains: Legends and Truth* explained what Earth and Water scholars knew about how volcanic mountain ranges arose, what minerals they contained, and how the Oromondo people had come to worship the periodic eruptions and see them as the will of their Fire Spirit, Pozhar. Over centuries the priest class, who called themselves Pozhar's Magi, had sprinkled more and more cooled lava into their flour; Driscoll believed that even if the Magi's Powers came from Pozhar, the heavy metals contained in the lava gave them their hallucinations. The tremendous pressure exerted by the volcanic forces also provided Oromondo with a rich trove of precious metals and gemstones.

The more Thalen read about the metallic ores present in volcanic ranges and the history of Oromondo mining, the more assured he grew about his hypothesis regarding the various blights that had afflicted this realm over the last years. Only poisoned water sources could account for the variety and widespread nature of these afflictions affecting livestock, crops, people, and especially unborn babes throughout the country. As the Oros dug ever deeper for riches, they would have disturbed layers of rock containing cadmium and lead; the mine tailings had polluted the water. Certain segments of the population lived closer to contaminated streams or were more susceptible to the minerals' damage.

But if Thalen's theory that the Oros had polluted their own water was correct, how could he keep the Raiders and their horses healthy? Here, the second book provided hope. Although he could not read the ancient language, the book contained maps of what had to be rivers *and springs*. The mining may have polluted the rivers, but if the natural springs came from aquifers deep below the surface, their water should be healthy. Would the springs still gush in the same places? Had time, erosion, or human structures covered them over? Could he find them? The Raiders could melt snow while their path kept them high up in the mountains; the pinch would come when they descended in altitude.

But how long would it take for Thalen to find these springs? The night before they ventured through the pass he had every container filled with sweet Mellie water. He cupped his hands in a small stream and drank his fill, savoring it, even though the cold hurt his teeth.

No wonder the Weirs worship sweet water.

In the early morning, Thalen formally thanked the last Mellie escorts for all their assistance and generosity. In symbolic repayment, Thalen gave the Mellies two of the Raiders' mares. This clan comprised the last link in the chain, a chain that would bring the next shipment of supplies here to the Mellie side of the Needle, which would serve as the Raiders' depot.

Thalen then set about arranging his men, women, and horses in the order they would file through the pass. He put Tel-bein and Adair, his best scouts, first. Right behind them his brawniest fighters, for if Oros were watching this defile, archers would be of no use—no room to pull a bow. He needed Weddle with his staff, Ooma with her knives, and his sword masters—Kran, Jothile, and Kambey—to overpower them. After this group he placed himself, with Tristo, who had settled into serving as his adjutant and message carrier. Gentain and the cavalrymen controlled the horses in the middle, because the last thing they needed were horses getting spooked or claustrophobic. Cook, Cookie, Cerf, the Mellie girls, and Yislan followed the horsemen. Sergeant Codek, with his calm steadiness, would bring up the rear.

He nodded at Tel-bein and Adair to proceed, then spoke to the rest.

"Raiders. It should take us most of the day to traverse this pass, walking the horses through. If there has been a rockslide or some other obstacle blocks the way, we might have to back out, since I'm told we won't find anyplace wide enough to turn around. Assuming we do get through, on the other side we'll be in the Oros' Land. We have chosen this route because it was unguarded the last time the Mellies snuck through, but keep your wits about you; we can't know what awaits us."

Thalen's gaze swept his assembled troop. "Keep quiet in the Needle; all our noise will echo against the rock face. But this is what we came for. Let's go." Drawing himself to his full height, he waved the line forward.

His soldiers nodded or muttered agreement. The Mellie girls rubbed the bridge of each other's noses, a curious gesture he would have to ask them about sometime. Did it mean "good fortune"?

Thalen entered the opening of the gap. Within a few strides the light grew dimmer; the rock face closed in on both sides. You could see only the sky, way up above, and the butt of the horse in front of you. Sandy grit covered the ground, interspersed with gravel or larger rocks. So far, nothing Dish couldn't handle.

Thalen calmed his nerves by examining the rock face with care, wishing that Tutor Irinia were with him to read the mountain's story. Had an earthquake made this pass? Were any of these black streaks obsidian? Not likely; he thought that obsidian came from dried lava.

"We're being buried alive," Tristo whispered.

"Hmm? No. Nothing like. Plenty of air here." How could he get the boy's mind off their claustrophobic surroundings?

"I wonder," he whispered back to Tristo, "if the wind ever blows directly through this passageway. If so, the gorge would act something like a whistle; I'll bet it would make a characteristic note. Did I ever tell you I can play the flute, Tristo?" he asked.

"No," said Tristo, without much interest.

"I played the flute for years. What's your favorite tune?"

Tristo gradually warmed to the topic, and they had a whispered conversation about Yosta bar songs that distracted the boy.

"I don't think I know 'Hop to the Mead.' Hum the beginning for me." Humming worked like a charm to calm Tristo.

Sometimes the walls pressed in even closer. Sometimes the horses balked at a thin patch and they had to whip them through.

Without a view of the sky, Thalen couldn't tell time. After a few hours they came to a slight widening of the crevasse and he called a halt. They let the horses breathe and switch their tails, and the men stretched and reached for water or into their saddlebags for food. They tightened the straps holding the packages on the horses.

A short time after they started up again, Thalen heard an ominous rumbling. He realized that way up high above them, on the mountains' surface, snow and rocks gathered energy and began to slide. An avalanche! But the Raiders had no means of escape because they boxed one another in. They were completely trapped.

As the rumbling increased, horses neighed and some of the Raiders yelped in fright. The shaking increased; clumps of snow and small rocks began tumbling into Needle Pass.

A few of the horses reared; he saw Literoy and Rowe pulling down the reins.

"Cover your head!" Thalen shouted, demonstrating.

The men waited, crouched down, arms over their heads. The rumbling rose in ferocity, even making the stone walls shudder. But after a few heart-stopping minutes it was clear that the heart of the avalanche had missed them, depositing most of its sliding snow some distance behind the end of the line.

"All right back here," Sergeant Codek called.

"Check your horses," Gentain added, because in their own fright some of the beasts had kicked out against the rock walls. Sulky Sukie had bitten the horse in front of her.

Thalen gave the men a few minutes to pull themselves together and then relayed the signal to move ahead. The pass's floor, which had always angled up, became even more steep. Their calf muscles began to burn, and their breathing grew more ragged.

They were all bone-weary, man and beast, when the whisper "Opening ahead" moved from Raider to Raider.

If Oros actually had been guarding the Needle they would all have been slaughtered, because they came out so tired and so blinded by the extra light of the open air of a late afternoon. They tumbled out of the defile onto a landscape completely different from what they had left in the morning. Here they saw snow and sharply angled sheer rock, with steep peaks opposite and crowding in on all sides. A chilling, ferocious landscape, brutal and unwelcoming.

When he exited the pass, Gentain ran up beside Thalen. "We need to tend the horses, and they need water so bad. I like that stand of trees down yonder."

Thalen assented, because the tree line below them offered a modicum of cover. Slipping precariously and making terrible clatters that echoed off the surrounding rock faces, they traversed the bare rock to an area where evergreens grew sparsely. They dismounted, took the baggage off the horses, and salved their mounts' scrapes. Thalen sent six Raiders clambering behind them to gather the snow into every container they owned.

Once water-gathering was underway, Thalen had the sure-footed Mellie girls lead him out from the trees to a nearby ledge where he could get a good look around.

Below them the land fell off precipitously down, down, down into a valley through which ran a creek swiftly plunging over a bed of boulders. A rutted dirt road paralleled the water. Thalen then glanced upriver and saw in the near distance the mouth of a mine, with a cluster of buildings. On the other side of the creek more jagged rocks reached toward the sky. In the folds of the canyons across, he spied more mines, access roads, and the spire of a Magi watchtower, though the town that served it hid behind a mountain's outskirts.

Thalen studied the shapes of the peaks and compared them to the images he had formed in his mind from studying maps, experiencing deep dismay because the pictures did not match up. Then he understood the cause of his confusion: he was now gazing southeast, and the maps he had memorized had been drawn facing north. So he had to try to rotate the maps in his mind, a task that required all his concentration.

Meanwhile, Eli-anna and Eldie crept around the ledge on their stomachs. Eldie threw a pebble at Thalen to get his attention and pointed toward a mine across the valley. The last rays of the sun glinted off metal, but Thalen couldn't make out anything more.

"Eli-anna, I've got a spyglass in Dish's left saddlebag. If you can't find it, Tristo will help you. Fetch it please."

When she brought it Thalen focused on the mine entrance, a group of buildings that might hold tools and such, some dwellings, and a convoy of wagons, mostly filled. He also saw a squad of Oro soldiers lounging around the wagons; likely their armor had drawn the light and Eldie's attention.

He forced himself to move his glass away from the men, looking for the tailings from the mine. To the left of the mine entrance he saw a pile of crushed rock. Snow and rain had run through this pile, making a slurry that coursed downhill. Thalen followed the downhill trail; as much as he could tell in the winter landscape all vegetation on either side was dead.

Turning his spyglass back to the wagons Thalen discerned that the workers had almost finished loading. This had to be a mining convoy, probably preparing to start at dawn. He traced the wagon track down from the mine and followed the switchback route it would take to reach the main road in the valley. He sent Eldie back for Codek.

When his second-in-command crawled out to join him on the ledge, Thalen said, "I see an Oro shipment coming down the mountain across from us in the morning. Can we ambush it?"

Codek studied the terrain and made his lips vibrate in a disparaging huff. "Commander, let this one go. It would take us all night to get down within reach, and some of the horses are in no shape for the trek off this muckshit mountain. Also, after we hit the Oros, what then? We need a hidey-hole—a camp so the horses aren't burdened with all these supplies. We don't want to fuckin' waste ourselves on the first day!"

Thalen sighed. "Finally we're here, and our target is right in front of us. I itch to engage." He pushed the hair that had blown onto his face out of his way. "But aye. We have come too far to be rash. All right then. Let's rejoin the others."

By the time they returned to the stand of trees, the mountains had cut off the remnants of daylight. They dug a fire pit to melt the snow for the horses, but Thalen insisted that men wave hats and blankets to disperse the smoke.

Codek posted watch. Thalen walked among the men, checking on them. Two of the younger cavalrymen, Jothile and Literoy, admitted that they felt nauseous; Thalen reassured them that this was just a side effect of the altitude and they'd feel better as soon as the Raiders moved lower. Rowe was pissed that Sukie had bitten his sweet mare, but Thalen jollied him out of it. Gentain reported that all but two of the horses would be fit to ride tomorrow and to compensate, the Mellie girls would double up and he'd put Tristo in front of someone lightweight, such as Fedak.

Thalen had Tristo rig his tent behind two of the broadest trees and bring him a lantern turned low, his vellum, and ink. With his books open and recalling what he had seen, Thalen started redrawing the map of this area of the mountain range from their current perspective.

Since Tristo hadn't set up his desk, Thalen had to hunch over, drawing on the ground. This reminded him of something, but he couldn't quite remember when he had done this before.

Tristo interrupted him with a tin cup of brandy. Cookie had decided the brandy weighed down the horses and they had plenty in reserve. After the tension of the day, liquor went down with a welcome warmth; Thalen savored the sweet taste of pears.

"Commander, really you must stop now," Tristo nagged as second watch started. "Or you'll be too tired tomorrow."

Reluctantly, Thalen gave up for the time being. Before drawing his blankets close around him he looked outside. Master and Apprentice moons looked so huge up here in the thin air. Instead of providing comfort they seemed determined to point out the Raiders.

"Look! There they are!" the moons shouted. "Invaders in the Land!"

Horses: 26–2 (gifts to Mellies)=24

PART
TWO

Reign of Regent Matwyck,
Year 13

13

Slagos to Alpetar

The dirty rainsquall sent Kestrel to the Blue Parrot while awaiting the sighting of a major cargo vessel from Rortherrod, because the wind blew so whichaway no one could guess when the ship would arrive. A Dock Street lass knew where to find her if the ship approached.

Kestrel called a greeting to Zillie, who poured her some mead, handed her a basket of the bread she knew she loved, and ran off to take more orders.

Surveying the low-ceilinged room, Kestrel sipped her drink and broke off chunks of bread. Lots of folk crammed the tavern tonight, deciding that the foul night called for lamps and company. Kestrel nodded across the room at two of her own drivers and recognized the blacksmith and his family. Other diners must be fisherfolk who had raced the storm into harbor.

Two older men with weatherworn skin sat at the counter close to her. Kestrel overheard their conversation.

"I heard this rumor from the mate on a Yosta boat that a squad of Free States devils has gone to Oromondo to fight the Oros there," said one to his chum.

"Aye, I heard the same from my brother-in-marriage—you know he's got kin in Yosta. Being led by some sprout who they say has the wit of a man twice his age."

"Sorry to impose," Kestrel addressed the fishermen. "Do you know how I could find out more about this?"

"Huh." The fisherman considered, chewing his food. "I heard one of the big merchants in Pilagos has set up as their headquarters. What was that name? Something about olives."

Zillie had returned with Kestrel's trencher and overheard the last sentences. "Do you ken it could be Olet's Olive Oil and Spicery? Famous trader in Pilagos. I get a lot of supplies from him."

"That's it exactly," said the man. "But what's your interest?" he asked Kestrel.

"I have a major score to settle with the Oros," she said.

"Aye, aye, as do many."

"Buy you a drink if you tell me all you know?" Kestrel offered.

"Pshaw. Save your coin, darlin'. We brought in heavy nets today. But shift over this way and we'll tell you what little we know."

When she got a moment, Zillie came over to join them. "You folk still jawing about the Raiders?"

"Raiders, is it?" asked Kestrel.

"Aye, that's what those folks from Pilagos call them," said Zillie.

"Now, how do you know that?" asked one of the fishermen.

"Heard that table of Pilagos folk talking about them not two moments ago," said Zillie with triumph, pointing across the room at a group of men. "You being concerned, want me to introduce you?" she asked Kestrel.

Kestrel said "Aye," and stood up, but at that moment the messenger burst in.

"Stable master, the *Ruler of Rortherrod*'s been sighted by the harbor watch."

"Then best get the drays out. Zillie, got a meat pie for a hungry girl?" Zillie winked at the wet messenger and handed her a pie. The Dock Street drivers across the room had noted Kestrel's movement and already crammed in their last mouthfuls. Kestrel tipped her cap to Zillie and the fishermen and then grabbed her cloak.

The cart horses returned miserable and muddy, and Kestrel had to stay late to make sure they were all groomed well and to jolly them out of their complaints. Then she dismissed the workers and headed back to her lodgings.

In the morning the rain had passed. Since *Ruler* had berthed last night, Kestrel had the morning free. The air smelled fresh, the spring sun lifted a mist off the greenery, and flowers had opened their faces; she took her late fastbreak to Vertia's Courtyard.

Gardener was sitting in the front stone yard when she arrived.

"Well met," he said when he heard her step.

"Good morn, Gardener. Did you sleep well in that storm? Everything looks extra lush."

"I had strange dreams," he said. "Perchance it was the storm. But I dreamed that a cup of water turned into a hawk and flew off to a land of snowcapped mountains, and then the mountains burst into flame."

Kestrel thought that other people's dreams were always boring, and she was hardly listening as she fed the crumbs of her scone to a parrot.

"Burst into flame!" said the parrot. "Burst into flame!"

"Be quiet, you," said Gardener severely.

Kestrel sat silent for a long moment, smelling the lilacs, savoring the beauty of the courtyard.

"I didn't sleep well either, because I've a problem on my mind. Gardener, I've been wondering if I should leave Slagos." She sighed. "Actually, I know I should leave. But it's hard. I seem to have spent my life just getting comfortable somewhere and then having to run away."

"Would you be running away?"

"Not this time. This time I'd be running *toward* a duty I've put off. I never meant to come to the Green Isles, much less stay so long. I was headed to Liddlecup."

Gardener said, "Often I have a seedling. I put it in a bed, and it thrives and puts down roots, and then I transplant it to a bigger bed, or a sunnier space, or somewhere drier—you catch my drift. Every time I transplant it, I can almost hear the plant's stress and shock, but in each new plot it grows more and more, until I finally discover exactly where that plant is meant to be. Slagos has been just a temporary garden bed for you . . . like a way station. Did you grow stronger here?"

"You know I have."

"Aye. I hear it in your voice and in your step. In my terms, you came here a seedling and will leave a sapling. With the right nurture, you will grow to a towering tree. You come from fine stock. How I wish I could see that!"

Gardener turned to his Spirit's statue. "Vertia, the Bountiful, may we grow strong in thy favor."

"But I still feel so unprepared for trials ahead. I wish—I wish you would come with me, Gardener." She covered his gnarled hand with her own.

"I belong here, child, and would wilt if I tried to leave. Besides," he continued, "I'm not the only one who sees you. Wherever you go, you will find companion plants." He squeezed her hand.

Kestrel rolled her eyes at Gardener's metaphors; although he couldn't see her gentle mockery he sensed it nonetheless and gave her the gentlest of cuffs on her chin.

She gave her week's notice at Dock Street that afternoon. She recommended one of the drivers be promoted to her position, and she spent a deal of time training her.

Kestrel readied her supplies, including plant hair dyes in various combinations, and watched for her chance for a ship. She haunted the broadsheets, the Blue Parrot, other taverns, and the wharf, trying to figure out sailing schedules, taking care to keep her cap on, her head down, and her senses alert for Weirandale's network of spies. Now was when she felt most exposed and vulnerable, because instead of being tucked away in the Dock Street yard or Vertia's Garden, she stood out as a young woman out and about in public places, asking questions. Still, she reasoned, plenty of people from foreign lands with all colors of hair and all styles of dress thronged the wharf area.

While she searched for ships headed north toward her grandfather and uncles in Lortherrod, she continually mulled over the daring of those intrepid "Raiders." But even if she wanted to join up with them, assisting them with her Talent (which was pure foolishness, she reminded herself every time her thoughts strayed in that direction), she had no way to travel to Oromondo. Commercial ship traffic to Oromondo had been embargoed by every realm in solidarity with the occupied Free States.

One morning, while she stood on the wharf scanning noticeboards, a white parrot with a yellow throat flew in front of her and perched on the top of the wooden slat.

"If she's here, we'll find her, never you worry," said the parrot in an unfamiliar male voice. Alerted, Kestrel glanced around, spying the harbormaster heading straight toward her.

She scanned her surroundings, thinking fast.

Yellow dog! Black dog! Start a loud fight right now! And get tangled up in the legs of that man in the dark surcoat who walks this way!

The yellow dog instantly lunged for the neck of the black dog, who responded with equal aggression. Their fight sounded furious and created chaos; in their heedless dives and rolls they took out the legs of the harbormaster. He fell on his hands, swearing at the curs.

By the time the dogs ceased their battle and slunk off chastised, Kestrel had ducked into a nearby storefront.

Shaking, she looked around, discovering that she had entered a tiny smoke shop. The proprietor stared at her hopefully.

"How can I serve ye, darlin'?" asked the owner.

"I'd like . . . a cheap pipe and a packet of cloves," said Kestrel, recalling that she had seen Zillie smoke this at the end of a long day.

"One of these?" He showed her an array of pipes. Though she hated to part with the coin, Kestrel quickly chose the one that looked the most like Zillie's. She paid for her purchase, tucked it in her belt, and was almost out the door when the owner stopped her.

"Wait, darlin'," said the owner.

Kestrel's heart froze. "Why?"

"Didn't you say you needed cloves?"

"Oh, aye," she said, and forced herself to smile. "Thanks for reminding me." She bought a small wrapped packet.

Kestrel opened the packet and packed the pipe, as she had seen Zillie do. Surely a Weir princella would not walk around town smoking a pipe. The owner offered her a light. She drew on the pipe; the smoke made her cough and made her eyes burn. The owner guffawed, but not unkindly.

As she turned to the entrance door, she saw the owner's battered straw hat hanging on a peg. The harbormaster had just seen her in Wilim's gray cloth cap.

"My cap is too hot for today, and it doesn't give me enough shade," Kestrel said, trying hard to sound casual. "I'm late meeting my beau. Could I buy your toppie?"

"My *toppie*? Why, that's a torn old thing. You can pick up a new one at the street vendors just over yonder."

"Please," said Kestrel, and she held out a coin easily worth twice what the hat must have cost him new. Just then a crowd of noisy sailors pushed in the small shop, elbowing her aside and shouting requests.

"Half a tick," the owner said to them. He handed Kestrel the toppie. "You've got the sun-touch, darlin'. You be sure to get out of the light, you hear now?"

"I will," Kestrel promised him, firmly placing the overlarge straw hat on her head and tucking her gray cap in her belt.

She walked purposefully out of the shop, scanning for the harbormaster through gaps in the straw. She saw him down the quay, talking to a man wearing a sword, who must be one of the few Green Isles watchmen.

The white parrot flew onto her shoulder. "I just spotted a gal of about the right age. And Hetthold says she seeks a ship to Lortherrod!" The parrot changed to another voice. "Keep your eyes peeled to find her again. We'll have to monitor all ships headed northeast."

The harbormaster and his companion scanned the quay in all directions. Fear dug its claws into Kestrel. The hat and pipe might help her escape today, but what about the next time she came to the harbor or when she tried to board a Lorther vessel?

Directly across from the pipe shop, a Green Isles ship, *Island Song,* swung on long hawsers. Kestrel heard a dockworker with a crate on his back call to the ship's mate at the head of the gangplank. "Where you off to from here?"

"Alpetar. The arse end of nowhere."

Kestrel saw the map that Tutor Ryton had made her study as a child. *Alpetar abuts Oromondo's southern border.*

Her mind moved on to a thought so startling that her lips unclenched around the pipe. It tumbled through the air, and she had to catch it in her hand before it smashed on the quay.

I could lend my Talent to Thalen's Raiders. I could attack the Oros in their lair, just as the terriers worked with me to track the groundhogs.

Trying to saunter nonchalantly, Kestrel walked up the gang-plank of *Island Song* and asked to see the shipmaster.

"I would like to book passage to Alpetar," she said to the man in his tiny cabin cluttered with papers, dirty clothing, and liquor bottles.

"We ain't a passenger ship," he said.

"I understand; I don't expect a private stateroom."

"You would have to bunk in with the crew in steerage. If you was a man, I might consider it, but I can't take no woman."

"Why not?"

"Can't be responsible. *Them's sailors.*"

"I can take care of myself."

"Humph. Why do you want to go to Alpetar, anyways? T'aint nothing left there but goats. We only stop in Tar's Basin to pick up bundles of goat hair."

"That's my business."

"You waste my time, gal. I got a ship to provision." As he gestured in the direction of a clutter of papers, Kestrel spotted the vine tattoo around his left wrist.

"And I have to get to Alpetar. If you need a vouchsafe, ask Gardener."

"You know Gardener?" The shipmaster leaned backward in his chair, and his forehead wrinkled.

"Yes, I know him well. Gardener'll tell you that Vertia wants you to carry me wherever I wish to go."

"We-ll, now." The shipmaster rubbed his chin. "You got the fare?"

"You just told me that you have no stateroom. How much can meals and water cost?"

The man laughed without friendliness. "Ain't you the feisty one. The fee will be two golden grapes. Take it or leave it. We sail on the evening tide."

The price was exorbitant, but Kestrel had no choice. When

she reappeared on deck she no longer saw the harbormaster. She threaded a path away from the quay, stopped at a local greengrocer's, and then ran up to her lodgings.

She used lemon juice to bleach out the brown dye coloring her hair. Then she made a paste of chamomile and honey, applied it, and left it on. She packed up her few belongings and tidied her room, the place that had been her safe, private refuge for several moons. When the afternoon waned and she could wait no longer she rinsed the mixture out. While wet, her hair just looked dark, but as she rubbed it dry the speckled mirror on her wall showed definite yellow streaks in a colorless background. She figured this would do for now; she would try to dye it again before arrival.

Covering up her changed hair in the battered toppie, throwing her sack over her shoulder, and tying her money purse (holding five golden grapes and some change) around her neck, she left her lodging. Her landlords were out, but she was paid up with them.

She stopped at Vertia's Garden, finding Gardener tying a lei of flowers around the statue's neck.

"Gardener, I'm leaving. I mean I'm leaving Slagos. I'm leaving right away."

"I know, my dear."

"You won't forget me, will you?"

"Never." He put his hand on the top of her head. "And Vertia's Blessing will go with you."

Kestrel trotted down the hill to the Blue Parrot to bid farewell to Zillie.

Zillie hugged her. "Darlin', I don't understand you at all, but you've nestled in my heart. Wait—let me give you something to take with you." She filled a sack with the bread Kestrel favored and a jug with her best wine.

"I have something for you too," said Kestrel, presenting her with the pipe and cloves.

Zillie exclaimed over the gift and packed herself a pipe.

"I know it's the dinner rush, but could you walk me down to the harbor?" Kestrel asked Zillie.

"Why not? Do me good to get a bit of air. Do my customers good not to take me so for granted. But will you let me stop a moment for an errand?"

While Zillie gave the cook some instructions, Kestrel addressed the resident dogs.

Terriers, will you escort us and cavort around? I don't want the harbormaster to see a lone woman again.

Let's go! Let's go! the young terrier yapped.

One could stretch one's legs, agreed the older dog.

Kestrel waited outside the herbalist's with the dogs while Zillie ran inside.

"Here," said Zillie, exiting and forcing a little sack into Kestrel's hands. "A traveling woman's friend. These herbs will lighten your courses, or even stop them altogether."

Kestrel tucked the sack away carefully, embarrassed but grateful.

If the harbormaster or any of his confederates monitored the quay, they made no effort to accost the little party at the gangplank of a ship heading south.

Sharing Zillie's bread and wine with *Island Song*'s first and second mates led them to conclude that Kestrel would be safer and more comfortable bunking in with them than with the rest of the crew, and they strung her a hammock in their joint cabin. The only drawback to the arrangement was that the second mate started to flirt on their first night at sea.

Kestrel said, "I appreciate the compliment of your regard, but I do not seek that kind of companionship."

He tried to laugh her rejection away, but Kestrel stared him down. Afterward, he desisted, and fortunately he was too good-natured to stay sullen for long.

Kestrel did not fall ill on this voyage, and sometimes she actually enjoyed sailing. When she went out on deck to survey the scenery, she saw a disturbance in the water to the starboard.

"What's that?" she asked a barefoot, nut-brown sailor with green sideburn hair, pointing to silver flashes in the ship's wake.

"Where? There? A school of dolphins," said the man. "Queer, you know; they seem to have picked us up almost right outside of Slagos. Been following us ever since."

All through the days the dolphins shadowed the ship as if drawn to it. They jumped and cavorted, delighting everyone with their antics.

Queen! Queen! Watch one jump!

No, watch this one!

This one will jump the highest for you!

Queen! Queen! Didst thou see?

The sailors said the dolphins brought the ship good luck. Certainly they had strong winds that blew them southwest in record time.

Finally, *Island Song* pulled into Tar's Basin, an unimpressive port in Alpetar. While the sailors concentrated on loading bales of goat hair, Kestrel bid the mates farewell and disembarked on a rickety wharf into a street that held only two dozen modest stone buildings with thatched roofs.

An inquiry led her to the only horse dealer in town. The man's hair looked quite different from Kestrel's poor dye job: it was a gleaming yellow-white with most of the sides hanging in separated, rolled strands. He had a meager choice of steeds for sale. Kestrel stroked a few muzzles, but none of his horses had the strength of body and spirit she required. Then, in an outdoor pen, she spotted a large, reddish pony with a shaggy coat and an even shaggier mane that fell over her fetlock. She hadn't seen its like before.

"Oh, that? That there's an Alpie pony," said the dealer. "I calls her Butter. Bred to take the heights of our mountains. She won't work up any speed, and her trot will ruin your back, but she is sure-footed and she'll never quit on you."

Butter? Butter? Were you meant for me?

Serve thee faithfully, Your Majesty.

"I'll take her," said Kestrel, "and a saddle and saddlebags, if you've got some that fit." From the one store in town, called Everything You Desire, she spent the last of her coin, filling the bags with food supplies (and lemons, chamomile leaves, bergamot oil, and coal tar). She set off from the harbor on Butter at midday in spring, homesick for the spring wildflowers and birds in Wyndton. The road in front of her cut through open fields and grasslands.

Three stray dogs followed her out of Tar's Basin and didn't leave off even when the town started to dwindle behind them. Kestrel turned backward in her saddle to examine them. The pack leader was a female hound; two male herders trailed behind her, one large and fluffy, and the other smaller, with one blue eye and one brown and a less showy coat.

Dogs. Don't follow me. I have a long, dangerous journey ahead. I can't feed you. I can't protect you.

We will guard thee and hunt for thee, sent the hound. *This land brimes with dangers. We will protect* thee.

Warm thee, Your Majesty, sent the big herder. *Our coats be so soft.*

Love thee, sent the smallest dog.

Every human needs a dog, the female insisted.

Kestrel realized that some of her loneliness since leaving Wyndton stemmed from the lack of a dog. She had always had a dog, from the pack that had lived with her in her palace chambers to Gili and Baki in Wyndton.

She smiled and spoke out loud. "My thoughts exactly. Well then, I welcome your comradeship. Come up here where I can get a good look at you."

The dogs joyously bounded in front of the pony. "Let's see. I will call you 'Didi,' 'Jaki,' and 'Laki.' We five, we'll be *Kestrel's* Raiders. We are off to invade Weirandale's sworn enemy and bring vengeance."

Butter broke wind at these exalted sentiments, shook her thick mane, and kept her steady, plodding pace. But the dogs wagged their tails so hard their hindquarters wiggled, and the hound let out a few enthusiastic bays, like a trumpet announcing an attack.

14

Sweetmeadow, Alpetar

Gunnit was up in the Middle Pasture with the hamlet's goats. Since he was nine summers old, he took a turn with the herd in the day-time; an older boy or one of the men would watch at night and sleep in the lean-to that provided partial shelter from the nearly constant winds that swept the foothills of the Obsidian Mountains.

Proud of his new responsibility, Gunnit watched the sky for birds of prey that might try to steal a kid, though he knew that the kids were too heavy to be easily carried off. He played with the frisky ones that jumped about and practiced their headbutting. Periodi-cally, he lay down on the warm ground, watched the clouds as fluffy as fleece, and made grass whistles.

When friendly old Daisy came close to him, *bleat*ing, Gunnit scratched her behind her horns, and he pulled off the brambles stuck to Pansy's coat. Even though the morning was still new, he grabbed his rucksack and attacked the packet of bread spread with creamy cheese and herbs that his mother had prepared for him at dawn. When Gunnit wanted to hear his own voice, he talked to Taffy, the donkey they pastured with the goats to protect them, who moved his ears as if he listened. Mostly he kept jumping up to chase any too-adventurous kid away from the rocky escarpment on the western edge of the large meadow. They probably wouldn't fall—their mothers didn't—but Gunnit didn't want anything to happen while he was on duty.

For what must have been the twentieth time, Gunnit had jumped up to move Petunia's brown-faced twins away from the drop-off. If one stood near the western edge of the pasture, the wind often carried sounds from the hamlet below. Gunnit heard the Sweetmeadow dogs barking their fool heads off—probably a visiting peddler. Gunnit felt sorry for himself that he would miss the rare opportunity of seeing a newcomer and his exciting display of goods; peddlers only happened along their tiny hamlet once or twice a year. But he was not a child any longer, to be dazzled by toys or sweets.

"Get along now," he told the twins sternly, making the most of his authority, stretching his shepherd's crook and his arms wide and herding them toward the middle of the meadow.

Then he walked back to the edge to see if he could hear anything else. A confused sound reached him of loud voices and maybe a clang of metal on metal. The wind dropped away, and though he strained for a few minutes he heard nothing but a nearby woodpecker.

Suddenly, a fresh gust brought the sound of high-pitched screaming. People screaming, with all their might. Children, women. In the hollow between other wails Gunnit heard one that he recognized as belonging to his sister, Linnie, three summers older than he.

Gunnit stood riveted to the spot for a moment; his mind couldn't process what could be happening. His father—many of the fathers—should be about the village; they wouldn't allow a peddler to frighten or threaten anyone. A renewed, stronger gust brought redoubled screams and the sound of keening and crying. Even Taffy rolled his eyes and snorted in alarm. Startled out of his stupor, Gunnit dropped his shepherd's staff and leapt toward the steep path—not the broad, gentler one on which they drove the herd, but the rocky plunge, tricky to navigate—that the village used for quicker access to the Middle Pasture.

Gunnit ran and slid down the rocks and loose dirt as fast as he could go, stopping only when one of his clogs fell off. The path wound around the hillside away from the village; so for the second half of his descent he heard nothing except his breath coming in gasps and the percussive small rockslides he started. Even pushing himself to his limit, it took him more than half an hour to near the valley floor where the hamlet of eleven houses—Gunnit's whole world—stood.

And by then, it was all over. When his path met up with the lane that ran from the narrow mountain pass through the center of town and thence to the High Road in the south, Gunnit saw that coming from Oromondo the ground had been all churned up by a large group of hoof- and footprints. Then he spotted the first of the bodies: Edderel's two dogs, their heads nearly severed off their necks. More dead dogs (one of which had the white-and-black silky coat of his family's longtime herder—*don't look, don't look*), then the first murdered woman (*was that Dame Idda, who did the village doctoring?*), three children whose heads had been smashed in against houses, leaving blood dripping down the walls. (*No, No!*) Mabbit, the biggest and most forceful of the fathers, lay sightless to the sky, his treasured, ancient sword now useless by his side and a dead man garbed in a helmet and a breastplate decorated with flames a couple paces away.

"Linnie!" Gunnit shouted, spying her yellow pinafore apron a few paces farther down the center lane. But as he got closer he saw she had been stabbed repeatedly, savagely, in the stomach and chest; the yellow stained with red; her face wore a dull look it never wore in life. At this sight, Gunnit broke, sobbing, screaming, "Ma! Ma!" and raced to his family's thatched cottage. It looked as though it had been quickly ransacked, but it stood empty. Where were his mother, father, or older brother?

Gunnit backed out of the empty house and stood, eyes streaming, heart pounding, in the lane. He heard soft voices from the house opposite, so he dashed across: "Dame Joolyn, Dame Saggeta!!!" Dame Saggeta—whom he had always liked less than the softer Dame Joolyn—met him at the doorway, blocking his entrance, though he still caught a glimpse of a sight he wished he hadn't seen: Joolyn sitting on the floor, naked except for a shawl wrapped around her, rocking back and forth and moaning. Dame Saggeta had blood spatters on her, but she looked alive, unscathed, and grim. He had never been so relieved to see anyone in his life, and she must have felt the same way, for she snatched him close.

"Gunnit, Gunnit, how did you survive, boy?"

"I was up with the goats. What happened? Linnie! Where's my ma? Oh, where's my ma? Where's my da? I heard Linnie screaming!"

Dame Saggeta's body shook. "A troop of Oro filth rode in; they kidnapped all the older boys and men; butchered everyone else; took the horses and whatever foodstuffs they could find. Joolyn's alive, but she's badly hurt."

Dame Saggeta pulled him out of her embrace to look him in the eyes. "Gunnit, I need to care for her. Can you search to see if anyone else survived? Could other folks have hid away?"

Gunnit swallowed down his tears and nodded. Dame Saggeta gave him another swift hug and turned back into her hut.

The boy dragged himself down the hamlet's center, trying not to see the scattered bodies of friends and neighbors.

Two houses down, at a cottage set back a piece from the road, a door was barred. Gunnit knocked and then pounded; then he leaned against the door and started yelling. "It's me, Gunnit. Is anybody there? They're all gone. Open the door; oh, please, open the door."

Gramps Dobbely unbarred the door. Above his stringy beard, half of his face was puffed and cut, just beginning to redden, but otherwise he looked as spry as ever. Mother Dobbely, who had not been right in the head for many years, sat on top of a quilt chest, holding on to it with an iron grip.

"Gone, eh?" said Gramps. "Mother now, you'd best get up. Wouldn't do to suffocate them chill'ens," and although he was thin and small he gently moved her considerable bulk into her rocking chair. Out of the chest clambered four of their grandchildren: Aleen, seven; her brother, Alloon, three; and their girl cousins Sheleen, four, and Doraleen, two summers. All wore their fine, flyaway, mostly yellow hair cut in lopsided bangs in the front.

Sheleen complained because Doraleen had wee-weed on them, while Alloon, seeking comfort, sucked his thumb. Gramps explained to Gunnit how he had hidden the children at the first noise and told how he'd faced down the stinking Oro son of a turd that had come to their house. Gunnit briefly relayed what he knew; he didn't tell Aleen, the eldest, that he had seen her father dead in the dirt, but he did awkwardly pat her upper back, and he ruffled Sheleen's sweat-dampened hair off her neck.

Mother Dobbely—the crisis making her more lucid than usual—gave all the children a cup of milk from her milk jug and a hard biscuit. The nourishment made Gunnit feel a mite stronger. Then Mother Dobbely took her youngest grandbabes, Alloon and Doraleen, in her faded apron on her big lap and started rocking them, crooning tunelessly.

Gramps told Aleen to bar the door behind him; he grabbed a poker and a small knife and accompanied Gunnit on his search mission. Unlike Gunnit, Gramps did not look away from the bodies on the ground; he checked if any were breathing; and he kept a mental tally as they went. Gramps sighed heavily over his daughter and daughter-in-marriage and softly covered their faces with their pinafores. In two houses they found nothing and no one. One of the dogs stirred, so Gunnit raced to it, hoping it was only wounded. But he was in his death throes; all they could do was hold his head and speak kindly as the light went out of his eyes.

In their circuit they came to Gunnit's home again, and Gramps insisted they go in, though Gunnit hung back. He heard Gramps rummaging around, and then heard him say, "Ah, there you be, Dame Linnsie!" Gunnit rushed inside and saw that his mother was on her bed; he had missed her, hidden by rumpled bedclothes. Her clothes were all disarrayed and her eyes were closed. But she breathed.

"Water," snapped Gramps, as he propped her head up and started surveying for wounds. Heart leaping, Gunnit got a skipper of water from the bucket and held it to her lips. She wouldn't drink. "Douse her!" ordered Gramps, and Gunnit threw the whole skipper in her face. His heart lifted out of his chest as she opened her eyes. "Ma! Ma!" he cried, trying to hug her. But her eyes wouldn't focus, and Gramps held him off with the hand that wasn't holding her up.

"Easy, easy, lad. I reckon your ma took a hard knock on her noggin. Let me tend her a bit. You get on to the other houses and look in them outbuildings too." Gramps handed him the poker.

Gunnit obeyed, dragging his feet, but once back in the street, he dashed over to Dame Saggeta. "My ma's alive but she needs you," he shouted at her, and he felt a smidge of comfort to see her head over to help Gramps.

Three houses later he found Limpett. Limpett wasn't the three-summers-old boy's real name; the older lads just called him that because of the way he always clung to them and tagged along. His ma lay by the hearth (*she baked the best spice bread in the village*), a cooking knife in her hand, but her own chest gaping open. (*No, I won't look.*) Reluctantly, Gunnit stepped around the body to open the clothes cupboard in the sleeping room, and lo and behold, out tumbled Limpett from where his mother had hidden him. Gunnit had just the presence of mind to put his hand over Limpett's eyes to spare him the sight when Limpett grabbed him around the legs in his ain't-never-going-to-let-go grip. Gunnit grabbed something to tie around his eyes, picked him up, and took him back over to Mother Dobbely. Limpett screamed his head off when Gunnit tried to pry his arms off from around his neck, but Mother D. and Aleen finally pulled him free.

"I'll be back soon, Limpett, I promise," Gunnit said. "I have a few more houses to check. You mind Aleen, now."

Gunnit was on the last house when he heard a muffled wail. He found Dame Mollie's new babe, wrapped in blankets and stuffed inside a larder cupboard. Once again, a child hidden by a quick-thinking ma. He plucked the baby out of its too-warm hideaway. It was about five moons, and Gunnit (who didn't pay much attention to babies), didn't recollect its name or whether it was a boy or girl; he just remembered that it was Dame Mollie's first, and she set the world by it. He figured that he didn't need to cover its eyes, so he carried it with him as he finished his searching. The babe fingered his shirt collar and grabbed at his hair.

The only other living thing he found in the various lean-tos, sheds, and jakes was a puppy. In a shed beyond the main street, Gunnit heard rapid breathing. He bent to look under a broken crate and found Kiki cowering in the shadow. He knew this dog; she belonged to Nimmet, Gunnit's best friend in Sweetmeadow, companion of a thousand games and confidences. Wimmie, his sister, looked like Nimmet, with freckles on her nose, and she climbed trees like a champion. To Gunnit she was the prettiest girl in the village, and sometimes he reckoned he would marry her when he grew up.

Yellow curls soaked in blood. Don't remember. Didn't see that.

When the dog recognized Gunnit she peed and showed her belly. "There, there, I'll take care of you, Kiki," Gunnit murmured. "You're not a coward; you're just smarter than the rest." Kiki frantically jumped at Gunnit, trying to lick his face, and Baby laughed and clapped its hands when Kiki's eager tongue licked its face too.

Holding Baby and with Kiki so hungry to be close to him she kept getting tangled in his legs, Gunnit walked back to his own house. Gramps and Dame Saggeta now had his mother sitting up in a chair they had set outside the front door. They had wrapped her yellow-and-brown springy hair in a rough bandage that dripped blood in the back. Red from the cuts on her arms had stained the sleeves of her mohair dress, and her blue pinafore's top fell, ripped, into her lap. Gramps held a bottle of elderberry mash; some had dribbled down his mother's chin.

"Ma, I'm here," Gunnit whispered, kneeling by her side. His ma hugged him into her neck, her soft gray eyes brimming with tears, but didn't seem able to talk. He placed Baby in her lap, so he could pull her closer with both arms.

After a minute he realized that over their heads Dame Saggeta and Gramps were discussing what to do next. "We *have* to leave. They poisoned the well water with bodies," said Dame Saggeta. "We have got to get out of here. For the children, for Joolyn and Linnsie, we cannot spend even a night here. It's too much to ask. And they might come back."

Gramps was gradually being persuaded. "We-ell. I do have my wagon. And them Oros ain't gonna eat my plow horses; I turned them out in Near Pasture, not in the corral where t'other ones was."

Dame Saggeta turned to Gunnit, treating him as an equal, even though he was only a kid. "What do you think?"

"What about my da and brother and the other menfolk? When they escape and return? How will they find us?"

Dame Saggeta's eyes misted, but she said to Gunnit, "We'll leave them a note."

"We's a goin' to need a heap of things: food and clothes and tools and such. And milk. You can't have all these young'uns and no milk," said Gramps. At that exact moment everyone realized that Baby had started fussing in Gunnit's mother's lap, exactly the kind of baby fussing that means, "I'm hungry and I'm fixing to wail."

Dame Saggeta crouched a bit, her face serious, so she could look Gunnit squarely in the eye. "Gunnit, you've already done more than a boy should have to today. You up for more?"

"Yes'm," said Gunnit, though what he really wanted to do was sit down in the dirt and wail louder than the hungry baby.

"Good lad," said Dame Saggeta. "Now we need you to climb back up to Middle Pasture and bring down the best milk goats," she said.

"And Gunnit," Gramps added, "you got to take them young'uns with you. Aleen might help us gather things, but the others will get in the way, and, besides, they can't see *this*."

"Can't Mother Dobbely care for them?"

"You know they ain't safe alone with Ma. But you don't have to take that babe; looks like Linnsie's coming round enough to hang on to this one." And indeed, Gunnit's ma had started patting away the baby's fussiness and had even given it her finger to suck on.

So Gunnit went back to the Dobbelys' cottage and rounded up the little kids. Mother D. had lost her focus; she tried to spoon ash into Alloon's mouth. Aleen helped him make blindfolds for the children, and she tied them together like beads on a string to Gunnit's belt. Kiki followed the little troupe closely.

The hike up to Middle Pasture was almost half a league uphill on the broad way (the little legs couldn't handle the rocky shortcut). This trek became one of the most miserable parts of the unspeakable day. It had gotten hot; the four tykes were frightened, cranky, and tired; they all wanted to be carried; and they whined and carried on. Two-summers-old Doraleen got too heavy for Gunnit, yet when he set her down and told her to walk she sat in the dirt and wailed. Gunnit praised, pleaded, and cajoled until he had no more cajoling in him, and then he spanked them all and bullied them up the last leg of the path.

The little ones settled down a bit in the sunshine beaming into Middle Pasture's wildflowers. Gunnit found his rucksack where he'd dropped it and shared the rest of his sandwich out. The water in his water bag did the children just as much good. Gunnit made a game of squirting Daisy's milk into their open mouths and made sure they each got a few good gulps.

Gunnit had to choose the best milk goats. He wanted to take Daisy, but he recognized that she was too old to travel. He chose Pansy and Violet. Fortunately, he had the rope that had tied the children together, because he hadn't thought to bring one. He wouldn't let himself think about what would happen to the rest of the herd without the villagers' care. And then he noticed Taffy. Taffy was just a donkey, but wouldn't he be useful as another mount?

The downhill trip was easier. Without a saddle or bridle it was tricky to ride Taffy, but by grabbing handfuls of his coarse mane in one hand, Sheleen, who at four was the biggest, could stay on and still have another hand to clutch Alloon and keep him from slipping off sideways. Gunnit put Doraleen inside his rucksack (praying it wouldn't rip), which distributed her weight better on his back and left his hands free to pull Limpett.

A ways from the hamlet they were met by Aleen slowly trekking up in their direction. Although he knew it was petty, Gunnit had almost been envying her working with the adults rather than the squalling children, but she looked as if she had been puking and her face was etched with tear tracks, so any complaint died on his lips.

"They were getting worried about you all," she said. "They are mostly ready. They sent me to tell you there's no need to circle round." She walked by Taffy and steadied the riders; Gunnit put on his last spurt of energy and even picked up Limpett. They marched into the hamlet with their heads held up.

Although the sandy ground showed red-brown blotches every-where, now no bodies lay in sight. Gramps had hitched his broad brown-with-white-stockings plow horses to a wagon. The wagon had a straw mattress in it, and a random collection of hastily-piled-up possessions. Dame Saggeta, with her hair now covered in a white kerchief, clapped her hands at the sight of Taffy and sent Gunnit to find tack for him. In Edderel's shed, he found a saddle and bridle that would do and even saddlebags and waterskins.

The sun started to lower over the mountaintops. His mother milked Pansy and Violet and calmed down the frantic baby with a bottle that had a finger of a glove fixed on it. Dame Saggeta took Gunnit into his own house to show him that she had indeed written a note and tacked it up.

To the Men of Sweetmeadow:
12 of us survived.
We have gone to find a safer place.
When we settle, we will send word of our whereabouts.
We love you.
May Saulé light your path and protect you wherever you be.

Gunnit wiped the tears from his face, not really caring whether she saw them or not.

The children were confused; they whimpered for supper and their mothers. Dame Saggeta loaded them and Dame Joolyn into the back of the wagon. Gramps helped Mother D. climb onto the seat beside him and tied Pansy and Violet off the back. Kiki, the puppy, Dame Saggeta, Aleen, and Gunnit would walk; Linnsie, holding the baby, who turned out to be a girl named Addigale, would ride Taffy, at least for now, while her head pounded so.

Saggeta turned to Gramps. "Someone ought to say something."

Gramps sighed and addressed the survivors. "Chill'ens, you all hush now. Sweetmeadow has been a wonderful home for us, but nothing lasts forever. Your mothers and fathers, your dogs, the other villagers loved you right hard. That there"—he pointed to Mabbit's house—"is where they will sleep now. We are going to light a fire so that no critter will disturb their final rest. When you see the sparks fly, you think of their souls flying free to the sky, up up up to join Saulė."

He struck his tinder and set a hank of straw alight. Dashing forward and then springing back, he threw the straw into the cottage. The flames lit something that the grown-ups had already prepared. The house went *swoosh* and burst into flame.

Some of the little ones hollered with excitement, but Limpett wailed, his whole face scrunched up with misery. Gramps climbed into the wagon and clucked the horses, and they moved slowly toward the High Road, the flaming house and the lifeless village behind them.

Aleen walked with Gunnit a ways; they were both so tuckered out that they stumbled. Finally, Gunnit offered her his hand for balance. Hers felt small and damp in his.

"Was it awful? What was the worst?" he whispered to her, not wanting to know but sensing she needed to confide in someone.

"Going through purses to find any valuables; it felt like stealing," she said. "I know they would want us to have the coins and such, but to take from my ma . . . my da. The grown-ups pulled the folks' bodies inside, but they asked me to drag the lighter dogs. . . . That's when I started puking and I just couldn't stop. My throat hurts like it's torn and so does my belly."

The refugees only made it a little ways that night. Gramps drove the wagon off the path into the soft grass at the verge. They unhitched the team and untied the goats, tethering them in the grass. Those in the back of the wagon were long asleep. The others sank down on coverlets on the ground and passed out from exhaustion. Gunnit snuggled close to his mother.

I am the only kid here who has got his ma, alive. I am the luckiest one of all.

His mother had baby Addigale on the other side of her. Kiki nestled against Gunnit's free side. Both babes, puppy and girl, whimpered now and again in their sleep.

15

Cascada

Marcot hated his father.

He understood the duty he owed his sire; he had no clear cause to complain of the way in which Matwyck treated him or his mother. His father had never struck them, never berated them, nor even publicly embarrassed them. His father invariably behaved with a proper politeness.

Yet Marcot sensed calculation behind every gesture and the lack of warmth in every smile. He saw the way his mother first shrank away from and then steeled herself to yield to her husband's touch. All genuineness, all spontaneity fled, replaced by careful calculation. His father's presence suffocated him.

And the people that the Lord Regent had chosen for his closest companions! Greedy, preening, power-hungry hypocrites with no concern save their own fortunes and advancement.

Since Lady Tenny's mysterious suicide had created a vacancy, his father had insisted that Marcot take a chair on the Circle Council. Old Lord Retzel had suffered a stroke, and his father packed him off to his country estate to wither away out of sight, replacing him with General Yurgn's son Burgn. While the water swirled in the center pool, the treasurer Prigent, Duchess Latlie, Lady Fanyah (who had once been a lady-in-waiting to Queen Cressa), General Yurgn, and his son Burgn sat around the table debating affairs of state with the Lord Regent. But Marcot saw precious little evidence that they cared about the people of Weirandale.

"But why?" Marcot persisted. "*Why* do you decline to join with King Rikil against the Oros? Doesn't the Treaty of Five Nations obligate us to unite against any future Oromondian aggression?"

"Wars drain the treasury, Lordling," said Prigent, with an unnecessary emphasis on the "ling."

"I understand that," said Marcot, "but surely continued Oro aggression costs too."

"Costly for the Free Staters, mayhap, but not for us," replied General Yurgn.

"But unchecked aggression anywhere erodes the rule of law everywhere," Marcot persisted. "And the price is not just borne by Free Staters but also by all international trade. Having gobbled up the Free States, what's to stop the Oros from further conquest? At present they mass right across the Ribbon from our shores."

"Listen to the lad," said Duchess Latlie. "So earnest, my Lord Regent. So bright. I do believe you've done a wonderful job with him."

Matwyck smiled at Latlie's compliment. "Marcot, without her queen, Weirandale is in no position to wage a foreign war. Our duty lies in keeping the nation intact and hale, to deliver to the queen when the hour of her return arrives." He tapped his fingertips together. "Besides, I mistrust King Rikil. He may want the riches of Oromondo or the Free States to increase Lortherrod's treasury. I will join no alliance with him."

Marcot desisted; once his father had spoken there was no point in prolonging a discussion. The conversation turned to other matters, including the recent death of the Duke of Crenovale.

"How did he die?" Marcot whispered to Lady Fanyah, since everyone else seemed ahead of him on the topic.

"A hunting accident," she whispered back. Marcot thought this strange because the last time he had conversed with the duke the latter had complained petulantly about how his gout kept him from riding. But Marcot had no chance to inquire further, because the Circle had launched into a debate as to who should rule the duchy, given that the duke had no surviving heirs. Fanyah, Yurgn, and Prigent all pressed his father about their respective favorites.

Matwyck finally burst out laughing. "You are under some misapprehension, my friends. *I* do not appoint dukes. Only the queen can do that, and only by having a male child. I might suggest that a caretaker be put in charge of the duchy, merely to keep order, mind you."

More discussion ensued. Marcot gathered that none of the council's candidates knew anything about the crops or trades particular to Crenovale; the decision hinged on "who is one of us," "who has the bearing," "who is the most reliable," and "who would be most grateful."

Marcot quickly grasped that "having the proper bearing" referred to Old Color. "What do you mean by 'reliable'?" he finally inquired.

No one would give him a straight answer. Marcot gradually deduced it meant who would be most prompt in paying kickbacks to the council members. He had trouble keeping his mouth from falling open and a harder time keeping his temper. He looked across the table to his father, who seemed to be enjoying the spectacle immensely. When he caught Marcot's eye he raised an eyebrow, as if to say, "You see, now, the venal fools I have to deal with?"

Marcot did see, but he also saw his father egging them on and pitting them against one another instead of putting a halt to this avarice.

Finally, the councilors agreed upon a suitably reliable, grateful, amber-haired candidate. Restless from the long meeting, the councilors stirred in their seats.

"Before we adjourn, I have just one tiny matter to bring up," said his father. "Rumors have reached me that the Sorrowers harbor seditionists. I think it would be prudent if I were named head prelate, so that I have more authority over religious matters."

Everyone's movements ceased, and the room grew totally still. Marcot had longed to escape the Circle Chamber, but he too registered this request as disquieting. General Yurgn's head snapped around, and his eyes squinted.

However, Lady Fanyah jumped in enthusiastically. "Of course, Lord Regent. Who better? This is only fitting. As you protect the realm, so you should protect the Waters."

Prigent chimed in, "I shall post the proclamation today, Lord Regent and Lord Prelate."

Since no one dared to voice an objection, the meeting finally adjourned. Marcot ducked out while Lady Fanyah accosted his father about giving her "adopted" (actually out-of-wedlock) baby boy a title.

He hurried back to their living quarters. His mother had been poorly over the last year, and he wished to see how she fared today. The healers who had examined her said her heart no longer beat properly. What could be done about this led to wrangling disagreements. One prescribed rest, another exertion; one hot baths, another cold; one a trip to the seashore and another a trip to the mountains; one leeches and another drinking calves' blood.

Tirinella took all the doctoring without complaint. But she told Marcot that she wished to leave court and return to their country house. Marcot's father, with some reason, argued that the healers in the countryside would not be as skilled, and that if she left his side, he could not supervise her care. Marcot believed that his mother's only hope lay in getting out from under this very supervision, but this was one of the many topics that could not be discussed in his family.

Marcot rapped his knuckles lightly on the door of his mother's sitting room. "Mother," he said softly. "Are you awake?"

"Enter," called Tirinella.

She reclined on a couch; a book had slipped from her hands onto the floor. Her caramel face had lost the glow of health, her lips had taken on a blue tinge, and her chest rose and fell rapidly.

"What can I do for you, Mother?" he said, sitting beside her.

She smiled at him and raised her hand to smooth his hair. "I want for nothing," she answered.

Marcot got her to drink a little wine and eventually to eat a pudding. She asked him about the council meeting, and Marcot told her it had been productive. Long ago they had entered into some unspoken agreement: neither of them would complain about their lots in life, and most especially neither of them would utter a word against the Lord Regent. If they acknowledged how unhappy they were under his thumb, they might be compelled to strive for change. And change was too frightening to contemplate.

Later, when his father joined them, he shared Marcot's concern about his mother's condition. He fixed her tonic himself and bid her drink it all down. He wanted to fetch all the healers and only relented when she insisted that she could not bear their fussing over her this evening.

In the morning, his mother seemed stronger. She joined Marcot and Matwyck at the fastbreak table.

"My lord husband, I do believe it would do my heart good to see the house, to check on my grounds, and to find out how the community school is doing. Would you permit me to travel to the country today?"

A look of something like pain shadowed his father's face. He looked down for several seconds as if mastering himself.

"My lady-wife, if 'tis your desire to subject yourself to the stress of travel, of course *my* wishes shall not stand in your way. What can I do to make your journey more comfortable?"

"I would like Marcot to escort me, my lord. I shall not keep him for more than a few days. I know you want him with you here in Cascada."

"Would you like me to escort you, my lady-wife?" asked his father. Marcot heard something like a note of hopefulness in his voice.

His mother answered, "Of course, my husband, your company would be my greatest joy. But I cannot presume to take you away from your duties of state."

In the coded, polite fencing that passed for his parents' marriage, Marcot's mother had rejected his father's offer.

"Very well. I will make all the arrangements," said Matwyck, just a tad abruptly. "Son, be ready to escort your mother in an hour. I would not have her kept waiting when she has made her preferences so clear. Here, my dear, let me fix you your tonic before you depart."

Marcot bowed to his father and left the room to collect some belongings.

In an hour, much of the court witnessed Lord Regent Matwyck solicitously helping his wife into her velvet upholstered carriage, personally tucking a blanket around her, and kissing her hands with devotion. Marcot shook hands with his father, seating himself beside his mother. Early on, his mother dozed against his shoulder; as they neared her family home she gazed avidly out the carriage window. Neither of them spoke about anything except the scenery for the duration of the journey.

When they reached their estate, a well-proportioned stone manse surrounded by beautifully tended grounds, his mother retired to rest from the trip. Marcot summoned the local goody, who also served as the nearest healer. She was an old woman now—stout and wrinkled. Marcot had not seen her for years, though he vaguely remembered her ministrations when he was a lad.

When Marcot told her of his mother's illness she replied pertly,

"I'm hardly surprised. Her ladyship's mother had a bad heart, and 'twas a weak heart that led her brother to die of just a wee touch of grippe. I'll pop up and give her a look-see. Don't bother to show me the way, lad, I've known this house since before you were born. In fact, I was there *when* you were born." She poked Marcot's belly familiarly, a gesture he resented, but he had more serious things on his mind.

After Marcot had paced around for some time, the healer found him in the library.

"I have given your mother's maid two bottles. One contains a tincture of garden cress. Your mother's heart is not working well enough to drain the humors out of her body. This will help right away. The other is oil of poppy. Folk with bad hearts wake in the night finding it hard to breathe and they get frightened. Just a drop of the poppy oil will relieve this breathlessness and help her get the rest she needs."

"What should she do about exercise, leeches, baths, or travel? The healers in Cascada gave us contradictory advice."

"Bless you, boy, Lady Tirinella should do whatever pleases her. None of those things are going to affect her heart. Also, there's a tincture I've taken away from her: Nargis knows what those Cascada dunderheads were thinking of!"

Marcot nodded. "I found it hard to have much confidence in any of those healers because they contradicted one another so often."

"Your ma said you should sup without her; she will see you in the morning. By the by, how's your right wrist, Lordling? I set it when you fell off your horse as a wee tyke. You always had a weakness for fine horses—I hear you still spend a fortune on them these days."

"My wrist?" Marcot said vaguely.

"Don't look so glum, Little Lordling. That heart will kill her someday, but we have no way of knowing when. I have seen folks with weaker hearts than your ma's last for many seasons. You knows where to send for me if you need me." And the healer bustled herself away.

In the morning, his mother appeared well. She bubbled over with delight to be back in her house and exclaimed over every tree's growth and every old possession.

"Marcot, I want you to return to Cascada tomorrow," she told him.

"I'd rather stay here with you," he replied.

"I know, Son, but that's impossible. You have a duty to your father. Come now. Lying in my dear old bedchamber last night I came up with a plan. I need to write your father."

Tirinella sat at her own mother's antique, delicate writing table and pulled out some notepaper. In a few moments she passed the letter to her son to read.

My lord husband,

I have arrived safely and feel that the country air is doing me a world of good. You would be happy to see how much improved my color is already.

I feel so much better that 'tis no need to keep Marcot from his duties, so as promised, I am sending him back to you.

While I don't feel it advisable to return to court, as soon as your work may permit, I hope you will visit me here. Perchance in two weeks, on the anniversary of our wedding? By then I am sure I will be healthy enough to allay your tender concerns.

Your dutiful Lady-wife, Tirinella

Postscript, I wonder if Marcot could better prepare to serve by seeing more of Weirandale? With me out of danger in the country air, a tour of the duchies might be great training for him?

Marcot looked at his mother. "You have bought my freedom by inviting him here."

"In a fashion," she answered, avoiding his eyes, "but he will not remain long. He finds the countryside tedious. He will visit and leave, visit and leave, and in between his stays I will be able to relax and enjoy my old home and estate. And I have sent you away, so I have cut the tug of competition with him over your love."

"I love *you,* Mother," said Marcot. "Not him."

"Hush, my son. I know that. You know that. Even he knows that. But 'tis a fact best not spoken aloud."

"Would you die without me at your side?" Marcot's bitter tone came from his grief.

"I will join the Water's Flow more easily knowing that you are out from under his gaze. It was my blindness, Marcot, marrying him, and I should be the one to pay the price. Not you."

"But sending me away now doesn't free me. Eventually, I would have to return from my tour of the duchies, and then I would be back under his orders, under his gaze."

"Let us not worry about far-off times." She smoothed his hair down, something she'd been doing since he was a little boy. "Let us have midmeal in the garden, stroll to my cunning footbridge, and enjoy to the fullest our day alone together."

They did enjoy the charmed day, while her garden showed its colors and the stream gleamed in the spring sunshine. In the evening Marcot and his mother played simple duets on their harps as they had used to do when he was young. His mother even felt well enough to dine with him, though he suspected that the color in her cheeks came from paint rather than the flush of health.

The next morning, early, he bid her farewell.

Heavy of heart, Marcot rode back to the capital on horseback and reported to his father. The Lord Regent received his wife's note eagerly and questioned his son about her improved health.

"My lord father, what do you think about the notion of my taking a tour of the duchies?" Marcot asked.

"And why not? Do you good to meet the people and see the whole picture. You could check on one or two things for me. I would like having information I can trust, not reports about harvests or tithes that turn out to be figments."

Marcot readied his kit for an extended journey. His father insisted on sending two guards with him, but he allowed Marcot to pick them, which Marcot appreciated, since this indicated they were unlikely to be his father's spies.

16

Alpetar

The strangely desolate High Road yawned before Butter, Kestrel's Alpetar pony. Close to the coast she had passed through two sizeable communities of sloped-roof cottages, goat pens, and businesses that straddled the major thoroughfare. The denizens' hair was brown, or brown with yellow streaks. All of them, male and female, wore wide pants and loose shirts woven out of an undyed yarn. The women's shoulder-to-ankle pinafores, however, provided a rich bouquet of colors, and Kestrel noticed that they all boasted large patch pockets. Men also wore aprons that tied around their necks and stopped before their knees. These were of darker colors and thicker canvas, and Kestrel saw tools sticking out of their pockets and loops.

The people pasted on neutral expressions as she passed, but Kestrel could sense their wariness of an outsider, so she mimicked their polite half smiles and chose not to engage with them. In the central squares—recognizable by their size and because they offered a sundial—she stopped for water at the public troughs. The dogs clustered close to the pony, but no one bothered her.

As she moved farther inland, occasionally she saw the smoke of a hamlet rise above the foothills or south of her on the plains, but few people traveled the major road. On the infrequent occasions when Kestrel passed a wagon or a rider, the driver would noncommittally incline his head, and she would return the gesture without seeking more conversation.

The landscape still tumbled about with more open meadows than woodlands. The road bordered fields that must once have been tilled and now lay fallow, with spring robins pecking out worms amongst the flourishing weeds. By dint of careful scavenging Kestrel found potatoes growing on their own, as well as turnips and beets. Although in mid-spring they hadn't reached any size, she pulled out as many as her saddlebags would hold. Butter loved carrots—greens and root—so she kept her eyes peeled for their distinctive leaf.

Wild animals and birds in this country peered at her, but they showed the same wariness as the folk. Kestrel could have addressed them, but since she had enough company with her three dogs and pony, she paid them no mind.

The land sloped, climbing toward the sharp Obsidian Mountains, which grew ever so slightly closer. The days passed slowly, with the pony's plodding footsteps and the ring of cicadas supplying a monotonous background. Although her battered toppie broke in three places, Kestrel wore it to provide some shade from the steady sunshine.

Didi, the hound, usually loped out front, while Jaki and Laki trotted close to Butter, either guarding her flanks or herding her forward. So it was Didi who first scented the group ahead and doubled back to warn her.

Humans ahead, she sent. *Puppies. Females.*

Slow as Butter trod, Kestrel kept gaining on the party in front of her, at first barely visible under the bowl of a deep blue sky. Soon, however, Kestrel could make out a wagon, a donkey, and light-haired people walking. As Butter drew nigh she could discern that the walkers were children and women. She saw only one man, driving the wagon.

A young herding dog with the group smelled Kestrel's party and commenced yipping frantically. When the folk realized she gained on them, they halted to wait for her to catch up. Kestrel tried to judge how much of a threat this party might be. A boy held a sword much too heavy for him; one woman clutched at a knife in her waistband; but they were basically defenseless against any serious danger and they knew it. Sorrow and fear weighed down their shoulders and made it hard to lift their feet.

"Good day to you," called Kestrel as she came within speaking distance.

"And to you," said the woman who held the knife. Her eyes regarded Kestrel warily.

Kestrel's dogs rushed up to sniff the puppy, who flopped down and showed her belly, wagging her tail frantically. The puppy sent to her, *Your Majesty? One sees thee! So hungry. So scared. Thou wilt surely help us?*

Kestrel sighed at the thought of delay, but she couldn't just pass these people, leaving them to whatever misery had been inflicted on them.

"How go your travels?" she asked, addressing no one in particular.

"I want my ma!" cried a little boy, who then burst into wails.

Kestrel was now close enough to pick out worrisome details about these travelers. The women riding in the wagon bed wore bloodstained clothing. Tear tracks etched the children's dusty faces.

"What happened to you?" Kestrel asked.

"An Oro press-gang stormed our village. Kidnapped our menfolk; kilt a good many; stole our horses; fouled our well," said the woman who appeared to be their leader.

"Oh!" Kestrel exclaimed, her hand flying to her mouth. "How horrible!"

"Kilt our dogs. That there's the only one left," said the older boy.

"And I see you've got injured and little ones?"

"Five chill'ens under five summers. And two of our women hurt something awful," said the elderly man, with a kind of perverse pride.

Kestrel suppressed a shudder.

"Who might you be?" asked the lead woman.

"Call me . . . 'Finch,'" she replied, deciding that a new name would be appropriate for each new land.

"I'm stiff from riding," Finch continued, sliding off of Butter. "Anybody want to ride my pony? Her name is Butter. I would walk a spell with you for the company; it's awful lonesome traveling alone." She put two of the children on Butter and walked alongside the square-faced woman who still had a spark of willpower left in her.

Saggeta introduced herself and the others and told Finch about the raid five days earlier. They had eaten all the supplies they had brought from Sweetmeadow and now only had the goats' milk and occasional foraged vegetables. The traumatized, hungry children fretted; Mother D. required almost as much care; and the women riding in the wagon—Dame Joolyn and Dame Linnsie—could hardly bear up from their injuries. Gramps, the two older children, and she were doing what they could to care for everyone, but she didn't know how much longer they could keep going.

Aghast, Finch took the full measure of their suffering. Here was the true result of conflict—not the lays Stahlia had taught her with their tales of heroics and glory—but starving, traumatized children and folk stretched past what they could bear, yet still plodding on.

"I don't understand. Don't you have guards to patrol the passes? A duke—or a mayor—some kind of official to take you in and protect you?"

"You're not from here, I gather," said Saggeta, gazing pointedly at Finch's poor dye job. "We've heard about gentry and magistrates and armies and such in other lands. But all those things require tithing. There's some more organized cities, way far on the west coast, but not hereabouts. We're simple goatherds and spinners. We live independent. We take care of ourselves and each other.

"What about you?" Saggeta addressed her. "The High Road is a strange place for a woman alone. Are you lost?"

Finch shook her head. "I'm not lost," she said, "though my path doesn't run straight."

"Dame, what's your dogs called?" interrupted a girl. Finch told her and watched her brighten up a bit petting Jaki and Laki.

Kiki, the puppy, wouldn't leave Finch alone; she kept running ahead of her and flopping down in the dirt to show her belly. When she squatted down to rub the soft, flat stomach, Kiki's squirming made figures in the dirt.

"It's my turn to ride the pony! My turn! *My* turn!" shouted a boy on the verge of a tantrum. Finch picked him up and jollied him a bit. Then she got all the children singing songs, which made the road pass more quickly.

The afternoon was still young when Finch spotted a good place by a stream to camp. On her own she would have continued on until sunset, which lacked some hours, but all her companions staggered with weariness. Someone had to take care of this group, or these people would not survive.

A queen's duty is to succor these innocents.

She and the boy, Gunnit, unhitched the draught horses, who had been allowed to grow fat and lazy. Finch rebuked the good-for-nothings as they watered them and turned them out to graze. The donkey was a more supportive soul, fiercely protective of the two goats.

Saggeta had gotten a rudimentary camp organized around a large fire. Mother D. had taken out a frying pan, but stared at it as if she didn't understand its purpose. Finch fetched her own sack of flour and gave it to the older woman, asking, "Do you think you could use some goat's milk and make flat cakes?"

Then Finch organized the children in a game of spotting wild greens and depositing their harvest into Linnsie's apron. She sent her hound Didi out to capture as many rabbits as possible. Afterward, with seven-summers-old Aleen's help, she got all the children stripped down and bathed in the river. She scrubbed out the filthiest of the clothes and laid the garments out to dry on rocks. Finch let Gunnit and Aleen have a few quiet moments without pestering little ones, soaking their sore feet in the cold water, as she steered the cleaner and refreshed naked tykes up to the campsite.

Flat cakes with ramps and new dandelion leaves made an odd combination, but satisfied their hollow stomachs more than a few swallows of milk. Soon the only people awake were Saggeta, Gunnit, and Finch. Laki patrolled the outskirts of their jumbled campsite.

"You've done a wonderful job," Finch said to Saggeta and the boy. "Without you, they would all have perished." Their efforts had been thankless thus far; her recognition and praise fell on them like water on parched tomatoes.

"I know a few things about surviving in the countryside," Finch continued, "and tomorrow, first thing, I want to search for some willow bark for your injured. You both turn in; my dogs will guard us so you don't need to set a watch."

She woke twice in the middle of the night: once when the baby cried and once when Gramps stepped on everyone while trying to get out of camp to pee. She knew that Didi had returned because she heard her licking young Kiki's paws. She made a mental note to check the puppy's paws in the morning; then she fell back asleep.

In the pearly morning light, while the children still slept, Finch shook Linnsie and Joolyn awake so she could take them down to the stream alone. This was not the Nargis River, but all clean flowing water held out the possibility of healing and renewal. A mist rose off the clear, still surface, and the slanted sunbeams appeared as dense shafts. They startled a heron when they neared the water; it flew off on wide blue-gray wings, gazing at them with sad reproach for disturbing its fishing.

Finch helped the women disrobe and washed the flesh wounds on their forearms, relieved at not finding signs of infection.

"Saggeta did a good job of cleaning your cuts," she noted. The knot on the back of Linnsie's head was as big as an egg, but it seemed to be healing. Joolyn's sprains and bruises might pain her less after a cool soak.

Both Linnsie and Joolyn spoke little, perhaps wary of confiding in a stranger. Finch let them be, hoping that they might find solace in each other and the cool water, while she headed downstream a ways, searching for a willow. She didn't spot the species she was accustomed to, but she paused over a midsize shrub abloom with catkins, because it resembled the "pussy willows" that Nana used to cut for her. When she peeled off a bit of the bark and chewed it, the familiar, bitter taste made her turn down her mouth. She used her knife to peel off multiple pieces of the soft bark, and just for fun, cut a big bouquet of the slender limbs with their soft blossoms.

As she headed back up the stream she overheard the two Alpie women's soft conversation echoing off the water.

"But what if there's a babe?" Joolyn asked Linnsie. "How could I carry his child?"

In gossip swirling around the Blue Parrot, Finch had heard that the blights affecting Oromondo had affected the men's fertility. Did the Sweetmeadow women know this? And even if they did, wouldn't they still worry themselves sick?

Finch deliberately stepped on a stick, making it crack to announce her return, and the bathing women looked up at her.

"Look at all this willow bark I gathered!" Finch held out her full hands with deliberate cheer. "And aren't these pretty? Do you know the name of this shrub?"

"Oh, that's goat willow," said Linnsie. "The children might like the catkins. I didn't know about the bark. . . ."

"Oh, yes, it'll be a great pain reliever." Finch added casually, "And I had another thought about an herb that might help us. I've seen pennyroyal growing wild everywhere along the road. I could brew a strong tea."

"Pennyroyal?" asked Joolyn, confused.

"Aye. Many women travelers take comfort in knowing they can control the timing of their courses."

"Does pennyroyal tea . . . bring on your courses . . . no matter what?" asked Joolyn.

"Sometimes it takes a few days," Finch cautioned, "but the herbalist I studied with swore by it. I had a friend named Zillie, she took lovers by the score, and she was never troubled with pregnancies."

The bathers exchanged glances, and some of the lines of strain in their faces smoothed away.

Gunnit had renewed the fire and had a kettle of water boiling, for which Finch silently blessed him. She was pleased to note that Linnsie felt better enough to praise him too. Finch brewed her willow bark and pennyroyal tisanes. Everyone broke their fast on tiny potatoes and carrots stewed soft in warm goat's milk. Didi had brought back two rabbits, but since they would take time to cook, Finch decided to keep them until supper.

Sipping their willow bark tea all day long, Linnsie and Joolyn perked up a bit, and all the travelers felt vicarious relief. Finch told the plow horses that they ought to be ashamed for walking so slowly a short-legged pony gained on them and forbade them from grazing when they ought to be pulling, so they set a brisker pace. Didi caught a third rabbit during the day, while Laki and Kiki managed to corner a fat squirrel, which Kiki carried to Gunnit with enormous pride.

In the midafternoon the travelers halted again. This time they feasted on rabbit stew with wild onions and burdock roots. The dogs got the whole squirrel and the rabbit entrails. Finch asked her canine pack to be sure Kiki ate more of a share than her low status would normally allot. She also treated the puppy's travel-sore paws with some oil, though she had to do this while dodging around her licking tongue.

"This is sure a sweet pup you've got here," she told Gunnit, who sat next to her on the ground.

"I guess she's mine now, but she belonged to my friend." Gunnit told her about Nimmet and Wimmie; Finch intuited that the vision of their dead bodies haunted him.

"To die so young!" Finch sniffed and wiped her cheeks. "And for you, to lose such friends! To have to see such horrors!"

Gunnit could make no reply; he hid his face in Kiki's fur.

"What kind of monsters roam our world?" Finch said to herself. Then louder, "I will get vengeance for them and for you, Gunnit."

"Will you?" he asked, trusting her.

"I vow."

She changed the subject before he could inquire how a solitary woman could take on the Oros. "But Nimmet would be glad you are taking care of his dog, and you should be happy to have her. Kiki needs to ride in the wagon for a day or two; let those paws heal up. In fact, I think you and Aleen should ride a spell and take a rest. Don't let them fool you; those lazy horses are plenty strong enough for the extra weight."

After eating, the children each found a grown-up lap to settle into. They begged for a story. Finch thought that taking their mind off their troubles was a good idea. She looked at Linnsie, who, as the mother of three, must be a practiced storyteller.

"Long ago, so long ago that the days are lost in the ripples of time," Linnsie began, "Saulė, Spirit of the Sun, tired of roaming the skies endlessly. Saulė longed for a place to call home, where the Spirit could drink dandelion kefir and rest undisturbed from never-ending travels."

Gunnit interrupted with a groan. "Ma, not again!" but the other children hushed him.

Linnsie continued, "Day after day Saulė roamed over the earth looking for the perfect place. Sometimes the Spirit would climb down from the skies to try a place for a night or two, but Saulė was never satisfied. Flat fields were too flat and mountaintops too spiky. Forests poked into Saulė just like when you try to sleep on pine cones.

"Then one day, just at twilight, Saulė paused over Alpetar. In between two of our highest mountains Saulė saw a high meadow, a perfect round bowl shape, blazing with buttercups. Saulė climbed down from the sky and tried out this meadow: it fit perfectly. The Spirit decided that this would be home.

"And ever after, Saulė roams the skies from here to there"—Linnsie pointed east and west—"during the day, shedding its sunlight on many lands. But come nightfall, the Spirit sleeps in Saulė's Basin, here in Alpetar. And each morning and night, Saulė kisses the people of Alpetar." Linnsie kissed the baby in her lap. Finch followed suit by kissing the top of Limpett's head; he nestled more tightly against her.

"Linnsie," asked Finch, "does Saulė grant your people special abilities?"

"Our legends say that Saulė gives us Rising."

"What?"

"Where you come from, do children play sitting on a plank, balanced in the middle, one up and one down?"

"Oh, aye. We call that a seesaw."

"Ah. We call it 'pushing the beam.' We think of people as feeling despair or cheerfulness. What our Spirit does is grant us the ability to Rise from sorrows—to push the beam up. Some people are stronger in this ability than others." Linnsie's glance swept over the children meditatively, as if weighing which did or did not have this Talent.

Optimism, thought Finch. *As Lautan traditionally allots Anticipation, so Saulė gives Optimism.*

"I know that," said Aleen. "Ma always said that's why we will always reach for joy. But I want another story—a new story."

"A new story," Finch said. "Hmm. Has anyone ever told you about the land of Weirandale and how it got its queen?"

"Tell it now," commanded Alloon.

"Long ago, so long ago that the days are lost in the ripples of time, Nargis, the Spirit of Fresh Water, had already chosen a home. Nargis delighted in a lake of the clearest, deepest water, on top of a mountain in a land we now call Weirandale. People lived in that land too—not many, because this was so long ago there were no cities, just scattered villages and farms. Nargis had no reason to pay much attention to these people. After all, to a mighty, immortal Spirit their lives were not significant. Nargis was more interested in lakes and rivers, ponds and springs, rainfall and waterfalls. The Spirit loved to watch waters' movement: the white foam or slow eddies, the ripples and plinks, plinks, plinks!" Finch's hands imitated the water's movements. "Nargis had quite enough to pay attention to, without worrying about *people.*

"But there was a farming family that lived fairly close to Nargis Mountain and Nargis Lake. One day, a group of rough-looking men came to the farmhouse door. They said they were very hungry—would the family feed them? The father was suspicious and wanted to turn them away, but the grandmother overruled him: 'No, we must be generous to all travelers; all travelers have guest right.' So, the family welcomed the strangers and fed them a hearty supper and gave them shelter.

"Everyone then went to sleep except for Cayla, the clever young daughter. She was about your age, Aleen. Instead of lying on her cot, she crept outside into the crook of a tree for safety, and the family's cats, always curious about what she was doing, came with her.

"In the middle of the night the men, who were very bad men—"

Damnation. I can't tell these children the ruffians murdered the family. Fool. I should have told them about Catorie the Swimmer.

"What? What did they do?" asked Limpett, impatient when she paused.

"They—they *robbed* the generous family. And . . . they tied them up. Cayla witnessed what happened. She wanted to run away and save herself, but her baby sister, a baby just like Addigale there, was still in the house. But Cayla was incredibly brave. You know what she did? She crept through the dark to the window near the cradle, reached in, and grabbed the baby!"

"That's what I would do," said Gunnit.

"I know," Finch agreed, then returned to her story.

"The bad men saw her, and they ran after her. Cayla ran and ran and ran. And her cats raced after her, crying because they couldn't keep up. The bad men were big and strong and had longer legs, but Cayla kept running. Every time Cayla tried to hide in a bush, the baby started crying too, and the noise alerted their pursuers, but Cayla would not put down her sister. She headed in the direction of Nargis Mountain. She had heard that the mountain was enchanted, and she thought that this enchantment might stop the—the robbers, but they kept following. They were getting closer and closer to her as the night waned and daylight approached. Cayla heard the noise of Water, and she was smart enough to think that the noise would cover up the sound of her crying sister, so she headed toward the sound.

"She burst out of the woods to see the most beautiful waterfall in the world. Sheets of water came tumbling down the mountain, and rainbows trembled in the air. But the sun—ah, your Saulé— had risen, and the bad travelers would be able to see her. So Cayla did another incredibly brave thing. Holding the baby close to her"— Finch imitated by grabbing both arms around Limpett—"she ran straight into the stream of the waterfall."

"Cold!" interrupted Gunnit, with a big shiver.

Finch nodded. "'Nargis, protect us,' Cayla pleaded.

"And Nargis noticed the girl-child. She saw how brave and clever she had been, and how selfless, to save her sister. And she knew that the grandmother had been just, to offer succor to travelers, and that the travelers had broken guest right by doing the family harm. Thus, she felt inclined to help her.

"'If I protect you,' asked Nargis, 'what will you do in return?'

"'I will pledge to watch over your Waters,' said Cayla. 'I will keep your Waters clean and pure, and I will never waste them or take them for granted.'

"And Nargis was touched, because even in those days, too many people were heedless of the gift of Water, throwing carcasses or offal into rivers. And she started to love this sweet child.

"So Nargis threw up clouds of mist around the waterfall, and the bad men couldn't see Cayla or her baby sister, and eventually they gave up searching for them and went away.

"For safety, Cayla stayed in the waterfall most of the day. When she finally came out she was so very, very cold. Her lips were blue; her fingers were blue; her nose was blue—even her hair had turned blue. When she warmed up, her skin went back to normal brown—but you know what? Her hair stayed blue, as blue as the Waters of Nargis Lake." Here, Finch paused and ran her hands through her own short, ratty hair.

"Then what?" prompted Aleen.

"Cayla grew up to be as brave and clever and generous as she promised to be as a girl. As Cayla got older, everyone noticed she had a very special Talent for persuading people to make sensible choices. She convinced all the folk to band together against robbers and highwaymen, to come to each other's aid whenever somebody was attacked or a fire broke out. She encouraged the people to work together to build roads. And she never forgot her promise: she convinced everyone to honor Nargis's Water.

"Years went by. Cayla married and had a little girl—and you

know what? That little girl also had blue hair. And then that little girl grew up and had another little girl who had blue hair. And Cayla's granddaughter, Carra the Royal, became the first queen of Weirandale, and set about turning Weirandale into a just, prosperous, and peaceful realm."

"That's a good story," said Aleen with a yawn. "I hope all the robbers got the trots."

"What happened to the cats?" asked Limpett. "I like cats. I want to have a kitty. Can I have a kitty?"

"No one knows. Some say that Nargis turned them into bigger cats, who didn't have to fear men. It's an old tale. I'm not even sure there were any cats. That's just the way I remember it."

The exhausted children soon drifted off.

In the night Jaki woke Finch by prodding her with his nose. *Wolves,* he said. Finch strained her ears, but she heard no howling. However, Taffy, ears twitching, agreed with Jaki. For an anxious hour the dog, the donkey, and the woman monitored the sounds and smells; finally they concluded the wolf pack had moved farther away.

Finch had a hard time falling back to sleep; she stared at the stars but saw visions of a wolf attack. She didn't think she could dissuade wolves—wolves, like coyotes, had such a strong prey drive that they wouldn't listen to her. Even if she could save the children by throwing them in the wagon, the loss of a goat or a mount would mean disaster for this band because its hold on life was so tenuous.

On the morrow they faced an actual—not imagined—disaster, because while traversing a particularly rough patch of road the wagon wheel went up over a small rock, and when it came down the old axle snapped in two.

Gramps looked through the tools he had brought and shamefacedly admitted he had forgotten to bring an axe. Although they could see a stand of conifers in the distance, they blanched at the prospect of trying to fell one. Finch examined Gunnit's sword but guessed that the brittle old metal would shatter at the first swing at a tree.

If this were not trouble enough, Didi trotted up to Finch and told her, *People coming. Many men.* In the distance she could just make out the dust cloud moving down the road, headed straight toward them.

Finch ordered the women and children to lie flat in a ditch at the side of road. She unhitched the plow horses. Mother D., today in a contrary mood, refused to get down off the canted wagon. Finch allowed Gunnit, Gramps, and Saggeta to back her up, though she placed more faith in the fighting skills of the animals.

A rider—perhaps the travelers' advance scout—rode by the broken wagon. He touched his hat in a rudimentary greeting but didn't stop. He wore a black hat with a pink feather, and a black leather sleeveless vest that showed off his bare, muscular, toffee-colored arms. *Pellish,* thought Finch, though she wasn't sure she had ever seen a Pellishman before. She also couldn't help but notice that the man looked rather dashing.

In perhaps half an hour the bulk of the other party of travelers came into view. It was a caravan of high freight wagons, flanked by outriders. The first two wagons just passed them by, ignoring the ragged group. But the third pulled up.

The driver, a man with braided brown hair with one streak of pink, climbed down. Finch gripped her dagger so tightly her hand cramped. Tail wagging, Kiki approached the man (though Finch's older and more suspicious dogs stayed at her side watching). The man crouched, stroked Kiki a moment, studiously ignoring the people but regarding the wagon closely, and then stooped down to spy out the broken axle. He straightened up and brought his hands to his mouth and made a piercing whistle through his fingers. One of the outriders, a man wearing a fancier embossed black vest with a prominent pink hat feather, rode up.

Still looking away from the band of four wary people, the driver quietly conferred with the rider, who called a halt to the whole wagon train. The drivers dismounted; several started a fire and broke out an enormous kettle tripod and foodstuffs. Meanwhile, the first driver marched to one of the last wagons and pulled out a spare, ready-cut axle. He and several fellows prepared to fix the wagon, but they needed to get Mother Dobbely down. The leader approached her, bowed low, doffing his hat to show the pink on the left side of his head, and addressed her in an accented voice. "Dame, you would be more comfortable by the fire. We have food and drink. Pray, will you join us?"

Mother D. let them escort her to the cook fire. Finch watched as the men hoisted up the wagon, replaced the broken axle, and trimmed it to fit. She strode forward, holding out her hand to the driver. "I want to thank you for your help."

He recoiled from her hand. "We never touch young females who are not family. Your fellows are welcome to join us for a repast of midmeal. All of your party—even those who hide in the ditch." He nodded at some small-sized clothes visible in the wagon bed. "You've younglings with you. Something tasty would not go amiss this day?"

Saggeta called those who were hiding to come out. The drivers fussed over the little children, running their hands through their yellowish hair, fingering it. Gunnit, however, pulled away from the men, scowling.

In the meantime the cooks had prepared a thick sauce that they served over fried cornmeal. Everyone ate heartily, without any of the conversation or pleasantries that normally would ensue while breaking bread. The drivers asked the travelers no questions and offered no information about themselves.

After all had eaten, the Pellishmen put full bowls down for the dogs. Then the man who had stopped originally talked to another; the second returned with a large bag of oats on his shoulder and another of flour, which he loaded into the back of their now-repaired wagon.

Despite all these kindnesses, Gunnit had not lost his wariness of these strangers.

"What is it?" Finch asked the boy.

"Their eyes," he replied.

Finch realized that the men would not look any of the adults in the face, yet they feasted their gaze on the small children.

She wondered if the Pellish just missed their own families. Or if they were as intrigued by the yellowish hair as she was by their pink strands.

The cook pot had been stashed away. Most of the men returned to their wagons, tightening up harnesses, checking the fastenings, but some eight remained clustered around the travelers. They helped rehitch the fat plow horses. Their leader ceremoniously led Mother D. back to the wagon. Gramps, from inside the wagon bed, and Gunnit, from the ground, assisted Joolyn and Linnsie in climbing aboard.

Yet when Linnsie reached out for baby Addigale, who was being cuddled by a Pellishman, Finch observed that the man pretended not to notice. Glancing around, she noticed that each man had one of the tykes in his grasp.

A wave of ice surged through Finch's chest: these men intended to keep the children. They thought they had "bought" them with two sacks of grain and an axle.

Did they intend to sell them? Enslave them? Abuse them?

More than twenty men altogether. All armed.

Her mind raced, looking for a plan. *I am not helpless. Think! What weapons do I have?*

Finch's Talent had matured enough to brush the minds of the four dogs, two goats, pony, and donkey, warning them to prepare to defend their herd.

Butter answered with a toss of her head, *We are ready but we be few.*

Then Finch thought of the Pellish horses.

I haven't had a chance to gain their trust; I have never touched or spoken to them.

Summoning all her Talent, she reached out to the thirty-three Pellish horses all at once: *On my command you will run forward as fast as you can.*

Some of the horses started at this strange voice in their heads or pranced a few steps.

Finch wanted to warn Gunnit and Saggeta. She turned her back and pulled her knife out of her belt. She saw their eyes follow her movement. Gunnit sauntered closer to Saggeta, whispering.

Finch walked straight over to the first Pellishman who still held Limpett in his arms. "Thanks," she said. "I'll take the lad. Limpett, come to me!" The combination of the dagger in her right hand and Didi at her heels, slunk low and menacing, made the man hesitate just enough so that Limpett, reaching for Finch with his arms, wiggled out of his grasp. But the man who had lost the boy to Finch wasn't going to give him up so easily. He drew his sword from his scabbard with a menacing grin.

Saggeta, following Finch's lead, had simultaneously approached the man who held Doraleen against his chest; he ignored her, turned his back, and started to stride away.

Seeing this caravan driver walking off with her cousin, Aleen shrilled, "Where are you going? Give her back to us!"

Her scream shattered the facade of friendliness. Jaki sprang at Doraleen's abductor, jaws sinking deep into his calf. The man cursed, roughly dropped the child, and pulled his sword. His comrade came at Jaki from behind, pulling his dagger; another man headed over to scoop up Doraleen as she lay in the dirt, still pulling in air for an enormous protest. In a whirlwind of commotion and growls, the three other dogs attacked the adversary who menaced Finch and Limpett. Meanwhile, the goats, Violet and Pansy, each pinning a foe in a glare, took several steps in reverse, tucked their heads down, and charged with all their might, knocking the men to the ground with unexpectedly strong headbutts.

The Pellish who stood by the carriages or who had climbed up to their wagon seats or saddles turned around to come to the aid of their eight fellows.

Finch Commanded the Pellish horses: *NOW! RUN!*

Carrying the outriders and the wagons in a mad dash forward, all of the horses obeyed. A few of the riders and drivers pulled on the reins so fiercely that the horses reared, crashing one wagon on its side.

While the Pellishmen near the carriages stared openmouthed at this catastrophe and three of the would-be kidnappers near the refugees ran after their wagons and mounts with curses, Finch, Gunnit, and Saggeta waylaid those who still held on to Sweetmeadow children. Saggeta ran after the man who had hoisted four-summers-old Sheleen over his shoulder like another bag of grain and kicked his feet out from under him. Saggeta's kick sent him sprawling face forward on his belly—which was lucky because Sheleen ended up cushioned on his back. A Pellishman grabbed Aleen's arm; she bit him as viciously as she could, and because he was further distracted by Butter—who was kicking him—Aleen managed to yank away.

The man who held Alloon wouldn't give him up without a fight; he reached for his sword in a side scabbard. But Alloon, who began kicking and punching with his little fists, encumbered him, and Finch managed to stab him deep in the groin with her dagger. As he crumpled in pain, she grabbed the boy away from him.

The kidnapper who had enfolded Addigale gently a moment ago now held the babe upside down by one leg, moving her about jerkily as if threatening to dash her brains out.

"Hey, you!" called Gunnit, getting the man's attention as the boy made a wild swipe with his heavy sword. Meanwhile, Taffy trotted up behind the baby-snatcher and took a deep bite out of his buttocks. The Pellishman yelped in surprise and pain and started to swirl about at the donkey, which allowed Gunnit, dropping the sword, to grab Addigale and pull her out of his grasp.

"Gramps! Catch!" they shouted as they freed each child, tossing him or her to Gramps, who threw the children into the wagon bed, then jumped up on the seat.

Finch pushed Gunnit toward Taffy and Saggeta to Butter.

Run, run, run as fast as you can, she ordered all their mounts. *Goats! Follow the wagon!*

Then she looked to the dogs. Led by Didi, they still assailed the downed Pellishmen to keep them from regaining their feet or counterattacking.

Stop, dogs. Follow me. She started to run, leaving the road for the cover and broken ground of the field.

Finch sent to the Pellish horses—some might have been out of range of her thoughts now: *Whatever you do: refuse to turn around. You Will Not pursue us.*

After the terror of the last few minutes, running felt good because it burned off the fear and fury coursing through her. Finch slowed her pace enough to look behind her at the battleground on the road. Tended by two standing comrades, three Pellishmen sat or lay in the dirt; none made any move to chase after the fleeing travelers.

She cut across country and ran up an incline to where she could see the road ahead curved around a switchback. The refugee party waited for her there. She saw all of them hoisting Pansy into the wagon; the goat must have been falling behind. When, panting, Finch reached the wagon herself, she braced her arms and tried to hop in. But after her run she did not have the strength. Linnsie and Joolyn each grabbed one of her arms and yanked her aboard.

With Finch safely inside, Saggeta shouted, "Go! Go!" The plow horses put on their best speed ever while the other animals gamely trotted behind.

Didi sent, *No men following.*

Finch lay on her back, her breath coming in ragged gasps. Doraleen and Addigale were wailing, while Alloon pounded on the wagon side and shrieked, "Go! Go!" Limpett strangled Joolyn with a death-grip hug and his face buried in her neck.

Finch regained her wind, propped herself up on her elbows, and took stock.

"Are you all right?" shouted Linnsie over the noise of the panicked children and the creaking wagon.

"Yeah, I think so," answered Finch. "Is there some water? What about all of you?"

Aleen cried out, "You saved us!" She threw her arms around Finch and started to sob. Aleen crying was such a new sight that other children quieted in round-eyed shock.

"Me?" said Finch, stroking the seven-summers-old's back. The adults needed Gunnit's and Aleen's help so much that they had all forgotten how young they really were. "Hardly. 'Twas that swarm of—of horseflies that made their horses go crazy. Wasn't that the greatest stroke of luck? And what about them dogs? And Taffy? Did you see our brave goats?"

She took some big swigs of water and got Aleen to drink a little too, which helped her regain control. Addigale, comforted in Linnsie's arms, had subsided into hiccups. Finch splashed a little water over Doraleen's face, hot from all her screaming, and was rewarded with a surprised ghost of a smile.

"Me! Me!" cried Alloon, so she wet a kerchief and washed his and Limpett's faces, the cool, fresh water providing a measure of comfort.

Pansy, the goat, chose *this* moment to piss all over the wagon bed. This struck the children as outrageously funny, and they started to laugh uproariously. Whenever the laughter died down one of them would make pissing noises, and off they'd go again into gales.

Finch lay back on the jolting, piss-smelly wagon bed and looked up at the Alpetar sun, overcome with relief and joy.

As a Weir princella, beloved of Nargis, Finch took the liberty of teasing another Spirit. *Saulė, I should have let the Pellish take them all.*

17

Cascada

Matwyck sat at his desk in his office, looking over reports, as he waited the few moments for his next appointment. He would have liked to reread the letter from Marcot about his travels and discoveries and compose a short note to Tirinella about his plan to visit her next week, but duty always came before personal matters. He prided himself on never shirking his work and using his time efficiently.

Today's meetings were going quite well from his perspective: he told the palace employee that due to the pressures of economizing, his services were no longer required, thanked him for his efforts, wished him well, shook his hand in both of his own to convey warmth, and walked him to the door, where Prigent appeared with a small bag of coin as severance. Most of the workers were too shocked to protest or argue. Of course he could have had Prigent handle the whole chore, but he wanted to judge personally if any of the people he fired were going to be troublesome. Perchance he had been hasty when he exempted all his supporters among the nobility from taxes, but that move had won him many powerful allies. Economizing on excess staff would not solve the realm's budgetary shortfalls, but it had the secondary advantage of removing people with alternate circles of power.

Heathclaw knocked to admit Royal Chronicler Sewel. Matwyck had cut the staffing of the Chronicler's Office twice already—why pay for royal chroniclers when no queen lived in residence? Each time the shitwit had protested vehemently, arguing that his office was charged with preserving older manuscripts and working with the Cascada abbey.

Matwyck had decided that it was high time to pull out this thorn. The tiny man was as stubborn and arrogant as someone twice his size.

Sewel entered without fuss, but his jaw was already clenched.

Matwyck pointed to the chair opposite, with a smile that in earlier meetings had been cordial and sympathetic.

"I have summoned you, Sewel, to inform you that as of today, your services will no longer be required."

"You are discharging me?"

"Regrettably, yes," said Matwyck.

"My deputy will take over?" asked Sewel.

"Actually, no. I am also discharging your deputy and your secretary."

"Then you are closing the Chronicler's Office completely?"

"Regrettably, yes. Although you refuse to accept the logic, it is a shameful waste to keep this office open now when Weirandale has another form of government."

"And how do you describe this new government?"

"'A democratic regency.' I serve because I've been called to this office by the people who vote."

"And when the queen returns?"

"Then we will reconsider, but in the meantime I must husband Weirandale's resources. They have been entrusted to me, so I cannot fritter them away on trivialities that run on the fumes and habits of tradition."

Sewel rose to his feet, and his voice escalated in pitch and volume. "Are you husbanding Weirandale's resources when you create a personal guard for yourself and when you throw lavish parties for the gentry? Are you husbanding our resources when you bribe different factions to spy on one another?"

"Surely such things are no concern of yours," said Matwyck. "I do not justify my decisions to a scribe." He controlled his anger; never allowing emotion to dominate him was his greatest strength. "Now. I thank you for your years of service to the realm." Matwyck stood up, but he broke his pattern by not shaking Sewel's hand—instead he put his own hand out, palm up. "The key to the Royal Library, if you please."

Sewel stood up, ignored Matwyck's hand, and exited the office. Prigent was waiting with his bag of coin, but Sewel brushed past him.

"Chronicler Sewel!" Matwyck called after him. "I demand that you halt and give me the key."

"Lord Regent," Sewel replied, turning his neck, "you have discharged me. I am no longer in your employ. I will accept no monies from you or your underlings, yet I will maintain my post in the library. I was hired by Queen Cressa. I serve at the queen's pleasure, thus I will carry on, unpaid and alone. My duty is to guard the queens' volumes from prying eyes."

Matwyck followed him into the anteroom, making *tsk*ing sounds with his tongue. "I insist that you turn over the key and leave the palace at once."

"You have no jurisdiction over my actions," replied Sewel.

"By what authority do you defy me?" asked Matwyck, his voice growing louder.

They currently stood in the midst of the outer chamber, and the clerks copying proclamations or filling in ledgers paused to gape at this argument. These people belonged to Matwyck, but by chance two kitchen maids had just wheeled in a cart with mulled wine and scones, and workers from other rooms had gathered around for refreshments.

Sewel said loudly, "I am merely staying at my post. Are you threatening me?" Sewel looked around at all the observers. "If I mysteriously sicken or disappear or have an accident, you will all know who ordered my assassination."

Matwyck forced himself to relax his face and unclench his fists. He walked over to the cart and took a glass. Deliberately, he also made a show of choosing a scone. The wait made Sewel positively snort with rage.

"Such a lovely repast," Matwyck said to the maids. "You've arranged the treats in such an appetizing way. These tidbits serve an important function because they refresh us from our labors. Every person in the palace must do his or *her* little mite to support our realm. Efficiently and with the least possible expense."

The women beamed at his praise and dropped curtsies.

"Chronicler Sewel," Matwyck said, when he was certain his voice would sound eminently reasonable, "I have told you that the palace no longer requires your services. Your reaction makes me fear you have lost your reason. I counsel you to consult a healer posthaste; perchance your irrationality indicates you are ill. If you would acquiesce, I would gladly send one of our healers to examine you.

"I regret your ill health, but I, *I* have much more pressing affairs that require my attention."

The rest of the day's dismissals proceeded smoothly. Matwyck crossed each name off his list with a tidy line. Discharging some of the garden staff meant that the Palace Gardens could not be kept up—he would tell the head gardener to concentrate on the formal entrance for appearances.

The nursemaid Nana was not on the list; his chamberlain had convinced him that her knowledge of the palace inventory was irreplaceable. Only Nana knew enough about the silverware to point out that a footman had been stealing spoons.

By evening Matwyck was able to put Sewel's defiance out of his mind as a petty annoyance. He had had the man followed intermittently: outside of his duties, he lived a solitary life. No, Sewel had no charisma to rally the masses, and he had already given up his most valuable knowledge a few moons ago, when Matwyck had placed his hand on the Truth Stone.

Yurgn had already sent spies to all the ends of the earth, searching for a young woman who could talk to animals.

18

Oromondo

Coming down from the high peaks, leaning way back in their saddles to help the horses negotiate the steep, rocky trails, the Raiders had hidden from Oro patrols or caravans by day and traveled in the cold half light of twilight or dawn. At sunrise of the third day, when they could no longer find any snow and their waterskins held only droplets, Thalen led them to a dell a short way above the valley floor, a spot that his book indicated held an ancestral spring.

A decrepit farmhouse fronted the road; behind it sat a small pond whose mudbanks showed the tracks of many animals. Though Thalen was elated, he acted nonchalant, as if he had never doubted his ability to find safe water. Their horses sucked greedily as the men refilled their water bags.

Codek and a handful of Raiders ambushed the farmhouse inhabitants just in the act of rising for the day: an elderly farmer, his wife, and her ancient mother, all with short, frizzy white hair and hanging, stained garb. They tied the family up, blindfolding them securely, and searched the house and outbuildings, finding the only other inhabitants to be two equally aged cows. Cookie milked the cows, but the yield was too meager to share out, so she gave it all to Tristo, with gibes about the boy still growing.

A back storeroom to the barn yielded nothing that tempted the Raiders.

"We can't make this farm our base," Thalen addressed the men who stood near him in the light that fingered into the storeroom. "It's too close to the road and has no cover. Get some rest. We'll move out after sunset."

The day slipped by slowly. As the afternoon started to wane, Thalen and Tristo checked through their supplies.

"Our lantern oil is low," Tristo remarked.

"Right. Maybe the householders have more, or some candles. Let's go check."

They walked in the back door of the farmhouse living quarters. The floor sloped, and the wood ceiling loomed so low that Thalen had to watch his head. Gentain and Cerf stood inside, arguing with Vatuxen, the Jígat cavalryman with a big nose and deep-set eyes, who had been assigned to watch the trussed-up homeowners. The argument raged so intensely that no one noted Thalen and Tristo's entrance.

"Go outside, Vatuxen," said Cerf. "You don't have to see this."

"But Sarge told me to watch the Oros. He said nothing about killing them," Vatuxen answered stoutly.

"Sarge didn't lose his two daughters," replied Gentain, "cut to pieces."

"Nor his sons and his wife," added Cerf, pulling out a long dagger with gleaming edges. "I'll give these here a clean, quick end. Which is more than any Oro deserves." He settled his out-of-place beaver hat more tightly on his brow, which had the effect of throwing a shadow on his face.

The captive farmer struggled in his bonds and rattled his rickety chair, while the wife sniffled with tears. The oldest lady slumped in her chair, either unconscious or pretending to be.

The lack of sound sleep and too much dehydration had made Thalen fuzzy-headed. He found the scene before him disorienting and hard to grasp. Cerf and Gentain were not young hotheads; they were the adults among the Raiders, his considerate healer and equally gentle horse master.

"Gentlemen," Thalen interrupted in a low tone.

Cerf looked up to see Thalen and smiled grimly, but without shame. "We came here to kill Oros. To cause havoc. To get revenge. We might as well start now. These farmers aren't innocent—they probably have sons among the Protectors. It could be that their son is the man who kilt your brother in the Rout. It could be that he kilt one of my boys."

"We've ridden a far way, Commander," Gentain added. "Might as well get started now. Aye, these three are just old civilians. But why should one Oro life be spared while we seek to take others?"

Temptation tugged at Thalen. One might be able to argue it was more ethical to take the life of the elderly rather than a young soldier: these farmers didn't have many years left. And didn't he owe a debt to Gentain's girls, Cerf's sons, and Harthen? Wasn't this why the Raiders had invaded Oromondo, to kill and cause havoc?

"Sarge wouldn't like this at all," Vatuxen spoke into the tense air.

"You're right," said Cerf. "Sergeant Codek plays by military rules. But military procedure led the Free States straight into the Rout and Occupation. Commander Thalen is more unconventional, more daring, which is why we stand here, with an opportunity we shouldn't waste. Nothing is assured: the commander keeps telling us we are on a sacrifice mission. So let's make sure our journey and our gamble count right now while we have a chance. Stand aside, Vatuxen. Or better yet, go outside. Gentain and I can deal with this without help."

Thalen stood paralyzed with indecision. But from behind him, Tristo burst out laughing. The other four men crowded in the dim room turned to him befuddled. Tristo's laughter redoubled; his eyes grew wet. Then he started jiggling from one foot to the other.

"Tristo, what—" Thalen began.

"Ooooo! I gotta pee!" Tristo flung open the door, yanked down his breeches, and relieved himself in the yard with a noisy splash. The men gaped in amazement at Tristo's naked rear as his shoulders still heaved.

"You guys!" Tristo said to Cerf and Gentain as he pulled up his breeches. "Did you practice that? The knife and all? For a moment there I really thought you was gonna do it! 'Stand aside, Vatuxen!' This was the best mummers play I've ever seen! Bet these Oros peed their pants too! You already evened the score on these old codgers— you scared them to death! I tell you, that was prime. 'Stand aside, Vatuxen!' You guys put on a show like that in Yosta's Square and I swear you'd stroll away rich! I wisht all the fellas could have seen this."

Mastering his manic glee, Tristo wiped his teary face with the fingertips of both hands and caught Thalen's eye. "Commander, didn't we come in here for some candles?"

Thalen came back to himself. "Look around in the cupboards, you lackwit."

He cleared his throat. "Cerf and Gentain—if and when you want to kill a captive, you will discuss the issue with Sergeant Codek or me." Thalen rolled some tension out of his neck. "The fact that you snuck around behind our backs demonstrates that beneath your rationalizations, you knew this was wrong.

"I sympathize with the need for retribution. You shall have it. But I shall choose the targets and the time and place. *Do you understand?*"

Cerf sheathed his knife, and they both nodded.

"We'll say no more about this—this mummers play. Go get ready to ride."

When the older men had left the cabin Thalen briefly set a hand on the cavalryman's shoulder. "Well done, Vatuxen. Really."

"Yeah, well, there's right and there's not," said Vatuxen.

"True, but vengeance and grief have a way of blurring the line between them."

Thalen turned to Tristo, whose hands bristled full of candles. "Tristo—"

"See all the candles I found? I'm *resourceful*."

Thalen grinned. "Take your haul and go pack up."

Thalen looked around the spare room for anything else that might be of use. He grabbed the only two books in sight: a pamphlet entitled, *Pozhar's People,* and a thicker volume with the words *Sacrifice and Sanctity* engraved on its cover. Then he walked over to the blindfolded Oro captives. He considered them a moment, taking in their shabby clothes and their wrinkled skin. He heard the wife's frightened intake of breath at his physical proximity.

"Vatuxen, give them each a drink of water. Then loosen their bonds just enough so that with effort and sweat they'll be able to free themselves eventually."

Reluctantly, the Raiders left the precious water hole behind. During that night's ride, Gentain rode abreast of Dishwater.

"Commander. I want to apologize." He looked away. "It's like a sickness sometimes. I hear my girls screaming in my head, screaming for me to help them. They must have screamed for me, and I never came. I set the sickness aside for a while, but it always comes back."

"I know what it feels like," said Thalen. "Truly, I do. Only it's my mother I hear."

And he also knew that he was really the one to blame, because he was the one who continually stoked the men's need for vengeance.

Death came to their enemies soon enough. A day later, while spread out searching for another spring, Kambey's squad of eight unexpectedly ran straight into a patrol of Oro guards flanking a wagon of metal ore. As Kambey later related, both parties startled at the encounter, but the Raiders drew their weapons first. These Oros, anticipating no danger, wore only breastplates. Weddle took down two with his quarterstaff before they even knew what was happening. Eldie, mounted, drew her bow and with lightning speed sent arrows into eyes and throats. The strong swordsmen in the squad, Kambey, Cook, Rowe, and Jothile, made short work of the Oros still standing openmouthed in astonishment that their destruction had caught up with them out of nowhere on a mild spring day.

When Wareth fetched the other two squads to the site of the skirmish, Thalen ordered the aurochs loosened and the Oro weapons harvested.

"Leave the bodies here. Burn the wagon. We want the Oros to know that danger is stalking them."

Though the Raiders canvassed the whole area where this second spring once coursed, they found no sign of water. Their water bags soon hung empty. They licked their dry lips and tried to calm their agitated horses.

Thalen led his increasingly parched company deeper into the heart of Oromondo, around the outflanking arms of FireThorn, one of the towering volcanic mountains, which occasionally spewed small plumes of ash and smoke. The riders' mouths grew chalky, and their temples pounded with piercing headaches. All their horses became lethargic and stumbled. Thirst was their constant companion, riding along with them, grinning an evil grin, impinging on every breath and mocking every step. Yislan, the archer, swayed in his saddle.

"Pass the word," Thalen said. "Dehydration causes dizziness. Don't let anyone fall off or lag behind."

To their right, down a steep embankment, their road followed a tumbling river, white and boisterous with snowmelt. Cautiously, their shadows etched by moonlight, the Raiders crossed a substantial wooden bridge, their horses' hooves making a clatter loud enough to wake the souls of those sacrificed to FireThorn.

On the other side of the bridge, the bank to the river sloped more gradually and the Raiders' thirsty horses were so desperate to drink that they yanked at their reins and ignored their riders' kicks.

"Hold them back!" Thalen ordered, knowing that this big river must carry the effluent of many mines. "The water's poison. You can't let them drink!"

While the other riders kicked their horses forward, away from temptation, Tristo wasn't strong enough to hold back his lively mare; Wareth had to grab Peaches's bridle and pull her away from the river.

Thalen quickly led the Raiders away from the water's siren call, deeper into enemy territory in the shadow of another volcano, the one the Oros called FireSky. As the horizon brightened, Tel-bein and Adair pointed to wisps of smoke indicating farms or towns.

"We can't be caught in daylight out here in the open," Codek warned Thalen.

"Any minute now," Thalen murmured, watching the ground carefully, praying his ancient map had not led them astray again. Finally, he spied a glint of water, a stream about a pace across meandering out of a canyon mouth. To keep Dishwater's head up until he could verify the source, Thalen kicked him into a gallop and led the men pounding upstream between the arms of the mountain. The canyon—sometimes so narrow it had no verge and they squeezed between towering boulders—tunneled deep between arms of sheer gray rock.

Abruptly, the canyon ended in a jagged rock face. Thalen jumped off of Dish and crashed through a thick stand of wizened trees and thornbushes. There he found the water's fount, a spring bubbling up from the aquifer below.

"Go ahead and drink," he called, though now the men could not have stopped their frantic horses even if they tried. Thalen cupped his own hands in wonder in the flow of safe, clean water. His throat was so swollen it was hard to swallow the first sips. He choked on the third mouthful. But after that he got down a series of soothing gulps. As if from far away, he heard Cerf cautioning everyone to drink slowly.

After he had slaked his most urgent thirst, Thalen looked around, appraising the location. Lush ferns, greens, and moss had taken advantage of the water. A few audacious saplings grew from the creek floor or out of rock ledges.

"What do you think, Codek?"

Water dripping from his chin and sparkling on his sideburns, his sergeant grunted, "Probably ain't gonna find anything better."

Thalen took a step onto a small boulder to use it as a pedestal. The rising sun had crept over the canyon edge, casting a bit of a glow into the defile. The water, however, still ran in shadow, and it reflected the canyon walls' dark tones. Thalen pitched his voice loud. "Raiders, listen up. This will be Ink Creek Canyon Camp. The spring is fast enough to provide what we need, and it is unpeopled and far from the roads. This will be our home base."

The water revived the parched horses and men. The Raiders saw to their mounts, taking off loads and tack, currying out the dust and burrs, washing off the sweat with buckets of cold, clean water. Once that task was accomplished, many men eased themselves out of their boots, breeches, and shirts and stood in the calf-high stream, soaking their feet, scrubbing off the worst of the caked-in dirt from their own faces, necks, and forearms. Cerf passed around cakes of soap.

Thalen dunked his whole head in the rivulet, letting the icy water flow through his sweat-matted hair. Then he joined his companions in the gravel on the creek's edge, relaxing. He barely registered that Codek had set to business, establishing the cooking area closest to the spring's mouth. The men's sleeping area came next, then his own tent, while the sergeant situated the women's sleeping area across the water and behind a stand of firs next to the rock face. A long and skinny corral for the horses occupied the greenest side of the downstream canyon, with a long and skinny practice yard across from it. Men stirred about, getting settled.

"Commander, your tent is ready for you," Tristo interrupted his half doze.

Thalen stifled a sigh and pulled himself to his feet.

Cook approached. "Can we start a fire? A hot meal would taste pretty fine. There's plenty of firewood."

Thalen looked up and around. High above, FireSky let off a stream of smoke, so Thalen reasoned that the smoke from their cooking would go unnoticed.

Thalen settled himself in his chair at his makeshift desk and rubbed his gritty eyes.

Adair appeared at the tent flap. "I've scouted the rear of the canyon. It's solid rock and too sheer. No one can attack us from behind, but we also don't have a way to flee if we're boxed in."

"Then we better not get boxed in. Tell Codek to set a watch at the front door. But not you scouts. I want all of you to get some sleep."

Gentain came to him to report that Peaches had colic—probably from lack of water—and they were walking her around and hoping for the best.

"Here, Commander," said Cookie, bringing him a restorative mug of tisane.

"Cookie, I need an inventory of your food supplies."

"Uh-huh," she said. "But let's get some food in our bellies first."

For supper that night they had a fire and a hot meal. The cook fire area had already been established as their gathering place. Raiders leaned against saddles or supply packages, smoking pipes and chatting in small clumps. Literoy broke out his fife and played some cheerful tunes.

After enjoying his own supper, Thalen stood up and stretched, then he gathered up Tel-bein, Wareth, and Adair.

"I want you three to ride out after moonrise. That wagon we burned counts for naught; it might not even be noticed. We need a bigger statement that will frighten the Oros. Ride out, spread out, survey the surroundings, and find me something sweet."

The scouts rode off, and Codek changed the watch at the canyon's entrance. Deep within Ink Creek Canyon the mountain's arms protected the Raiders from the cold wind that had plagued them since their landing in Metos. Relieved by his success in finding sweet water, Thalen drifted off to sleep listening to the song of the creek.

The next day Codek set the men to repairing torn tack, sharpening and oiling their weapons, mending their clothes, and cutting juniper brooms to brush away their tracks. Cerf insisted that their clothes needed a good wash if their skin was to stay healthy. Ragged, wet clothing soon hung from every bush and draped every large boulder. Even though this was the first day in moons when they hadn't been on the move, and plenty of details needed attention, by afternoon Kambey had the men practicing their swordplay and archery in a gravel practice area. At night Gentain supervised taking the horses out in small squads to feed in the green hollows on the mountain's arms. Per Thalen's orders, the men shoveled the horses' dung into canvas sacks and lugged it back into the canyon, both for secrecy and for extra fuel when their wood supply ran out.

In preparation for battle, Thalen sat down with Cerf and *Basic Battlefield Healing*. Together they reviewed the most dangerous arteries and how to stanch the bleeding.

"Commander, you don't have to assist me," said Cerf. "I could get someone else who doesn't have your duties."

But Thalen was reluctant to cede his self-assigned position as Cerf's second. Partly, he realized, this was to make his lie to his mother about working with the healers come true. Partly, he wanted his hands to help save his men.

During the second night in Ink Creek Canyon, Adair shook Thalen awake.

"Commander, we spotted a sizeable Oro caravan and patrol."

"Show me," said Thalen, rubbing his face and unrolling a map.

In the predawn light Thalen left the worn-out scouts to guard Ink Creek Camp and roused the rest of the company. Watered, rested, and freed from their burdens of supplies, the horses frisked about. A hard ride out of the redoubt and then a few leagues due east brought them to the chosen spot where the road passed through a cramped ravine.

Thalen arranged his archers—Eldie, Eli-anna, Yislan, and Cookie—on both sides of the roadway with a plentiful supply of arrows.

"Stay down on your bellies until the fighting starts."

He had the men quickly cut down trees to blockade the narrowest span of the road by making an abatis of sharpened pine limbs and sticks.

"Codek, Ooma, and—and you, Fedak, position yourselves on the far side of the barrier, just in case the Oros break through. It's your job to keep them from escaping."

Then he hid the main force of the Raiders' cavalry down a draw off the main road.

They finished their preparations just in time: the caravan's dust cloud became visible before they had rubbed the pine sap off their hands or the sweat off their faces with their neck wraps. The ground shook as two dozen Oro foot soldiers, a wagon pulled by aurochs, and two officers mounted on the same ugly beasts passed their hideaway and rode into the trap the Raiders had prepared.

This will be my first sortie as commander.

He waited until he heard the twang of arrows, shouts of shock, and the bellows of the beasts. Then, with the wolfhound leaping and growling at his side, Thalen pulled Quinith's grandfather's rapier and spurred Dishwater.

"Raiders, charge!"

Some of the Oros were trying to batter down the abatis, but the majority had turned backward to flee the punishing onslaught of arrows from above, so they ran straight into the mounted Raiders. The enemy wore breastplates and carried pikes. Caught by surprise, however, they had no space or time to form up; most of them gaped at the thundering coursers and never even leveled their weapons.

Thalen found that Kambey's training had strengthened his blows. His rapier flashed through the air where he wanted to take it. Thalen stabbed the Oro he engaged straight through his unprotected neck. He freed the rapier with a jerk, and his backhanded motion accidentally slashed the arm of another enemy, severing an artery. Out of the corner of his eye he saw Jothile take advantage of the man's shock to behead him. An Oro officer mounted on an aurochs pulled his sword; though the ravine walls barely stretched wide enough for this maneuver, Thalen and Kambey closed on him from either side. Thalen parried a flurry of panicked and wild strikes as Kambey leaned in and hacked the man's leg clear off at the thigh. The enemy officer screamed.

Dishwater carried Thalen past the lines of Oros until he found himself just behind the wagon, which was trapped in place, unable to turn around. Though the driver whipped the aurochs forward, the oxen balked at the sharp barrier. Without hesitation, Thalen skewered the driver from behind in the kidneys. Neither pity nor bloodlust touched him: this skirmish was only an unpleasant task that had to be completed. These Oros were not the ones who had murdered Harthen and his mother, but their deaths would save Free Staters' lives.

The noise of the skirmish echoed against the ravine wall, but in minutes comparative silence fell. Thalen heard only the gasps of the winded Raiders and the moans of the injured.

Codek's voice broke the quiet with the order Thalen realized *he* should have uttered: "Look to our wounded!"

Rowe lay dead, his neck broken. But Thalen had no time to

grieve, because blood was spurting out of Literoy, Gentain, and Kran. Cerf and Thalen swiftly tied tourniquets and bandages. Then Thalen sent Tristo and Eli-anna to escort the injured and Cerf straight back to Ink Creek Canyon for serious patching up.

Thalen regarded the Oro wounded who lay scattered on the ground. One man tried to crawl away; another held his hands up, whispering a plea for mercy.

"What do we do with their wounded?" asked Codek.

"We can't care for them, and we don't want them telling any tales," Thalen sighed, pulling his hair out of his eyes, and absently accepting his hat, which had fallen off, from Cook. "They need to be put down."

A few cavalrymen gaped at him, but Thalen walked resolutely over to the closest Oro lying supine on the ground but still breathing. He was just a young boy, his white-and-brown curls streaked with dirt, his lips gray with blood loss. The tear tracks down his caramel cheeks almost undid Thalen, but he tightened his grip on his sword.

I'm glad you have your eyes closed. It's over now. No more pain. Not the pain of dying, nor the pain of living.

Holding the boy's hand to provide a semblance of comfort, Thalen aimed the point and sliced the lad's throat.

After he had demonstrated his own willingness to engage in this distasteful task, Thalen looked up. "Any volunteers for the rest?"

"I'll do it," said Ooma.

"Good. You have steady hands. Make it quick and easy." Thalen watched her croon, "Hush now," to the next soldier with almost maternal tenderness.

Eldie and Yislan retrieved their arrows, but Cookie was too busy vomiting to help. The Raiders scavenged the Oro weaponry, more to keep it from their enemies than because they wanted it.

"Fedak, Weddle, and Britmank, dismantle the abatis—I don't want the Oros to see it. Then set the logs and the wagon alight. Cut loose those aurochs and drive them all around the area to trample our tracks."

"Everyone, scatter widely and erase your own hoofprints with care. When you get close to the canyon, find a rocky bank, and ride your horses in through the water."

Back at Ink Creek Camp, Literoy's arm slash turned out to be bloody, long, and jagged but fairly shallow. Gentain, however, had lost two fingers and a chunk of skin on the outside of his left hand. Kran's injury was the most serious: a pike point had penetrated deep into the meat of his thigh, and infection might set in. Cerf heated up his knife. With two Raiders sitting on top of Kran and a leather between Kran's teeth, Cerf painstakingly cauterized the depths of the wound. Lesser injuries on knuckles and faces kept Cerf washing, sewing, and bandaging for hours.

After the injured had been dealt with, the Raiders buried Rowe deep in the canyon's dirt and gravel.

Thalen read the Raiders' mood from their faces: sorrow for their comrade, concern for their wounded, but elation that they had won the day and relief that they had so successfully—after moons of travel and hardship—begun their actual mission. Thalen broke out the brandy for everyone and sat awhile with Rowe's particular mates—Vatuxen, Britmank, and Literoy—toasting his memory.

Toward evening, Kambey and Codek came to his tent to analyze the battle.

"The archers did more than half the work for us," Codek enthused. He mimed pulling a bow. "Those Mellie girls!"

"Some horses balked," said Kambey. "When Gentain is back on his feet, we've got to set up more mounted drills. Weddle and his staff—Spirits save us! A one-man death squad."

"I've had a long chat with Cookie," said Codek. "I'll wager she'll handle the next skirmish with a stronger stomach. You'd think that as a cook, someone who deals with butchered meat every day . . ."

"No," said Kambey, "this is completely different. I'm just glad more of the Raiders didn't lose their fastbreaks."

Thalen was glad that he hadn't shown such weakness.

Tally: 24-1 (Rowe)=23
Horses: 24

19

Alpetar

Finch felt exhausted, not because she and the Sweetmeadow refugees had traveled so far this day, but because wrangling the children could be so tiresome. Yet she could not fall asleep. The High Road their group followed, which for so long had approached or paralleled the Obsidian Mountains, had started to curve southward, the wrong direction for her.

She heard a rustling in the woods, too large to be one of the customary nocturnal creatures but apparently not a threat, because the dogs snored on peacefully. Moving slowly so as not to wake the others, she got up to investigate, walking a short way out of their campsite.

Finch looked around. She saw nothing. A slight rustle overhead made her shift her gaze upward, where she spotted a large screech owl perched on the branch of a pine.

Your Majesty. The owl turned its head sideways one direction and then the other. *What bringst thee into one's territory?*

I am on my way to Oromondo, the Land of the Fire Mountains.
How might one aid thee?

I need a guide to help me find a path through the peaks. And once there I need to find a particular group of men.

One does not leave this wood. But the hawks know those mountains well. One will find thee reliable escorts. Watch the skies.

The owl stared at her for a long moment; then he unfurled his surprisingly large wings and swooped away.

Hawks. What a fool I am! I could have had them scouting ahead for us this whole time. Gardener told me about hawks in his dream. Stupid, stupid, lackwit!

Finch made her way back to her sleeping blanket. She looked up at the cloudy half moons, troubled. What had been keeping her awake was her knowledge that she would have to part ways with her fellow travelers. Already they had slowed her down. If she were going to join up with these Raiders to fight the Oros, she would have to leave the villagers to their fate. She felt torn in two.

They are so defenseless. They need me. I make a difference in their lives—I can even save their lives. They look to me for protection.

The chance to be *a leader* had been an intoxicating experience for Finch. The refugees followed and trusted her. And she also knew in these weeks she had lifted them up from their lowest point. Each day they grew stronger.

Though if she were honest with herself, it wasn't just concern about their welfare that made her reluctant to leave the Sweetmeadow group. In the two weeks she had traveled with them, she had become so fond of them, and they provided her with fellowship, a family. To strike off alone again now—what a bleak prospect! And what would happen to these precious friends?

What would Gardener counsel?

That Alpetar only served as another temporary garden bed for me, and these folk only temporary companion plants. Oh, drought damn him and his adages!

Finch sighed and thrashed around in her blanket some more. Turning north solo would be pulling herself out by the roots again.

Yet she really had no choice if she were going to lend her Talents to the fight against the Oros.

Finch gave up trying to sleep and went to sit by the embers of the fire, her blanket thrown around her. Jaki came and lay behind her so she could recline against his furry bulk. She stared into the flames until her eyes smarted from the smoke; Jaki's solid heartbeat thrummed through her chest.

Alloon woke her by prying one of her eyes open. From the looks of things the others had been up for hours; everyone's belongings had been packed away and the team hitched to the wagon.

"She's awake," cried Alloon.

"That's because you woke her, twit," said Gunnit. He brought Finch a cup of milk and some fried dough, both of which he had kept somewhat warm. "You ain't ill, are you, Finch?" he asked.

"No. Just tired. Looks like you are ready to move. Pull out, and I'll catch up with you." Finch started eating slowly as the grown-ups rounded up the kids and bumped the wagon back onto the road. Then she made a show of getting up, packing up her blanket, and starting to ready Butter while they could still see her.

The moment the wagon passed out of sight, she looked up at the sky. High overhead two hawks circled. They immediately dove down, landing on two different branches of the tree in front of her. They had cruel beaks, sharp talons, and yellow eyes. These birds were predators, not pets.

Your Majesty, said the female of the breeding pair of black-tailed hawks. *We are here to guide thee.*

Is there a road or a path into Oromondo near here?

No roads, no paths. A deer trail for part of the way.

Is there a pass?

Not in this part of the mountains.

How will I get over them then?

Thou wilt climb. We shall show thee the way.

All right. I will take leave of my companions; then I will follow you.

Finch whistled up the dogs and mounted up on Butter. In less than half an hour she had caught up with the Sweetmeadow caravan.

"Finch!!!" cried the children. "Your turn to sing us a song."

"Not right now, urchins. Saggeta, I would speak with you."

The princella dismounted from Butter and walked with Saggeta at the rear of the procession. Saggeta looked at her curiously but waited until she was ready to speak.

Finch steeled herself. "I ran into you on the road. We were well met. But now my path takes me in another direction from yours."

Saggeta was stricken. "How will we survive without you? You have become our leader and our protector."

"*You* are their leader, Saggeta. You were before, and you can be again. As for protection, I have decided to leave the two herders, Laki and Jaki, with you. They'll support Kiki in guarding you. You'll have three watchdogs."

"No, no. We can't take your dogs," Saggeta protested. "You may need them. A young woman, all alone . . ."

"I will keep Didi as a hunter, because I don't want to take any of your provisions. Just Didi will do for me."

They walked a few steps in glum silence. "When are you leaving?" Saggeta asked.

"No point in delay. I'll say my farewells now."

The children cried and pouted. Gunnit scowled at her as if she had betrayed him. Gramps tried to wheedle her into staying.

Linnsie took the news the most stoically; she even rebuked the children. "You don't own Finch. If she says she has to leave us, well then she has to leave us. We should be grateful for all she has done for us, rather than such carrying on. Now, give her a kiss."

Finch accepted multiple kisses and hugs. Then she silently instructed all the animals in their duties to these humans; Taffy, the donkey, was greatly relieved that Laki would remain with them, because the small herder and he had forged a tight bond.

"May Saulė light your way!" her friends called after her with choked throats. Aleen's voice sounded very shrill.

With a lump in her throat, Finch rode Butter off the road and turned her head northward. She heard footsteps behind her: Gunnit ran pell-mell after the pony.

"I didn't want you to go thinking me ungrateful. I will never forget you, Finch, not as long as I live. I wish I had something to give you, as a present I mean."

In desperation, he grabbed the knit cap off his head. "Here, take this." She took the ragged hat as if it were the costly gift of a king.

Finch regarded Gunnit seriously. "You are a very brave, capable boy. I am proud to have known you." She reached into her saddlebag and pulled out Tilim's toy soldier, the one keepsake that she had grabbed from the Wyndton home the night she fled. "You are too old to play with this, but mayhap you would like to keep it as a remembrance? It belonged to another boy whom I am very fond of."

Instead of hugging him, she shook his hand, as she would have shaken the hand of a man grown.

Then she mounted up on Butter, kicked the pony into her jolting trot, and sped away before her heart pulled her back to her Sweetmeadow friends.

With just Butter and Didi her day passed so quietly. The northward deer track climbed steadily, and the mountains loomed over her as she got closer. Butter plodded on, seemingly unaffected by the incline and the thinning air. Didi caught a rabbit, which Finch cooked for her supper, giving Didi the entrails. She made herself a grass whistle, but it was a poor substitute for the children's chatter. Butter chomped contentedly by her side.

Near the trail ran a stream of icy snowmelt, pouring down from the high peaks in front of her, so Finch had plenty of water. Most of the second and third day, her route climbed steeply near the stream. Looking down, she saw the foothills, meadows, and plains of Alpetar behind her; clouds cast a pattern of moving shadows. The hawks helped out by feeding the dog squirrels, mice, and even lizards. Thus Didi could concentrate on catching Finch a rock grouse, which took a lot of plucking but made a tasty change. The grass thinned, no longer providing as much forage for Butter, but the pony did not grumble.

The terrain turned to all rock on the fourth day. As the horse trader had promised, Butter was sure-footed, never slipping even when a boulder beneath her proved unstable. No grass grew this high up. Finch had stuffed her saddlebags against this eventuality, but her provisions didn't last long. She searched the bottom of her bags, finding two wizened carrots and crumbs of sugar and salt; she gave this to Butter in her cupped hand. When it was gone, Finch scratched the pony behind her ears and pulled her fluffy mane out of her eyes. "That's all there is, girl. That's all I have," she said aloud. Her own voice sounded strange to her in the windswept silence of the upper altitude.

On the fifth day, Didi and Finch shared a snake the hawks dropped for them. With no vegetation to burn, Finch forced herself to chew the meat raw. Butter drank water. The mountain peaks reared right up in their faces. Though it was summer, it grew frigid at night. Finch slept in all of her clothing, sandwiched next to the dog. The pony slept on her feet for all but an hour; when she lay down she provided a windbreak. Gunnit's warm cap proved to be a blessing.

In the afternoon of the sixth day, they came to a nearly sheer rock face. Finch studied it with dismay. She saw no way to get the pony and dog up this barrier. She ventured first to the left and then the right; the face continued as far as she could see. She summoned the hawks.

You have brought me to a dead end.

We have brought thee to the easiest route into the Land of the Fire Mountains.

*But I can't ride my pony up a cliff. A dog cannot climb. There must
be places where the way is not so steep.*

Men with metal guard those places. A human can climb.

Finch looked closely at the cliff. Could she climb that? Possibly. She could see a multitude of crevices, handholds, and shallow ledges. Probably.

But doing so would mean leaving Butter and Didi behind. She glanced from Butter, twitching her ears, to Didi, stretched out panting. She loved them both; she needed their companionship. But her need was selfish—she had no food for them, and she was leading them into danger. Sending them back down into Alpetar would ensure their safety.

Finch rubbed a few self-pitying tears off her cheeks. She unsaddled and unbridled the pony, then used her knife to cut Butter's reins, making herself some leather straps. The straps secured to her back her blanket, her waterskin, a pan, her tinderbox, her hair tinctures, and a few other oddments. Then she turned Butter and carefully used the rest of the leather to tie her mane up neatly.

I must leave you now. Didi, you and Butter head down the mountain. You can catch up to Laki and Jaki and the human puppies and females. Stay together and watch out for each other.

Shouldst we stay with thee, Majesty? Thou hast no fur. Thou can nay hunt. Thou art helpless without this one and the stocky equine.

No, where I'm going you can't follow. What I have to do, you can't be any part of. I must go alone. She kissed Butter's soft nose and scratched her behind her mobile ears. *Don't argue. Get along now, while there's still some light left.*

She knelt to cup Didi's soft head in her hands.

Get along now.

The animals obeyed her command, though both turned back to look at her several times. Watching them grow smaller as they swiftly descended, she felt as abandoned, as lonely as if she were the last person in Ennea Món.

She turned to look at the sheer rock. "May the Waters keep me," she said aloud.

Hawks! Lead me up!

The hawks learned that she needed them to perch about three paces ahead of her, indicating the deepest fissures or most secure perches. The first section of the cliff had a bit of a slope, so though she moved slowly, Finch wasn't too frightened. Mostly, she grew tired. The air was so thin she could not catch her breath, and her muscles burned from the continuous exertion. Her crude rucksack banged against her back uncomfortably and the leather stretched, forcing her to readjust it constantly.

Toward the middle of the cliff the incline vanished and she faced a sheer wall. She had a moment, looking down after an awkward reach to a tiny foothold, when the height terrified her, freezing her in place. But she couldn't stay where she was, so she took some deep breaths and pushed herself onward.

Twice she followed what looked like a promising seam in the rock only to reach a place where she could find no further footholds or handholds. She had to back down, her heart in her mouth, and try another route. The hawks did their best to guide her.

She had climbed for more than an hour, and her muscles trembled with fatigue. Her fingers no longer had the strength to steady her as she moved her weight from one slight crevice to another place where the rock face barely jutted out. She lost her balance and started sliding, her instinctive scream snatched away by the wind.

The tiny ledge she'd stood on three steps earlier broke her fall. She leaned into the rock face, grabbing with hands, elbows, and shoulders—even her chin—to keep her momentum from carrying her off her thin perch. Her scraped skin burned in a dozen places.

Hawks! Take me another way!

There be no better route.

I can't do it!

The hawks had no answer.

I can't do it!

Again, the hawks had no answer. These birds didn't care if she lived or fell. They obeyed the order to guide her, but they felt no reverence or affection for her. Finch didn't think that hawks ate human flesh, but sourly she wondered if they would sample her carcass if she crashed on the rocks below.

Anger proved to be a good motivator. With enormous effort, Finch renavigated the tricky last patch and pulled herself, shaking, over the top of the cliff. She hugged the more level ground while she sucked the thin air in great gasps and then looked around. Before her she saw only more barren rock, though the slope ahead now was gradual enough for hiking.

When the sun sank behind a mountaintop, night fell like the shutter of a lantern, leaving her in blackness. The hawks led Finch to a crevice on the bald top of the mountain; it was actually just a fold in the rock. She could half recline with her blanket wrapped around her.

At least this fold faced out of the wind, because as temperatures plummeted during the night, exposure would have taken her.

As soon as the sky paled she continued her trek, since moving helped her warm her cold and stiff body. The terrain eventually leveled out; she could see she was on a plateau on top of the world. Gazing northward she had a fine view of more snowcapped mountains, stretching off into the distance. The peaks looked so jagged and majestic, Finch could imagine developing a deep connection to this countryside.

She ate some snow, but the barren rocks provided nothing more. She trudged through the day, sometimes climbing small rises, other times descending. By late afternoon, however, her route clearly inclined downward; the hawks guided her to a sheltered hollow. Dead fir trees provided enough wood for a welcome fire, and the hawks dropped her two chipmunks. Roasted, these rodents provided little meat, but Finch scarfed the mouthfuls gratefully.

It snowed overnight, just enough to make Finch's way slippery and dangerous and to render her boots sopping. She grabbed half a handful of snow once in a while to quench her thirst. After a while she reentered the tree line. Recalling her lessons from Lem and Rooks, she gathered as much lichen as she could scrape from the tree trunks. Weakening from hunger, she halted in the midafternoon, built a small fire, and boiled the lichen in her saucepan with snow. It tasted bitter, but she knew it would fill her stomach and provide some sustenance. She took off her wet boots and attempted to dry them on sticks over the embers.

In the morning, she slipped past some border markers. She had now entered Oromondo.

20

Ink Creek Canyon

Tally: 23
Horses: 24

"Tell me, Tristo," Thalen said, "what are those black-and-white ribbons everybody is now wearing?"

"Like this?" smiled Tristo, showing off the scrap of fabric. It looked like a piece of one of the white silk Jígat neck drapes, onto which someone had roughly added black striations. "Don't you recognize the pattern? We copied it from the bracelet you wear. It's our insignia! This is what shows that we belong to Thalen's Raiders."

"I see," said Thalen, trying to keep his pleasure from being too obvious.

In their days in the canyon, the soldiers refined their techniques. Kran, who recovered from his thigh wound, had the inspiration of preparing the pointed stakes for an abatis ahead of time. The Raiders sharpened them and hardened them in their coals. They had a small and precious amount of metal wire that they would use to lash these points to any trees they could fell near an ambush, and thus quickly set up a secure and impenetrable barrier. Meanwhile Gentain (with his bulky bandaged hand) and the cavalry ran the horses through drills, while Kambey and Codek kept the men at fencing and archery.

Thalen sent the scouts out every night and from their reports mapped every possible site where the terrain might be in their favor.

Acting on the scouts' information, Thalen led his troop out for skirmishes. They slaughtered a pair of post riders from ambush. On the principle that anything he could learn about the enemy would be helpful, Thalen scavenged the bags full of letters.

Their later foray out of the canyon, to attack a squad of Protectors herding a string of aurochs toward the wooden bridge and the mining camps, turned chaotic when the animals stampeded. Latof's horse took an auroch's horn in the chest and went down, spilling his rider; subsequent rampaging animals trampled the cavalryman. When hostilities ceased, Latof's broken body was such a grisly sight that Codek had to hold Ooma back from taking revenge upon the living beasts. Thinking both of her anger and of their need for supplies, Thalen ordered her to cut out the tongues of all the dead aurochs.

At the funeral in Ink Creek Canyon, Thalen tried to read his comrades' faces and postures. He saw less shock and sorrow than with the earlier deaths and more grim determination.

Afterward, in his tent, Thalen said to Codek, "We've stung them several times now. Someday soon they will send a larger force of their home guard to investigate."

"Do they even know what's going on out here in the arse-end of the world?" his sergeant asked.

"We're not that far from Wûnum, which is a fairly major town. And I'm counting on the Oros being completely incensed by the thought of invaders in their fuckin' Land."

"What kind of force will we face?" Wareth asked, joining their conversation.

"If I were their commander I'd send fifty, maybe one hundred."

"But you've seen the enemy," Codek added. "The ones today reminded me of Tristo. Underfed boys. Maybe a few crippled veterans or old-timers mixed in. They sent all their strong soldiers to the Free States."

"Riiight," said Wareth, a bit doubtfully. "So do we hunker down in here?"

"No," said Thalen. "We figure out how to kill them all. If they wanted them alive, they shouldn't send them after us."

Later, Thalen found no Oro name on his maps, so he dubbed the broad roadway that paralleled the Iron River "River Road." The Raiders had turned south at the "Miners Bridge" to hug the outskirts of FireSky on their way to Ink Creek Canyon, but the road continued straight along the river, which gathered into itself more and more tributaries, flowing through the central valley of Oromondo. The river and the road coursed together southeast to Wûnum, and then straightened out and broadened so that eventually both met Femturan and the sea.

"If they march in numbers, they'll come from the garrison in Wûnum up River Road," Thalen said to his scouts, tracing the route on the map.

"How do you know they've got a major garrison in Wûnum?" Wareth asked.

"The post dispatches," Thalen answered.

"You've read them all?" asked Wareth, giving a low whistle of surprise.

"Twice. Now pay attention. Around here on my maps, Fire-Thorn spreads out a spur. You're looking for a spot where the Oros can't get off the road—where one side is steep and one side is river."

"Why don't we just ambush them in the same ravine we used before?" Codek asked.

Adair answered for Thalen, "They can't be that dumb."

"No, they can't," Thalen agreed. "But they'll feel safe on River Road—they've marched it a hundred times, up to the mines and Oro towers and back. It's obviously open and airy. They'll slog along it confidently. We'll use *the river* as if it were a second cliff wall."

"But it's not—I mean, men and horses can ford the river," Wareth said the obvious.

Codek looked up at Thalen, scrunched his eyes, and grinned. "You can't ford a deep river at any pace. They'll ride straight into our archers."

"Aye," said Thalen. "I'm more worried about blocking the road before and aft, to cut off escape."

Thalen sent Wareth, Adair, and Tel-bein out to find him the best spot along River Road, south of the bridge.

Wareth returned in a day in high spirits, though his clothing looked rumpled and wrinkled.

"'Mander, we all agree: we found the place for the ambush!"

"Draw it out for me," Thalen ordered, and he squatted down. Several other Raiders clustered around them as Wareth described

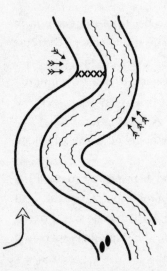

how FireThorn jutted out toward the riverbed, forcing the Iron River into a deeper channel. He drew three looping bends and told them that the southern verge of River Road loomed too steep for man or oxen to climb.

"And you can't see around the turns, so they wouldn't be able to spot our abatis up ahead."

"This time, they'll be sending out scouts," Thalen said, thinking aloud. "We'll have to be sure they don't report back."

"Yeah, ah, well, here's the catch—

we can't get to the far bank any way but by swimming. We tried crossing at Miners Bridge and following the river's edge—you run into solid cliffs. I mean, maybe you could find a way of climbing FireThorn and coming down where you want to be, but that would take a lot of time and be awful chancy."

"So you swam the river?"

"Yeah. The rocks are too sharp for horses. And the water is *free*-zing—I mean, my nuts shrunk into peas, and I'd thought I'd lose my toes or fingers. The current's kind of wicked. But Adair and I made it across and then back in one piece. Adair stayed there, waiting for Tel-bein. He'll rush back here with any news."

"Good job. The question is: can our archers cross the river, keeping their bows and arrows dry?" Thalen let some gravel dribble through his hands, then rose up from his crouch.

"Tristo!" he called. "Gather all the rope in the camp. Steal leather from reins if you need to and work with Wareth to make something that will stretch across the Iron River. And then set to work on oil-cloth sacks."

Thalen then gathered all the Raiders together near the cook pit. "Who's a strong swimmer? Who has no fear of the water? I need someone to swim across and tie a rope to help others follow behind him."

Fedak, one of the Vígat cavalry, a wiry man with short dark hair, volunteered with a slow smile. "My father was a bargeman on the Sutter. I grew up swimming the river day in and day out. 'Otter,' my chums called me. My father thought I'd go to sea or something. . . ."

"This river might be colder and running faster," Thalen warned.

"Oh, that Sutter runs pretty cold and wild at its headwaters. 'Sides, if Wareth and Adair can do it, I can do it. Consider it bagged."

Wareth made a face of mock hurt. Eldie stood up. She and her sister still refused to speak to the Raiders out of the penance they'd set themselves in honor of their dead sister, so instead she made a series of hand gestures. One looked like flowing water, and one pointed to herself and her sister. Then she shook her head decisively.

"You don't swim?" Thalen asked. "And neither does Eli-anna? Then we'll put you two above the road, and send others across. Yislan and Cookie, can you swim? Are you willing?"

Both nodded, reluctantly.

Thalen said, "Fedak and Wareth, you'll ford the river and stay with them. You're both middling with your bows, but the distance should be very short. Just don't waste arrows."

The next day, shortly after dawn, Adair galloped in on his mare, Brandy. His horse's sides heaved, and Adair also showed the strain of his race back to the canyon. "Tel-bein has returned from Wûnum. He counted sixty-four pikemen, and lost track of the officers with them. More than ten. They march the River Road, just as you predicted. He saw something else—a big, shiny black box that men carried. This just confused him; he had no idea what it is."

Thalen pushed his hair out of his face. "Black box? Some kind of weapon? Did he say how big it was?"

Adair shook his head.

"Never mind. Tristo, get him something to eat and take his poor horse to Gentain. Then Adair, you're to turn in. We're riding at dusk, to get in position for tomorrow. I want you and Tristo to guard the camp when we leave."

Tristo started to protest, but Thalen would have none of it. "Raiders, I need you *here,* with food and a fire burning. We'll surely have wounded this time, and your efforts may keep them alive."

The Raiders rode out cautiously and caught a few hours of sleep in a dark hollow close to River Road. Thalen waited until sunrise the next day to send Fedak across the turbulent water at the chosen spot. True to his word, Fedak swam the current without much difficulty, and he tied their rope securely around a tree on the far bank. They found nothing on the roadside to hold the rope, so Kran and Weddle, both big heavy men, wrapped the loose end around themselves and braced themselves to keep it out of the wet. The Raiders had fabricated sacks of oilcloth with leather loops to slip along the rope. They filled these sacks with bows and quivers, and Wareth dived in to push the oilcloth sacks along the rope until he and the weapons made it to the other bank and Fedak grabbed his hand and pulled him from the current.

"Don't get too excited now, fellas," Cookie said as she untied her now-colorless skirt and bodice, revealing equally colorless under-clothes that hung shapelessly from her reduced frame. She also took off the ridiculous feminine bonnet she always wore, revealing thin brown hair mashed down on her scalp, and handed it to her husband. She stepped out into the freezing water, her mouth making a silent "Oo!" in shock. With her hands on the rope guide, she crossed to the far side safely. Yislan followed her, with more curses. Once those two were across, Fedak rolled in the rope and kept it with them on the far side.

Thalen exhaled. He had four archers lying in wait across the Iron River. Tel-bein, Eldie, and Eli-anna would take up position on the hill abutting River Road with their bows. The cross fire would be deadly.

While Thalen supervised the river crossing, Kambey had led a squad to a stand of fir trees. They chopped these down, dragged them to the road, and constructed the abatis around a curve, using river boulders to weigh it in place. Then they lashed their hardened spars onto the logs with their metal wire. The barrier bristled for-biddingly.

Thalen tried to consider complications. *But what if some other party travels River Road today? We can't undo the barrier and put it back quickly. We'll have to kill them too.*

"Cerf," he ordered, "I want you to scout west toward Miners Bridge—when you hear sounds of battle, gallop back. You must hold the west end of the abatis. Jothile, you do the same to the east: you'll be our scout for the enemy. Let us know if anyone is coming."

Thalen now had the problem of hiding the remaining Raiders so that the Oros wouldn't see them as they marched up the road. But no convenient draws or byways intersected River Road. Thalen kicked Dishwater and galloped down a ways. Nothing presented itself as a convenient hideaway. Standing up in his saddle he could see the road ahead, the river on his right, and a sloping hillside to his left that held only dead, spindly trees and low growth.

Has the polluted river water killed most of the trees? There's not enough cover for the horses. This is my fault: I should have specified this need to the scouts. It's too late now to move or back down.

Thalen galloped back to the cluster of Raiders.

"Everyone—except you, Gentain—dismount with your weapons. Gentain, you're going to have to lead the horses up that way until you find a place that keeps them out of sight. And stay with them. Can't have them giving away our location by making a noisy fuss. The rest of you, smooth out our prints and follow me."

Thalen led his remaining men and Ooma to a slight depression where two hillsides met.

"Spread out and lie down, wiggle behind scrub, take off anything that will whip about in the wind. Maki, lie down. Stay."

Thalen had everyone arranged in as good a position as he could manage. *Two scouts, watching both directions. Seven archers as the main force. A barrier blocking the front, and eleven of us to close the back door.* From now on they just had to wait. Thalen didn't know if the Oro soldiers would come in ten minutes or in ten hours. Tel-bein had reported they marched at a fair clip, but Thalen had read about Oro troops stopping for long prayer sessions.

Waiting, straining one's ears, thinking about killing, dying, and pain was not an easy thing to do.

Someone threw a small rock at Thalen, who lifted his face from hiding it in his arms. Literoy touched his ear and pointed west, toward the far side of the abatis. Thalen motioned for him to go investigate and for the others to keep their hiding place.

Thalen heard a muffled noise, but with his head in the earth he couldn't tell what. Then more noises—what must have been voices. One shout, snatched away by the wind.

In a few moments Literoy reappeared, carefully crawling on his belly back down the hill behind scrub. He caught Thalen's glance and held up two fingers, then made an archery gesture.

Two Oros had approached the far side of the abatis. The archers had taken care of them.

Grass prickled Thalen's neck, and sweat dripped down his nose. Ants walked over his hands and up his sleeve. His mouth tasted like dirt. He raised his head to check on his comrades. Vatuxen and Britmank, who had formed a deep friendship with each other, were lying together behind a bush. Ooma had found a great patch of gorse. Cook's hand gripped his bow so tightly his veins stood out. Maki had his head up, sniffing the wind.

"Put your head down, you fool dog," Thalen whispered to it. Maki ignored him.

Codek has a water bag. If I don't hear anything in another minute, I'll crawl to him for a drink.

Thalen was glad that he was with other Raiders through this difficult wait. He realized that it had to be extra hard on Gentain, Cerf, and Jothile, stationed all alone.

I must remember to thank those I send out for solitary jobs. If I live.

Thalen heard a blackbird's song, far off in the distance. Songbirds rarely whistled in this blighted land. Was that a real bird, or Jothile's way of sending a warning? Then he felt a vibration through the ground. He didn't need Codek's sharp whisper, "Steady lads, someone's coming now." He felt Maki's body quiver, and he put a hand on the dog's back to keep him still.

Soon enough he detected the stamp of feet. A squad of men trod by the Raiders' hiding place chatting casually to one another: these must be the forward scouts. Thalen assumed his archers would deal with these.

Twenty minutes later the ground shook more dramatically. He heard a symphony of footfalls, a squeaking wagon, and men cursing at aurochs. Sound bounced around in this river valley, making extra reverberations. Maki growled in his throat, and Thalen had to hold him back, but the approaching enemy made much too much noise for him to be heard. The column marched past their hiding place and around the first bend of the road. As soon as the rear guard passed, Thalen tensed his muscles to spring up. A quick look around him showed that Codek had burrs and seedpods stuck in his sideburns, Ooma had pulled out her long knives, and Weddle already had his quarterstaff braced against the ground.

Thalen stood up, grabbing his bow, which he'd placed just at hand.

"Wait!" Thalen barked in a whisper to the others, his voice coming out hoarse with strain. "Let the head of the column bunch up at the barrier. We don't want to give the game away!"

Another minute passed, and then, above the ordinary sounds of the company on the move, they heard men scream.

Thalen and his companions threw themselves onto River Road to cut off retreat. Maki streaked ahead and out of sight, followed by Weddle and Ooma, who both dashed forward, overwhelmed by their battle lust.

Codek counted off a steadying cadence in a low voice that carried: "One, two, three, four. One, two, three, four." Nine Raiders marched forward to the beat, arrows nocked. When they came around the bend, Thalen saw a blur of bodies heading in their direction.

"Loose!" shouted Codek.

They fired and readied another arrow. "Loose!" shouted Codek.

The hindmost Oros had just learned that retreating backward didn't lead to safety. They paused, uncertain. The marching Raiders advanced, then loosed again. Thalen had to aim away from Weddle, whose quarterstaff wreaked a rippling wave of havoc amongst the

mail of enemy soldiers. He couldn't see Ooma at all, but he suspected her location wherever he saw Oros unexpectedly sink to the
ground. A maddened aurochs came charging straight at them, an
officer sprouting arrows slumped on its back.

"Just let him through!" Thalen shouted. The Raiders dodged to
either side, then re-formed across the road and marched forward
once more.

"Loose!" Codek yelled.

The Oros realized that they were surrounded. Splashes and
bellows indicated they tried the river.

"Form pikes!" an officer shouted. Eight pikemen had the presence
of mind to stand abreast and level their long spears at the advancing
Raiders. And another eight formed up right behind their comrades.

"Shoot at will," Codek shouted.

The Raiders had closed enough distance that Thalen could see
the enemies as individuals. They wore their breastplates and helmets. He shot one boy in the thigh, then swiftly pulled another arrow from his quiver and shot an old man straight in the face.

"Charge!" screamed an enemy officer. And a wall of two layers
of pikemen—desperate to escape—ran at them pell-mell. Although
most of the Raiders had quicker reflexes than he and fired repeatedly, Thalen got off only one more arrow, then dropped his bow and
pulled his rapier.

Too many. We're all going to die.

The wave of bodies crashed together.

Kambey's incessant drilling allowed Thalen's muscles to move
without thought. Thalen blocked a wavering pike downward, stepped
in, twirled around, and broke the man's arm. He then struck up into
the crotch of the pikeman in the second line. An officer stabbed him
with a sword, but his point wasn't sharp enough to penetrate Thalen's
quilted doublet at an oblique angle. It slid sideways up the canvas,
nicking Thalen's neck but giving him time to strike deeply into the
man's right leg. The blood made the road slick as he tried to regain his

balance. Thalen slipped, breaking his fall with his left hand but keeping his grip on his rapier.

"We're coming!" Jothile shouted from behind. Jothile and Gentain, mounted, pounded up to join the fray. Their arrows frightened the pikemen into slowing their forward charge. And something else bulled into the melee, sowing fear and causing the enemy line to buckle: Gentain had brought with him three of the Raiders' most stalwart or aggressive horses.

Dish nosed Thalen on the ground. Grabbing onto the stirrup allowed Thalen to gain his feet. Vaulting himself into his saddle gave him a feeling of control.

"Press them forward!" he shouted, standing tall in his stirrups and pointing with his rapier.

A few Oros had broken through their line and escaped down River Road. But Vatuxen now sat astride a bay, and Kran had gotten himself up on the big black mare Sulky Sukie, so five mounted Raiders stretched across the roadway, essentially closing it off again. They trotted into the bunched crowd, slashing down on enemies, while hand-to-hand battles continued on the ground. As the Raiders pushed the fleeing Oros around a curve and back into the view of the archers still lying in wait, Thalen could see the wagon and bodies piled up in front of the barricade and many bodies snagged on the rocks in the Iron River.

Brutal fighting continued for a few more minutes. Then, all at once, the Raiders faced no more resistance: those Oros still alive dropped their weapons and raised their hands.

"Look to our wounded!" Thalen shouted.

Weddle, who swung his staff so vehemently, was dead, blood gushing from scores of wounds. Literoy, the chatty fife player, one of the most popular Raiders, also lay sightless to the sun. Then someone called "Commander!" and Thalen rushed to another crumpled figure.

Codek lay curled on his side, his hands holding the pike that had punctured his ancient, rusted breastplate and sunk deep into his belly. He had a cross expression on his face. Thalen knelt by his sergeant's body, pulling the burrs off his sideburns as if this tidying up would breathe life back into his inert body.

No. You can't die. I can't do this without you. I should have chosen a better site. All these deaths are my fault. Codek!!!

Somehow Cerf had threaded himself around the abatis. "Thalen! I need your help! We must save the living!"

Five injured Raiders sprawled on the road, bleeding but still alive. Thalen helped Cerf bandage and put pressure on the wounds; poor Gentain had again been injured, and Britmank was in sad shape. The Mellie girls departed for Ink Creek Canyon, each riding double on a battle charger with a slumping Raider in front. Cerf pulled down Vatuxen's breeches and sewed up the slash in his buttocks right then and there; afterward the healer grabbed the horse Jothile held and raced off to care for the casualties.

Ooma's slash across her ribs turned out not to be very deep. Once Thalen had wrapped it up tight with his neck drape she growled at his further ministrations. Thalen looked at the bumps and shallow cuts on Cook's head, deciding these held no danger, but he was concerned about the fact that Cook's eyes wouldn't focus and he couldn't stand on his own.

"Just sit still, Cook. Give it some time."

Leaving the other Raiders to complete the after-battle chores such as harvesting auroch tongue, putting down enemies, and throwing weapons into the water, Thalen drifted back to kneel numbly next to Codek's body, wondering if the older man had known how much he relied upon him. Wareth, water dripping from face and clothing, appeared at his side.

"Oh, Spirit fuckin' no! Sarge! Sarge!" Wareth pulled out the pike and tried to pull Codek's clothes to cover up the pool of black blood.

Someone called, "Commander, we need you! It's important."

"I'll stay with him, 'Mander," Wareth sobbed with his hands over his eyes. "You go. Go on."

Fedak, who must have swum back with Wareth, helped Tel-bein shift some packed bodies so Thalen could walk up the road without stepping on people. Close to the front of the line sat a shiny palanquin constructed of black wood and encrusted with jewels. Inside the palanquin a white-haired woman in silk lay sprawled back against the black leather seat, a Mellie arrow shot clean through her heart.

"Who is she? I mean, what is she?" Tel-bein asked Thalen.

Thalen wanted to stop thinking, just turn his mind off, but he couldn't. "We've killed a Magi," he said softly. "Number Four." He gestured toward the number encrusted on her tabard. "Probably on her way to her tower at Fourcaster."

He looked at the open door of the coach. "When they hit the abatis, they set down her palanquin. She started to get out. If you archers hadn't taken her out instantly, she'd have killed us all."

Tel-bein made a soft clicking noise with his tongue on the roof of his mouth. "Eli-anna's mark," he said, pointing at the arrow's fletching.

Thalen automatically began to search the palanquin for dispatches. Shouts from across the river interrupted their inspection of the scene.

"Hey! Hey! You forgot us! We need to cross back over," shouted Cookie. Thalen realized it might have been an hour since the fighting stopped, and all that time the two archers who were weaker swimmers had waited on the opposite bank.

When Wareth and Fedak had swum back, they'd dropped the rope by the rocks. Now, Fedak and Kran picked it up and wrapped it around their bodies. Cookie pushed the oil sacks of bows across and climbed out of the water shivering violently. They let the rope go slack into the water a minute while Ooma searched for a blood-free cloak to wrap around Cookie. Then the two braced the rope around their bodies again and shouted, "Yislan! Come across! We're ready for you."

Yislan held on with his right hand, holding his repeating cross-bow above his head with his left. He had crossed about halfway when a knot in the water-soaked rope slipped loose and the rope pieces separated with a forceful spring. Yislan yelped and went under, still holding his bow up. Cookie screamed.

"Drop it! Swim! Kick!" Ooma hollered.

"Yislan! Drop the damned bow!" Thalen shouted.

But Yislan didn't have the strength. Wareth and Fedak were rushing toward the river when the survivors watched him sink, surface some four paces later, sink again, and then get swept away by the tumbling white water.

Tally: 23–5 (Latof, Weddle, Literoy, Yislan, and Codek)=18
Horses: 24–2=22

21

Sutterdam

Sumroth had set his headquarters up in Sutterdam, which had a large port and warehouses full of foodstuffs; he saw no reason for himself to move deeper into the Free States. He was tired of constant travel. He dispatched sixth-flamers in his command to conquer and loot Fígat, Wígat, and Jígat.

He kept a large office in the Council Hall as a base of operations. High-ceilinged and offering a long balcony where Sumroth could get fresh air or pace, it was as good a room as any for a man more accustomed to activity than desk work. From here Sumroth parceled out to his underlings specific functions, such as keeping order, supervising the slaves, maintaining modes of transport, gathering food, and overseeing harbor activities.

In general, morale soared as his men enjoyed full rations. His officers reported little trouble from the subdued populace, and if Protectors encountered truculence, they put it down decisively. These Free Staters were weaklings and poor fighters, but they lived comfortably, and his men savored their featherbeds and fine dishware after so many moons of severe conditions.

Unlike the majority of Oromondo officers, Sumroth did not choose a comfort woman from the captives. His forbearance arose not from moral scruples; he just found the slighter-framed Free States women unappealing, and without white highlights their brown hair looked like mud. They reminded him of boys or children, so the idea of sex with them turned his stomach. At night he dreamed of Zea's lush curves. Every shipload of food he sent home he pictured as feeding his wife, restoring her to the plump lusciousness of her youth. He sent her a letter on most of the ships that sailed to Drintoolia.

He had learned from the heedlessness of the Protectors who'd looted Alpetar some years earlier. Sumroth was careful to ensure that working farms, ranches, and dairies be well-maintained, even expanded. Businesses related to processing food he allowed to keep functioning, but he closed others and transferred their workers to toil the fields. Dressmakers mended fishing nets; bookmakers salted venison. He intended the Free States to serve as a colony of Oromondo for years to come as a perpetually fertile breadbasket.

Sumroth was reading dull reports at the conference table he used as a desk when an underling announced, "Priest, sir, asking to see you."

"What now?" Sumroth grumbled. "Make him wait until after I've finished this paperwork."

Sumroth intended to keep the man dancing for a while, but he found he couldn't concentrate, knowing that this aggravating meeting would have to be endured.

"Send in the priest," he shouted to his guard.

Thirty-two priests had accompanied his army. Sumroth didn't mind them so long as they stayed out of his way. They had been quiet during the journey and the military maneuvers, but they had started to assert themselves once his army settled in the Free States, annoying Sumroth with their requests and complaints.

He thought he'd seen this particular man before, but he couldn't be sure.

"General Sumroth." The man bowed low.

"Yes, yes. Get on with it, Brethren," Sumroth said.

"We are turning local churches into Citadels of Flames," said the priest.

"So?"

"They were sites of heathen practices before," he said.

"Sounds right."

"They must be reconsecrated," said the priest.

"Very well. Go off and do it. Why come to me about religious rituals?"

"Then we have your permission?" The man looked relieved.

"Of course. And don't bother me about such things again."

"Thank you, General." The man bowed and headed swiftly toward the door. Something about his haste made Sumroth suspicious.

"Wait . . . one moment. *How* do you reconsecrate a heathen temple?"

"With an offering to Pozhar."

"Don't make me pull this information out of you," Sumroth snapped.

"Yes, General. That is, no, General. We offer Pozhar a sacrifice, which we burn on the altar."

Sumroth squinted his eyes.

"A child will do, General. We need not deprive you of the service of slaves. But the babes that Free States women care for, they just hamper the mother's efficiency. By offering the child to Pozhar we can purge the building of all contaminants and free the mother of the burden of caring for it."

"You would burn Free States babies?"

"Yes, General. We realize that this might—um—disturb the populace, which is why we felt we needed to inform you before we began. In case, for instance, the slaves grew restless, or otherwise—"

"How many?"

"Per citadel? That's hard to say. Often it only takes one sacrifice to drive out the foreign pollution; I've read that on rare occasions it can take as many as eight."

"No, you fool! And how many churches do you plan to reconsecrate?"

"That's hard to know, General. The 'Chamen Pyramids we find particularly easy to convert, but the Dwellings of Lautan, which are all built around saltwater fissures, may prove inhospitable. And naturally the Ghibli Wind Mills are just impossible. Totally unsuitable."

"Guess," said Sumroth, with a thin smile that the priest didn't notice.

"Perchance we'll end up with one hundred new citadels spread throughout every corner of this pagan land," he said with pride.

Sumroth recalled the smell of burning flesh from the executions he had had to perform when he wore only four flames. Well, now he wore seven. Actually, he would summon the tattooist and award himself an eighth for his services to the Land. With eight flames he would be the highest-ranking Oro military officer in centuries. And he deserved this honor.

I have had enough of bowing and scraping to dictates of fanatics. They didn't win my victories. They aren't feeding the Land.

Sumroth slapped his hands down on the table to seal his private decision.

"No. You do not have my permission. You will not incinerate any babies. In fact, if you touch a hair on any of the slaves' heads—of any age—I'll gut you and your thirty-one fellows."

"But—but—General, how can we consecrate the citadels?"

"That's your problem."

"May we use sheep?"

"Are you barking mad? Mutton is too valuable as food."

"But, but—"

"You may use aurochs if you must. But that's all the time I have to spend on such matters." Sumroth called out, "Third-Flamer! Show this man out of the building!"

Sumroth strode out on his balcony and paced about.

Well Pozhar, here I am. Strike me down if you find me so blasphemous.

When nothing untoward happened, Sumroth returned to his tedious paperwork.

Some days later the eight-flame general had his adjutants around him at morning meeting going through reports when a young officer burst into the room.

"A thousand pardons, Lord General."

Sumroth glanced up in annoyance. He had no idea who this officer might be or why he felt entitled to such a breach of protocol.

"What is the meaning of this interruption, Fourth-Flamer?"

"Lord General, I serve as warden of the petrels."

"What?"

A sixth-flamer prompted his memory. "You recollect, Lord General, that our allies, the Pellish, gave us these birds, these petrels, to serve as message carriers. This officer here tends the perches they fly to."

Sumroth was angry about the interruption and angrier that he had to be publicly reminded about those damn birds.

"You," he said, pointing. "You had better have received a message of utmost import, or I will have your head."

"Aye sir, Lord General," said the officer. He laid a tiny, rolled-up parchment on the table in front of Sumroth.

Invaders in The Land. Magi 4 kilt. Return with your best legions at once.

1 2 3 5 6 7 8

He turned his furious gaze back on the bird warden. "When did this arrive?"

"This morning. Not an hour ago, Lord General."

"How long does it take the birds to fly here?"

"A few days, at most."

"Have you gotten other messages?"

"Yes, sir. Routine matters. And I have sent back reports on our great victories."

"How do you know this is authentic? How do I know it is authentic? Maybe the Free Staters forged it? Maybe you forged it!"

The commander wet his lips, but he stood his ground. "Lord General, here is the string that tied the note to the bird's leg." He pulled out of his belt purse a slender red braid and placed it in front of the general. Sumroth's closer examination revealed it was not string, but finely wrought metal, and it only looked red because the wire passed through eight small rubies, each cut intricately and differently, with a skill only Oromondo jewel-smiths possessed. Cunning and unmistakable: only the Eight had access to such craft, yet cared so little about worldly riches as to put them to utilitarian tasks.

Sumroth rose and walked to the balcony doorway, giving himself a moment to think.

He deliberately strode the long way around the table and returned to his chair.

"Fourth-Flamer, you have done your duty. Now leave us."

Sumroth turned to the high-ranking officers sitting around him. "Gentlemen, our plans have changed. Here are my orders."

Umrat should relocate from Jutterdam to take command of the Free States from this seat in Sutterdam. Supported by six thousand troops, Sumroth would set sail for Drintoolia, the closest deepwater harbor, as soon as the men could be mustered and the ships readied. This would leave close to three thousand soldiers under Umrat's control, more than enough to keep order in these vanquished states, though he should concentrate his forces in the cities and forget about remote areas. Food shipments to Drintoolia must continue from Sutterdam, Jutterdam, and Yosta.

Sumroth expected to root out and squash these invaders quickly. Ergo, his ships would remain in Drintoolia, at the ready to return him and his legions to the Free States and beyond. This excursion should take only a few weeks—two or three moons at most.

He found the news shocking but not without certain advantages. Returning to Oromondo meant that he could see Zea. Perchance he could even bring her back to Sutterdam afterward. The Magi would not approve, but if he relieved them of their fears of these invading vermin, they could hardly forbid it.

Sumroth would like Zea to sleep in a featherbed and drink sweet wine.

After he squashed the invaders, Sumroth would leave some of his legions behind to protect Oromondo, so that nothing of this nature ever happened again. And he intended to seed the Land with logical, hardheaded military men, loyal to him.

PART
THREE

*Reign of Regent Matwyck,
Year 13*

SUMMER

22

The Western Duchies

Marcot, riding his best horse, with two guards as escorts and a servant/groomsman who led both the second-best horse and a packhorse of luggage, headed northwest, keeping to the well-maintained post roads. His first major destination, like that of so many travelers in Weirandale, was the hallowed environs of Nargis Mountain. The mountain thrust upward from some scattered foothills, solitary and majestic, over twenty leagues northwest of the capital city. Occasionally its summit was shrouded in fog or clouds; more often its rocky face gleamed in the sunlight.

The Abbey of the Waters sat three-quarters of the way down from the peak in the mountain's valley. Lord Consort Birchtrum had constructed it some three hundred years ago, seeking solace after the death of his wife, Queen Cirnessa the Enchanter. The stone building had been constructed in two halves: with the abbey proper on one side and the guest quarters on the other. An arched bridge over the Nargis River, which tumbled with white froth down a waterfall, linked the two structures. Visitors came to listen to the roar of the waters and stand in the spray from the cataract to refresh themselves from their burdens.

No fence or rule prevented anyone from hiking farther up Nargis Mountain or seeking to find the source of the sacred river, but travelers who ventured on the foothills inevitably turned back—some sense of trespass cooling their ardor and curiosity.

The lordling's party arrived just as the sun slipped into the western foothills. He stood for an hour on the bridge in the twilight, the thundering Water surrounding him evidence of its Power, praying chiefly for his mother, but including his baffling father in his thoughts, hoping Matwyck would find more warmth in his chilly heart.

He stayed at the abbey an extra day, to feast his eyes on the summit and the river. But like most travelers, he found the guesthouse's stone beds and plain meals discouraged casual loitering. He gave the abbess a large donation and led his group west from the duchy of Riverine into Lakevale.

His father's clerks had sent tidings to all the duchies, alerting the gentry of his travels. For politeness's sake, Marcot stopped for a week with the duke and duchess of Lakevale, though he found them insufferable toadies (managing to insert professions of loyalty to the Lord Regent into even the most banal comments). Also, the duchess kept throwing her marriageable daughter his way, and though Marcot had nothing against the young woman, he was determined to avoid entanglements. So he found his visit less than restful.

Marcot also felt duty-bound to stop at the immense manor of the Retzel family, where he discovered a hunt in full swing and the great hall thronging with visiting gentry from the younger, faster set. The new Lord Retzel, who had succeeded when his father passed away, and his wife, Lady Dinista, who had once served as a lady-in-waiting to Queen Cressa, professed delight at Marcot's fortuitous arrival and insisted on his joining their festivities.

As a keen huntsman, Marcot relished the sport during the day. He brought down an eight-point buck and was proud of his skill, though the unctuous compliments that the other guests showered upon him ultimately took away his joy.

That night Marcot found himself in the Retzels' dining hall for Feast of Mayhem, with guests dressed in all manner of guises, such as chimney sweeps or peasant girls or bootblacks. By the second course, dinner descended into drunkenness and licentiousness. The young man found the display distasteful and endured teasing about his prudishness to retire—solo—early.

The next day, while most of the guests slept late, he asked to bid leave of Lady Dinista. She still lounged in bed, but she sent word that he should enter.

"So, you are leaving us as rudely as you appeared?" she said to him, her eyes mocking, her pink lace shawl negligently fastened, allowing Marcot to see bite-shaped bruises all over her neck and upper bosom.

"My apologies, Lady. I—I have far to travel if I am going to send the Lord Regent the reports he requested."

"Ah! You are your father's son, after all," she remarked, a comment so ambiguous and disturbing that Marcot turned it over in his mind for many leagues.

Marcot turned his traveling party south through Lakevale, trying to escape his troubled thoughts by enjoying the vistas of large lakes that hosted flocks of waterfowl. His party of four stopped at nights at the inns along the Royal Highway. Most offered comfortable hospitality, and in the evenings Marcot joined any well-bred travelers over meals of freshwater fish or duck in the common rooms. If the inn or company looked lower class, Marcot kept to the company of his guards, who were decent chaps if not stimulating conversationalists.

As they crossed into Maritima in early summer, Marcot enjoyed the coastal views and the quaint seaside towns that flecked the shores of the Ribbon. When he reached the ducal estate, he determined to pay a courtesy call. He had not met the duke and duchess previously—he gathered some bad blood with his father kept them from attending court functions in Cascada.

The ducal couple received him on a second-floor, awning-covered balcony that looked out over the town and eventually the waters of the Ribbon Passage. Duke Favian was a short, tidy man dressed in a cravat tied in a manner many decades out of style, precise in his manner and movements; he sat in a straight-backed chair, while the duchess perched herself on a low hassock and leaned back against her husband's legs. Duchess Gahoa was much taller than her husband; she wore some wispy, colorless, floating garment and pinned her hair in an eccentric, blowsy style. As they conversed with their guest, her husband periodically tried to tuck her tumbling locks behind her ear or catch them up with her hairpins.

They inquired about his travels, and Marcot told them about the houses he'd visited; the farmlands, vineyards, and water mills; and how beautiful the lakes looked reflecting summer greenery.

"Yes, yes," said Duchess Gahoa, "but the people . . ."

"What my lovey means to ask is whether your travels have allowed you to become better acquainted with the people of Weirandale?"

"Why, certainly," Marcot replied. "I've spent time with people I knew only in passing, and I'm making new friends, such as yourselves."

"Not the *gentry,* dear boy, but . . ."

"Oh, you mean the common people. Well, in many inns I've had long conversations with other travelers. I've learned a great deal about the concerns of trade and business. I've heard all about the roads, and the need to provide security against ruffians. Of course, on the estates I've spoken to the laborers, inquired about their conditions and such."

"I'd be very astonished," said Duke Favian with a touch of tart-ness, "if you received forthright answers."

Marcot realized that the workers and servants he'd spoken to had—to a person—been reluctant to talk to him, staring down at their feet or shooting glances at his guards or the resident nobles standing beside him.

"Well no," he admitted, "I don't think I did."

"Such a pity," said the duchess, "to travel so far and not really profit . . ." She waved her hand in a broad arc.

". . . From getting to know Weirs outside of Cascada." Marcot finished her sentence for her and sat back in his seat with the heat of embarrassment burning his cheeks.

"We've heard that many of the under schools . . . Did you find? . . . Lack of funds . . ."

Marcot recalled the extravagant, wasteful feast at the Retzel manor. He had not thought to examine any of the schools he had blithely passed by.

"Begging your pardon, Lordling," said Duke Favian. "I don't mean to be rude, but near every moon we get another decree from Cascada trying to squash people's discontent and telling them to turn their problems over to Nargis. Instead of suppressing his citizens, the Lord Regent should be listening to their troubles and as-suaging them. That's what a queen would do. In fact, that's what old Queen Catreena *did*."

"Though listening in itself is not always . . ."

Marcot had begun to get the pattern of the duchess's trailing sentences. They might appear vague, but they pointed at uncom-fortable truths. He recalled his cursory questions to the workers while the Duke of Lakevale pointed out his new dyke, a dyke that must have taken so much backbreaking labor, and he felt his ears burning.

"The Lord Regent believes that a heavy hand can solve all problems. He's mistaken, and he'll find this out, sooner or later," said Duke Favian. "Perchance *you'd* be wise to find out sooner, meaning no offense, Lordling."

"I take no offense, Duke, but I do marvel at your candidness. Few speak this plainly these days, at least to me."

The duchess laughed and leaned forward to pat Marcot's cheek with a hand with long fingers. "Oh, dear boy, what is it you imagine your father could possibly, possibly . . ."

"What my lovey means, Lordling, is we two are going to die soon." The duke waved away Marcot's polite protestation. "Come. Come. That's obvious. The Lord Regent is just waiting us out. As long as we're together, we don't give a peach stone over who thunders at us or sends us nasty letters. Matwyck probably won't send assassins to kill us, but if he did, as long as we're together, we'll be content."

"That's right, lovey," agreed Duchess Gahoa, and she leaned her head on his knee, causing more hair to fall down.

Marcot desperately wanted to shift the subject away from his father having people murdered.

"How would I go about listening to the people? How could I get them to really talk to me?"

"Do you think . . . ?" the duchess asked her husband.

"Leave it to me to make some arrangements," said the duke, and he slapped his knees and changed his tone of voice into bluff heartiness. "Now, Lordling Marcot, perchance you'd do me the honor? Would it please you to tour the house and grounds before we dine? I'd love to show you the new millstone I installed!"

The duchess burst out into girlish giggles at her husband's impersonation of a typical nobleman.

"Will you while away the tour with sardonic digs about high taxes and little cutting remarks about your neighbors?" Marcot asked.

"If you insist," said Duke Favian with a theatrical sigh. Then his tone became normal and solicitous. "Lovey, will you be all right if I show our handsome young visitor around for a few hours?"

"You sneak! You really want to see his . . ."

The duke winked at Marcot. "I *am* an admirer of horseflesh, and my chamberlain, Hooper, was watching out the window when you rode up. But don't fret, lovey: I promise I won't mount up." He turned to Marcot, explaining, "An unfortunate incident ten years ago. Broke my elbow. She'll never let me forget."

"Will you be back for our rest . . . ?"

"Of course. But don't wait for me; go lie down now."

"First, I have to see to . . ." The duchess's wide gesture encompassed everything, as if she felt duty-bound to fix the whole world.

"No, lovey, the household staff can put on a dinner for our special guest without you fluttering about. You need to rest so you bewitch us all in the candlelight." Favian kissed his wife's hand as a leave-taking, and Marcot found himself doing the same.

The estate was modest in comparison to some, but very well kept, and the duke spoiled Marcot's horses with sugar lumps and fulsome endearments. At dinner they were joined by local notables: his hosts had considerately seated an expert horse breeder on Marcot's right. The duchess, sitting at the foot of the table on his left, had changed into another formless and colorless gown, but an antique collar of pearls and dangling pearl earbobs added glamour in the candlelight. The woman across from him was the duchess's second cousin; Marcot found her conversation less delightful, since it consisted mostly of complaints about how the new cider and bread taxes placed an un-due burden on the poor. Thus, he felt relief when—claiming his wife's fatigue—the duke dismissed all the guests at the end of the courses.

The duke, duchess, and Marcot lingered over their dessert wines. The conversation, which ranged from conditions in Maritima, to their memories of Queen Catreena and Queen Cressa, to the story of how they met, kept Marcot intrigued.

As Marcot assisted the duchess from her chair at the end of the evening, she patted his cheek again. "Do you see, lovey," Gahoa sighed to her husband, "what we missed?"

"Now, now. Don't go distressing yourself, lovey," said the duke. To Marcot he murmured, "When she drinks wine she grieves over the children we never had." Duke Favian took his wife's arm, "Couldn't be helped. We've had each other. You can't know, if we'd had a likely young son like the lordling here, you would have made a fuss over him and I might have been jealous of your attention."

As the elderly couple shuffled down the hallway, Marcot overheard the duchess quavering, "But no one to leave the duchy to . . . No one to watch over our people . . . Who will distribute gifts at Solstice Fest? Who will see that young mothers get the care . . ."

"You drank a wee bit too much, lovey. Wine always makes you sad. But we had such a nice dinner with our young guest, didn't we? Let me put you to bed. You know you'll feel better in the morning."

The next morning, the duke's chamberlain, Hooper, attended Marcot after his morning tray.

"If I may suggest, Lordling, your guards and servant will be quite safe in the manor house. If you'd care to accompany me, I have commissions at several establishments in Queen's Harbor, and I could introduce you to some people there."

"Ah. This must be the duke's plan of providing me more access to common folk."

"Indeed, sir. And with your indulgence, Lordling, the duchess suggested that you alter your appearance. The cut of one's jacket can forestall confidences." He held out a shabby jacket and a shapeless cap.

"People will be less likely to talk openly in front of me if they see I'm nobility?" said Marcot, accepting the garments and pulling his nose down from the wrinkling that had been his first reaction.

"Indeed, sir."

Marcot acquiesced, slipping out of his silk dressing jacket and putting on the commoner's clothes. "What will I learn, Hooper, if folk speak to me?"

"You may learn how much the people suffer under the yoke of the Lord Regent. Or folk may speak to you about how his functionaries abuse their power to steal and bully."

23

Oromondo

Finch lost track of how long she hiked up and down the high peaks of Oromondo. The lonely, hungry days faded into one another, as did the unchanging vistas of the jagged, rocky peaks.

Usually she closed her mind to small animals, because their chatter was just incessant and annoying. But in this extremity she reached out to squirrels, asking them to share their stores of nuts. The squirrels generously heaped tiny piles of their depleted winter caches around her morning and night. Finch was so touched that she asked the hawks not to hunt squirrels for her, but snakes instead. These nuts, the occasional rattlesnake (which she stewed to tenderize), and whatever greens or lichens she could scavenge fueled her heavy exertion. Often the ascents were so steep that she had to halt every ten paces to catch her breath or the descents so sloped she had to catch onto trees and saplings to break her downward momentum.

As she moved farther into Oromondo the hawks warned against some of the streams, thus when she wasn't famished she longed for water. Her mind may have wandered: she saw red eyes in the dark.

Hawks! Have you seen any red-eyed bats?

We captured some bats the other nightfall for our meal. Wouldst thou like us to catch some for you?

No! Just don't let any bats swarm me.

Her clothes became tattered and dirty, and her hair—which she continued to dye a muted yellow—became matted. The friendly animals didn't care. Larger game was scarce; she saw no deer, elk, or moose. But whenever she stopped for the night raccoons would creep out to visit; these bandits would crawl up and down her arms or sort through her few possessions curiously with their cunning black paws. She never considered killing this company for food, because their visits kept her from succumbing to the solitude. Once a red fox brought out her kits for the Queen's Blessing; Finch fell asleep curled around the soft little bundles as the mother kept watch, a proud gleam in her eye.

Other animals showed hostility. At a safe water hole Finch stumbled into a solo male wolf who snarled at her. He refused to speak with her. She had to back off until he had drunk his fill.

After this encounter, she feared the wolf stalked her as prey. The hawks did not see him in the day, but they retired at night. For the next three nights, she slept—or tried to sleep—on tree branches that stretched high enough off the ground. The fourth night, she was so weary that she slept on the ground, but she entreated a skunk to wake her if a wolf approached. She made it through the night without alarms, so she dared to hope that the predator had moved on to other game.

On top of her loneliness, exhaustion, and hunger, her boots became her most serious problem. After getting thoroughly soaked in the snow, the leather warped, forming ridges that rubbed against her heels. Eventually Finch cut the backs with her knife to relieve the pressure, but her skin could not recover. No matter how much she soaked her feet, tried to fashion poultices of wild garlic, or wrapped them in fabric torn from her clothes, blisters rose and festered. Every step became painful. Using sticks for crutches, she hobbled on. Every twenty paces she thought about sitting down and giving up.

Why didn't I sail for Lortherrod? Was I too proud to show up on the door of unknown relatives, asking for help? As if I could be of any assistance to these Raiders. Even with my Talent, I can hardly keep myself alive. I can barely walk. A footsore fool is what I am.

Penetrating deeper into the country, at times Finch crossed roads or came within sight of peaked roof dwellings, but she never had a close call in terms of encounters with local inhabitants. The hawks offered cold companionship, but they proved themselves able scouts, leading her in a zigzag away from mines, farms, traveled roads, or villages.

As the days passed by, Finch grew concerned, however, about whether they understood her request to rendezvous with the Free States Raiders. The hawks confessed they were not able to tell one human from another.

Eventually, they brought an eagle to meet her. He was a magnificent bird with a black head and reddish tail feathers. His wingspan, counting from one of his flight feathers to the other side, stretched longer than Butter.

Your Majesty. The Eagle bowed.

Your Majesty. Finch acknowledged the eagle with a bow in return. This pleased him; he preened his chest feathers for a long moment.

How may one be of service?

I seek a particular group of men. These would not wear the metal that the Oros wear. They would ride horses. Their hair would not be white. And they would often stay hidden from other men.

One has seen the humankine thou seek in my flights.

Are they far from here? she asked with rising hope.

Far? Not for an eagle.

Ah, but few creatures can fly as magnificently as you, Lord of the Skies. Will you lead me to these men?

One will explain to the hawks where they nest. And . . . one will keep an eye on thy progress.

You are generous, Lord of the Skies.

The eagle basked in her compliment. He turned his head from side to side, taking extended looks at her with his fierce yellow eyes.

If thou needst assistance, Little Majesty, thou hast only to call. Then he opened those long wings.

Thereafter, the hawks set out with new purpose, leading Finch in the direction of a tall mountain that must once have been an active volcano, for its top was hollowed out and it issued whispers of smoke. She skirted more roads and small hamlets. In the sloping valleys she crossed farms, though none looked prosperous. One evening Finch asked a placid cow to hold still while she milked it. Nothing had ever tasted as good to her as those mouthfuls of warm milk, and nearby skylarks soothed her with their song.

Just as night approached the hawks led her to the mouth of a canyon from which a small stream burbled steadily.

The men thou seek nest in the end of this cleft in the mountain.

Are you certain?

We saw them and their horses. And the eagle has confirmed this.

Ah. Well, then. Hawks, you have led me most faithfully; I am grateful for your assistance. To accommodate me, you have traveled far from your home territory in Alpetar. Return to it now with my thanks and my blessing.

Like arrows finally loosed from a bow, the hawks flew off toward the first stars in the evening sky.

Standing stock-still, Finch took her bearings. She examined the mouth of the ravine and decided where, if she were defending an encampment, she would place her watchmen. Sure enough, after a time she saw slight movement in both locations. She delayed until midnight, and then, using all the woodcraft that Rooks had once taught her in Anders Wood, she embraced the shadows and slipped past the lookouts.

She followed the stream's patter. The water stretched two to three paces in width and rose above ankle depth. The rocky ravine walls loosely paralleled the stream, sometimes pressing in close like a tunnel, sometimes creating a broader valley floor. The princella heard and saw no signs of people.

She hobbled awhile longer, but her feet hurt so. She did not feel up to meeting armed strangers or frightening them in the dark, so she decided it would be best to hole up for the night and resume searching for their camp in the daylight. She climbed a small rise that lifted her off the streambed floor. On the rise's far side she found a natural depression where moss and ferns grew thick and leaf debris had settled. Pulling Gunnit's cap down over her head, wrapping her tattered blanket around herself, Finch lay down and let exhaustion pull her under.

24

Ink Creek Canyon

Finch woke to the touch of cold metal on her throat. A large man stood over her, blocking the light; it was his sword that had disturbed her.

"Easy now, lad," he said. "Ya move quick and I'll slit your throat. I need to know how ya found this canyon and how many ya brought with you."

"I'm alone," said Finch.

"Uhh," said the soldier and leaned to spit to the side. "Get up, slow-like, with both your hands on top of your cap."

Finch obeyed his orders. The man shook out her blanket and patted her down, confiscating her dagger. He gestured toward her boots. Finch yanked them on, not allowing herself to wince. The man used her own knife to cut the leather that once was Butter's reins into a smaller piece. Then, watching her warily and keeping the knife open, he sheathed his sword and tightly bound her wrists together. He gestured some paces away to where a mare stood, ears cocked forward, making soft huffing noises.

"Climb up in front of the saddle."

The horse was tall. Finch tried to hoist herself up and slipped back to the earth. She tried again, but she couldn't lift her foot into a stirrup almost level with her rib cage. On the third try, the man assisted her by pushing her rump. Then he swung himself up behind her, turned the horse into the depth of the canyon, and nudged the mare into a canter. The sun lit the silhouette of the top of the ravine wall, a bright flash against gray rock.

On a fast horse it took only moments before they entered an orderly campsite. Another man grabbed the horse's reins and questioned her captor.

"What you got there, Kran?"

"A spy! Better fetch the commander."

"Is our hideout discovered?"

"Fetch the commander, will ya? And the new sarge."

Kran yanked Finch off the mare and held her roughly by the upper arm. A sparse crowd gathered, regarding her with curiosity and wariness.

A tall man exited a nearby tent. The first thing she noticed was his eyes, blue and intense under straight brows; then his jawbone, triangular and clean-shaven; and his hair, unruly with coarse curls. He must have just been washing for morning, because a couple of water drops trickled down his hazelnut-brown neck. He still held a towel in his hand.

"Kran, report."

"I was riding out to relieve Jothile on guard duty when the mare starts acting funny-like, as if she smelled something. I gave her her head and I found this lad here in a hollow, sound asleep. Thought I ought to bring him back for questioning, sir."

"It's a woman, Kran. Was there anyone else?"

"What? Really? I'll be blowed." Kran shook his head slightly. "Ah, no. Not that I could see. Sir."

"Are our guards on the posts? Have they been killed?"

"Don't know, sir. I came straight home."

"Tel-bein, go check on them," said the commander to an older man, "and if they are alive, ask them how this girl sauntered past them. Also, check for any other signs of trouble. Take Eli-anna with you."

All the time he was talking, the commander's blue eyes never left their steady survey of Finch.

A slender lad came up to him and took the towel he still grasped unknowingly from his hand.

"Who are you?" the commander asked his captive.

"Skylark," she answered.

"Where are you from?"

"Alpetar."

"Where in Alpetar?"

"Sweetmeadow."

"I have seen Sweetmeadow on a map. A farming town on the flatlands."

"No," she said, "a herding village in the mountains."

The commander nodded. "Why are you here?"

"The Oros raided my village, murdered my kin, molested two of our women, kidnapped our menfolk, stole our horses, kilt my friends, and kilt our dogs. I don't know what happened . . . to my father, my brother . . ." She cleared her throat. "Probably they're dead. I want to join up with you. I want vengeance against the Oros."

"When was this?"

"I don't know exactly. More than a moon ago."

"Where were you when these Oros raided? How did you survive?"

"I was up in Middle Pasture with the goats."

"In Alpetar they use women as shepherds?"

"I was taking my brother, Gunnit, his midmeal. He had forgotten it that morning."

"Were you and Gunnit the only survivors?"

"No. Gramps and Ma Dobbely survived, and Saggeta, Joolyn, and Linnsie. And some babes that had been hidden away."

"So, a parcel of survivors. Who was killed?"

"My sister—my sister, Linnie. Stabbed six times. My friends, Wimmie and Nimmet, I've known them all my life—their heads, against a wall—their little heads, their yellow hair . . . And the Oro filth, they threw the bodies of my aunt and uncle down a well." Her voice shook with anger. "Do you want me to name the dogs too?"

"Give me her cap," growled a bald man with an earring. Her captor, Kran, pulled the cap off her head and threw it to him.

Skylark worried that the men would notice her hair was not the shiny yellow shades of the Alpies she had met. But the bald soldier inspected the cap. "The wool is Alpetar cashmere. Some words embroidered inside." He moved the cap closer and farther until his eyes could focus: "'Gunnit, my dearest.'"

Skylark had never examined the inside of the cap. She stretched her hand out for it back, but the older man ignored her request.

The commander continued, "The names of the dogs will not be necessary." He looked up at the sky, then returned his gaze to her eyes. "What bothers me is how you knew about us. How did you know we Raiders were even in Oromondo? This canyon is hidden away, and no one should suspect we are hiding here. How could you, an Alpetar girl alone on foot, come unerringly to the right place?"

Fool! Lackwit, she berated herself. *Never to have anticipated this simple question. No one in Alpetar has even heard about these Raiders— only people in the Free States and Green Isles.*

A large wolfhound loped up, interrupting the interrogation by growling at Kran. The growl escalated.

"Maki, it's me, Kran. You know me."

"Maki, stop it!" ordered the commander.

The wolfhound shook off the order. His eyes fixated on Kran while the hair on the back of his neck stood straight up. His growl grew lower and fearsome, coloring the air with threat. Everyone froze with astonishment.

Skylark said to her captor, "Let go of me or pull your sword, because he's about to go for your throat."

Kran dropped her arm. The dog subsided instantly. He crawled inch by inch on his belly, wagging his tail, toward Skylark. When she bent down to stroke him, the dog bit through the bonds that held her wrists.

Your Majesty! No one will hurt thee while one breathes.

I appreciate your devotion, wolfhound. But I didn't want humans to know of my Talent. You have caused enough trouble for now. Go over there and lie down.

The dog obeyed. The people in the surrounding crowd were shocked by the dog's actions. The commander stared at her even more intently.

"Why did my dog react that way to Kran? He has always accepted all the men in this troop. Why did he behave that way with you?"

Skylark could see no way out of this predicament but something like the truth.

"I have a way with beasts. They like me. In fact, I found you with the help of an eagle."

Some of the onlookers laughed.

"I find that hard to believe," said the commander.

"Give me some moments and I'll prove it."

Lord of the Skies, do you hear my call? I need you to come to me. Does my Talent stretch to your height and distance? Lord of the Skies?

While Skylark called the eagle, the lad brought the commander a small leather strap, and he tied his brown hair—a little longer than hers—at the neck. Then someone brought him a cup of tisane with a smoky-spicy-sweet aroma; the smell haunted Skylark.

With a rush of wind the eagle appeared in the sky above the

ravine. With a flair for drama Skylark might have predicted, he flew five paces over the heads of the assembled crowd, banked sharply, and landed near Skylark. He stared at them all with his haughty gaze.

"Commander," she said, "I have the honor of introducing the Lord of the Skies. It would be appropriate to bow."

The commander bowed to the eagle. Some of the assembled men were too flabbergasted to move, but others followed suit.

"Lord of the Skies," said Skylark aloud, "I would like to introduce you to— You haven't told me your name."

"Thalen of Sutterdam, commander of the Raiders."

"To Commander Thalen of Sutterdam."

The eagle bobbed his head and turned his neck this way and that, looking at the people.

Why didst thou interrupt one's hunt, Little Majesty?

Sorry to disturb you, but these men might have kilt me if I hadn't explained how I found them and their hideout. Will you suffer me to touch you?

A strange request. . . . One would be honored.

Skylark moved closer to the bird. His head was level with her heart. She stroked the feathers on the back of his head; they felt wiry. He leaned into her touch, much like a cat leans into a stroke. After a few moments, however, he decided he had had enough.

Art thou safe now?

Without waiting for her reply, he opened his wings and flew off over the rim of the canyon, the sun glinting through his wings.

"I have never met someone with such a way with beasts," commented Commander Thalen.

"Really?" said Skylark. She forced herself to shrug. "We live closely among animals. At home, Mabbit could herd the whole flock with a word."

"None of the books I've read about Alpetar mention this skill. Is it inherited Magic?"

Skylark called his bluff. "Books about Alpetar? I don't know of any."

The tall commander chuckled at that. "Sounds like an interesting place."

A man in the back of the crowd spoke up. "Sir, even in other lands, folk vary in their connections with animals. Horse masters and hunting masters, for instance."

Commander Thalen looked around him at the young lad and the older man with an earring who still held Gunnit's cap. "Kambey? Tristo?"

Earring said, "Even *if* her story be true. Still . . . look at her. She's a scrawny thing, without the muscles to fight. What good would she be to us? Just another mouth to feed or another woman to cause trouble amongst the men. We would never have taken her in Yosta. You know that Codek would never have accepted her."

The commander nodded.

The lad smiled at her—a dazzling, confiding smile. "Skylark, huh? How could you help us? What good would you be to Thalen's Raiders?"

"I could ask birds to scout for us. Would that be helpful? To know where the enemy is at all times?"

"You can call other birds besides that pet?" asked the tall commander.

"He's much too proud to be anyone's pet. And aye. Would you like me to gather all the crows nearby? Or all the jays?" This was the Talent she had to offer the Raiders; this was her way to make a contribution.

"Not at this moment. I want to hear from the scouts I sent out. Kran, return to where you found her. Examine the ground and fetch any belongings you find. Tristo, get her some food and then bring her to my tent."

Thalen turned, breaking up the gathering. Tristo took her to the cooking area, filled a plate of corn mush for her, poured some jam on it, and got her a cup of tisane. Skylark tried to eat the warm, wonderful mush as slowly as possible while he watched her and casually built a tower out of pebbles. When she'd finished, Tristo let her wash her face and hands in the running creek and then led her to the command tent. Its front flap was tied open to the light and air. Inside she saw utilitarian furnishings: a desk, chair, camp bed, and a footstool.

The air carried the metallic charge of an argument. "Shall I tie her up, Commander?" Earring asked when Skylark appeared. "Shall I post a guard?"

"I don't think that's necessary," said Tristo. "Just a feeling I have."

"All right. Skylark, stand at attention over there until I say differently," ordered the commander, indicating a spot in the tent two paces from his chair.

Ignoring her presence, he sat at his desk and consulted some books and maps. At one point he traced his finger along a route and added up some figures.

The scout he sent out first returned. She saw now that the man's hair was shaven up from his neck and that its brown included strands of deep purple that some people termed plum.

Mellie plum to hail your chum clanged in her mind.

"The lookouts are alive, though quite chagrined," said Tel-bein. "They swear they didn't nap on duty. She must have some forest skill to have gotten by them. Eli-anna back-traced her trail almost a league. No other footprints, no horse or aurochs, though a wolf followed her at a distance, no doubt choosing its moment."

"Thank you, Tel-bein, Eli-anna." The commander dismissed them and resumed his desk work.

Skylark's feet throbbed so in her boots it seemed to take forever for Kran to return. He came in with her blanket tied in a bundle, and Earring followed him into the tent. The commander cut the leather of the bundle. The three men examined each of her few belongings one by one: the battered green wool cloak Stahlia had made for her Winter Solstice present three years ago; her bottle of coal-tar hair tincture; bundles of herbs; a store of acorns; tinderbox; whetstone; her extra pairs of underdrawers and hose; a waterskin; and the saucepan. The latter, which she had bought at the general store in Tar's Basin, had an artisanal name scribed on the bottom: "Alpetar Smithies."

Good thing I gave Gunnit that toy soldier. It had a Weir uniform and the name of the shop in Gulltown.

The filthy, torn blanket was knit of the same wool as the cap. Kran added her nondescript knife to the top of the pile and even the leather bits of Butter's reins. Skylark didn't like these strangers pawing over her things, but she wasn't in any position to protest.

"Any thoughts?" the commander asked the others. "I don't see anything that contradicts her story."

The tall leader laid the stuff aside and dismissed his confederates. He picked up his paperwork once more.

Skylark had never stood at attention before. She discovered how hard it could be just to stand upright and still, with her hands clasped behind her back. Her muscles protested. She wanted to break the pose, but she suspected this to be some test as to her endurance or compliance. Gritting her teeth, Skylark focused her eyes on one splotch on the canvas tent, and concentrated just on breathing.

Her feet throbbed with each heartbeat. She placed all her weight on one, counted to one hundred, and then switched to the other foot. Then she tried reciting the names of all the queens of Weirandale in her mind. On the other foot she attempted to reel them off in reverse order, but she couldn't manage the task.

Maki trotted into the tent. The wolfhound started snuffling at her feet and then licked at the places where she had cut open her boots. The commander noticed.

"This looks ill," he said. He went to the tent flap and called out to someone, "Fetch a basin of hot water and track down Cerf.

"Come now, sit down," he said. Gingerly she stepped to the stool he indicated and collapsed onto it. The commander examined her boots, noticing the blood soaking through the layers of padding cushioning the blisters. He pulled out his own knife.

"I am going to cut off your boots. I'll be as gentle as I can."

With care he cut through the leather. Skylark had wrapped the area about her ankles where the boot tops rubbed with strips from a shirt, but blood had soaked through there too. He kept slicing, peeling the boot away from her heel—rubbed almost to the bone—and then opening up the top of the boot and freeing her blistered, oozing toes.

Tristo appeared bearing the basin of hot water. Kneeling down, the boy pulled away her ineffective bandages, sucked in a breath at the ugliness of the wounds, and moved her feet into the basin. A whimper broke through her clenched lips when the warm water hit her broken skin.

Thalen said to Tristo, "Go see what's keeping Cerf." To Skylark he said, "You *have* trekked hundreds of leagues."

A thin-faced man with slate-gray eyes, wearing a leather apron, entered the tent within a few moments. He had brought a satchel of supplies with him. He washed each foot and inspected it in the sunlight coming in the tent flap. Then he called for another basin of hot water and added unguents. In the meantime someone brought another mug of tisane. The healer poured some brandy into it and handed it to Skylark. She concentrated just on holding it steady with both hands.

While Cerf was wrapping her feet and ankles in tight, clean bandages, the commander and Earring conferred outside the tent. Skylark overheard, "Are you satisfied now?" The commander's voice sounded angry. "Has she given enough proof of her stamina and willpower for you?"

Earring answered defensively, "I didn't know about her feet, Commander."

"No, I realize that." His tone moderated. "But we both should have been wiser. No one slogs all those leagues afoot without paying a price. If she isn't tough enough to join us I do not know who is. Besides—what other choice is there? Are you prepared to either kill her in cold blood or throw her out for the Oros to find and question?"

Earring coughed. "You've dealt with other . . . situations without such mercy."

"True enough. But a wise comrade, Vatuxen, once told me there's right and there's wrong. I haven't completely lost my moral compass. Yet."

The commander reentered the tent. The healer said to him, "The only way her feet are going to recover is if she stays off them. Completely. She needs to be carried everywhere she goes. She needs to lie down with her feet raised up in the air. I won't use up my milk of the poppy on chafed feet, no matter how grisly. When the skin closes up, the pain will lessen. She's undernourished too; she'll heal quicker if we feed her well. I'll change her bandages tomorrow. Fetch me if she starts to fever—but I doubt that's in store."

Skylark felt woozy, from pain, stress, and the brandy. She thought she heard the commander say, "Until she proves trustworthy, someone should keep an eye on her at all times."

A different large man in an apron came into the tent and picked her up, one arm under her knees, another under her back, as easily as if she were the toddler Doraleen.

He carried her to an area of the camp that smelled of fir needles, where some bedrolls were stretched out. He laid her down as tenderly as she would have lain down Limpett, propping her aching feet up on a saddle.

She had been naive to think that all she had to do was find the Raiders. The Raiders might be as much danger to her as the Oros. Why would they trust her or treat her kindly?

Maki appeared, poking her with his long nose, snuffling her ears, her neck, her mouth, and her body. Once he'd memorized her scent, Skylark bid him lie down and interlaced her fingers in his fur. For the first time in weeks she had a dog beside her. And beneath Maki's loud breathing she heard the constant melody of the rushing creek. Even though she worried about being accepted and her feet throbbed with sharper pains after being disturbed, a deep comfort washed over her.

25

Alpetar

Peddler tucked Saulė's Mirror away into its small velvet pouch. If he caught the first rays of morning light or the last gleams of the day on the silvered surface, the Spirit granted him a vision of far-off events. These images, however, appeared unlabeled as to time or place, thus Peddler found himself frantically wrestling with their elusiveness. The Mirror had shown, for instance, a group of Alpetar men and boys slaving to load heavy ore carts, and later, he had seen their bodies, lifeless in the dirt. Where were they working? When had they died? Who were they?

He had seen a party of travelers, forlornly tramping the High Road with a big wagon. On three occasions the Mirror had focused on the oldest boy, as if he was of special import.

Another evening he had been shown the Nargis heir shivering in her sleep in a tiny seam of rock, warmed by an Alpetar cap and a woven blanket. Peddler was not sure how he knew her identity— he just recognized her, as if her face was already imprinted in his mind.

Each time he was granted one of these visions he had wanted to intervene—to rescue or at least offer companionship. But he was only human; the Agency Saulė granted him did not lend him any magical ability to move from place to place any faster than his donkey, Aurora, could pull his cart. And the visual clues did not offer specific information about exactly where to search.

So he considered the Mirror's images as almost a curse; snatches of information about crises that he knew about but felt powerless to affect. He was bold enough to want to take action—he thought that Saulė had chosen him for his courage and initiative even more than his faith—but this summer, time and again, he had found himself wrong-footed and out of position.

He patted Aurora. "Do you reckon, old friend, that this time we can get to the right place at the right time? You're going have to pick up them feet and step lively now."

Two days earlier the Sweetmeadow refugees had come upon a hamlet along the High Road. The town was half-empty and many buildings had been burned; only a few families still lived there. By dint of much persuasion, they had exchanged some of their valuables for food, an axe, and a replacement bottle for Addigale. But this was obviously not a place where the party wanted to settle, so they returned to their wandering.

This afternoon the refugees made camp in a field off the thoroughfare. Green leaves sprouting from broken furrows signaled an abandoned patch of vegetables, and Gunnit set the children to digging while the women gathered wood and started a fire and Gramps unhitched the draught horses. Addigale—wet, hungry, or just fussy—began to wail, getting on everyone's nerves, so he sent four-summers-old Sheleen, who had a way of making funny faces and setting the babe to giggling, to tend her on her blanket.

Gunnit saw Laki and Jaki, who had been nosing the soil, stop and scent the air. Then the herding dogs started barking and streaked northward into a half-wooded meadow.

"What is it?" Dame Saggeta cast down her armful of wood next to him and peered anxiously after the dogs.

"Dunno, but I hope it's nothing bad." Gunnit and Saggeta followed the dogs a few paces across the field, but they did not want to leave the others unprotected. The boy wished he hadn't dropped his sword and left it behind during their encounter with the Pellish.

"Look!" Gunnit shouted, pointing. "It's Butter!"

Butter and Didi had to contend with the other dogs leaping on them enthusiastically. Didi got bowled over more than once; each time she rose with dignity and shook herself off. The pair marched themselves straight to the Sweetmeadow group. Then the children mobbed them, each hugging a part of the pony or dog in their grimy, clutching arms. Aleen wrapped her arms around the pony's neck, while Doraleen embraced her front hooves and Limpett grabbed her tail. Alloon basically threw himself on top of Didi, hugging her with all his weight.

"All right now, urchins, back off. Let us have a look at them and make sure they are hale," said Saggeta. She pointed Gunnit to Didi while she examined the pony. Before he could reach the hound, however, Kiki pushed herself between Gunnit's legs, so excited she peed; the older dog greeted the puppy with a swift lick on her muzzle.

Didi stood still with a wagging tail as Gunnit ran his hands over her, examining her for wounds or ailments. He pulled off a couple of briars and ticks but found nothing seriously wrong.

Saggeta finished her inspection of Butter. "Oh my, she needs currying! Fetch the brush and a bucket of water, Aleen. Any longer and she'd have wicked skin ulcers."

"But where's Finch?" asked Limpett, his voice trembling.

Dame Saggeta put her hands on her hips. "That, I don't know. But I'd bet a goat she wasn't forced to give up the animals too quickly. Look at these braids in Butter's mane, each tied with a bit of cut leather. One, two, three . . . six."

"We have six children with us," Joolyn commented.

"Seven, if you count the babe," Gunnit said. "Did she forget Addigale?"

Limpett had walked around Butter. He pointed as he called shrilly, "I see another in her tail!"

"Aye," said Dame Saggeta. "Seven children, seven plaits. Pretty clear if you ask me. She went on her way by another means, and she sent these two back to us."

"She's not hurt, Limpett," Gunnit reassured the tyke. "And isn't it great for us, to have Butter and Didi again? Why don't you give Didi a kiss on her head? She likes that." Limpett kissed the top of Didi's head solemnly, as if he were kissing all the people he had lost.

This happy reunion was not the only event that befell them; others were more somber. A stroke hit Ma Dobbely a couple of days later. They stopped for a spell to try to care for the elderly woman. That night another stroke shook her like a dog shaking a varmint, and this one carried her off.

Gunnit helped Gramps Dobbely build a pyre. Gunnit supposed he should have felt sad, but he had no love for her. After all they had been through, all the death and trials, even her grandkids were wrung out of tears. The only one who grieved was Gramps, but Gunnit figured that caring for her had been so time-consuming he might come out even in the end. For himself, although he supposed he should have felt more sorrow over a woman he'd known his entire life, Gunnit thought that Butter and Didi's return way overbalanced Ma Dobbely's loss.

Then, three days later Sheleen stepped in a field hornets' nest. Gunnit counted twenty-seven stings. Her lips swelled up as thick as squirrels' tails, and her eyes swelled up so much she couldn't even cry. Dame Saggeta looked fearsome worried; she sent Gunnit and Gramps on horseback to see if they could find help. After casting around in panic, riding in one direction and then another, finally they saw the smoke of chimneys from a cluster of three cottages south of the road. When they explained the emergency, a stringy older woman there grabbed some herbs and agreed to follow them to their campsite. By the time they returned, Sheleen's throat had almost closed tight. Dame Aalooka handed his ma her herbs and told her to brew some tea, and then she cut a bunch of cattail reeds. She had an awful time getting one of these down Sheleen's throat, because the girl kept gagging and resisting and the reeds kept breaking or bending. After several tries, she got one in. Gunnit could hear each desperate breath whistling through the straw.

For hours, the women took turns holding Sheleen in their laps, spooning chamomile and willow bark tea into her mouth. Most of it just trickled out, but they just kept pouring the liquid into the child. As the day waned, with Gramps in the way, Gunnit and Aleen fed the other little ones and tried to get them to sleep. Upset, the tykes couldn't relax, so his ma came and patted Addigale and Limpett on their backs until they finally dropped off.

The sun had set by the time Sheleen frantically wriggled herself out of Dame Joolyn's grasp, yanked the reed out of her own throat with a choking noise, and threw up a cup of liquid. Then she knelt on the ground, with her head lowered, panting.

Aalooka put her ear to Sheleen's back and listened to her breathe and cough.

"She lost the medicine. And doesn't she need the reed?" Gunnit asked the dame. "Do you have to get one back in?"

"Nope," said Dame Aalooka with a relieved smile. "I'm sure she absorbed a lot of the tea. If that much liquid can come up, air can get down too. You can let her rest now. But give her more tea whenever she wakes. And keep wet clothes soaked in the lavender water on all the stings."

"We don't know how to thank you," said Dame Saggeta, bursting into sobs, a sight that actually made Gunnit more frightened than anything that had happened earlier.

"Truly, dame," said Gunnit. "Sheleen's a wretched nuisance, but she's one of us."

"Never you all mind," said Dame Aalooka. "I'm just pleased to have been able to lend a hand." She paused. "I wish I could invite you all to settle with my family but we're just barely getting by. . . ."

"That's all right," said Gunnit's ma. "You've done us an incomparable service as it is."

Ma Dobbely's death and Sheleen's close escape made Gunnit even more anxious and watchful. He watched the road before and behind them carefully and looked to the dogs for warning of any danger. Dame Saggeta noticed his keeping guard, and told him that he was her "right hand." The responsibility of protecting the band weighed heavily on him.

One morning Gunnit saw a horse-drawn cart approaching from a side road that led north into the steeper foothills. As it drew nearer he saw it was a peddler's cart, painted white with big yellow suns, pulled by a donkey with bells around its neck. The driver's hair shone every shade of yellow—from the palest to the brightest—elaborately divided into separate thin strands, all of which ended in tiny bells. The cart itself creaked, but when the man pulled up and dismounted, the boy could hear that whenever he moved the bells created a pleasing jingle. He had a round face and big eyes of a shockingly bright green.

The dogs raced to him as if he were their long-lost master. Gunnit decided that even without their eager approval he would have trusted this stranger.

"Travelers! Well met! I'm excited to see you," the man called. "Where do you all hail from?"

They halted to talk with him and told him their tale. He sat on a rock, tapping one foot on the ground. The dogs clustered around him, and he scratched their ears abstractedly.

Remembering what Finch had taught him, Gunnit slipped the bits out of all the horses' mouths to allow them to graze comfortably while all this confabbing took place. He untied Pansy and Violet too, knowing that if they strayed the dogs would herd them back.

"My goodness! What a story. Start over and tell it to me again, would you?" the peddler asked. This time he often broke in with questions, such as, "Had you ever seen Oros in your parts before?" and, "This woman, Finch—did she say where she was from or where she was going?"

"Have you heard about more raiding parties?" Saggeta asked him.

"Not in these parts," said the peddler. "But Oros have been raiding the borders at will since the Incursion, three years past. They take men for workers and steal any food they can find."

"Have you heard anything of the menfolk kidnapped from Sweetmeadow?" asked Gunnit's mother, twisting her hands.

"I'm sorry, dame." He shook his head and rubbed his beard, which also had bells tied in it. Doraleen climbed into his lap and batted at the bells. The peddler rubbed her back with the same absent patience as he petted the dogs.

Doraleen misses her father. We all miss our fathers.

"Ah me, 'tis a very sad tale. I'm so sorry about your losses. What troubles you folks have suffered! The question now is what to do with you all." He stroked his beard again, and his bells tinkled. He sat up straighter as he came to a decision.

"I just come down from my favorite hamlet on my whole circuit. 'Tis called Cloverfield. As far as I know, there ain't been no Oros round this way and no Pellish neither. That's probably because the Temple of Saulė sits above Cloverfield in the Bowl of the Sun."

"The Bowl of the Sun lies near here?" his ma asked with eyes going wide, and Gunnit knew she was thinking of her favorite tale.

"Oh, yes," said the man, his green eyes twinkling. "Did you think the story was just a legend? Well, I guess I did too, when I was younger, afore I learned different. But we have to have a temple somewhere for Saulė, right? I know we're not a church-building folk, but doesn't the Spirit who lights our days deserve at least one special place?"

The peddler didn't give the travelers a chance to respond. "Kindly folk, them that live in Cloverfield. And rather prosperous, as herders go. I suggest you perch there. Either for a spell or for always. The village would welcome you, of that I am certain."

Saggeta polled the adults, Gunnit, and Aleen. They were all weary of the open road and yearned for a place to call home.

"We'll take your advice and thank you for it," she said to the stranger.

"That's fine." He nodded, pleased. "'Tis two days' ride north from here. Let me give the little ones something to brighten the last stage of their journey." From the back of his cart he pulled out a box of colorful bracelets; tiny bells tuned to different pitches dangled from each. He encouraged each of the children (even baby Addigale) to choose one, which they joyously clasped on their wrists.

Yet when Gunnit approached the box, the man shook his head. Gunnit consoled himself with the thought that he was too grown for children's toys.

While the children were showing off their prizes to the adults and trying out the sounds of their bells, the peddler beckoned Gunnit behind the cart.

"I have something special for you. What's your name again?"

"I'm Gunnit."

"Pleased to meet you, Gunnit." The man shook his hand. "You can call me 'Peddler.' I've been told to keep a lookout for a lad like you."

"Told?" asked Gunnit. "How could anyone tell you about me? Who told you about me?"

The man didn't answer; maybe he didn't hear because he had turned around and rummaged in the back of his cart, noisily tossing around things that clattered and clunked.

"Ah-ha!" he said as he turned around with a small white silk pouch in his grasp. He handed it to Gunnit, who opened it. Inside lay another bracelet, formed in a stiff cuff, though this had no bells, only a dangling charm fashioned to look like the sun. At first Gunnit felt disappointed because this didn't make music, but looking closer he saw that both the bracelet and the charm were made of lustrous gold that grabbed the daylight and bounced it back again. This was a special present indeed.

The peddler clasped it on Gunnit's left wrist and then mimed that Gunnit should push it farther up his arm. Wonderingly, because the circlet fit his thin wrist perfectly, Gunnit pushed the bracelet under his shirt over his forearm (amazingly, it slid easily), over his bony elbow, and then up to the muscle of his upper arm.

The peddler nodded, quite pleased. "Kissed by the Sun, you are, Gunnit. Kissed by the Sun."

Gunnit had no idea what this meant, but he nodded.

Peddler grabbed another package from the back of his wagon, and he and Gunnit joined the rest of the travelers.

"I have to be off," he said, liberally handing out boiled sweets to everyone, even Gramps.

Gunnit had lost all memory of treats; the candy in his mouth tasted so sweet it lifted his heart. He saw the tykes' eyes similarly shine with pleasure.

"You follow the side road toward the mountains and at the fork turn left," Peddler said, pointing. "Actually, you can't get lost because the right fork leads to Cloverfield too, but it's a longer route."

"Thank you kindly," said Saggeta. "Your gifts have been a boon, and your advice even more valuable. May Saulé light your road."

"I wish you happier days. We'll meet again," said the man, looking at Gunnit significantly, and he climbed up to his wagon's seat.

"May the Sun light your way!" they called after him.

The route climbed steeply, and normally the little ones would have chafed at the exertion, but the thought that they were nearly somewhere cheered everyone up.

Soon enough they saw a hamlet nestled at the base of even higher hills, backed by rocky and white-capped mountains. The hills were traced with dirt and rock paths leading to higher meadows, from which came the familiar bleating of goats. Blooms of white and yellow yarrow and blue larkspur speckled the green forage.

Gunnit saw at a glance that the community was bigger than Sweetmeadow had been. Many more thatched cottages clustered companionably together.

As the refugees rode into the center of town—a cobbled square with an ancient sundial in the middle—the seventy-odd villagers poured out of their houses or left their tasks to surround the refugees. They offered food and drink and a warm welcome. Dame Saggeta spoke for the group, and the Cloverfield folk listened to their story with horror, sympathy, and admiration on their faces.

The travelers might have felt overwhelmed or shamed by the outpouring of generosity, but they were proud of the skills they had to offer (including their stamina and their courage), and their healthy animals, which would be welcome additions to any hamlet.

Conveniently, one thatched stone house presently sat empty, so his mother, himself, baby Addigale, and Limpett lodged there. The village banded together to construct a new house for Dame Saggeta and Dame Joolyn; the women had decided to raise Sheleen and Doraleen, which was awful good of them, given that the girls were not their real kin. An older Cloverfield couple invited Gramps, Aleen, and Alloon to share their home. Their mounts and goats joined the hamlet's corral and flock. Didi, Jaki, and Laki moved at will amongst the three cottages, or patrolled the village perimeter, always a little more wary, a little more on guard than the other village dogs. Kiki, however, was never more than a few steps away from Gunnit's leg.

Gunnit often found himself encircled by young followers, having to tell of his adventures over and over.

When he took his turn herding Cloverfield's goats, at first he felt fearsome anxious whenever he left the village houses, lest something awful happen in his absence. Gradually, he relaxed and it became wonderfully boring to spend the day in the sunny pasture with Taffy browsing nearby and come back to supper with Ma and the little ones. Limpett looked up to him with a gaze near worship (he was glad his mother had adopted Limpett and not that brat Alloon), and baby Addigale giggled sweetly when she was warm and fed and someone shook a bell bracelet for her. Gunnit would hold her in his arms after dinner, giving his mother a break and taking on the role of big brother.

But often Gunnit thought about the dangerous world around him. He questioned why Saulė had allowed the raid on Sweetmeadow to happen in the first place. He worried over whether he would ever see his father and brother again. Now that they had reached safety he missed his sister Linnie and the companionship of Wimmie and Nimmet more than ever.

Sometimes Aleen and he would wander off to talk alone, mostly to confirm that their six weeks on the High Road had been real. Aleen told him that the peddler they had met was held in high regard in Cloverfield. Folk even whispered that he might be someone important to the Temple of Saulė. None of the villagers had ever seen this famous temple, he learned. Every time a person overcome with curiosity tried to climb higher to find it, their path twisted around queer-like and led them back down to the village.

Gunnit pondered whether they would ever meet this peddler

again. Maybe he would come back at the turn of the seasons. He also wondered if he would ever see Finch again. He asked the dogs and Butter, but they could not say. Kiki wagged her tail at the name "Finch," but then that fool dog wagged her tail whenever he looked at her.

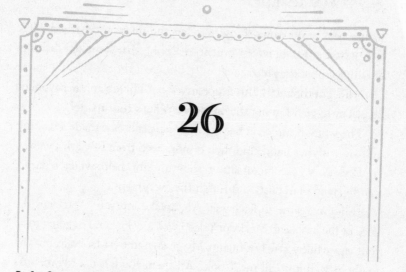

26

Ink Creek Canyon

When Skylark woke, the wolfhound had left her side. Moving in her sleep, she'd shifted her feet off the saddle, but the bandages still looked clean, even if red had seeped through around the right ankle and at both heels.

She stirred on the bedroll, relieved beyond measure that she did not need to hobble all day long.

She propped herself up on her elbows to look around. Three other blankets lay near her. All of her own things were neatly piled close at hand, with the exception of her tattered blanket. Although she could hear voices not far off, she couldn't see anyone through the scrim of evergreen needles.

She called the dog, *Come to me, Maki; I want you.* The large gray beast appeared quickly, beads of water on his feet and his yellow eyes looking around for any threat. He reminded her of some dogs from her childhood in the palace, and she wondered if she had owned wolfhounds then.

As she hoped might happen, the dog rushing to her attracted human notice. A graceful woman wearing a bracer on her arm and with a bow and arrows slung over her shoulders approached. Sky-lark stared at her in astonishment, realizing that some of her locks of hair were a deep plum color.

"Hey," said Skylark, finding her voice. "There's another woman here! I'm so glad I'm not the only one. What's your name?"

The woman smiled at her but did not speak. She made a waiting gesture with her hand, and then disappeared from Skylark's view.

Skylark was contemplating shouting for help when a large, middle-aged man bustled through the evergreens.

"Eli-anna came to fetch me. Ah, awake are you? You slept the sleep of the innocent. Me, I don't sleep well any longer. I'm going to be your legs while you're healing up. My given name is Moorvale, but you might as well just call me 'Cook.' All them Raiders do. My missus's name is Maribel, but these clever, clever chaps, they call her 'Cookie.'"

"I'm grateful for your help, Cook," Skylark answered.

Cook continued. "I'll wager 'bout now your bladder is fit to burst." He hoisted her up in his arms again and took her to the privy area. Afterward, he carried her to the stream for a wash, and then to the head of the creek, where a cooking station had been set up. He kept up a steady river of talk all the while; he told her about those Mellie gals, about the problems with the water in Oromondo, about the tavern he and his missus used to own, about their grown children, and about which dishes he and his missus prided them-selves on. "An army's fuel is good eats. And them that's wounded won't heal without nourishment. So you might say *we're* the most essential Raiders."

He placed her near the fire (burned down to embers and smell-ing decidedly of horse dung), propped her feet up on a saddle, and moved a sack of oats for her to rest her back against; then he brought her some porridge and a cup of tisane. Maki showed up again, reset-tling himself at her side, watching her every move.

Cook went back to peeling potatoes. "Now our provisions are running a little low. Not so low as to fret, but low enough. Wareth—

he's the commander's boon companion from before-times—he's gone with Eldie to fetch a load of supplies. Dangerous trip; sure hope they make it through. Could be some beans this time. Beans is mighty good in soups, mighty good in stews." He waved his paring knife at Skylark to make his point. "Course with beans some bacon goes mighty fine, but we never knows what they will send. Me and the missus, we just gotta im-pro-vise."

"What does that black-and-white armband mean, Cook?" Skylark asked.

"Oh, this? We all made one and put it on. This is our insignia as Raiders. It copies something our commander wears."

The smiling boy from the day before showed up.

"Hey, Cook, I need some tisane for the commander."

"Help yourself," Cook replied.

"Hey, Skylark, how are the feet? How are you? I'm Tristo, the commander's aide."

"I'm doing well, thank you for asking," she replied.

"Hey, you need anything?" Tristo examined her closely. "How about a clean shirt? I'll find you one, and then scrub the one you've got on. I think Eli-anna washed your blanket earlier; I saw it drying on some rocks."

"I would be grateful for something fresh," Skylark replied, looking down at her grimy and torn covering. "I cut up my extra shirt for bandages."

"Say, never saw the like of when that eagle came a-swooping down. Did you raise it from a chick or something?"

"Hardly. I just met the eagle a couple of weeks ago."

"You're joshing, right? Come on, you can tell me—I'm nobody around here. I was sure you found it with a broken wing and nursed it back to health. I've heard of stories like that."

"Sorry. Nothing of that sort," she said.

"Well, Maki is taken with you. Never saw him leave the commander for someone else before. I'll let you in on a secret: he's not a very nice dog." Tristo wrinkled his nose and stuck out his tongue at the wolfhound. Turning to Cook, he continued, "Hey, we're supposed to put some meat on our lark. You could fry her some of those potatoes all crispy like you do?"

"These taters are for the soup. You can't ask me to make special dishes for just one soldier. We've had wounded before and will again."

Tristo winked at Skylark. "Aww, come on, Cook. Her feet look real nasty, and she won't heal if you don't feed her, and your fried potatoes taste better than a mess of porridge. If you won't make 'em, I bet Cookie will do it. Her fried taters are even better than yours. She im-pro-vises with wild onion. I'll go fetch her. I think she's target practicing."

"You will take the commander his tisane whilst it's hot and stop plaguing me, or I will fry *you* in the pan!" said Cook. But he did grab a skillet and start melting lard in it.

The potatoes reminded Skylark of Stahlia's good cookery. With her stomach full, Skylark began to grow drowsy again. Cook took her back to her bedroll.

She dozed for a while. When she woke, the same plum-haired woman had brought a large bucket of warm water. She wouldn't speak to Skylark, but her touch and smile were friendly. She gave Skylark a rag bath—with real soap!—and helped her change into the clean green cambric shirt that had miraculously appeared. The shirt was way too large, so they rolled up the sleeves and tied it at her waist and laced her bodice over it. Then the woman used the rest of the soapy water to wash Skylark's hair, which felt lovely. She even had a wooden comb, and she patiently worked through all the knots. She finished her ministrations by rubbing some kind of oil into Skylark's chafed arms and hands.

"Oh, thank you," Skylark said. "I feel so much better."

Cook came to fetch her for midmeal: potato soup with wild onions and bits of some tough, unknown meat. Others of the troop filtered to the cook fire in small groups. Some ignored her or gave her slantwise, almost suspicious glances, but most greeted her with amiable curiosity. Gentain, the horse master, with a wounded hand and a patch over his eye, introduced himself and sat beside her.

"It was me that convinced the commander that some folk are just better with animals than others. They have a sense. Though I have never seen *your* like. Are you as good with horses as you are with dogs and birds?" he asked.

"I guess I am."

"Then when you're up to it, I would like you to work with some of ours. Been a harder time for the horses even than the men, and I'm not what I used to be."

"I came here to lend my skill to helping out. If the healer lets me sit a horse, maybe tomorrow?"

"No hurry, no hurry," he said. "When you're fit."

"Tell me, Gentain, I haven't seen the commander today. Doesn't he eat with the troop?"

"Sure, but often he reads or studies his maps."

The bald-headed, earring-wearing man came to sit next to her, telling her his name was Sergeant Kambey. "I meant no offense yesterday morning. In the last battle we lost our real sergeant, an old-fashioned coot; he never wanted women in a battle camp. The loss is so fresh—I think of him often and I try to replace him. But I was wrong yesterday. I hope we're square." He held out his hand, beefy with muscle and shiny with calluses.

Skylark shook it. "Of course we're square."

After midmeal, Cook took her back to her bedroll again. Skylark woke to Cerf cutting off her bandages. "Hmmpf," he grunted.

"What does that mean?" she asked. She couldn't see her feet from this angle.

A stocky woman had shown up by Cerf's side. She grinned a

wicked grin and spoke with a hoarse voice. "It means your ankles look nasty and your feet look as if an imp put 'em through a mangle."

"Ooma! Who was it healed you up last time?" Cerf chided. "I can tend boot chafing and blisters."

Cerf addressed his patient. "I'm going to put on another unguent; it may sting some. I'm running low on this, so when it burns, count yourself lucky. Believe me, infection hurts worse. Then I'll wrap on some fresh bandages."

As he was finishing up, Skylark asked, "May I sit a horse on the morrow? That way I could move myself around and be useful."

"Not tomorrow, no. We want to keep your feet raised up—not down in stirrups around horseshit. Not until the skin closes up. You'd undo all my efforts. Just take it easy and enjoy the rest."

Ooma settled herself cross-legged where Skylark could see her. "Cerf's actually got some skill at this game. Follow his advice. Last time I was stabbed in a skirmish I didn't listen to his yammering, so I paid a price." She pulled up her leather weskit to show a bright red, puckered scar across her brown belly.

Skylark asked Ooma about the fight, which Ooma was happy to recount in harrowing detail, including the deaths of several of the Raiders.

"You ain't never kilt no one, have you, bird gal?" Ooma asked shrewdly.

"I've stabbed a man, but I didn't stick around to see if he died." She gave Ooma an abbreviated version of the fight with the Pellish to get back the tykes.

"I'll bet the bastard died. Britmank, one of our cavalry boys, came home from River Road with a belly wound and Cerf couldn't save him. Barely pulled Gentain through; he fevered for a week.

"Good to know you've some grit. Though rescuing your own kin is a mite different from swooping down on a fella just minding his own business, even if he be a stinkin' Oro. Your fighting abilities ain't no concern of mine. Kambey'll test you.

"By the by, we put you here, in the women's camp, with me and the Mellie gals, so's no one would bother you. Actually, all the men are great chaps, and no one's getting drunk on this holiday, so you might be safe, naked as a babe in the middle of the men's bedrolls, but why dangle catnip in front of cats?

"Cook won't forget about you, but if you need somethin', whistle low and me or Eli-anna will wait on you like you's a duchess." Ooma chortled at the last thought, and Skylark smiled to herself at the irony.

No one had time to keep her company or to explain the many questions Skylark had about their mission and success. She heard the noises of people busy with activities or practicing with swords. Bored and less sleepy, she wished she could read a book (perchance one of the ones she saw in the commander's tent), but she figured Alpie girls didn't read much.

Kambey did stop by. When he questioned her about her training, Ooma's conversation had forewarned her to have answers prepared. An Alpetar girl would have no experience with a sword, but a modicum of skill at archery would not compromise her disguise. Obviously, she couldn't shoot targets lying prone, so Kambey postponed testing her skill.

Skylark spent a lot of time gazing at the fluffy clouds in the sky, listening to the birds, and now that she was finally here, safe and fed, worrying about how the Sweetmeadow refugees might be faring. She was pretty certain that Didi would have guided Butter safely to them; she was counting on sharp-eyed Saggeta to notice the braids and conclude that she had proceeded by some other means.

Every time she thought of Wyndton she felt as if she were probing a deep toothache; she would quickly shift her thoughts elsewhere.

Maki kept her company only intermittently. This was not a sweet dog, like her old, beloved Gili. Maki had been bred to kill and had lived most of his life in a kennel, and his bonds with humans were shallow. His heart was even colder than Baki's, her guardian in Wyndton. But he recognized who she was and honored her, which was a balm in and of itself.

It's important to be recognized. How many parts have I played? Chickadee, pampered heir to the throne, keeping my Talent hidden from my mother's enemies. Low-class, orphaned Wren, pretending not to be quick in school, hiding in Percia's shadow. Kestrel, confident boss of the carter's yard. Finch, mysterious traveler, savior of refugees. Now, Skylark, vengeance-seeker from Sweetmeadow.

I've become skilled at playacting, but I'm getting confused as to who I really am.

That night, Commander Thalen joined the assembled company around the cook fire. The men stood when he approached them, hardened older soldiers showing respect. Skylark did not want to be judged rude; she hoped that everyone understood about her infirmity.

"As you were," Thalen said. Skylark watched him closely. The commander thanked Cookie for the food and then wandered amongst them, passing a word here and there, always looking a person straight in the face, and even occasionally resting a hand on a shoulder. Eventually he made his way round the group to where she sat next to Gentain. He squatted on his heels to be level with her face.

"Doing all right? Feet healing?" he asked.

"Yes, sir."

"Our scouts returned, so we will be riding out tomorrow. I need the dog, if you can spare him."

"Of course, sir."

"When I get back, we will confer about how your birds might help us."

"Yes, sir." He rose. Skylark burst out, "Come back safely, sir."

He turned and knelt down again. He spoke quietly so that only she could hear, his eyes unreadable, since his face was turned away from the cooking coals that illuminated only his profile. "Raider, likely we are all going to die here. You have to accept that or you are of no use to us. But I have no intention of dying tomorrow. Our job is not finished."

Skylark felt both rebuked and reassured.

Most of the troop rode out before dawn, but the commander ordered Cerf and Cook to stay behind. Cook never neglected her, but she could tell his mind was elsewhere. Cerf changed her bandages around midday and told her that on the morrow she could sit a horse if she kept her feet out of the stirrups and wore clean hose over the dressings that she changed frequently. He also gave her some clothes to rip into bandages to replenish his supply. Skylark was glad for the activity, because the day passed slowly.

In the early afternoon, a Raider she had not seen before materialized by her side near the cook fire. A slight figure, he moved with quiet grace; she had not even heard his approach. His light brown hair was pulled back into a long tail that reached to the middle of his back.

"Milady Duchess of Alpetar, let me introduce myself. I am Adair of Wígat," he said in a cheerful, joking tone, making a little bow. "I am the Raiders' best scout (though Tel-bein gives me a run for that title), and I am acknowledged as the Raiders' best cobbler, 'cause I'm their *only* cobbler. And *you,* our commander told me, are in dire need of a new pair of boots."

Skylark couldn't help laughing. "That I am. They cut my boots to ribbons. This deprived me of the satisfaction of roasting them."

"Ah. A sad tale. Though roasted boots are not very tasty, I can assure you, since I've had occasion to try them. I am going to make you a pair custom to your feet that will feel like the softest silk and never cause you a moment's pain. How's that for an offer?"

"I would be forever in your debt."

"I'm sure we can think of some way for you to repay that debt." The flirtation in his tone was light enough not to be ribald, but unambiguous.

Skylark felt her cheeks flushing.

"As it please you, Milady Duchess, I need to get a rough estimate of the size of your feet to start cutting the leather. I brought some measuring tools, though we'll wait until you are completely healed up for exact measurements."

Skylark allowed him to measure her feet, ankles, and calves. He hummed as he did so and seemed in no hurry.

"Why aren't you out with the others?" she asked, to turn the subject.

"I was the one who found the target, so the commander ordered me to get some rest. Scouts often work ahead of the battle. And these days Commander Thalen always leaves some people behind to keep camp and prepare for the casualties."

"When will they be back?"

"Depends. The wounded will return first. The rest of the Raiders will trickle in singly, the better not to be followed."

Adair sat down next to her. "I was out searching again for a sweet-water spring, like the one in this ravine. I found one this time, but it had waned to just a swamp, not running strong enough for us to use as a second camp. On my way back, though, I cut to the north, and I saw in the distance, as pretty as you please, a sizeable Oro town. And in the middle, ruling the view, I spy a fuckin' enormous Citadel of Flames. Commander wants to burn these to the ground. So, for a day and night I hid in a gully and watched to see how well the town was guarded, and then I scurried back here.

"Only to find out that we had taken on a new recruit in my absence. And a pretty one at that! I have heard a bit about you: won't you tell me your story? I especially want to hear about them 'evil' boots."

Skylark laughed. She told Adair her story from the Sweetmeadow raid onward, being very careful to tell him the same things she had told others. He listened so attentively that she found herself confessing to him more detail about how these events affected her:

how shocked she was by the rapes; how troublesome and miserable the children were; and how frightened she was when the Pellish caravan drivers tried to steal them. And then her deep loneliness, hunger, and pain during her solitary trek. Adair turned out to be a great listener, since he nodded in all the right places, clucked with sympathy, and threw his head back to laugh about the goat piss. He had a twinkle in his eye and the nicest white teeth.

For the first time in her life, Skylark felt the urge to confide in someone about her true identity. She had to bite the words back.

Skylark asked how he happened to be here and how he became a scout. He had grown up in a woodland village where all the children's games had involved hiding in the trees. His father had apprenticed him to a traveling cobbler, and for a while he liked the work, and then he tired of it. When he was seventeen he had run off.

As they sat talking, FireSky rumbled loudly. It belched a plume of lava and ash high up into the sky. Adair sprang to his feet to check if this was the precursor to a larger eruption, but the mountain spoke no further.

"What do you think?" Skylark asked him.

"Oh, just a little indigestion," he answered with breezy confidence.

Cook strode up to them carrying a large sack. "That woke us up, didn't it?" He said to Adair, "Don't you want to ride to the front of the ravine to watch for the wounded? Skylark, I need you to cut up these mushrooms."

Clearly, Cook had decided it was high time to break up this growing intimacy. Adair took the interruption good-naturedly.

"Just so everybody knows that I spent half a day on hands and knees, harvesting those mushrooms. I expect a double portion tonight for me and milady." He winked at her and glided off, his own boots noiseless on the ground.

Cook watched him go. "He's a charmer, that one," he commented neutrally.

Skylark was looking down at the mushrooms when a large shadow passed overhead. The eagle settled a few paces from her.

Your Majesty. How art thy wounded claws?

They are healing. It is good of you to pay me this visit, Lord of the Skies.

Yes. One now takes an interest in thee and thy flock. One watched a battle between men a few turns ago. Wouldst thou tell the humans not to burn dead aurochs or horses? We would feast on them.

Of course. Could you tell who won the battle?

Thy nest mates. They slew many of the other nest. And started a large fire.

Lord of the Skies, do you know of another water spring where the water is safe? A place like this where people and horses can hide?

One knows all the sweet water in these mountains.

Are such springs far from here?

Far? One does not understand thee.

Lord of the Skies, do you know the distance a horse travels in a day?

Sometimes horses go fast; sometimes they hardly move at all.

Yes, and they go slowly if they have to climb up mountains. But can you think of any hidden nests that have sweet water within one or two 'horse-days' of here?

One has never considered water as separated by 'horse-days.' One will fly to one's water sources, considering thy need.

That would be extremely kind of you. Could you also find hawks that would serve me, who would watch the movements of the other men for me? I would not think of asking you to do such a chore, but perchance you could select some lesser birds?

Thou art full of requests, Little Majesty. Look skyward in the morn. The eagle flew off.

Skylark had finished the mushrooms by the time Cook reappeared. She told him the eagle's report on the battle, and they shared the news with Cerf. Cook had made just a small batch of corn fritters for the four of them. He poured some plum preserves on top.

"Waiting behind is one of the hardest things," he said morosely.

"Commander makes us take turns. Each of us would prefer to be out with the action rather than hanging back in suspense, not knowing who's been wounded or who's been kilt. We have lost some grand chaps already. Grand chaps. Each of 'em."

"I find it helps to keep my mind on my work," said Cerf. "After I saw to the picketed horses I've been boiling my knives and needles and readying all my tools. Got lanterns to prepare now, as it's clear they won't be back until dark. Can you hold a lantern steady, Skylark, if Cook sets you next to someone? You won't faint at the sight of blood, will you?"

"I can help—I want to help. That's why I am here." Skylark had never seen anyone badly injured, but since she was supposed to have survived the raid at Sweetmeadow, she couldn't admit this.

Cook said, "I'll get a mess of mushroom soup prepared. At the first sign of their return I'll put the kettle in the coals. Them that ain't injured will be hungry. Hungry from all the hard work of riding and fighting, and hungry because cheating death one more time leaves you needing good eats."

Cerf had just readied his lanterns when Adair came riding in at a gallop leading a horse carrying an injured rider slumped over. A few minutes later Eli-anna splashed up the creek, riding double with a figure gushing blood. Then more injured streamed in.

With practiced routine, Cerf had each casualty laid out on pallets in the infirmary tent and suspended a big lantern from the tent pole. The Raiders who were hale fetched clean water to wash the wounds. Cerf prioritized the cases and set to work. Cook moved Skylark, kneeling on a blanket, to wherever Cerf wanted her to hold a second lantern. Skylark barely recognized the boy who had gotten her potatoes and a clean shirt. His brown face had lost all color; his clothing was caked with black blood; his left arm missing. Cerf sewed closed a jagged flap of skin and then burned the area with a hot knife. The smell made vomit rise in her throat, but she managed to remain stoic.

Outside the tent and down the canyon, a horse screaming in fear distracted Skylark. She felt physical relief when the screaming quieted.

Holding a lantern up is a simple task, but her arms started to tire and cramp. When Cook moved her to the next patient he kneaded her shoulders for a blessed moment in his big strong hands. When, despite all her efforts, her arms started trembling, Cerf called out, "I need a new lantern holder; this one's used up." Ooma, looking unwounded but grim, took the lantern from Skylark.

Cook was busy, feeding the survivors and providing tisane to those helping with the nursing or the horses. So Kran, the man who had captured her, slung Skylark on her stomach over his shoulder, holding onto the back of her legs, and carried her to her bedroll.

"How many died? How many injured?" she asked his broad, sweaty, slightly sooty back.

"Two dead outright. Lots injured. I dunno how many is bad off. We'll see in the light. Cerf's an awful good healer, but he can't save 'em all."

"The commander?"

"He's not back yet."

Though it was past midnight, Skylark could not sleep. The blood, the moans of pain, and the sense of emergency haunted her. She called Maki to her.

Has the commander returned? Is he all right?

Hurting, but not bleeding.

Despite herself, she saw the drops of water slowly dripping down the commander's bare neck, and she felt his touch as he guided her to the stool. She barely knew the man, but she felt completely invested in his welfare.

Will you stay with me awhile? she asked the dog.

As thou wish. Unless master calls one to guard the ravine entrance.

Why? Were the Raiders followed?

Not this time. If their enemy had scent hounds . . .

Maki's instinct was astute. They had stayed hidden this long only because the Oros did not have dogs. She would have to talk to Commander Thalen about making it a priority to kill any Oro dogs they spotted.

Eli-anna approached, silent as a shadow. She sat on her bedroll, her upper body shaking. Skylark wiggled on her rear, using her elbows as leverage, until she was close enough to reach out to the other woman. Eli-anna let Skylark take her hand. When Skylark knew for certain that the Mellie woman was weeping, she laced her arm around her back. Eventually, she persuaded Eli-anna to lie down.

As Skylark was drifting off she felt someone lift her feet and elevate them on top of a saddle. It was probably Eli-anna—except it couldn't have been, because she still held her hand.

27

Androvale

Duke Naven and his wife were shocked when a messenger arrived giving them notice that Lord Matwyck's son, Marcot, intended to visit them on the morrow.

"I wonder if he is like his father," Naven fretted. "Is he going to count our heads of cattle and look at my books, and raise his eyebrows at me, trying to find me out guilty?"

"Mayhap he will be more like his mother, with amber hair and a gracious manner," said the duchess. "You forget that I met Lady Tirinella at the Election Fest, and was most impressed with her. A lovely lady indeed. The son must be grown. Would he do for our Alavena? Actually, I wouldn't mind if he chooses any one of our girls."

"Don't go setting your cap for him as a son-in-marriage before we find out what kind of man he is," said the duke. "I'll leave you to finish your meal and dream of gowns; I must talk to my chamberlain."

Attended by a small escort, Marcot arrived at the manor house in the afternoon of the next day. The duke was relieved that the young man was nothing like Lord Matwyck; he had softer features, and his gray eyes were gentle. His hair was brown on the sides, but amber on the top, and the palace barber had made the most of this by cutting the sides short and leaving the top covered with long and wavy curls.

"I trust I am not disturbing the peace of your household," said Marcot. "And regret that I didn't send notice of my visit sooner. The truth is that I am traveling the duchies with no definite plan; I rarely know where I shall be from one moment to the next."

He turned to the duchess. "Pray do not fuss on my account. I need no elegance and no fine feasts. I am not the Lord Regent, merely his kinsman."

"You are very welcome, Lordling," said Duke Naven, and found himself meaning the words. "Are you traveling on business or for pleasure?"

"Actually, I'm traveling for education. I have seen so little of Weirandale in my life, and I dislike the tedium of court. I have been enjoying traversing the land and learning about the duchies."

"Ah, well then! I could talk to you about Androvale for days. I'm sure it is the loveliest and best of the eleven. Would you care to see my new barns or taste this year's fresh strawberry wine?"

"Fie, my lord husband!" said the duchess. "Won't you let an over-heated traveler wash the dust from his throat afore you take him tramping in your beloved fields and barns? Lordling Marcot, you are welcome here indeed. How fares your lady mother?"

"Do you know my mother?" he asked eagerly.

"Aye, though not a close acquaintance. We met in Cascada some years ago."

His face fell a little. "My lady mother is but poorly. 'Tis another reason I travel."

Seeing a shadow on the young man's face, the duke said, "Lordling, let our home be your home. Come, come, I will give you a chance to freshen up, and a glass of my famous strawberry wine, and *then* take you on a tour."

The duke took the measure of the man through the circuit of his holdings. Marcot showed genuine interest in Naven's property and plans for future improvements. He also shared information on farming methods he had seen in his tour of the Western Duchies. They had quite a long—and to Naven, fascinating—chat about fertilization and irrigation. Marcot agreed with him that the key point was to get the water to the roots, not the leaves.

At the evening meal (Naven noticed that his two eldest daughters were garbed in their newest dresses), the young man was polite but not in the least flirtatious. Marcot stressed that he hoped he would be treated like a member of the family and asked Naven's youngest two if they would oblige him with a game of Oblongs and Squares after supper.

Ah, thought the duke. *If he has been traveling to each of the duchies he has had many a duchette paraded before him. He has learned to deflect the attention in a gentlemanly way. Good. I would hate for my girls to have Matwyck as their father-in-marriage, even if the son is a catch.*

Marcot stayed at the manor house for three days. On the third, fearing their guest might be growing bored and wanting to show him more of Androvale, Duke Naven offered to take him on a ride through the countryside. The lordling agreed. Indeed, in the morning he made an appearance dressed down in unprepossessing clothes, even going so far as to cover up his amber hair. He explained that country people were more chatty with him if he laid aside his normal garb.

They rode through Anders Wood, admiring the stands of hardwood, listening to the birdcalls, and enjoying the coolness in the summer's heat. Naven then led his guest through several farming hamlets, talking to the locals about soil conditions and the roads, tithes, cattle diseases, and tomato blights.

Most of the farm families invited them in to sample their ale, cheese, or garden harvest. Marcot appreciated their hospitality, praised their goods, patted their infants, and made a fuss over their prized poultry. Naven's people would be pleased with *this* visitor from Cascada.

In the late afternoon, Naven steered the way to Wyndton.

"There is a householder here I visit regularly," explained the duke. "The missus is a weaver, truly one of the best in Weirandale. Mayhap she has something up on her loom today. Besides, I look in whenever I be in town; I take an interest in the family since the father died."

Marcot was amenable.

"Missus?" called the duke as they rode into Stahlia's yard.

Duke Naven had always somewhat fancied Stahlia (though of course he would never poach his man's wife—besides, he had enough trouble maneuvering between the two paramours he already juggled); today he thought she looked older and more care-worn than when he last saw her, which helped him substitute concern for attraction. He was gratified at how happy she was to greet her unexpected guests. She showed them the tapestry she was currently working on, which was her rendering of Queen Cressa leading the Allied Fleet against the Pellish pirates. Naven was struck by the craft and artistry of the piece, which showed the queen, with a determined expression, holding her sword aloft at the bow of her warship, flanked by her consort and her brother, the waves high and angry and the sun piercing through clouds.

"Stirring, don't you think?" Naven turned to Lordling Marcot.

"Oh, indeed!" Marcot enthused.

Duke Naven inquired how the family was faring and was satisfied that they had all they needed, especially since the daughter had opened a school to teach dancing and was bringing in a small second income. The party had moved into the yard, saying their farewells, when one of the lordling's guards interrupted, "A rider nears."

"'Tis only my daughter, returning from Wyndton," said the missus quickly, as if the guards would react too protectively.

Percia, surprised to see visitors, rode up on a chestnut gelding. One of the guards held the horse's head; Marcot politely sprang to offer the young woman a hand down from her saddle. Naven saw the girl look flustered at the handsome young stranger's attentiveness.

"Percia, my lass," said Duke Naven, "may I present Lordling Marcot, a young acquaintance from Cascada. Marcot, 'tis my honor to introduce you to Maid Percia, the daughter of Wilim and Stahlia, and the fairest dancer in my duchy."

The young people exchanged a few words. Naven didn't listen to their talk but noticed their demeanors; Marcot, who had been calm and self-possessed during all other visits, suddenly stumbled over his words. Percia's eyelashes fluttered as she looked down. Duke Naven rubbed his hands with a bit of roguish glee.

"On second thought," said Duke Naven to Stahlia. "You offered us mead some moments ago? I do feel a mite dry, and the refreshment would not taste amiss before our long ride back."

He offered Missus Stahlia his arm. This perforce led Lordling Marcot to offer his arm to the pretty young woman.

28

Ink Creek Canyon

*Tally: 18 – 1 (Britmank) + 1 (Skylark) – 2 (Cookie and
Tel-bein) = 16
Horses: 22 (only 18 in camp—two packhorses gone with
Wareth)*

Thalen woke the morning after the raid with a foul taste in his
mouth and a pounding headache. At first, confused, he thought he
had taken a blow to the head. Then when he tried to sit up the piercing pain reminded him that the wallop had been to the back of his
ribs, and he had doctored himself with too much brandy rather than
pull Cerf away from Raiders with life-threatening injuries.

"Tristo!!" he called. No response. "Tristo!" he yelled louder, and
with ill temper. His aide did not enter his tent; Eli-anna did. Thalen
looked at her befuddled and then the image of the boy's arm, shorn
off right below the shoulder, came rushing back to him.

"Did he survive?" Thalen choked out.

Eli-anna nodded. He looked at her more closely, realizing that
her face had changed. *Tel-bein.*

Despite his agony, Thalen rose, unsteadily, and reached for Eli-anna. He clasped her two hands within his larger ones and stared into her eyes.

"Your uncle was a valiant man, a skilled scout, and a hero for his people. His arrows saved the mission yesterday. He will be sorely missed and forever honored in our hearts."

Eli-anna nodded, her eyes brimming with tears, and she then looked away.

"We all weep over our losses, Eli-anna," Thalen sighed. "They deserve our tears.

"Now. I need to tour the camp. Yet I don't want the men to see me like this. Will you help me? I need hot water, tisane, and a bandage large enough to wind around my chest."

She nodded and melted away. Thalen sat slumped in his chair with his head in his hands. *Two. Tel-bein and Cookie. Tel-bein is the worst loss militarily, but losing Cookie will devastate morale.*

He relived the Battle of Fûli in his mind. They had reached the town before sunrise. Thalen had split the Raiders into three squads and sent them into position. They had struck a little shy of midday.

The Raiders had let the women and the few children flee, but they had killed two dozen men and soldiers in confused hand-to-hand fighting in the streets—fighting that seemed to go on for hours because the villagers knew how to use their buildings to their advantage. Thalen himself had crossed swords a dozen times with a stalwart Oro officer, but ultimately Kambey's training had prevailed; he had drawn the poor bastard closer with an off-balance feint and then struck the killing blow.

The big prize Thalen had aimed for was not the Oros' miserable lives, but rather their Citadel of Flames. This huge, hexagonal stone structure sat on the top of a rise, making it highly visible for leagues. The flames of rubies and other jewels embedded in exterior mosaics glowed when struck by light.

Once the Raiders secured the town, Thalen tended the wounded—

including Tristo, who had lost an arm!—and dispersed the men, asking only Kambey to stay with him. Inside the citadel he tried to catalogue the details and their significance. A mosaic of eight peaks decorated one wall, while the wall across from it showed a city dominated by a large tower. Flames of beaten gold and silver soared above both mountains and tower. In the front of the church he saw an altar of coals, still glowing red. On the tenet that he should always gather all the information about his enemies that he could, Thalen grabbed an ornate religious tome lying open on a pedestal near the altar.

After this survey, Thalen and Kambey carried in Cookie's and Tel-bein's bodies, laying them down gently and closing their eyes. Near the coals they found stores of oil. Splashing the oil around the church made it easy to send the building up in a towering pyre, a fitting honor to their fallen friends.

As Thalen backed away from the heat, astonished at the size of the conflagration, an Oro woman snuck up on him from a side street and clobbered him with an axe handle in the back.

Thalen had doubled over; a second blow to his head might have finished him. But Kambey dispatched his assailant with one thrust of his sword. With Kambey's help, Thalen was barely able to get atop Dishwater. The ride home had been a blur of misery, but he had sworn his sergeant to secrecy for the night.

He had left survivors this time: people who could describe the Raiders. Even so, and even though an Oro woman had almost killed him, he felt that sparing the women, children, and enemy wounded had been the right thing to do. But what kind of life had he left them? A life where half their relatives were gone and their church burnt to the ground. Would it have been more merciful to put an end to them?

Eli-anna returned, and Thalen pulled himself into an upright position. She brought a basin of hot water and a mug of tisane. She shaved and washed Thalen herself. He could not move enough to get his arms out of yesterday's shirt, crusted with sweat, smoke, and ash, and splattered with blood, so Eli-anna drew her knife and cut it off him. Thalen could only turn his neck enough to catch a glimpse of the red-and-purple bruising on his back. Eli-anna produced one of Cookie's aprons that she had also fetched, winding it around Thalen's torso tightly as he pressed his lips together. He could not move his arms enough to put on another shirt, so she grabbed his cloak and fastened it around his neck.

Thalen nodded his thanks at her and strode out of his tent with as much dignity as he could muster. He went first to check on the wounded in the infirmary tent. Cerf, eyes bloodshot, teetering on his feet, took his commander around the bedrolls. Tristo still lived, though in a deep, poppy-induced sleep. Ooma sat nearby, gripping Tristo's one remaining hand tightly. The blade that had struck Jothile in the neck had miraculously missed all major arteries, and a line of neat, black stitches marched from ear to collarbone. Vatuxen, who had taken a pike deep into his chest, lolled unconscious; Cerf told Thalen that it was likely he would not survive.

Thalen stroked Vatuxen's hair back off his forehead. "Well done, Vatuxen," he said with a catch in his voice. "Really. Couldn't have done it without you."

Then his next duty was to comfort the living. Thalen sought out Cook, who obviously already knew his wife had fallen. Cook was sitting a ways apart from everyone, slowly scraping the burned soup off the bottom of a pot.

"Moorvale, she was a wonder," Thalen said. "We all knew that, from the very beginning, from that first day in Yosta. And then crossing the Iron River. If we needed any more proof, we had it yesterday, when she rushed in to rescue Tristo. The boy had lost his arm to an Oro sword and was just about to lose his head, when Cookie dived for the man's ankles and sent him sprawling. Before we could reach them, another Oro had gotten to her. It was quick— I'm not just saying that to comfort you. She was gone before I lifted her from the ground. She did *not* suffer. Not one minute.

"Kran and Ooma saw this too; you can ask them if you want confirmation. And you should know this: Kran killed the Oro who took Cookie from us, while Ooma gutted the man who maimed Tristo. So our vengeance was swift and thorough."

Cook made no response. Thalen stood a long moment with his hand on his shoulder, giving him a chance to talk or not. Then he left him to grieve in his own way.

Thalen forced himself to eat a bowl of lumpy porridge, deducing that someone unskilled had boiled it this morning. Afterward he went back to sit by Tristo; Ooma shifted over to make room for him near the pallet. Tristo looked ghastly, but his chest still rose and fell in a strong rhythm. Thalen thought that if he could somehow save this youngster, that would make up for helplessly watching Harthen die. He knew this bargain was totally irrational, but he placed his hand on the boy's heart, willing it to keep beating.

After a time he returned to his tent and sent for Kambey, who showed up with stitches on the bridge of his nose, his chin, the backs of his hands, and possibly other places hidden by his clothing.

"We're down to sixteen—*if* you count the new girl and assume that Wareth and Eldie survive," Thalen muttered. "Fifteen, once Vatuxen dies. And most of us not fit to fight or ride. The citadel was a prize target, but we paid for it. I wish I knew if this gamble has paid off, if the Oro forces have left the Free States."

"Wareth's due back any day. And he might be bringing reinforcements."

Thalen answered grimly, "*If* he returns. If he doesn't we will soon be out of food."

Kambey added, with gallows humor, "Look at it this way. Fewer mouths to feed, specially since we are down a cook."

Thalen was in too much pain for any kind of humor. "Should we have brought the bodies back? Feels wrong, not to have funerals this time."

"Commander, we are too few now, too few to fetch bodies back and too few to dig the graves. Too few, too injured, to have proper funerals. Leave off this second-guessing."

Thalen said, "We can only bank on the Oros' stupidity so long. One day soon they are going to track us back here, and we'll be caught like rats in a trap. We need a new camp, away from our last targets. Maybe we need to move farther into the Iron Valley. But we've lost one of our best scouts. I am out of ideas on how to find fresh water, and we can't go bumbling around settlements full of Oros without a set destination or hideout."

Kambey said, "You need some doctoring. I'm going to fetch Cerf."

Soon Cerf stepped in the tent, unwrapped the apron, and poked around Thalen's ribs.

"Most of this ugly swelling is just bruising," he pronounced. "The blow hit a well-muscled area. But I'd wager one or two of your ribs are cracked."

"How long until I can ride or fight?"

"Two, three weeks until you can ride at more than a walk without risk of setback. It will be at least six weeks until the bones knit well enough for you to use that arm."

"*Six weeks?*"

"Sorry, no one can make bone knit faster."

"How long will it pain like this? My mind is clouded."

"Let me give you some milk of the poppy."

"I don't want to be drugged. I need my wits about me."

Cerf asked, "Can you think through the pain?"

"Not really," Thalen admitted.

"I'll give you half a dose for now," said Cerf, "but you'll need more later, and then I won't put up with any arguments."

After swallowing the liquid Thalen felt the shooting pain with each breath ease some. He closed his eyes in relief. "Better. Now, I order you to get some rest, Cerf. You're no good to your patients in this condition."

Cerf barked a laugh. "Not true. I was just some good to *you*. Nonetheless, I am off to catch some sleep."

Thalen took a woozy turn around the camp to show himself to the men and check on conditions. Gentain and Fedak were working on the horses. In the crisis last night, many had not been seen to properly. Thalen felt a flash of guilt for just tumbling off Dishwater and neglecting even to remove his saddle.

The Alpetar girl sat astride the small gray filly they had previously used mostly as a pack animal, with her feet covered by too-large wool hose.

She was rubbing horses' noses and talking to them softly. She called out to Gentain, who stood nearby mixing a concoction, "What do you call this one with the white blaze?"

He looked up from his work. "That's Pastry."

"Pastry's cinch has been too loose; it chafed her belly."

"Right," he answered.

She called out again. "This big bay, she needs a gentler rider. Whoever's been riding her is scaring her more than the Oros do."

Gentain looked up from the liniment he was slathering around the inflamed knee of the brown horse named Funnel. "The horse is Sandy; the rider's Kran. He rides horses as if they were aurochs. I give up on which mount to give him."

The girl considered. She nudged her mare around the milling herd and stopped before a black horse. "Have you tried this one?"

"Sulky Sukie. Oh, she's a handful, that one. Kicks and bites, but she won't show her teeth to me, so often I ride her myself."

"If she bit Kran that would teach him not to kick so hard or rein in so abruptly. These two would be a match for one another. And the one you're tending now gets jealous whenever you ride Sukie."

Probably the poppy juice had made Thalen a bit giddy, because he laughed aloud at this. The noise called attention to his presence, though, and everyone saluted him.

"Gentain, did you care for Dish?" Thalen asked. "I neglected him last night."

"Aye, Commander. Washed the soot off him too. See? He's no worse for wear. And I've got the book you stashed in your saddlebag whenever you want it."

Thalen was relieved. "Report."

Gentain replied, "Two horses didn't return from this raid. Apple Pie—such a sweet gal!—and Quackers—who isn't the worst loss. But we will have the whole string back in fighting shape within a week. Gotta bring down this inflamed tendon here."

Gentain moved closer to Thalen and spoke to him in a low tone. "Sir, when Skylark asks the horses to stand still whilst we doctor them, they stand like a statue. I ain't never seen the like. Can you assign her to help me with the string?"

Thalen looked at the Alpetar girl. He had been planning to talk to her about something, but his cloudy haze wouldn't let him remember what. "Skylark," he called her over. "Report."

"Yes, sir." She rode the filly over to where Thalen stood. "Sir, I have a corps of six long-tailed hawks ready and waiting instructions. You could dispatch them to watch the mouth of the ravine and give your men more rest rather than waste them on guard duty. I have also sent the eagle to measure the distance between here and other safe water in order to give you a choice of alternate camps. I hope I haven't overstepped. The biggest difficulty I am having is getting birds to understand distance in human terms."

Thalen stared at her, frowning, his fogged mind taking a few beats to catch up to the meaning of her statements.

"Gentain, I am afraid you will have to share this Raider. I need her. Send Fedak to find Kambey and tell him to meet us by the cook fire. Skylark, ride your mare there and have Cook set you up as before."

Thalen took advantage of the short walk through the campground to pull his muddled thoughts together. Thalen and Kambey conferred with Skylark over a pot of burnt tisane and some soda biscuits. She sent her hawks out. Thalen didn't really believe her promises, but he saw no harm in giving them a try.

"Could the eagle fly to Drintoolia?" Thalen asked. "Could he check if any big ships have docked? What I want to know more than anything is if our attacks have prompted the Magi to call back the army occupying the Free States."

"I will ask him when he visits next."

Thalen's ribs had rebuilt their fierce pain. He looked in on Tristo once more and then sent Eli-anna to Cerf's bedroll for another dose of painkiller. Either this was something stronger than before, or his limited activity had worn him out, because after he took the medicine, Thalen's pain floated away and he collapsed on his stomach on his camp bed.

Kambey's pushing through the tent flaps woke him. Kambey gestured with his palms to stay lying still and pulled the stool up near the head of the bed. He rubbed his hands and looked very pleased with himself.

"Commander, I have buckets of good news. Buckets! That Alpie girl—she's like a Magi herself. Or a sorceress. I mean, really, she's uncanny. The hawks came back almost immediately after you went to sleep. They've spotted Wareth! As far as that bird girl can figure, seven people and supplies will be here late tonight. Also, the eagle just came back with two white owls for night guard duty. Owls as guards! And there's more! The eagle will return in the morning to talk to you both about water and about the survey of Drintoolia."

Thalen rubbed his eyes. "Things were looking pretty black there, old friend."

"Aye," agreed Kambey.

"Tristo?"

Kambey smiled from ear to ear. "Actually, forget all this other news. *He* is why I disturbed you. Opened his eyes a few minutes ago and asked for potatoes."

Thalen shook his head with wonderment.

Kambey rose. "Someone will fetch you some supper in a bit. Since Wareth's been spotted, Cook went whole hog. Maybe it's good for him to be busy. Then Cerf will be in to check on you."

His healer came in just as Thalen, idly rereading *A Leader's Duties* in his head, was finishing his food.

"Good to see you eating, sir. No nausea, no vomiting, I take it?"

"No. How are the injured, Cerf?"

"You mean the *other injured,* sir. You're on the casualty list too," his healer replied a little huffily. "Vatuxen's slipped lower; he won't last the night. Adair is now keeping the deathwatch. But everyone else is on the mend."

Cerf untied the bandage, prodded and poked, and retied it straight and tight. "Now, I am going to give you more milk of the poppy, because most everything hurts worst in the night. We'll start easing off in a day or two."

"Leave it on the table and first have someone carry Skylark in to see me. I'll take it after I've had a word with her."

Kambey brought the girl clinging to his back like a child riding a horse. He dropped her on the stool and placed the upended basin on the ground to serve as a clean footrest, keeping her feet off the dirt.

Thalen looked at this young woman in the flickering lantern light. Someone had given her a black-and-white armband, which she had tied on her left arm. In addition to being shorter than average, she was slender, without womanly curves. He noticed for the first time that her brown brows were arched and velvety and her lashes long and full. They didn't match the ugly straw shade of her mop but he recalled from his reading that Old Colors only showed in some men's beards and in the hair of the top of one's head. Whether naturally or because of her weight loss, cheekbones showed through skin without baby fat. Her taffy-colored skin was weather-chapped and her lips peeling.

Automatically, the student in him wished he could go through the library holdings in Alpetar. A small country, mostly of goatherds, which had stayed out of the battles for Power. No army to speak of and no central government. Alpies worship the Sun that warms their high grazing grounds. As for Magic . . .

She met his gaze steadily, but her eyes gave nothing away. Their silence had grown long.

"Report," he ordered, because it was the first word that came into his head.

She told him things he had already heard and added more details about the owls.

"You like owls?"

"When I was a girl there was an owl, Speckles, I counted as a friend. I am really pleased to have these two guarding us. Owls will eat corn from my hand. If corn is included in the new supplies, may I treat them?"

"Sure."

A long pause stretched between them. Thalen kept staring into her eyes, weighing her truthfulness against all his knowledge and instinct.

"Will there be anything else, sir?"

Thalen spoke on top of her, "I know you have secrets, Skylark. What I have to know is, will they affect my men or my mission?"

"Commander," she answered, "I want what you want, to take vengeance on the Oros. They killed my kin and destroyed my country. You and your men have naught to fear from me. You trusted me, fed me, and nursed me when I was close to all in. I sought you out to lend my Talents to your cause."

This woman must be blessed by the Alpie Sun Spirit with some manner of Magic. (Oh, Deganah, forgive me for arguing with you so pigheadedly.) But she is not working for the Oros.

"All right, then."

After Kambey carried her off, Thalen drank down his medicine, which dulled not only the roaring pain in his back but also the piercing new pain in his heart over Tel-bein, Cookie, and Vatuxen, and the old wounds from the many losses that he always carried about with him. He blew out his lantern. He dreamt of being at midmeal with all of his family, laughing at one of Harthen's pranks. His mother was wearing her flowered hat at the table, which was quite peculiar, but she smiled at him and brushed his hair off his forehead.

Tally: 16 (assuming Wareth and Eldie live) — Vatuxen = 15
Horses: unknown

29

Drintoolia, the Coast of Melladrin

Sumroth expected his Free States trading ship, flying the Oromondian flag and the Authority Firebolt, to be met by Brigadier Chumelle, whom he had left in charge of Drintoolia, the largest harbor on the coast of Melladrin. He did not expect one of the Magi to be personally awaiting him in his black palanquin encrusted with "3"s formed from rubies. He brushed his hands down his uniform and fluffed his hair up as he marched to the glittering conveyance.

The general knew Three from his escort trip to the Pellish coast so many years ago. The years had not been good to him; though his eyes still burned brightly, the Magi had lost all his hair, and sores studded his lips. Instead of mitigating his menace, his disfigurement added to it.

"Your Divinity," Sumroth bowed. "I am honored you have met me at the ship."

"Honoring you was the last thing on Our mind, General," Three sniped. "Oh, We know you conquered Melladrin and the infidel Free States. All hail the great conquering hero! Yet this goes for naught, if while the Protectors are drinking wine and rutting with savages in Sutterdam, *terrorists have entered the Land!*"

Sumroth had not worked so hard and dutifully to be berated by a priest who had never held a halberd. Even a Magi who could incinerate him on the spot.

"I'd expect, Divinity," he responded coldly, "your magical Powers are enough to counter any threat to the Land. Since you have so little respect for the Protectors, you have come to tell me that our voyage has been in vain, and we should return whence we came?"

Three's mouth fell open, revealing that white, pus-filled sores covered every inch of his tongue and inner cheeks. With effort, Sumroth kept his face impassive.

That Three mastered his fury at being spoken to in this manner indicated how concerned the Eight must be. "General, let us start again," the Magi said. "Of course the Eight are proud of the achievements of our blessed Protectors, dearest to our hearts, the pride of Oromondo. We look forward to chanting blessings in thy name to Pozhar. However, Three has met your boat because time presses and We want most urgently to consult with a man of your experience. Pray, sit beside Three."

Sumroth dearly wanted to flee in any other direction, but he mastered himself to climb inside the palanquin, sensible of the honor granted to him.

"How long will it take to get the Protectors off those boats and marching?" the Magi asked.

"*Disembarking* six thousand from *ships,*" Sumroth stressed the words, for he was proud of learning a pinch of maritime terminology in Sutterdam, "should take all night. We also brought stores of food in large bales. Unloading the cargo, parceling foodstuffs for Protectors to carry, and hitching up aurochs wagons for the supplies we ferried across the sea to feed the Land will take even more time. We should be ready to march in . . . oh, three days' time."

"Not fast enough!" cried Three, reverting to his louder and critical tone. "Did you bring any horses?"

"Horses die quickly in Oromondo, as well you know, Divinity. I brought only enough for myself and my senior officers, whose accomplishments are such that we should no longer suffer the indignities of riding on aurochs."

"How many horses?" Three pressed.

Sumroth did not know, but he was unwilling to admit this to Three. "Oh, some dozens." He airily waved his hand.

"We want you to gather your best fighters and your best hunters of men, mount them on these horses, and leave with Us immediately. Three, himself, will ride one of your horses."

"Leave the bulk of the army behind? Leave the food behind?"

"Yes. We cannot wait for them to be ready to march. They can follow. You must have a capable brigadier to lead them? They won't get lost on their way to the Mouth of the Mountains?"

"What's the urgency, Your Divinity?" Sumroth furrowed his brow with confusion.

Three closed his eyes and sighed. "Three moons ago wagons were attacked and their Protectors slaughtered. Then post riders disappeared. We sent a regiment of Protectors safeguarded by Four, on her way to Fourcaster, to look into these raids. An enemy cut down Four. An arrow kilt her, inside the Land, before she could even defend herself!

"Then yestereve, We received a bird: these invaders have burned the Citadel of Flames at Fûli dedicated to FireMount. Burned our citadel!"

As most of his thoughts had bent toward seeing Zea, Sumroth had not given much consideration to these invaders during the voyage. If he'd pondered them at all, he'd assumed that his men would be chasing down a band of Mellies or Alpies who were taking advantage of the Protectors' thin ranks to raid from the borderlands. But

Fûli sat deep inside the Land; this could not be the work of a chance party of Mellies. The sacrilege disturbed the general sufficiently that he smothered his wrath over the Magi's haughty demeanor.

"You have hunted these invaders? You have seen them? Who are they?"

"We have found a few dead horses. No soldiers, no bodies. It is as if phantoms are committing these crimes. Moreover, six weeks ago Two had a vision. She said that a Power had entered the Land—a Power with the ability to drop Fire from the sky."

"That makes no sense," Sumroth said. "You Magi are the ones who can rain fire from the sky. I saw this that magnificent day on the Pellish coast, when you took down the Allied ships."

Three swallowed. "Some of Us believe these predations are the works of the ghosts of the Magi who signed the Treaty of Five Nations. That they may be angry We have broken their word. Some of Us believe this is a mistaken interpretation; We feel certain that this is a furtive invasion of earthly enemies. So. We need you to travel in great haste to the battle sites to investigate the cause. Such haste that Three himself will leave this palanquin behind and ride a horse. Once We know the cause there will be time enough for the Protectors and my sisters and brethren to squash it—if indeed the invaders be mortal."

"Do unquiet ghosts of men come back to walk the earth?" Sumroth asked doubtfully.

"We don't know," Three admitted. "But there is more Magic in the world than most scoffing people credit."

Sumroth swallowed, uneasy whether Three had read his mind. "I must give some orders. I will return shortly, Divinity." He exited the palanquin and found his high officers. He appointed a sixth-flamer as head of the main body of the army and told him to follow when the men, wagons, and supplies were in readiness. Locating which ship contained the horses proved more troublesome. They turned out to be stowed in three vessels that were currently waiting in the harbor for their turn to disembark. By dint of a great deal of yelling and cursing, Sumroth got the ship that was engaged in unloading to desist, row out of the way, and cede its position at the long wharf.

Sumroth returned to the Magi's palanquin. "The horses are coming, but it will take a little while to get sorted."

Finally, fifty horses were gathered near the quay and a crowd of Protectors were seeing to their needs. Now, Sumroth had to figure out how to choose their riders. Protectors had no training as hunters, trackers, or investigators.

The general turned to Brigadier Chumelle. "You have Mellie slaves and captives here in Drintoolia, I presume?"

Chumelle answered, "Only a few. Mellies never last long in captivity. They fight so to escape we have to kill them, or they starve themselves to death."

"I would question those you do have. In the meantime, work with my adjutants to choose about fifty men—the best riders and the smartest minds available."

As a city, Drintoolia was a wreck. Many of the buildings had fallen into rubble and a Ghibli Wind Mill stood in a central square with only wooden frames showing where its blades had once twirled. The few buildings that looked weatherproof had obviously been recently repaired by Chumelle and his troops. Sumroth had escorts lead him to the slave quarters. He found only three captives: one was ancient and frail; the second looked barely old enough to grow whiskers; the third was a real rascal, with a mop of light brown curls and calculating eyes.

Sumroth spoke to the rascal. "Do you want to earn your freedom, slave?"

The slave counted the tattoos above Sumroth's brow. "I would like to be free, High Officer, sir."

"I will give you your freedom if you perform a service for me."

"What service, High Officer, sir?"

"Some murderers have been killing innocents. I want you to help track them down."

"Here in Drintoolia, High Officer, sir? I could track the soldiers to their barracks easily enough."

"I am in too much of a hurry to bandy words with a slave. Do you want to get out of this stinking cell and work as a tracker, or do you want to stay here and starve?"

"I would rather not starve, High Officer, sir."

"Very well. Guards, unlock this cell. But tie his hands tightly. What is this piece of Mellie cheek called?"

The man answered himself. "My name is Eldo, High Officer, sir." And he flashed his rascal smile.

His officers had caught Sumroth's urgency, and with promptness they had chosen and readied the riders and horses.

As the sun sank lower in the sky, an odd grouping galloped southwest toward the Mouth of the Mountains: one Magi, one slave with hands bound in front, one general, and forty-seven of his fiercest soldiers.

30

The Scoláiríum

Rector Meakey sat on a fallen log, and the rest of the tutors sat in the mud in a cluster around Winka, the tavernkeep's young grand-daughter.

"They left, I tell ya," Winka insisted. "Two days ago. All the Oros left Latham. Umpah says they are 'deserting the provinces' and 'concatting their strength in the cities.'"

"'*Concentrating,*' my darling," Meakey corrected absently. "Does your grandfather know why?"

"Nah. But he waited two days to be sure they were really gone before sending me. They are really, truly gone."

Meakey stood up. "Then we will leave these caves and return to the Scoláiríum. This is fortune's blessing, as we would perish from tedium if we were to stay here much longer. Tutors, ladies, children, gather whatever we have here of value, and let us go home."

After more than half a year living in the woods, the procession's clothes were bedraggled and everyone's skin darker with rubbed-in grime. The campus that awaited them lay disordered and lifeless, but not otherwise overtly damaged. Hyllidore met them with tears running down his ruined face.

Meakey bid Hyllidore light the coal burner under the big water boiler for baths, knowing it would take hours to heat a quantity of water. In the meantime, she set all her people to sweeping and dusting their former quarters. The children made a beeline for the kitchen gardens, to see if any vegetables had survived untended, and then to the cellar storerooms, to check if any foodstuffs had been overlooked by Oro pillagers. Oros apparently did not care for olives; miraculously these stocks sat untouched. Their occupiers had also overlooked a cupboard full of sacks of buckwheat. By evening, the erstwhile forest-dwellers were bathed, dressed in clean clothes, and fortified by real food.

The following day, Meakey took a thorough tour of the campus. The empty laboratories proved to be in worse shape than the living quarters, with broken beakers and overturned shelves. Mice had overrun the tutors' offices, nibbling at books and parchment. Every surface in the kitchen, laundry building, and refectory sported a film of dirt, but otherwise these spaces waited undamaged.

Drawing in a deep breath, the headmaster entered the library. All the windows on the first floor had been smashed. In the center of the entrance rotunda sat a charred pile of the few books left behind when they emptied the library. Meakey found the scrawled profanities and lewd drawings on the marble walls more distressing than the loss of these stragglers.

The rector apportioned her followers into work crews: Irinia's crew would concentrate on the laboratories, Andreata's on Scholars' House, and she herself intended to see the Library of Humility scrubbed clean. Villagers came to help; their livelihood depended on the Scoláiríum, so the sooner this wealthy institution returned to normal, the sooner their lives might return to normal.

Ten days into restoring the Scoláiríum, an elderly woman riding a knock-kneed mule approached the front gates and asked for the rector. Meakey was pleased that she was able to receive her first visitor in her own office, now nearly restored to order, with two bowls of guppies on her desk (it being necessary, of course, to keep the females and males separate). Meakey herself wore earbobs made out of seahorses dyed purple; though slightly chipped, these lent her some of her former sparkle.

"So lovely to have a visitor! I am Rector Meakey. What can I do for you? And what can you do for us? Can you give us news of events in the rest of the Free States?"

The small woman was very elderly, with a shock of plum-colored hair above one ear mixed in with light brown. She was missing several of her teeth, which gave her mouth a puckered look. Her eyebrows straggled across her forehead, but underneath them her eyes gleamed bright.

"I have ridden here all the way around Clear Lake from Sutterdam," the visitor wheezed as she spoke. "I have a note that I am to entrust only to Rector Meakey."

"I am she," said Meakey, eagerly holding out her hand.

"So you say. But I am to give the note only to the person who can answer this question: 'The day you admitted a boy named Thalen to the Scoláiríum, *whom else* did you admit?'"

Meakey half whispered, "Gustie! And only our Gustie would have used 'whom.'"

She tore open the note but was crestfallen to discover she couldn't read a word because the message had been written in an ancient language. So she sent for Andreata, and for some wine for the woman who had traveled so far.

Tutor Andreata soon joined them in the rector's chamber. Scanning the note, Andreata said, "She wrote in Ancient Lorther." She haltingly read aloud, translating on the fly and not pausing to correct Gustie's errors.

¾ of Oros gone sucked away due to Thalen's battles. The remaining live in Yosta, Jutterdam, and Sutterdam. I am placed most fortunate at Command Top Place. I can free all the Sutterdam slaves and jailed people. However, I need a weapon of killing 100 Oro offcers at a dinner. You must fashion it excellent. Give to Mother Rellia. You can trust her. Make quick.

Andreata dropped the paper.

Meakey's smile stretched almost wide enough to reach her seahorse earbobs. "Don't be distressed, Andreata, even though the grammar leaves quite a bit to be desired in one of your star pupils. These are fabulous tidings. Our Gustie has a plan to kill many of the Oro officers and free the enslaved. One hopes that once Free States men are released from their imprisonment, they will deal with the remaining Oro soldiers."

Turning to her visitor she asked, "I assume you are this Mother Rellia? And the Defiance has a similar plan for Yosta and Jutterdam?"

Mother Rellia replied only, "This is very good wine."

The headmaster tapped her desktop with her fingernails. "What kind of weapon would kill every Oro and spare our Gustie or any other Free Stater in the room? And what do we have the capability of making in our current circumstances?

"Andreata, fetch the other tutors immediately to the main laboratory."

The scholars debated long into the evening, frequently rushing about to check on supplies or fetch a reference book. Ultimately, Meakey's own plan carried the day: she had enough stores of a paralytic jellyfish venom to poison eight score men. Even more importantly, because she had been working with this venom for many years, she had distilled a small amount of antidote. The antidote needed to be administered within five minutes of ingesting the poison before it made its way to the muscles working the lungs and the person suffocated.

"Mother Rellia, are you certain that you or someone can get into the banquet hall and deliver the antidote to our Gustie in time?" Meakey asked. "I would not offend you for all the treasures of Ennea Món, but you do not look particularly spry."

"No offense taken. I will find a spry and reliable substitute. For safety's sake, could you write back to Gustie everything she should know about this concoction in a note in that ancient tongue?"

Tutor Andreata was happy to do this. She wrote Gustie in Old Lorther that the venom needed to be delivered in a room temperature or cold liquid—heat would neutralize it.

Mother Rellia had not been stopped and searched on the way here, but for extra precaution Hyllidore fashioned a satchel with a false bottom to hold the vials. In the morning, they wished her on her way with prayers for the success of her mission, and buckwheat cakes wrapped in brown paper.

31

Ink Creek Canyon

In the morning, two days after the attack on the citadel in Fûli, Skylark lapped up the gossip around the porridge kettle that the commander's friend, Wareth, had ridden in during the night. He and Eli-anna's sister, Eldie, had had several close calls and had lost one horse in a fall off a steep embankment, but had managed to avoid all the Oro patrols. He had also brought five new men as reinforcements. Two of these turned out to be twin brothers that the commander had met before on some ferry. The news rippled through camp that Commander Thalen was overjoyed to find them again.

The commander's joy offset some of the anguish the troop suffered over Vatuxen's passing away.

A funeral made a grim welcome for the new Raiders. Cook wept throughout the short service, rubbing his face with his burn-scarred apron.

"We've lost so many cavalrymen," Cook choked out. "Brave chaps who fought to keep the States free. Literoy, Britmank, Rowe, Latof." He held up a finger as he said each name. "And now Vatuxen.

Vatuxen told me that he and Britmank had grown up in the same village and been chums since they were little lads."

The commander walked Cook some paces away and talked to him in a low voice.

A broad-shouldered man with curly brown hair and an open, smiling face strode over to Cinders. Skylark liked him immediately because he took the time to acknowledge her filly's greeting.

"Hey there, girl," he said, patting Cinders's neck. "I'm Wareth."

"Skylark," she said, leaning over to shake his hand. "I'm sorry I'm up here; my feet . . ."

"Oh, I've already heard the whole story," he grinned. Cinders nudged his chest, and he stroked her again. "I think Slown rode her originally. You've chosen well. She's a stout-hearted filly. Not as grand as my Custard," he said loyally, "but you're a good girl, aren't you now?" The horse snuffled against him.

"Skylark, I have a damn hard task because I have to tell Gentain about how Goldenrod slipped off a cliff. Even worse, I *gave away* one of his prizes, one of the horses he trained himself. I needed to make some recompense to the Mellies for all their help. They asked for a mare, and I gave them Acorn. Do you think Gentain will ever forgive me?"

"Will they treat Acorn well?"

"Oh, sure."

"Then Gentain will understand. He might even be relieved that she is away from the fighting."

Wareth grinned as if a load had lifted. "Better get this over with, then. See you around, new Raider."

Later in the morning, the eagle swooped in. He described the two closest water sources to Skylark. Together Adair and the commander studied maps, concluding that Adair would leave as soon as it was dark, with an owl as guide, to find these places and judge their suitability as new encampments.

Lord of the Skies, would you honor us with another exploration?

What didst thou do, Little Majesty, before thou hadst an eagle at thy beck and call?

I blundered blindly, Lord, and in great jeopardy.

This must be true. He nibbled at his folded wing feather. *What be it that thou wants to know this time?*

Skylark described the desire to find out if an Oromondo army had landed in Drintoolia and was on its way here. The eagle had never previously flown into Melladrin, but he understood what they were looking for in the harbor town.

Skylark asked Cook for a smoked fish as a token gift; the eagle snatched it from her hand. Then, opening his magnificent wings, he flew off to the northeast.

FireSky rumbled throughout the day, sending up more plumes of ash and smoke, making them all uneasy.

Before setting out on his new mission, Adair wanted to do a more exact fitting of Skylark's deerskin boots. Since her feet weren't totally healed, Skylark thought he was rushing the process a tad, but she rode Cinders over to the men's sleeping quarters. Adair's tools and the precut pieces of leather were at the foot of his bedroll. Skylark's feet were no longer swollen or bandaged, but she wore a dead Raider's thick hose to keep from disturbing the thin layer of healing skin. Cinders walked right up to the side of the bedroll so that Skylark could slide off without stepping in the dirt.

Adair sat down beside her and pulled off the hose with exquisite gentleness. He cautiously examined every healing blister and chafe. Then he pulled out a soft pair of ladies' hose.

"Where did you get those?" Skylark asked.

"Cookie's clothing. They were too big for you, but I restitched them. Here, try them on."

He stretched the stockings so wide they didn't touch her broken skin. They fit as if they had been darned just for her. With the tailored hose now protecting her feet, Adair remeasured the lasts and the leather, making little *tsk, tsk* noises, tracing her size against his first rough estimates. He seemed in no hurry. When he finally finished, they sat down together on the sun-warmed blanket. The new arrivals were napping while other men were off doing drills or other chores. Skylark was keenly aware that except for Cinders and a family of yammering blue jays, they were alone for the moment.

"It is awful kind of you to take such pains over these boots," she said.

Adair grinned. "How about one kiss as a reward?" he asked boldly.

"Adair!" she answered with mock shock. "We are in the middle of a war! Now is not the time for kissing."

"Now is exactly the time for kissing," said he, taking her hand and kissing her palm and then her wrist. "Anyone could be kilt anytime. I could be kilt; you could be kilt. Now is *not* the time for waiting or a long courtship." His kisses moved up her arm.

Skylark had never felt this tingly warmth before, and she gasped.

As if reading her mind, Adair whispered, "You're so . . . innocent. Don't you want your chance to know what lovemaking feels like?"

With her free hand, she untied the leather holding Adair's long ponytail.

He pushed her down on his bedroll, laying himself on top of her. He kissed her neck. "Yes?" he asked, smiling his warm smile, looking in her eyes, his loose hair now tumbling down, enfolding her as in a curtain.

Skylark did not know what to say. Her breath came short.

Cinders, stand between us and the rest of the camp. Make noise if anyone comes this way.

Adair kissed her more passionately. Skylark slipped her hands under his shirt in the back, feeling his skin's warmth and the movement of his muscles.

Before they could progress any further, Cinders neighed. Skylark pushed Adair away. Breathing heavily, they straightened their clothing, sharing secret smiles. Adair lifted her up by the waist to help her regain her perch on Cinders.

He kissed her hand again. "Milady, I want to make some progress on these boots. I will see you at mealtime."

Skylark rode back to the horse corral. Had anyone noticed how long she had been gone? Did she care if they had? Had they broken some rule? Did she care if they had? Did she want Adair, or was she just flattered that he wanted her? Men had shown interest in her before, but none had been as dashing and tempting as Adair.

At supper, the scout did not bother being discreet. Beaming, he brought her a dish and sat next to her. When they had finished eating, she stretched because her back was uncomfortable sitting on the ground. Using two arms, Adair pulled her waist, placing her in the hollow of his cross-legs so that she could lean against his chest. Skylark stiffened a moment in embarrassment, knowing how this would look to the rest of the Raiders and also angry at Adair's presumption toward a queen of Weirandale. Then, almost despite herself, she relaxed against him, luxuriating in the feeling of his warmth and his arm around her, an intimate closeness that penetrated deep to the marrow of her loneliness.

Kran was playing a simple air on the fife. Commander Thalen came out of his tent with his plate, which he returned to Cook with a compliment on the new food. He spent long minutes squatting on his heels talking to Tristo, who had recovered enough to be able to sit up and eat if someone cut up his food for him. The commander then walked about the men, pausing to converse quite a while with the newly arrived twins. He made his way over to Adair and Skylark.

"Adair, don't take any fool chances tonight. You can't leave me with Wareth as my only scout. It is a wonder that blunderer made it home to us."

"It was skill, not luck, that got Wareth and his squad back to us, and you know it," said Adair, sticking up for his fellow scout. "But I intend to return, Commander." He gave Skylark's arm a little squeeze in the dark.

The commander absolutely ignored their intimate posture, as if Raiders sat in one another's laps every day, or as if he didn't care at all.

He said to Skylark, "Balogun and Dalogun claim they love working with horses. I will leave it to you to judge if they are the best hands to help you and Gentain."

"Aye, sir," she answered.

After the meal, Skylark rode Cinders over to where Adair's roan, Brandy, was picketed.

Brandy, bring him back safely, she ordered. Then she briefed the female owl on the route to the water holes and told her to warn Adair of any enemies.

Adair swung himself onto Brandy's saddle. "Give us a kiss for luck, pretty duchess," he said, heedless of whomever was nearby.

Skylark kissed him. He gently traced her cheekbones with his index finger and then cantered off.

Neither the eagle nor Adair had returned in the morning. The eagle flew in late in the afternoon, thirsty and hungry. He drank at the stream and snatched up the two smoked fish Skylark offered. Then he preened his chest feathers for long moments.

Fetch the male you call Commander, he sent to her.

She did so. Commander Thalen bowed to the eagle, which pleased him. Skylark translated between them.

One saw large wooden buildings floating in the salt water. More humans in and around the town than mice in the fields. And men on horseback, already through the big passage you call the Mouth of the Mountains.

Thalen found this message puzzling. "What did they look like?"

Men look like men. Most wore shiny metal. One had a long black garment with red stars on it. One had his hands tied. That one looked like your mates.

"Skylark, ask him what he means by red stars?"

Not like stars in the black sky. Small red and yellow stars that wink in the light.

Skylark commented, "Commander, I think he saw jewels."

"What did he mean by 'our mates'?"

"Sir, 'mates' could mean females. Perchance he saw a Mellie."

"Ask him again, would you, how many men on horseback?"

"Sir, unfortunately, birds do not count, or at least not in the ways we count."

"Got it. Then ask him if there were more riders than us or fewer."

The eagle said more, many more.

Thalen bowed all the way down to the ground, though Skylark could tell this hurt his ribs. "Lord of the Skies, you have done us an incomparable service."

The eagle understood his gesture and his tone. He bobbed his head and turned it in a semicircle. Then he sailed off.

Thalen called Skylark, Sergeant Kambey, and Wareth to an immediate conference in his tent.

"Here is the situation," the commander said, pacing back and forth, though his hands had unconsciously moved to both sides of his lower chest. "The Oros have landed in Drintoolia with a large army. This is what we hoped for—this is what we sacrificed our friends to achieve!"

"Hooray!" shouted Wareth, and he hugged Skylark, and thumped Kambey and Thalen on their backs, though Thalen impatiently pushed him away.

"When you think about it," the commander said, already back to business, "you can assume such a force would be slow to get moving. However, they have already dispatched a small group of soldiers riding on horseback. At least one of the riders is a Magi and they have one Mellie with them. Your thoughts?"

Wareth asked, "How much magic do Magi have? Can't they just find us with their Powers?"

Thalen answered, "They can throw firebolts and they can start fires. They can transform people and things. They eat lava and see visions. Oros don't have Anticipation like some Lorthers; Pozhar's gift to its people is called Passion. But none of the books I've read say anything about miraculous Powers of seeking or finding."

Skylark, who had also read many books on Oromondo, silently agreed. She asked, "Sir, could you show us on your map how far away the riders were when the eagle spotted them?"

Thalen unrolled his map. "Somewhere hereabouts."

"I suspect that Oros have little skill at tracking," Kambey said, scratching the stitches on the back of one hand. "If they have a Mellie captive, they brought him to hunt for them."

"So they could be on us in two or three days?" Skylark asked.

"Aye. It could take them as much as four days. No matter. I would like to be gone by then." Thalen twirled his quill. "If their Mellie tracker finds us here, this box ravine is a death trap. Besides, I find the volcano's recent activity unsettling. Could be a burst of lava on our heads any day."

"I'm going to get the troop to pack up," said Kambey decisively. "We've all become too comfortable here. We must be ready to move out on a moment's notice."

"What about our wounded? Send Cerf to me to discuss whether they can be shifted."

"'Mander," said Wareth, "how is your injury? How much pain are you in today?"

Thalen did not answer Wareth's question. Instead, he barked,

"Skylark, what are you doing standing about on your feet? I gave you a direct order about that!"

"But my feet are much better, sir. Very little pain."

Kambey came to her defense. "Commander, if the whole weight of the Oro army is about to fall on us, it hardly matters much if her feet are perfectly healed. *I'm* not perfectly healed; *you're* not perfectly healed."

Thalen blazed up with anger. "My orders are always to be followed to the letter. She does not use those feet until Cerf says so."

"Aye, 'Mander. Up you go, Skylark." Wareth hoisted her up pickaback.

The commander's angry rebuke upset Skylark.

Not fair, not fair, not fair! How dare he? In my whole life, no one has ever spoken to me like that! No one speaks to a queen that way!

Adair would never treat me so rudely.

In the wee hours of the morning, Adair shook Skylark awake.

"You're back!" She threw her arms around him in relief.

Eldie and Eli-anna awoke at the noise and sat up, clutching their bows. Adair made a calming motion with his hands.

"Told you I was coming back, Duchess. And I found us the sweetest hideout. It won't be quite as easy to water the horses, but the place is much more secure."

"What did the commander say?"

"He said, 'Good job, go get some sleep.'"

"So what are you doing here? . . . Oh, no, you are not sleeping here in the women's camp!"

"I thought of it, but Ooma would gut me. Good thing she's on guard right now. Just give me a good night kiss or two."

They kissed multiple times, and then she managed to push him away. Adair melted away into the darkness. Skylark lay down with her heart pounding fast. She heard Eldie and Eli-anna giggling. She giggled too, flooded with relief at his safe return and drunk on so many kisses.

Cerf dropped by her bedroll in the morning. He examined her feet.

"I hear that Adair, among other things, is making you boots," he said dryly. "When they are finished, I want you to wrap here, here, and here, with these bandages. Then you are cleared for some walking, at least around the encampment. But ride your filly as much as you can and seek me out at *the least* sign of chafing, bleeding, or infection."

"I will, Cerf."

Skylark called Cinders to her, and Ooma easily hoisted her up. She rode to the cooking area, where Tristo stood next to the kettle, handing Cook ingredients with his left hand. His right arm stopped a bit below the shoulder, and the bandages around the amputation looked slightly pink.

"Should you be up?" she asked him in low tones as he handed her up a mug of tisane and a piece of fried bread.

"I need to move about," he answered her. "Going crazy on my pallet. I figure I can get away with a few hours before Cerf or the commander catch me out. It's not like your feet. I ain't using my stub, just my uninjured parts."

"Be careful," Skylark warned. "The commander's got a temper about healer's orders."

Tristo leaned a little closer to Skylark and whispered, "Don't let anyone give you crap about you and Adair."

He was about to say something else, but Cook called, "Tristo, we need more salt!"

Skylark turned Cinders to the horse herd. Gentain had started hectic preparations for their relocation. Packsaddles filled with the new supplies had to be tried on each horse to be sure they were balanced and fit, and Skylark was too short and too weak to throw these about. Yet with Balogun and Dalogun's assistance the work progressed smoothly. Skylark immediately liked the boys because they were quick and steady with the mounts. They kept up a constant, cheerful chatter. They introduced her to the new horses, all of which, oddly, had been named after spices: Pepper, Cloves, Cinnamon, Chili, and Anise.

Skylark suggested that from now on Tristo ride the smooth-gaited gelding Walnut instead of Peaches, the livelier mount he had favored before his maiming. Since the Raiders had some spare mounts, she also decided which ones should be used solely as pack animals and the order in which they would be strung together. Sulky Sukie had taken a firm dislike to some of the geldings; it was best to keep them separated.

Late in the morning, Kambey rounded up the five newcomers and Skylark and brought them to the practice area to assess their fighting skills. Skylark was nervous about her test. She had not trained with weapons for more than a year, and her half starvation had further weakened her muscles.

One of the new arrivals, a thin-faced, morose-looking man sporting a reddish-brown beard and wearing spectacles, hit the targets and parried Kambey's sword well enough, but Skylark learned that he had actually been chosen for his healing skills, to serve as Cerf's assistant. Balogun and Dalogun, who had gangly long arms, showed skill with their bows as advertised, hitting the bull's-eye each time. Yet they blundered haplessly with swords; Kambey took them both on at once and managed to knock the weapons out of their hands and spank them both with his own. That test dissolved into raucous laughter.

Kambey ordered, "I'm going to train you in the use of swords. But come a battle, you two are seconded to the Mellie girls, who now head up the archers. You follow their orders exactly—they point at what they want and if you do something dumb their scowls are as expressive as any curse."

The two others whom Wareth had brought held themselves ramrod straight. Skylark found it impossible to determine their hair color, because they both wore their hair so close-cropped. Thus far they had only nodded at her and glanced at her sideways. They gave their names as Shyrwin and Nollo.

"Guard experience, eh?" muttered Kambey. Their arrows smacked the target with resounding thuds, and their fencing skills impressed the weapons master. "You two have trained for years. Where did you serve?" Kambey asked.

"Hither and yon," said Shyrwin, whose smile did not reach his eyes.

"Mercenaries?" asked Kambey. "Why would you put yourselves at risk with us for no gain?"

"No gain?" said Shyrwin with a mirthless grin. "Don't tell me you ain't heard the tales of Oro jewels. The men that hired us said if we could pick up any kind of accidental-like, they'd be ours for the keeping."

"Besides," added Nollo, "we like to be where the action is."

"Now, what kind of fool wants that?" Kambey asked, but the men just shrugged. "All right, go back to whatever chores you were assigned."

With a consideration that surprised her, Kambey had saved her for last. "Now Skylark, you have proven your worth to the Raiders, but I need to know what you can do in a scrap." Kambey handed her a bow and arrow as she sat on Cinders. Her form and aim didn't shame her, but her arms did not have the muscle strength. The arrow dropped far short of the target.

"I can do naught with a sword," she told Kambey as he started to hand her one.

"What would you be able to fight with?" Kambey asked.

"A dagger?" she suggested meekly.

"Gal, you can't get close enough to an Oro. Your little arms aren't half long enough. Even on a horse. And what about their armor?"

"I have been thinking about that. Could you put my dagger on a stick, to extend my reach?"

"You mean a spear?"

"Ah! Yes, of course. I mean, yes, a spear."

"Humph." Kambey moved over to where he had several spears pointed into the dirt.

He handed the weapon to Skylark, who held it warily because she had never touched one before. "That looks ridiculous," growled the weapons master. "Steady it with your left and hold the weight in your right. Can you launch it at me?"

Skylark threw the spear. It only traveled a few paces and then fell with a harmless clatter.

Kambey picked it up, shaking his head. "If you can't pull a bow you don't have the muscles to launch a spear."

"Here, give it to me. Let me try something different," Skylark pleaded. "You be an Oro on foot. You use your sword."

Skylark told Cinders about this new game and then dropped the reins, leaving the choice of approach to the nimble little horse. Skylark concentrated all her strength on keeping a two-handed grip on the elongated dagger. Cinders feinted to the left and then came in on the right. Skylark touched Kambey's waist leather gently with the tip. Kambey whirled around with his sword, but Skylark ducked while Cinders danced away. Cinders then circled round and round Kambey erratically, allowing Skylark to connect with her spear again on the back of the neck.

"Enough!" Kambey called. "My guess is that the commander would soonest keep you in reserve, like Cerf, because your bird skills are too important. But in an all-out melee, you ride with me and the cavalry. *Cinders* might be able to take an enemy down."

At the noonday meal, Adair met her with the boots that just needed their rear seam stitched up. They slid on with a soft swish and fit her as if the royal cobbler had made them. The nearby comrades whistled with appreciation.

"Hey Adair, if I were as purty as lark girl, would you craft me a pair of boots like that?" asked Ooma.

Adair ignored her. "Do you like them, Milady Duchess?" he asked Skylark.

In front of everyone, Skylark gave him a lingering kiss. The assembly hooted and laughed.

Kran said, "Hey Skylark, if I fashioned you somethin' that noble, would I get a kiss that honeyed?"

Skylark threw the old hose she had in her hands at Kran, saying, "Not in a million moons, you big old bear. You're the clod who thought I was a lad."

The merriment was interrupted by one of the long-tailed hawks swooping down onto a tree behind Skylark.

Marching men and men on aurochs.

How many, where?

The hawk did not know how to answer, but eventually Skylark determined the hawk had spied a considerable force approaching from the east.

Did they have any dogs with them?

No canines.

For help with the location Skylark turned to Adair, who more than anyone else had scouted the environs of their camp.

He eventually decoded the locations from the hawks' descriptions. He took off for the command tent at a run. Kran boosted Skylark up on Cinders, and she met him there.

Thalen and Adair located the position of the battalion. This was not any of the forces that had just landed at Drintoolia, but reserves of pikemen who headed their way from Wûnum. They were angled so as to close in on the town that had been their last strike, the town where they had burned the large Citadel of Flames.

Commander Thalen traced a line from the Mouth of the Mountains southward.

"Fifty riders must not be enough muscle for Oros. The riders are just their hammer. This battalion of pikemen is their anvil. And *we* are supposed to be crushed between them. But they will have to find us first.

"Pass the word: we ride at nightfall."

32

Emerald Lake

Tally: 15 + 5 (Balogun, Dalogun, Pemphis, Shyrwin, Nollo) = 20
Horses: 22 – 2 (Wareth's trip) + 5 (spices) = 25

Thalen wondered if it was too risky to lead the Raiders out into the open when all of Oromondo was on the prowl for them. Or was it too risky to stay, knowing that their ravine was easily discoverable and they were too few to defend it against a large force?

The birds' sightings indicated that they had at least a day left of free movement. They had to seize this opportunity.

Kran, Fedak, and Dalogun lingered until last, following Thalen's orders about the encampment. Thalen asked Kran's crew to sweep up all the scattered dry horse dung and any other discards and then seed the piles with embers, which should ignite the fuel after they were well away. Fire meant everything to Oros. Knowing that Oros were deeply superstitious, Thalen wanted to confuse them about the identity of their invaders. He wanted to burn the ravine clean of all clues.

For the first league Adair had them walk their horses in Ink Creek. When he turned the file away from the stream, he asked the Mellie girls to dismount and use their juniper brooms to sweep the horse tracks. With practiced skill Adair led them to a rocky ledge that would not tell tales.

Although Dishwater swayed with his typical gentle gait, climbing the escarpment reignited the pain in Thalen's rib cage. He looked toward the back of the line, catching sight of Nollo and Shyrwin riding next to one another.

Wareth says they followed his orders but spoke little on the whole trip from Needle Pass. He is sure they were not from the Free States. Kambey says their fighting skills are too good for anyone but career soldiers.

I'll have to question them the first chance I get.

Turning around hurt his back. Thalen faced front again. By squinting, he could just make out the figures of people riding in front of him on the open rock.

There she is, up ahead behind Adair.

Kambey groused at me about her relations with Adair and wants me to put a stop to it. Codek would not have allowed this for a minute. Why have I delayed?

Thalen recalled her happy, glowing face as she sat in Adair's lap in the flickers of the cook fire.

Could I be jealous of Adair?

No. Hardly. No.

Really?

But why would I be jealous of Adair?

Thalen found Eldie and Eli-anna more attractive. They were tall and graceful; their long hair more fetching. He was awed by their incredible skill with their bows. Skylark's coloring looked off, and she was still bony. Her communicating with animals—however invaluable it had been to the Raiders—was plain uncanny. He was not sure he completely trusted her.

Yet. That glow on her face. As if she was lit up from inside by her Sun Spirit. I want her to lean against me. *I want to be the one holding her.*

Could I win her away from Adair? He is so graceful and confident, while I'm just clumsy. Besides, to even attempt such would be unseemly. I'm the commander. I can't lower myself to vie for a girl's attention. After how hard I've worked to win the men's regard—to throw it away over a strange girl!

Thalen's thoughts turned morose. He wondered if his longing really had to do with Skylark herself or whether it had just been too long since he'd experienced any tenderness. His affair with Deganah seemed a lifetime away.

Have I ever really been in love? Am I going to die out here, never having known love?

Are we all going to die out here? I never hazarded a plan to extract us. But. Tristo. Wareth. Eldie. Eli-anna. Skylark. The ferry boys. I have to keep them all alive. I have to see them safely out of enemy territory.

How can I keep them alive when thousands of Oros are about to descend on us? What kind of a leader am I, to bring them all into such danger?

He answered himself mercilessly: *This was the plan all along, to sacrifice ourselves in order to get the Oros out of the Free States. Now that it is time to pay the forfeit, I'm just writhing at the price.*

If I'm lucky, I'll die first and not have to witness their deaths.

And what's to stop the Oros from returning to the Free States after they've crushed us? Our deaths may—after all—count for nothing.

The troop had halted. Thalen was so distracted he didn't rein in. Dishwater stopped on his own rather than walk into Balogun's horse in front of him.

"Trouble?" Thalen asked, generally. Gentain behind him explained, "No, Cerf wants to check on the wounded."

Thalen struggled to get himself some water. He couldn't unlace his water bag without turning in a position that hurt his ribs too much. He might have dismounted, but he didn't feel up to the maneuver, so he gave up on the idea of getting himself a drink.

As he waited, he saw way off in the distance a bolt of lightning arc from cloud to ground. It was so far away; they didn't even hear the thunder.

Cerf rode up to him, the new man Pemphis, who carried a shaded lantern, by his side.

"Report, Cerf," Thalen commanded. "How are the wounded holding up? Jothile? Tristo?"

"No, sir," said Cerf. "In this area, you report to me. How are the ribs holding up?"

"Not too bad," lied Thalen.

Cerf had Pemphis uncover the light so he could see Thalen's face.

"Aye," said Cerf. "That's why your face looks so sweaty. Time for a dose. I had to treat Tristo too."

"Cerf, no. I can't doze off now. We're out in the open. I need to keep my wits about me."

"Commander. I doubt you have any wits. I order you to take this."

Thalen did not have the strength to argue. He drank the elixir down with secret gratitude.

When the horses started moving again, Thalen didn't care. He felt warm, relaxed, free of pain, and sheltered from the jealous and melancholy thoughts that had been plaguing him.

In a few minutes, he felt Dishwater halt and someone get up on the horse behind him, holding him around the waist so he would not slip off. It was someone strong enough to hold him and tall enough that he could relax backward, so it could not be Skylark.

But maybe it is. Maybe she is beside me and we are riding on the ferry over Clear Lake. The water is choppy in the fresh wind. And she is glowing with happiness because she is with me. *Because she wants to be with me more than with anyone else in Ennea Món.*

Thalen surfaced to consciousness to find that he was lying on his stomach on his bed in his tent. Experimentally he took a few deep breaths, discovering that the pain in his ribs had subsided to a manageable roar. Keeping still and taking in his surroundings, he heard the splash of rain on the tent fabric. Thalen smiled. This rain would wash away any hoofprints they had left.

Cautiously, he sat up and looked around. Tristo lay asleep nearby and Jothile a few paces away. His tent was not set up how he liked it—only Tristo knew his preferences—but at least the box with his books and maps had been brought inside out of the rain.

After a bit, Pemphis and Cerf came dashing through the flaps, bringing some food and checking on the patients. Thalen learned that they had ridden without incident, reaching this new hideout in midafternoon.

Pemphis probed his back while Cerf checked Tristo's breathing. "You didn't do any damage to your ribs; that pain you felt was just the sore muscles going into spasm. Here, let me rub it a moment." His strong touch kneaded away a nasty kink.

"Go back to sleep," urged Cerf. "It's now the middle of the night. There's naught to do in this rain."

Thalen followed this advice. It rained hard for an hour, the only rain he could recall since they'd arrived in this country.

In the morning, Cook brought his wounded charges some warm porridge. Thalen, Jothile, and Tristo ate it gratefully and chatted a spell.

"We should get up; I've got to survey this new camp." Thalen considered swinging his legs forward. All of a sudden a second cloudburst struck the tent cloth with a loud staccato.

"Wait a bit, Commander," Tristo urged.

Thalen drifted off to sleep again.

When the noise of the rain abated midday, Thalen felt hungry and clearheaded enough to be restless, so he set off to explore.

This encampment differed from the Ink Creek one. Dripping fir trees surrounded his tent, which his men had pitched on a rare, almost level spot of earth. Instead of a flat creek bed offering a clearing, in all directions sloped woods impeded Thalen's sight. From below came the sounds of horses, which caused him to turn uphill. Twenty steps brought Thalen to a hillcrest: ahead he saw a lake three times as large as Sutterdam Pottery filling a bowl in the rocks. The emerald-green water trembled under the continued assault of raindrops; craggy high peaks rose into the mist beyond.

Only a few flat spaces edged the lakeshore. Right in front of him stretched a ribbon of beach broken by big boulders cast about like a giant playing marbles. To his left, the water had carved out a rocky place under an overhang. This was obviously going to be the gathering place. A cluster of Raiders and a cook fire beckoned. Thalen strode over, greeting those already gathered together: Cook, Ooma, Wareth, Kambey, and Fedak.

Cook handed Thalen a plate of beans simmered with bacon and a mug of tisane.

He learned that they had climbed the mountain just before the rain started; with no time to set up the infirmary, they had put the wounded in his tent.

Cook had had the foresight to gather wood out of the wet. But in their haste to unload the horses when the storm hit, everything loaded on Patches had slipped off, smashed open, or tumbled away. They'd lost two bags of oats, a bag of beans, and other precious foodstuffs, washed away in the downpour.

Thalen took the loss philosophically. "Shame. But better that than any loss of men. Where is everyone?"

"Everyone scattered under trees to find dry spots," said Wareth.

"The hawks showed up right after dawn; they are watching both the path we rode up on and the back door escape, which is around behind the lake. The owls will take over at night. Those owls amaze me. Flying over and around us like white shadows, hooting softly, the entire ride." He whistled in appreciation. "'Mander, you were so dopey you missed quite a sight!"

Wareth was the one who held me up on Dishwater. Of course. I shouldn't feel disappointed; I should feel grateful for his solicitude.

"Why is the water that color?" asked Ooma. "Is it safe to drink?"

"It's completely clear," Thalen answered. "My guess is that some minerals from the mountainsides have eroded into it."

Cook threw some more logs on the embers, and the fire redoubled its heat.

"If you lean against this"—Wareth gestured at the rock wall—"it feels good." Thalen moved against the rock, feeling the heat unkink his rib muscles. Maki resettled himself close by, scratching his neck.

Thalen considered the new camp's attributes. It was far from any road, so quite secure, and it offered abundant water. He missed Ink Creek's sight lines however; his Raiders had scattered and hidden in the trees and slopes. And Kambey would find the beach area barely adequate for drilling.

As the afternoon wore on, more Raiders gathered around the cook fire and the food. The rain subsided into a fine mist. A person could sit in it now, even without a hat. Kran pulled out Literoy's fife and started to play softly. Balogun and Dalogun began singing bawdy bar songs, and many joined in. Nollo and Shyrwin joined the group, and Thalen reminded himself to question them tomorrow.

Tristo tottered up the hillcrest, unsteady on his feet. Like a mother hen, Ooma shooed two Raiders away from the sheltered rock and got the boy a bowl of food.

Eli-anna, Eldie, and Skylark emerged from the mist together. *So she was sleeping with the other women, not with Adair.* Thalen was ashamed of himself for keeping track. They sat on the far side of the fire in their threesome, Skylark's eyelashes catching tiny pearls of water. Gentain seated himself on the other side of her, which was perfectly fine with Thalen.

A rare urge to show off his musical skill stirred Thalen. "Could I use the fife, Kran?" Thalen trilled a few scales to warm up, checking if the soft blowing hurt his lungs.

"Whoa, Commander!" said Tristo. "You told me you could play, but not like that."

"That was a scale, muckwit," Thalen said affectionately. He started the familiar opening of "The Lay of Queen Carmena." Weir ballads were famous throughout Ennea Món, and this would be a change from bar songs.

Skylark sat up straight and eager, as if she had been touched with a hot brand. He raised his eyebrows at her, inviting her to sing along. She pointed up, meaning a higher key. He modulated upward, then nodded the count to her: one, two, three, four.

"The Waters of Weirandale," she began. Her voice was high but textured. She sang musically, without affectation. Her eyes lost their focus—as if she saw the story or remembered when she'd learned the lay. All the Raiders stopped talking, falling under the spell of the song's melody and epic tale. If they were surprised by Thalen's skill with the fife or Skylark's singing, everyone was totally shocked when Nollo started harmonizing with Skylark during the chorus. His fellow, Shyrwin, tried to shush him, but the music could not be denied.

Thalen played the lay all the way through to its beautiful end, when Carmena freed herself from her kidnappers and chose a loyal consort. By then, all of the Raiders had crowded around. They clapped and hooted their appreciation of their musicians. Thalen brought the fife to his forehead, looking in Skylark's eyes, and saluted her. She smiled her smile of liquid sunshine.

Then Adair—*where the devil did that thief come from?*—lifted her up and was clasping her within his arms, swinging her around in a circle.

33

Cascada

Nana and her stableman lover, Hiccuth, had a rare afternoon off together. The sun shone bright in the blue summer sky, so they sat on a bale of hay, leaning their backs against the outside wall of the stable. Hiccuth mended a mess of leather tack with an awl; Nana kept her hands busy letting out one of her gowns that had gotten just a wee bit too snug around her waist, though her weak eyes made the task an exercise in frustration.

"Drought!" she muttered, realizing that the row of stitches wandered crookedly and would need to be ripped out.

"Why don't you ask one of your friends amongst the tailors to do that? You're making a right mess of it."

"I don't know, but I will," sighed Nana, letting the material fall into her lap and raising her eyes to rest them on the nearby paddock, where a few of the horses cavorted and nibbled at thrice-eaten grass. A dog in the enclosure played a prance-and-run game with a young foal.

"You've let yer foot fall again," she nagged Hiccuth, worried about the arthritis in his knee. "Keep it raised up."

He just grunted at her, so she wiggled her rear to get down from the bale, built up the footrest out of straw, and replaced Hiccuth's left boot on the footrest to give the knee a rest. As she fussed, placing his boot just so, Hiccuth patted her head, but since he still held the awl in his hand the pat felt more like a poke. She climbed back on the bale, shifting her broad rear around quite a bit to get more comfortable.

"Did you hear what I heard?" she asked Hiccuth.

"Now, how would I know what you heard?"

"About the raid on the Central Market."

"Yep," he answered. "Sounds as if the guards went berserk—smashing stands, spoiling food, arresting people. What was the point?"

"To flex their muscles. Keep the merchants scared," Nana said. "Do you think it's true, what they're saying, that Matwyck intends to crown himself?"

"He wouldn't dare," answered Hiccuth. "Who told you that?"

"The maids burst with such tales, but I don't trust them. Fluttery, stupid girls, full of wild rumors. Think about it—the catamounts would rip him to pieces."

"If he didn't kill them first," said the stableman darkly.

"Oh, but Nargis would never allow such a thing. You need Nargis Ice to be queen. Nargis ain't about to give Matwyck no jewel of Nargis Ice!"

"You're right," he agreed, and he patted her thigh reassuringly. "There is smart you are."

"Those maids should shut their gossip holes and not get folks so riled up," Nana grumbled.

"You're right," said Hiccuth. "Lots of talk and dark rumor. Hard to know what's really happening."

"Easy to know what *should* have happened. Besi should have been appointed head cook," said Nana.

"We've been over this too many times. Besi ain't in their pocket," replied Hiccuth.

"It still galls me," she said.

"A lot of things gall you. Can't you put them aside and enjoy the sunshine with me?" said Hiccuth.

"Patience ain't never been my virtue," she snapped.

"You don't say," replied Hiccuth.

They were both quiet a moment. Hiccuth's awl made little pulling noises, but Nana had tossed her sewing aside.

"If I was Besi," said Nana, breaking into the peace, "I'd put rat poison in their suppers."

Hiccuth started to laugh.

"I would!" said Nana sharply. "What's so funny?"

"Peacefulness ain't your virtue either."

"I guess not. But don't think I ain't been pondering a way out of this fix. The trouble is that some meals they make a footman taste first. Or sometimes one of the undercooks."

"Poison's a coward's way," said Hiccuth. "Besides, you kill one, another will take his place."

"Right," said Nana. "The real trouble is, the people is quiet, just keeping their heads down, just accepting."

"I don't know about that," said Hiccuth. "I heard from the duke of Woodsdale's coachman that the folk in Gorseton, last time there was supposed to be an election for Lord Steward but they cancelled it again, they barricaded the center street with carts and threw cobblestones at the watch."

"Really? Or is that just gossip too? We rarely hear about what's going on outside of the city. This is such a huge realm. There could have been a successful revolt in one of the duchies, and that lot could keep the news from us."

Nana kicked her feet against the straw and puzzled over the problem of getting reliable information across the duchies. She sprang to her feet. "I'm sorry, but I've got to pop down to town."

"Hey!" said Hiccuth. "I thought we was doing pretty fine here together."

"I'll be back in time to spend some time in yer room."

"In my bed," smiled Hiccuth.

"No place I'd rather be, you old goat. I'll be back real soon. You just finish soaking up some sunshine."

A Sister of Sorrow told Nana that Brother Whitsury would be concluding an orientation for newcomers to the abbey any moment.

She waited on a bench in the hallway until he joined her.

"Nana! Is anything wrong?"

"No, but I need to talk to you. Can you take a turn around the Fountain with me? No one would mark us there."

"Whitsury," she said, as they strolled, "how do the Sorrowers feel about Matwyck naming himself prelate?"

"There's not five people in the country who don't see this as a travesty. Pensioning off our prelate! He's trying to get us under his control! He shut down the Harbor Abbey in Maritima and sent the Sorrowers in all directions."

"Why?"

"We believe because the abbey was helping the people and supporting them in their grievances."

Nana nodded. "Who knows what's going on at all the abbeys and in all the churches, all of them, everywhere?"

"Well, the supervisors write a report once a moon. It comes to the Prelate's Office at the Church of the Headwaters." Whitsury pointed to the grand church, a block from the Fountain, the official center of the worship of Nargis in Weirandale. "I've seen a few. The reports are pretty boring; they detail this much spent on food, three sisters sick, the townsfolk patched a roof, and so on."

"Could we use these letters to find out about resistance to Matwyck's decrees? Or mayhap even give a little poke in that direction?"

"Ahh, I see." Whitsury smiled with relief at discovering what Nana was aiming at. He walked a few more steps meditatively, clasping his hands behind his back. Nana looked up at the Water's arc, noting that today the highest point was at least a hand's length lower.

"No. The official reports would need to stay as boring as they are now. But some—most!—supervisors might be willing to include political information on a separate sheet. The Prelate's Office could just pull these out before passing the ordinary items on to our beloved regent. The Sorrowers who work in that office are probably the most outraged of anyone in the realm; I'm certain that getting their cooperation would be easy."

"I'd leave the arranging of all of this to you," said Nana.

"But what will we do with knowing that a certain city watch is mistreating their citizens, or that a duke is double-tithing his people?"

Nana replied, "Not much we can do right now. But we'd be building a network. And taking names. Because when the queen returns, justice will fall like—like a mighty cascade, and the flood will scour the streets of those who sold their souls.

"I just wanna be sure we know who's who."

34

Fûli, Oromondo

Riding horseback was faster than being carted by palanquin; Three found he enjoyed the freedom of movement and the ability to see in all directions. His muscles' weariness barely counted in comparison to the pain in his mouth and throat caused by the infernal sores. In six days, Magi Three and General Sumroth's riders reached Fûli. The battalion of reserves Three had ordered to the district met them there: thus Sumroth now had more than four hundred men under his command.

Three's heart raged at the sight of Fûli's destroyed Citadel of Flames. This had been one of the most sacred citadels of the Land, dating back centuries, one of the proudest offerings of Oromondo skill and reverence to Pozhar. Now it stood a blackened shell. Its ceiling had caved in and its steeple crashed to the ground. Rainwater puddles lay mixed with ashy residue on the floor of the once-magnificent structure. Close-by homes had also burned to their foundations.

Sumroth reported that the rain that had passed through three days ago had wiped out any obvious clues about the invaders. The men who had fought the invaders had either died of their wounds or fevered so their words were worthless; the only people they could question were the town's surviving women and children.

Sumroth, who possessed no social skills under the best of circumstances, was ham-fisted in handling the survivors. He and his men could not extract a straight story from any of them. Granted, they had been terrified, their relatives had been murdered, their town burned, and the rain had made them all the more miserable. But could they not agree on any one simple thing?

How many attackers were there? Some said five; some said fifty; one said five hundred. Were they men? Some said yes, of course; some said they were ghosts. Others said they were women! A few said they were Mellies, when everyone knew that Mellies were too frightened of the Magi Power to cross the border into the Land. Nearly all agreed they had seen horses. But one child said they rode in on owls, and when Sumroth told him to stop telling tales, he stuck to the story, even after he'd been cuffed a few times.

Three tried to take over the questioning himself, but the folk were so frightened by his appearance that he got only gibberish.

Once, before this plague ruined him, he had been a handsome man. Very handsome, in fact. His people would have been awed by his presence and confided in him gratefully, worshipfully. The worst thing about the plague was the constant pain, but the disfigurement also burned his pride and condemned him to isolation.

After the frustrating conversations, General Sumroth walked through Fûli, kicking at the debris. He fumed. "Irritating idiots! These are the people I work so hard to feed?" Three watched him, weighing his insolence against his usefulness.

Sumroth had the captive Mellie brought along. The man gazed around at the burned town with great interest.

"What do you see?" asked Sumroth.

"I see what you see, High Officer, sir," said the man.

"Don't parry words with me, slave. What do you see that I do not see? What would you do to find the villains who did this?"

"What would I do? I would send two men out from this town, riding in ever-larger circles, bending over and looking at the ground. Of course, it has rained. And of course, bringing all those soldiers in, you likely trampled on any evidence of your prey's entrance or exit. Still, that's the way to examine a site. If your riders find anything, call me. I'll be napping in the sun over there."

The Mellie moved over to a patch of sunlight that warmed a stone bench. Sumroth's hand went to his sword—he was ever too quick to solve problems with violence. Three stepped forward, ordering him to desist. They had brought this Mellie "tracker"; now they should see what he could ferret out. Sumroth chose riders for these circles; after they departed Three concentrated on his mourning prayers for the Citadel of Flames. They would rebuild it, grander than ever. This site was sacred.

If the invaders do turn out to be human, we will reconsecrate the site with their screams. I will use their blood and bones in the mortar. The vermin will rue the day they crossed into the Sacred Land.

At first, when the riders reported findings to the slave—a broken stick, a depression that could have been made by a horse—he rejected their significance. The day wore on; the riders ranged farther from Fûli. When the soldiers were so far they were almost out of sight, one of them came riding back in a lather.

"Your Divinity, General, we believe we have found a trail," he reported.

"Show me," Sumroth said. To other guards he snapped, "Bring the slave."

"We will come with you," said Three.

"As you wish," replied the general, rather too heedlessly.

The soldiers had carefully marked five places within several paces of one another: broken branches off a shrub, a deep hoofprint that had retained water, and so on. The trail led north.

"Very good, lads," said the Mellie lazily. "It's too late to follow this now. In the morning, we can see where this leads."

"Are you playing Us for a fool, slave? Are you deliberately wasting time?" asked Three.

"Wasting time? To what end, Your Divinity? If you would care to try to follow the trail in the dark, I am at your command, but I would counsel against it. Hard to track without light, especially a trail that's now more than a week old and one that's been rained on."

Sumroth and Three conferred.

"He's a knave, lying and tricking us, in league with the attackers," said the general.

"We shall see." Three held up his left index finger. A fine jet of flame arced out from his hand. The Magi walked closer to the Mellie; some Protectors held him when he tried to back away. With slow, deliberate care, Three singed off just the man's eyebrows. Three prided himself on his exquisite control—he could burn skin layer by layer—so far this burn would pain no worse than a slight cooking accident.

Three held the arc of flame just over the slave's right eye. "Slave, I could burn your eyelid off in a heartbeat and your eye would start to liquefy from heat transfer. Now, are you purposely delaying Us?"

The slave licked his lips with fear, but his voice did not falter. "I know no more about your enemies than you do. Following a trail in the dark is always a risk," he replied. "One could miss the spot where your quarry doubles back or turns."

Sumroth assented to the delay, but he had the horse troop ready to ride at first light. Three could have objected to Sumroth's cutting short morning prayers, but in these circumstances, he decided not to. The troop of fifty riders followed the trail northward some leagues, until it hit a small stream. Then the trail disappeared. For hours, the Mellie slave had the soldiers scouring the banks for any trace of where the horses had reemerged.

Three made up for missing morning prayers with a midday service. It was hot, standing in the plain without shade, but Three's heat came from his unquenchable passion. Some of the Protectors swayed with ardor during his fervent sermon, and Three felt on Fire.

Afterward, Sumroth ordered his Protectors to follow the stream itself. It led into a slender entryway in ravine walls.

They passed through the canyon opening, their horses ankle-deep in the water. Within a few moments they reached the end of the canyon, where an eerie sight greeted them. An immense conflagration had burned here. The Fire had torched every tree to cinders; scorch marks climbed the rock over the heads of the seated riders. All they could see were piles of rain-soaked cinders.

Magi Three stood up in his stirrups and rode all the way to the rear rock face, looking around with wonder and awe, trying to read the signs. He reached into a purse hung around his belt for a pinch of ground lava that he always carried with him. The grains tasted gritty and bitter; without wine to mix them in Three had a hard time swallowing any quantity down his throat.

He waited a few moments, ignoring his horse's tugging toward the spring, until his body began to ripple with the convulsions the ground lava produced. Three looked around the canyon and with the enhanced vision brought on by Pozhar's magic, he saw trembling cascades of Power flowing down the walls of the canyon. These looked distinct from the transparent flames that bespoke the recent presence of other Magi. The Power flowed down, not up, and the flames were not nearly as fierce.

Is this the aura of ghosts of dead Magi?

When Three turned his horse back to the Protectors, Sumroth's face was dark with anger, and his soldiers shifted on their feet.

Sumroth spoke authoritatively, "This could have been caused by a lightning strike; remember it rained three days ago. Or a seam of lava might have flowed down from FireSky."

One of the soldiers muttered, "But there's no lava flow anywhere."

The slave, Eldo, said under his breath, "Looks to me like a signal."

Sumroth wheeled on him. "A signal of what, slave? Of what? OF WHAT? That there has been a fire here, I know."

"Beg pardon, High Officer, sir. I am a stranger to your country and your faith. But to me it looks like a message that we should hunt these spirits no more, lest we be burnt to ash ourselves."

The words had been spoken aloud; the men exchanged looks. Sumroth pulled his whip and rode over to the slave. "Coward! Shit-wit!" He lashed the man with each curse. "I'll trample you like aurochs dung beneath my boot!"

Magi Three interrupted before Sumroth whipped the man to death. "General," he said sternly, "it is best that you leave this place, since it is holy to FireSky. Wait for Us outside the ravine."

After the Protectors had filed out, Magi Three stood up in his stirrups again and chanted a verse of reverence to the Spirit of Fire, though such singing made his throat hurt worse than ever. The top of the volcano spurted out high tongues of flame in answer.

The riders retreated from the canyon and headed back toward Fûli. General Sumroth and Three took stock. Magi Three concluded that there was nothing more to be gained from scouring the area around the wrecked city.

"We wish to confer with Our fellow Divinities at Femturan, General."

Sumroth had the temerity to sneer at Three. "Don't tell me that you are frightened by a little bit of fire, Divinity? Do you really believe that ghosts of the dead roam the Land?"

"General, you forget yourself much too often. Do not meddle with Powers you are too puny to understand."

"Powers! When I fetch the invaders' very human scalps to Femturan, Three, I expect to be greeted like a savior."

"General. As usual, you overstep your station. Have a care." Magi Three flicked his third finger off his thumb and pointed it at the medal Sumroth had been awarded for the Battle of the Mouth of the Mountains. The metal immediately started to glow red-hot.

Sumroth braved the branding metal for two long minutes; then he tore the honor from his smoking uniform, ripping his tunic, displaying his bare human chest and fear in front of his men.

"In the meantime, General, here are Our orders. Send a rider to Brigadier Chumelle. We want the Protectors you fetched back from the Free States and their food stores brought to Femturan whilst We decide on our next course of action."

"As you wish, Divinity," said Sumroth, though his tone of voice was still brash. And he had the temerity to tack on a request: "But would you take the Mellie dung with you? I mistrust him, and he has a bad effect on morale. I'd like him out of my craw. Your fellow Magi might also wish to question him more closely."

Three nodded, but he punished Sumroth's arrogance by making the latter's sword pommel shoot out hot sparks. Sumroth leapt up like a frightened cat and Three couldn't resist a small smirk as he walked away.

35

Emerald Lake

Skylark was working near the new corral (which was actually just a rope enclosure stretching around a big circle of trees), hanging wet horse blankets on tree limbs to dry, when a tan hedgehog with a white underbelly scampered onto a nearby rock.

Your Majesty! Your Majesty!

I'm busy, she tried to put off the two-pound mammal. If she stopped to listen to every little creature, she'd never have a moment's peace. Usually they wanted to brag about the size of their litters or scold people for approaching their nests. This hedgehog, however, would not be put off; she ran frantically around the rock in circles, shedding some of her quills in stress.

Your Majesty! Your Majesty! she called again in her mind. Her sending was so urgent that Skylark paused.

All right. I'm listening.

Last night a man came to the place where thou slept. He looked at thee.

Huh. Who was it? Was it Adair?

Not a hare, a man. A predator. Then a sleeping female humankine sat up. And the predator backed away.

That is curious. Skylark wanted to know who had trespassed into the women's sleeping area, but the rustle of the eagle's wings as it settled on a pine sent the hedgehog into terrified flight.

Good morn, Lord of the Skies. This is a wonderful new campsite. We are grateful to you for finding it. Do you have news for us?

From the sky I saw a small flock of men that flies toward the sun. The man who wears stars rides a horse. Another be a mate.

Skylark found this message opaque.

Come with me to consult with the commander.

She found Thalen standing on the sand beach, deep in conversation with Nollo and Shyrwin. The eagle flew to the top of the largest boulder, interrupting them with a glare in his yellow eyes.

When she relayed the eagle's message, Thalen decoded his sighting. "The Magi, the captive Mellie, and a few guards are riding toward Femturan! Ask the eagle if he saw any other soldiers between us and these riders."

Skylark got the answer. "No. Many soldiers move about near the mountains, but none are directly between that group and us."

Thalen had difficulty controlling his excitement. "To catch a Magi out in the open, so lightly guarded! I can't believe they are so confident as to risk this again! We will never have another chance like this." He jumped onto one of the boulders edging Emerald Lake, calling, "RAIDERS, TO ME!"

From around the lake or below the hillcrest, everyone came streaming around him.

"We have a chance—only a chance—of running down a lightly guarded Magi. They have a head start. We need our best fighters on our best mounts in two minutes, ready to ride breakneck. Kambey, you don't need to argue with me; I'm not the best fighter even when hale. Kambey leads and chooses the Raiders; Gentain chooses the horses; Skylark briefs the birds. Everyone! Set to!"

Without hesitation Kambey counted out, "Nollo, Shyrwin, Kran, Jothile, Adair, Eldie, and Eli-anna!"

Immediately, Gentain, Balogun, and Dalogun sprinted down to the corral to ready the horses. The chosen warriors dashed for their weapons. Others filled water bags or parceled out strips of preserved meat for their comrades.

Skylark led the hawks and eagle away from the bustle to inform them of the plan and ask for their help.

Wilt thou leave dead horses for us to eat? Horsemeat be tastier than aurochs, sent the eagle.

It will be so, Skylark agreed. She shouted this bargain to Kambey as he appeared from the men's sleeping quarters buckling on his sword. Then she ran down the hill to the corral. She checked Brandy's tack and cinch and held his head for Adair. Most of the Raiders converged there, passing up water and food and seeing off their comrades.

Before putting his foot in the stirrup, Adair kissed her hard on the mouth. "See you after I earn my keep, Milady Duchess!"

The riders took off down the thin path that led down the mountain. Caught up in the bustle, Maki started after them.

"No, Maki!" Skylark called out loud. "The horses may be galloping a long way—you can't keep up. Stay with me." The wolfhound looked after the horses, their excitement pulling at him. "No," she repeated. "We need you here to guard the camp."

The Raiders who had been left behind looked at one another in the sudden stillness.

"Well, that hurt my pride," said Wareth, and others agreed, laughing ruefully.

"Yet, tell you the truth, I'm relieved to miss this one," said Fedak.

"Why didn't he take me?" Ooma grumbled.

"You're one of the best fighters," said Gentain, "but it's going to be too fast a gallop for you." Turning to the sky, Gentain intoned, "Spirits on High, may they all return unscathed. Come on, lads, plenty for us to do. Hooves to check, muck to shovel, tack to mend."

The commander led a group of Raiders back to the lake, giving orders about moving the men's sleeping quarters to the far side of the water and gathering wood for the cooking fire.

The day grew hot and stretched on as if the sun would never travel over the sky. Slightly before sunset, when Skylark sat washing some clothes in the lake, the eagle circled down. He refused to talk to her until after he had drunk his fill. A crowd of anxious Raiders gathered around Skylark and the bird at the lakeshore.

Your fellows caught up with the small flock, the eagle finally deigned to tell her. *They slew them all, except for the mate. The horses were tasty, but none of the water near the kill site is good to drink.*

Were any of my fellows injured? Any killed?

Oh, aye, sent the eagle. *And fire shot out and roasted a man.*

Who? How badly?

One does nay learn the sounds you call each another, said the eagle huffily.

Isn't there anything you can tell me?

The horse with the white face was tasty.

The eagle was just being true to his nature, but this struck her as so cruel that she turned her back on him and walked away. She couldn't recall who had been riding Pastry.

Tristo grabbed her arm. "What did you learn?" She told the assembled crowd what little she knew. Then she whistled up Cinders and rode down the trail, to the place where the mountain's flanks reached a more level glen, to wait for the survivors and injured, even though she knew it was far too early to expect them. Maki loped by her side. She dismounted and sat on a rock, stroking his rough coat, letting Cinders browse among the sparse greenery. Over and over her mind hummed: *Who was it? Who died? Who lived?*

A couple of hours later Commander Thalen appeared out of the woods on Dishwater.

As always, he looked her straight in the eyes. "Would you rather wait alone?" he asked.

"Not necessary. You understand I'm not waiting just for Adair," she said. "I'm worried about Eli-anna and Eldie. And Kambey has been so kind. I—I'm not like the rest of you. I am not used to people dying on me. Or even horses." Her throat choked up.

The commander sighed. "Always before I have ridden with the fighters, never stayed behind with the injured. Aye, now I know how hard it is to wait in suspense. But as to death, I am getting used to it. Hardened to it. I no longer keep count of the men I have killed. Only the friends I've sent to their deaths."

Idly, Thalen scrounged on the ground for some small stones and tossed pebbles at a small pine. "All men will die. Yet sometimes it hurts more than others. Especially when it's someone young."

They sat in silence for long minutes.

Thalen used up his handful of pebbles and retied his fluffy, loose hair in its leather. He continued, confidingly, "I think I got into all of this because my little brother died, right in my arms, and I could do nothing to save him. Nothing at all. Grief has become my anchor, vengeance my sword. Now I am killing more and more Oros—some of them injured, begging boys, as young as Harthen."

"In Sweetmeadow Oros murdered Wimmie and Nimmet," said Skylark with heat in her voice. "And Linnie. And the dogs. To slaughter babes and dogs! There was no need—no reason. Some crimes are unbearable. It is right, it is *just,* to punish a people this brutal."

"I thought that way too, for a long time. But I discovered that when I kill an Oro it does not bring back Harthen's laughter. It does not bring back the brave Raiders who have already perished under *my* command or who are out there, perhaps dying tonight." The commander pressed his lips tightly together.

"It does not even slake my fury, which bursts forth with renewed force whenever I lose someone. Let me tell you something, Skylark (though everyone has to discover this for herself): vengeance may seem like a noble prize, but you grab for it, you grab for it, you grab for it, and it turns into a dagger blade that merely cuts your own hands."

Skylark pondered that thought.

"Doesn't it punish those who should be punished? Doesn't it deter aggression?"

"No. In this mission I kill people who never did me harm. And it seems to foster more and more killing. If I lose more people tonight—on a night when I didn't even ride with them—I will rue the order." He paused a moment. "'Specially if it should be Eldie or Eli-anna."

"Eldie and Eli-anna are soldiers, great soldiers—better than nearly all of the men; that's why they went today; they would not have you treat them differently."

"I understand that in my head. I know why Kambey chose to take them with him. But not in my heart. And it is not that they are women—or maybe that has something to do with my worry. They are the youngest out there tonight. Like Harthen, they are too young to die."

"Actually, no one is too young to die," Skylark demurred. "Babes die every day. The awful thing is not the dying, but the suffering beforehand. Especially to suffer alone. But by the Grace of the"—she caught herself—"Saulė this night it be not Eldie or Eli-anna."

A whistle through the woods warned them that Wareth had ridden down from camp to join them. He had brought them mugs and toted a metal pot of lentil soup. It was still warm, and it tasted delicious.

Skylark turned to Wareth. "The others, they call you the commander's 'boon companion.' Have you known each other since you were young?"

Wareth laughed. "It feels like we were both children that first night. What do you think, 'Mander, can I tell this new Raider the story?"

"Why not?" he answered.

So Wareth told the tale of the Rout and how he had been injured before it even truly started, and how, by luck, Thalen had caught his horse, and how they had coincidentally met up again at some creek. He was a good storyteller, and he got caught up in the performance, acting out all the parts. The commander sometimes corrected him, or told him to stop lying so baldly, but he also laughed and took over parts of the tale. This was the longest Skylark had spoken with either of them, and she felt honored to be included in their intimate circle. The moons rose, Daughter Moon circling Mother.

"Hush!" interrupted Skylark. They all froze, listening for a long moment.

"There's nothing out there. I have sharp hearing," Wareth said.

"Still, hush!" directed Skylark. "An owl is sending to me. He's too far. I can't quite hear him." She mounted Cinders and rode out into the darkling valley, straining for a sound that wasn't a sound, but rather a thought—a thought only she could receive. Maki loped close by her side.

Wareth and the commander followed Cinders's canter slowly, giving her room. Skylark closed more of the distance between herself and the owl.

Nestlings returning. Over here, the owl directed.

Skylark headed Cinders in the right direction, cantering over ground that sloped gradually downward. But once Cinders put on speed, Dishwater and Custard—who were both longer-legged—far outpaced the little filly. Skylark could not hear the owl's hoot over the horses' hooves, but she spied his white wings moving against the clouds in the north. Below him she made out small shapes.

The attack squad was returning at a crawl: their horses certainly would be exhausted; she hoped their injured weren't bleeding so heavily that speed was urgent. Skylark tried to count figures, but she was no scout; the gloom defeated her eyes. Squinting, she could just see that the commander and Wareth had reached the group and pulled up their horses. They were talking to the riders. She was too far behind; she could not catch any of their words. But she could use her Talent, even in the dark.

Brandy, where is your master?

Tied across one's back, Your Majesty. Cold and stiffening. His boots dig into one with each stride.

Skylark reined Cinders to an abrupt halt. She felt light-headed and her skin turned cold and clammy.

The commander raced Dishwater back to her, facing Skylark so their legs were parallel and barely brushing. He reached across the two mounts, almost as if to grab her hands, but instead at the last moment he took hold of the pommel of her saddle. "Raider," he said, gazing straight into her eyes, "they killed the enemy. They killed another Magi! But in the sortie we lost two comrades: Shyrwin and Adair."

Skylark sat still, unable to speak. Wareth and the survivors had resumed their slow pace in her direction.

"I'm sorry, Skylark," the commander said, and again made a motion as if he would take her hands, but refrained at the last second. Instead, he grabbed Cinders's reins and stroked the mare's neck.

Skylark made no audible reply. *Brandy, did he suffer?*

"Skylark. Did you hear me?" Thalen asked.

"Yes. But Brandy can't tell me how much he suffered."

"I think it was quick," said Thalen. "And I'd like to believe that his friends held him. You could ask the others, but I'd advise against it. Sometimes, not knowing is better."

She said out loud, through numb lips, "Adair *was* brave."

"Indeed," said Thalen, "and such a skilled scout. For what it's worth, he was very happy—these last weeks. He was always a cheerful companion, but since you joined us . . . Very, *deeply* happy."

"Eli-anna and Eldie?"

"Unscathed," said Thalen. "Nollo and Kran are injured, but not seriously. And, though it's hard to believe the coincidence, the Mellie scout they rescued turns out to be the girls' brother, whom they had given up for dead."

"Then we have *something* to thank the Waters for."

Catching her emotions, the hound at Cinders's hooves raised his throat in a mournful howl.

PART

FOUR

⌒

Reign of Regent Matwyck
Year 13

AUTUMN

36

Outside Cascada

Matwyck had arrived at his wife's country estate late in the night, summoned by tidings that her condition had worsened.

His valet shaved him and dressed him in a doublet of dark gray silk and matching trousers. His silk shirt of pearl white peeked through the slashing and at the cuffs. After a nice fastbreak—Tirinella's geese always laid the tastiest eggs—he consulted with the estate chamberlain. Then he went up to see his wife. She did look worse than his last visit; he noticed that her face had lost its burnished toffee tone, her breathing came more rapidly, and her fingers showed the swelling that last time only affected her ankles. Fortunately, the bedchamber had been kept orderly and held none of the sickroom odors that offended him. The roses he had made provision for lent the room just the right amount of scent.

Tirinella was asleep when he first entered. He sent the servants away and looked over her household account book from a comfortable chair placed near the head of her bed. He dozed off for a few moments and woke to find his wife staring at him.

Her eyes bothered him. They had always been luminous. Once

he had thought them her loveliest feature. That was before a shade of judgment and disappointment crept into their gray depths. All the reproaches she never uttered made their way into those dumb, pleading calf eyes, which in recent years held a look of disgust and horror.

"Ah! My lady-wife! You're awake," he said, just a little flustered. He reached for her cold hand and pressed his lips against the back of it, noticing that even that light pressure left an indentation. "I rode in last night and did not want to disturb you. I heard that you were going through a bad spell, my dear, and I wanted to lend you my strength. Surely you will rebound now that I am by your side."

She'd pulled her hand away from his, but said nothing. Her eyes fixated on his face.

Matwyck stood up to stretch and walked to the window. "It's a lovely day. You should see the trees ablaze with color. Would you like me to have you brought out to your garden for an hour? Isn't that a good idea? That would please you, I'm certain. I will give the orders."

He strode to the door and spoke to the servant and guard on duty outside.

"Now, my dear, before such a taxing excursion you must take your cordial. I have some right here. I had it mixed up fresh for you before I left the palace."

He poured some liquid out of a little vial into a glass by her bedside. He added a splash of wine from the decanter at hand.

She was too weak to pull herself up into a sitting position on her own. Repressing his distaste (and congratulating himself for hiding it well), Matwyck slid his arm under her shoulders and raised her up.

"Here, my dear, drink this down."

At first he thought she might defy him and keep her lips closed. Tirinella's eyes never left his face, but she slowly drank the liquid, down to the last drop.

"That's my good wife," Matwyck said, and he was grateful enough that she hadn't made a scene like the time before that he kissed her briefly on the top of her soft amber hair. "Now I'll go see about your treat, your trip outside."

Matwyck took his time, finding the exact right spot in the garden, warm in the sun, sheltered from the wind, and providing a pleasant overlook of shrubbery, trees, and brook.

She always loved this estate more than she loved me. It is generous of me to think of her preferences at this crisis. She's beyond noticing, but perchance the tale will travel.

"I shall stay out of the way as you shift her so as not to cause one speck of unnecessary strain," he told the estate chamberlain. "But set up a chair next to her for me, and come fetch me from the library the moment she is settled."

In the library Matwyck drank a mug of mulled wine as he idly passed his hand over leather-bound books on the wooden shelves. Tirinella's father, Lord Tanker, had had good taste. The furnishings in this room spoke of old money, a little too obvious for Matwyck's preferences, but the maple wood was well polished, the leather well buffed, and the silver candlesticks shone. Matwyck raised his cup to the portrait of the lord hanging on the wall. He had arranged for that proud old cock to die in a duel in the early years of Matwyck's marriage, shortly after the second time Lord Tanker had complained about some unsavory rumors concerning his son-in-marriage that had come his way. And when Tirinella had been distraught over her father's death, he had celebrated his victory by taking her, *right there,* on her father's desk. Afterward, he told her he wanted to distract her and convince her of his undying ardor, but really, of course, that sexual act had been his display of triumph and possession.

As he recalled, she had responded well to his passion. At any rate, she had ceased crying.

Had that look been in her eyes then? He couldn't recall.

Matwyck studied the portrait of his wife in her early years—she *had* been lovely. He took the heavy painting off the wall and moved it over to the desk. Surely the next time the servants came in they would notice that he'd been admiring her youthful beauty.

As he moved the picture he also caught sight of a portrait of Marcot.

When would the boy come home? As a grieving widower, wouldn't he be in his rights to request his son at his side? Or should he let him keep traveling, denying his own need and putting Marcot's preferences first?

He heard a knock at the door. He took a white lace kerchief out of his sleeve and balled it up in his hand. "Come in," he called, expecting to see some servant saying that Tirinella's move had been accomplished.

Instead, he recognized the local midwife, a woman he had clashed with repeatedly over the last year.

"What do *you* want?" he asked. "Don't complain about moving her out-of-doors. My lady-wife loves her estate, and she deserves to see it one last time."

The square-faced woman, dressed in faded woolens with a white cap, jerked her head and waved off the suggested topic with her hands. "I know what you've done," she said.

"You will address me as 'milord' or 'Lord Regent,' *woman*! And why did you not curtsey when you entered? I hold *you* responsible for Lady Tirinella's low condition! You've been looking after her these moons."

The goody did not quail. She actually stamped her foot. "For seasons I've wondered why her ladyship always worsened after your visits. Now I know." She pulled out of her apron the glass that Matwyck had just used to give Tirinella her tonic. She held it to her nose and ostentatiously took a sniff.

I'm slipping. Grief has upset me.

"I don't know what you think you 'know,' woman. *I know* that you have failed your patient, you have failed her son, you have failed the realm, and you have monstrously failed me!" And in an instant he grasped with a certainty why Tirinella had not borne him any more heirs. This blotch-faced female! She had provided his wife some means of killing his seed. She was the one who was truly to blame for his ruined marriage!

In two strides he reached the old lady. He slapped her face and with his backhand knocked the glass violently out of her hand, sending it crashing to the floor.

The woman took the blow stoutly, without falling over and without putting her hand to her cheek.

If she had cringed or begged, Matwyck would have desisted. Her audacity, however, enraged him. Though not often a physical man, Matwyck grabbed the bitch with two hands around her throat. An unseemly scuffle ensued. She kicked him hard in the shins; he tried to tighten his grip.

The door opened because one of his new guards, trained to be watchful of everything around the Lord Regent, had heard the sound of breakage and raised voices.

Matwyck let go of the goody, cleared his throat, settled his cravat, and pulled down his sleeves. "Guard, I have been sorely tried by this woman's impudence and incompetence at such a fraught moment. I must go to my lady-wife. You will detain this—this wretched excuse for a healer until such a time as I can deal with her."

"Listen to me!" Words tumbled out of the woman's choked throat.

"*And* since she has a foul tongue, here." He passed the guard his kerchief. "You will gag her and keep her gagged."

He noted with satisfaction that *now* the healer looked frightened. He pushed past her, moving down the hall, putting her vileness behind him. When the chamberlain approached, Matwyck raised his brows.

"Is my lady-wife settled? Has she asked for me? I must not be kept away from her. The moments are too precious to me."

The chamberlain told him that Lady Tirinella had been safely moved to the spot he had chosen. As Matwyck strode through the mansion doorway, a dusty rider dismounted with a satchel in the yard. "Milord, General Yurgn sent me with urgent dispatches."

"I doubt that anything the general could tell me is as urgent as my duty in the garden. Nevertheless, give them here." Matwyck continued on his way, carrying the letters, and sat in the armchair next to the bed that had been carried out on the green.

Tirinella's closed eyes fluttered restlessly as Matwyck read about bread riots in Maritima. Keeping the populace slightly hungry was prudent, because people busy searching for food can't revolt. Desperate people, however, have little left to lose. Finding the exact balance was quite tricky. Matwyck had been too gentle in quelling previous unrest. Apparently, the troublemakers all hailed from Chatlin-on-the-Sea, so he would order the entire community into exile in the far reaches of Prairyvale, while having the ringleaders hung. That would serve as an object lesson. And afterward he would send cart-loads of flour to Maritima to show his forgiveness.

The breeze blew a leaf on Tirinella's bedding, and Matwyck brushed it off. He couldn't tell whether she was conscious or not. Her breathing sounded very labored, and her nostrils flared with each breath. He watched her chest rise and fall for a few minutes under a white coverlet. Some of her hair had come out of its snood and lay upon the pillows.

He contemplated the pastoral view, which was quite pleasant, and his fingernails, which he could find no fault with.

No one tells you how boring death watches can be. You're supposed to sit by, but for how long? I have things to attend to.

He recalled that he had seen some tolerable books in Tanker's library. A copy of *The World Well Won: A Tragi-Comedie in Five Acts* would make time weigh less heavily if he had to sit idly by.

When he could tolerate his boredom and inactivity no longer, Matwyck decided to go inside to grab the book, answer Yurgn's messages, and order his midmeal. He leaned over for a formal kiss on Tirinella's forehead. Her hairline smelled, as it always had, of the lilac scent she favored, and for a moment Matwyck lost himself in memories of their youthful beddings and pillow confidences. He blinked his eyes several times and succeeded in making them tear up a little.

"I'm sorry, my dear, but this is best. You know it is," he whispered in her ear. "That's why you resumed taking your tonic. You should never have deprived me of more sons."

As he strode up the walk to the manor house he called to his wife's favorite maid. "Go sit with her; hold her hand. I want someone with her every moment. I don't want her to face the Waters without someone holding her hand."

37

Emerald Lake

Tally: 20-2 (Shyrwin and Adair)+1 (Eldo)=19
Horses: 25-1 (Pastry killed by Magi)=24

Thalen concluded that they were trapped. For two moons Oro troops patrolled the entire Iron Valley, watched the towns, and surrounded every Citadel of Flames. The Raiders could do nothing but lie low, hoping to stay hidden by their mountain lake on an arm of FireMount. Thalen couldn't send a resupply team to Needle Pass with any hope that it could sneak through such a robust cordon. And they couldn't take advantage of the Mellies' hunting skills. The men's morale sank as food supplies dwindled.

"I'm sorry, Gentain," Thalen said. "But we don't have any choice."

They stood by the makeshift corral that afternoon. Skylark and the ferry twins, who had been currying some horses a few steps away, heard his words (as he had intended) and froze midstroke.

"I know, sir," said Gentain. "I'll not fight you."

Thalen let go of the breath he'd unconsciously been holding in.

"Which one?" he asked.

"That's the thing," said Gentain. "Skylark and I can't decide."
He called to the girl, "Come, and explain the problem."

She came, a curry brush clutched in one hand.

"Probably we should choose Tater, that brown mare with the
white socks. See her, over there? She's got a strain in her rear right
leg that keeps flaring up, and she's in season, which makes her dis-
tractible. But the thing is, even though the leg hurts her, she's got
grit, and she'll push through the pain and do her best."

"Is there another option?" Thalen asked.

"There is," Skylark answered. "Patches, the piebald gelding over
behind Balogun."

"What's the matter with him?"

"Nothing," said Gentain. "He's hale and he should be fast."

"But he's not fast; he's mopey," added Skylark. "Depressed."

"Do horses get depressed?" This was a new concept for Thalen.

"Of course," said Skylark. "Horses are herd animals, and they
form deep attachments to their friends. Patches is a young horse,
and he was devoted to his mother, Pastry, who didn't return from
the race to kill the Magi. He's heartbroken."

"See? That's why, sir, we can't decide," said Gentain.

Thalen looked at Skylark and Gentain, both of whose faces
looked anguished at needing to choose one of their horses for
slaughter.

"I'll decide," said Thalen, taking the burden. "It's Patches."

"Very good, Commander," said Gentain. "Do you mind telling
me why?"

"You two are concentrating on the horses," he said. "I'm thinking about feeding the Raiders. Patches is larger, so more meat, and
younger, so more tender. If we are going to take a life, let's get the
most out of this sacrifice."

Gentain and Skylark both looked a little sheepish at this logic.

"Why don't you tie a lead to Patches and give him to me? Kambey

and I will take him away from the rest of the herd and up to Cook."
Thalen wanted to make this easier for his horse masters.

"Commander, I'd like to comfort him through the ordeal," said
Skylark.

"I promise you it will be quick," said Thalen.

"Even so."

"Very well."

They led the horse up the incline and found a little clearing away
from the lake but close enough to the cook fire. Cook and Kran had
already sharpened their best knives for butchering, and Kambey
had put a fine edge on his heaviest straight sword.

"How do you intend to kill him?" Skylark asked Kambey. She
said "kill" outright, as opposed to some indirect phrasing. If you
weren't listening for it, you wouldn't hear the slight quaver in
her voice.

"Cut his throat. We'll tie his legs and pull him down to the
ground so I can get right to here." Kambey touched the front of his
own neck.

"No, don't tie him or pull him down. That would just terrify
him." Skylark stroked the horse's neck a few times and murmured
to him. The big gelding folded his knees and set himself down on
the fir needles and leaf litter. Skylark rubbed his forehead and his
muzzle; though they didn't hear a command, the horse then pon-
derously stretched out on his side. Skylark knelt and leaned over the
horse's head, one hand resting lightly on his nose, the other behind
his ear, in such a way that her body blocked the sight of the others
and her smell filled his nostrils.

"Now," she said. And Kambey, who had been standing still
and patient, holding the sword hidden behind himself at the ready,
swung it in a terrible arc that severed the animal's neck in one blow.

The geyser of blood was horrendous. Even Thalen, who wasn't in
the arc's path, instinctively jumped backward. Cook came running
up with a big kettle to catch as much of it as possible. Maki, who

had been underfed in recent weeks, started frantically licking up the liquid puddling in the dirt.

"Fuck," said Kambey, quietly and forcefully. "Fucking fuck that." Thalen didn't know whether Kambey was referring to the blood that had splashed him or to having to kill the horse, but he didn't care because his attention was riveted on Skylark. She closed the animal's brown eyes as they grew glassy and stood up. She was drenched: hair, face, hands, and clothes. And her stance was none too steady—she swayed slightly as she stared down at the carcass.

"Tristo! Heat some water for washing and bring it to my tent," Thalen called; then he grabbed Skylark behind her elbow and steered her away from the grisly sight.

In his tent he poured brandy into a mug. "Drink."

She downed the contents. He grabbed his own towel and made a stab at rubbing the worst of the blood off her face, hair, and hands.

"Take off your clothes and throw them outside the tent door," he said. "Then you'll wash. I'll go rustle up some clean garb for you." He left her in privacy.

He sent Eli-anna to scrounge a change of clothes for Skylark. When he returned to the tent the bloody shirt and trousers were lying in the dirt, and he heard the sound of water splashing inside. He gathered up Skylark's stained clothes and started to wash them himself, scrubbing them furiously in a bucket on the lakeshore.

"Sir, let me finish that," Dalogun interrupted his thoughts. "You must have better things to do."

Thalen ceded his place over the wash bucket. "I'll check on Gentain," he said, heading down the trail.

Gentain now stood alone in the corral, methodically finishing the currying that had been interrupted.

"Gentain?"

"Aye, Commander?"

"He felt no pain, no fear. One blow. It was quick and peaceful."

"We should all have such a good death," Gentain replied, his voice firm. "I only wish I could have provided such for my daughters. My regrets don't circle round the horse, Commander. I have worse sorrows."

Thalen couldn't think of any possible reply to such a statement.

"But Commander," Gentain called as Thalen began to turn away, "with the oats gone, I can't keep the herd fed. This woods doesn't provide them enough to eat. Also, they need real exercise— more than we can give them just moving about on these skinny trails."

"What do you suggest?"

"Let me take the string out at night to nearby pasturelands. Say, half of them at a time, so if we get caught you still have enough mounts."

"That would be dangerous," Thalen said. "Let me think about it."

Thalen circled back to his tent, seeing that the door flap had been opened. Skylark sat unmoving on his stool, dressed in clean clothes.

Thalen squatted level with her face. "How are you?" he asked. He saw some spots of blood on her neck and hairline that she'd missed; he wiped them off with his fingers and the cuff of his sleeve. Skylark didn't seem to notice.

"Would it be all right for me to have a little more brandy?"

"Sure. I'll join you." He poured for both of them.

"Would you—would you talk to me?" she asked.

"What about?"

"About anything. A new topic to take my mind off this afternoon. I'm sorry; you must think me very weak. After all the Raiders who have died, to fuss about a horse."

"No, I think you're strong and brave. To hold his head like that. I hadn't considered there'd be so much blood."

He swirled the brandy in his mug. "Hmm. Let's go sit by the water. Do you know the history of how the Free States overthrew its monarchy?"

"No. Tell me," she said in a tone that was almost an order.

They climbed out onto the boulders. The lake water looked particularly green today. Thalen launched into the history of the indifference of the Iga Throne to the welfare of the people, of the pleas of the martyrs, their transformation into stone, the Bloody Rebellion, and the establishment of a new system of government. Skylark interrupted him constantly with questions. Why was the monarchy so corrupt and uncaring? Who had led the rebellion? How did the system of electors work? What were its strong points and its weaknesses? Why a four-hundred-year-old history of another land should interest an Alpie confused Thalen, but seeing animation come back into Skylark's face and light into her eyes pleased him so much he poured more brandy and launched into a description of Free States elections. She took off her boots and dangled her feet in the lake water as the setting sun turned the sky orange.

Underneath his chatter Thalen's mind ran on a different track. He had a powerful desire to kiss her.

Thalen immediately scoffed at the idea. *Kill her horse, ply her with liquor, and try to seduce her?* She was under his command, and that would be taking advantage in the worst way. Were Sergeant Codek still alive he'd be aghast. To even touch her would prove that Thalen should never have been made commander in the first place. It would dishonor all their sacrifices.

Thalen threw the last sip of brandy in his cup onto the shoreline.

Tristo appeared behind them. "Commander, Cook's calling."

Thalen's stomach had been rumbling at the smell of the cooking meat.

"Come on," he said to Skylark.

"You go," she said. "The water's almost warm tonight. I'd like to bathe in the lake for a few minutes."

Since Thalen had seen additional streaks of horse blood in her hair, he thought a more thorough wash was a good plan. He headed over to the cook fire, resolutely keeping his back turned to the lake, though boulders screened the section of the lake they had allotted as "the bathing corner." With effort, he wrenched his mind from dwelling on the cool water of Emerald Lake lapping against her body.

"Everything all right?" he asked Cook.

"I've had to threaten to chop off some greedy hands," he replied, "but Kran's a wonder at keeping my knives sharp."

"Eat slowly," Cerf counseled everyone. "Small portions, small bites. Otherwise, you'll all be sick and you'll end up worse than before."

Thalen hoped the men had the sense not to be too celebratory over their first hearty meal in days. As people grabbed plates and settled on the ground cross-legged, he nodded absently while Cerf spoke aloud some of his theories about diet.

The men concentrated on their horsemeat steaks with minimal chatter.

Thalen looked around. Balogun, Dalogun, and Gentain ate a little glumly, but steadily.

Skylark appeared from the lakeside. Her hair was now plastered down, and her clothes stuck to her damp body in a way he found disconcerting. Cook served her a small steak. Thalen watched Skylark lift her knife to her mouth and then put it down on the plate.

You need the meat as much as the rest of us. Don't let the sacrifice of the horse have been in vain.

"How long do you think Cook can stretch one horse?" Cerf asked, interrupting his thoughts.

"I haven't tried to calculate."

"I'm going to dry half of it for later if I have to stay up all night guarding it," Cook said with a glare. "Anyone who tries to steal a piece will get a kettle on the head!"

Eldie clasped Skylark's hand, stabbed some meat with her dagger, and then brought it to the girl's lips. For a few seconds Skylark kept her mouth closed; then the smell reached her empty stomach, and she acquiesced. Thalen thought he saw a spasm of nausea flit across her face, but she mastered it and began to chew. Eli-anna briefly rubbed Skylark's back.

"Good," whispered Cerf, and Thalen realized that he too had been watching the mini-drama. Glancing around at the men, he had a feeling that many of them had also been holding their breaths, hoping to see Skylark eat.

Such good men. Tough, but not hardened. My Raiders. Starting a liaison with Skylark would disrupt the group solidarity. It would be selfish, in so many ways.

After they cleaned their plates, they all wanted more, but Cerf was adamant.

"There'll be meat for fastbreak, lads," Cook promised. "Go to sleep and dream of food."

The troop rose and began to move about. Thalen approached Skylark, discovering that he was not the only one clustering around her.

"Why did you do it, when you knew it would be hard on you?" asked Pemphis, the Green Isles recruit.

"To be there with him to his last second. No one should die alone."

"What did you say to Patches at the end? What did he say to you?" asked Gentain.

"What is there to say?" Her voice sounded strong, her chin jutted up. "I told him he was a great horse, I loved him, and he was going to a place where his mother awaited him, with green grass and warm sunshine and the most delicious water on earth."

"And what did he say to you?" asked Wareth.

Skylark shook her head, unwilling to answer.

Thalen headed for his tent and cot, worn out from the day's events.

It's wonderful that she's so brave and bighearted. But I'd love her even if she shirked such a trial.

Love her?

Yes.

'Tis not just jealousy. Not just loneliness. Not just desire. She's nothing like I thought I wanted, but she's bewitched me.

The next day he mentioned Gentain's plan about the horses to Kambey.

"Ach. Whoever took the string would need the owls and Skylark to have any hope of making it out and back alive and unseen."

"How could we keep the Oros from seeing the cropped grass and the horse droppings?" asked Thalen.

"Search me," said Kambey. "Let's ask Skylark what she thinks about this plan."

Thalen sent Tristo to get her.

"Can you send out your hawks, scouting for pastureland that's not watched by Oro patrols?"

"I've already done so, Commander. There are three places that seem suitable. Shall I show you on your map?"

Thalen laid out his map on the table.

"This area northwest is enfolded within the arms of a mountain; it's probably the most secure, but the forage is likely to be thin. Over here, the hawks saw the best grass, but to get to that pasture we'd have to pass these dwellings, and soldiers bunk there these days. Now this field here, it's fairly isolated, but Oros patrol the road. We'd have to spot them coming, hide, and wait for them to pass by."

"What do you think of Gentain's urgency? Is he risking the whole troop because of his attachment to the horses?"

"Commander, actually, that depends upon *your* strategy. If you plan that we are just going to stay hidden until we're discovered or starve, then we should forget about the horses' health and just butcher them as they start to fail. If you foresee that the Raiders have more forays or even escape ahead, then we don't have a choice—we *must* get the herd more food and exercise."

Her dispassionate appraisal impressed Thalen.

"Right," he said. "Tonight we'll scout those three pastures with human eyes."

"Who's going out? Which horses should we get ready?"

"Saddle Dish—I intend to see for myself. And Cinders. And we'll take the owls with us."

When Kambey heard of the plan, he argued against Thalen putting himself at risk.

"Let me go instead, or Wareth."

"No, I need to see for myself."

"At least let me send some archers with you for protection."

"Our best hope lies in stealth. A smaller group leaves the lightest footprint and makes the least noise. Leave off, Kambey—these are my orders." Thalen could almost convince himself that he needed to judge the situation with his own eyes and that his stubbornness was not influenced by the opportunity of having more time alone with Skylark.

She was waiting for him in the sloping corral after supper, sitting on long-legged, dusty black Kettle, not the little filly she favored. She had had the sense to change into a dark-colored shirt, and she'd covered her yellowish hair with her ragged cap. An owl perched on her saddle pommel.

Thalen swung himself up on Dishwater and nodded to her, pretending to be all business, even though his heart had started to thump most uncomfortably.

"Why Kettle and not Cinders?" he asked.

"Because Cinders can't keep up with Dishwater if we have to run for it," she answered.

They walked the horses down the slope and then she led them north, following the owl that flew ahead of them in the light of two waning moons. They skirted some rock outcroppings and moved under cover of some evergreens. In less than half an hour, she reined in.

"This is the first location," she said, and they both dismounted. They stood in a valley between the arms of the mountain, and during their trek they had passed neither roads nor houses.

"You're right: this is quite isolated and secure," Thalen assessed. Dish and Kettle, both hungry, had immediately reached for mouthfuls.

"The horses like the fare," she said. "Can we give them a chance to eat a bit before we move on?"

"Sure." Thalen seated himself on the grass. Skylark slipped the bridles off the horses and then sat beside him.

"How are you holding up?" he asked. He wanted to know if her heart was broken over Adair, or if she still mourned the horse.

"I'm—I'm all right, sir," she said into the darkness, as if she'd read his unsaid questions. "It's just so very odd. The strange emptiness. Someone you care for is here one day, and then the next day, they're not. It's like a small hole has been rent in the fabric of your life. If this loss occurred in . . . Sweetmeadow, someplace where you saw the person every day for years, probably the pain would be more piercing. But everything has been passing strange for me these moons. My life doesn't have a pattern. In some ways all of this seems unreal."

"Tell me about your real life in Sweetmeadow."

"What do you want to know?"

"Well, tell me about your family."

So she told him about her sister, Linnie, who loved to dance; her younger brother, Gunnit, whom she'd helped raise; her mother who spun goat fiber into thread; and her father, who understood her better than anyone else. Her voice grew husky with longing.

"How did you learn the Weir songs?"

"My mother taught me; she used to sing them while she sat at her spinning wheel. How did you learn them?"

"My aunt knew them; she used to own an inn and would hire troubadours. She taught me to play the flute. Sometimes I thought she was the only one who really saw me."

"You care for her a lot, don't you?"

"Yes. She's still in the Free States, living under Oro Occupation." The thought brought Thalen back to the business at hand. "We should go scout the other pastures," he said.

The second location wouldn't do because several of the houses they skirted had cows that lowed as they passed. (The owls hadn't paid any attention to the cowsheds.)

"Shh, shh," Skylark whispered to the cows.

Thalen and Skylark moved on as quietly as they could. The third pasture, a large gentle meadow, grew thick with grasses and shrubs.

"We could graze our whole string here," Thalen said. "Plenty of forage."

"Yes, but the road's down there."

"Where? I can't see it in the dark."

Skylark sent one of the white owls to fly straight over the road. Thalen judged that because of the bushes, horses would be fairly well screened from sight here, especially if the owls gave warning.

"Let's wait here until an Oro patrol comes by and see how exposed Dish and Kettle are then."

"Yes, sir." She sat on the ground and he joined her, sitting a bit closer.

"Tell me about the school you went to and what you studied," she said.

Thalen obliged. He hadn't really spoken about the Scoláiríum to any of the men; he generally played down his education amongst the Raiders. He relished describing Meakey, Granilton, and Irinia to Skylark; and this untutored Alpie girl appeared to understand his attraction to the library. She made him tell her every detail about musical concerts.

They were so engrossed in their conversation that they forgot to be on guard for Oros. Kettle and Dish had wandered away from them, chomping contentedly. Suddenly, an owl hooted a warning. Would they be visible from the road?

"Down," Skylark whispered, and both horses immediately folded their legs and disappeared behind some bushes. Thalen and Skylark threw themselves on the earth behind some high grass. Thalen wiggled forward a pace and peered through the stalks.

In a moment, a squad of eight, mounted on aurochs, came thundering down the road. They wore mail, which gleamed from the flaming torches they carried.

"Good," he whispered. "They've created night blindness for themselves; they won't be able to see anything beyond their torches."

He watched until they passed and then scooted back to lie adjacent to Skylark.

"We'll wait a few minutes for them to get farther away. Then I want to ride down to the road on Dish and look up this way to see if Kettle or you are visible."

"Right." She now lay amidst the scratchy scrub on her back, staring up at the sky. The stars burned against the midnight silk, so far and yet so clear they looked almost touchable. She reached out her arm as if she could grab a handful.

"What do you call the moons in Alpetar?" he asked.

"'Mirror' and 'Jewel.' We believe that the moons shine because they reflect Saulė's light. See how little Jewel twinkles tonight? What do Free Staters call the moons?"

"'Master' and 'Apprentice.'"

"And Oros?" Skylark asked.

"'Furnace' and 'Firefly.' They've just got to get their fire imagery in."

"And they've only disgust for the smaller moon."

"True," Thalen agreed.

"Should we stay here until another patrol rides by to get their timing?" she whispered. Thalen thought he heard a note of hope in the question.

"No," he said, against all his own wishes. "After I test the sight lines we should head back."

They lay on the rough ground side by side without talking. He could hear Skylark's breathing, and he thought he could smell her scent: a mixture of horse, sweat, and some sweet herb. The starlight glinted in her eyes.

She suddenly reached toward him and pulled some grass seed from where it had tangled with his hair near his cheek.

Thalen rose to put some distance between them.

After he tested the pasture's visibility from the road—judging that even if an Oro squad came by without lanterns they'd need to have an owl's vision to see a horse on the hillside—the two headed back toward their hideaway. One of the snowy owls flew in front to show the way; another circled above to spy out any signs of the enemy. The path wound through isolated woods and scrub; Thalen concluded that it did not present much of a risk for a small, quiet string.

"Do you think we'll get out of here alive?" she asked, turning in her saddle and breaking in on his thoughts.

"That wasn't the original plan," Thalen admitted. "When I decided to come, it was a sacrifice play, like in Oblongs and Squares where you decide to give up some pieces for the greater strategy. Do they play Oblongs and Squares in Alpetar?"

"Oh, yes."

They rode in silence for some moments, just the thud of the hooves and the little creak of the saddles. Thalen continued, "A year ago, right after the Rout, I felt I had little to live for, but now . . . Now, I feel differently."

Skylark made no reply.

"I'll find a way to extricate us or die trying," Thalen said, aware of the grim irony in the pledge.

But how will I possibly save Skylark and the rest of the Raiders from the entire Oro army? How could I have been so cocksure and foolish— to risk these precious lives?

Horses: 24−1 (Patches—rest in peace) = 23

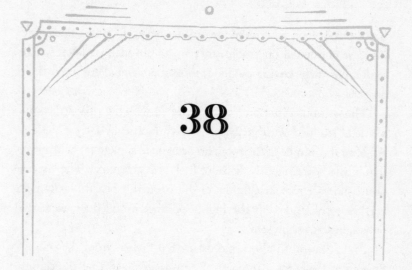

38

Femturan

After all his patrols in the area of the attacks came up empty, Sumroth was invited as an observer into the deliberations of the Magi over how best to counter this threat to the Land. To be allowed into the Fire Room constituted a high honor, but one that petrified the general. Standing in a dim corner of the enormous chamber, he pressed himself back against the wall.

Sumroth had climbed the nine flights with dread. He couldn't deny that the Magi possessed great Power—the burn on his chest had blistered and pained him. But it wasn't their magic that shook him; it was their irrationality. He did not look forward to more time with the Divinities.

The Fire Room was on the top floor of the Magi's gray metal tower, the Octagon, which dominated Femturan, rising sheer and powerful in the middle of the city, next door to the immense and ornate Citadel of Flames. A central spiral staircase carried occupants up and down the Octagon; each Magi had quarters and servants on a floor, with Eight's quarters on the ground floor and One's quarters at the top. The room where the Magi deliberated occupied the level above One's floor, where the tower sides began to taper. The spiral staircase continued one more story up to an open parapet, where sometimes their Divinities stood, took the air, and surveyed their domain.

The spacious Fire Room was furnished with high-backed chairs of metal studded with gems, placed symmetrically facing one another. In the middle of the room an octagonal, sunken pit held a Fire that burned continuously, without fuel, heat, or smoke. The last leg of the staircase rose straight out of this unearthly hearth. Its flames, and their reflections off the highly polished wood floor, were the only light sources present.

Except Sumroth also noticed tiny red flickers from the ceiling. Staring at them for a moment, Sumroth realized that the ceiling was papered over with bats, whose red eyes intermittently opened. With deliberate irreverence, he allowed his thoughts to wander to the effort the servants must expend keeping the floor and chairs so clean—unless the bats were somehow trained to shit into the fire pit and their guano was the fuel for the Fire? The fancy made him almost smile.

Today one of the throne chairs was empty because during the current emergency situation Magi Three had not yet been replaced. The new Four was a mere babe in her cradle, which for the meeting had been set by her attendants on her chair. Since the odd numbers signified males and the evens females, three female Magi—Two, Six, and Eight—faced three male Magi—One, Five, and Seven.

All six adults, whom Sumroth could recall from years past as normal-looking people, currently showed the effects of the blights, but their illnesses took different forms, from a tumor the size of an egg growing from One's skull, to Two's blindness, to Eight's withered hand. Their infirmities had not affected their fervor or their air of menace, however. Their eyes burned with anger.

One opened the discussion. "The tracks found after the attack on Our colleague Three conclusively indicate that these predations have been the work of men, not ghosts. But despite Our Protectors' efforts, no progress has been made toward finding these blasphemous invaders of the Land."

Two spoke next. "Our dreams offer confused images, and We have trouble reading them aright. Birds keep pecking out Our eyes. We face grave danger."

They kept silent for the amount of time Three might have taken to speak, as if they were listening to his ghost. The silence chilled Sumroth more than their speech. Then they all looked at the baby and listened to Four's babblings as if these constituted sense.

"It is time to put into action the countermeasures We have prepared," said Five.

"Yes, Five, We agree," said Six. "Guards, bring up one of Our woros."

"Fellow Divinities," Seven said, "we are in awe of the work you have accomplished to create these creatures. A most magnificent feat."

"Where men fail, the Power of the Eight shall succeed!" intoned the last Magi.

The Magi waited long minutes in silence except for the baby's little noises. Finally, Sumroth heard the clank of heavily armed Protectors' mail and a ferocious growling and thrashing. A metal knock vibrated the door.

"Enter," called One, his voice surprisingly strong.

Two Protectors wearing full suits of armor threw open the ornate double doors. In between them, shackled by metal chains and muzzled, thrashed a wolf. But this was hardly a normal wolf—its eyes glowed, and much of the fur on its head had fallen off in patches.

"And how is Our favorite today?" Two asked.

"Ravenous, Divinity," answered the keeper. Sumroth could well believe it. The wolf looked thin, noticeably, unhealthily bony. Even though it weighed less than either one of them, the keepers were having great difficulty controlling it. Sumroth placed his hand on his own dagger, just in case the wretched creature broke free.

After waiting during Three's and Four's turns, Five said, "Do We have a sufficiency of these weapons?"

"The Hallowed Number works in all matters," Magi Six answered.

Seven turned to glare at Sumroth in his corner. "Where you have failed, Our magicked beasts will prevail. Hunting dogs died out in the Land years ago. But wolves have proven immune to the blights. We captured some, bred them, worked on them over a period of years."

"They hunt only one kind of prey—men," Eight said.

"We are agreed on this strategy," Magi One spoke. "We will bait a trap for the invaders. In their loathsome pride they seek especial harm to Our Worship Citadels and Our Divine Persons."

"Thus," Two continued, "We will send out fifty soldiers flanking two men wearing Magi cloaks. *You* will wear one of these cloaks, General. Our Champion Tulsham, who will accompany you, will wear the other. We believe the infidels will not be able to resist such tempting targets, and they will show themselves."

Tulsham! Sumroth had never met the legendary fighter before. He had a reputation as Oromondo's greatest warrior because he had won the highest prize in the Combats the last time they were held. After this feat he had become the head of the Magi's personal security.

Sending Champion Tulsham on this mission was certainly an honor, but could it also connote that the Magi did not completely trust Sumroth or put their faith in his competence?

Silence. Baby cooing. "We have had a closed cage built that looks like a normal ore wagon. Except its cargo will be Our woros," Five added.

Magi Six picked up the thread. "When the infidels show themselves you will loose the woros. They will assist the Protectors in killing the intruders."

"Most importantly," said Seven, "they will track down any enemy who flee—track them to their lairs."

Eight turned to glare at Sumroth. "You will loose a cage of petrels, calling in reinforcements. You will destroy any remaining invaders."

Magi One did not deign to look at his general. "The Protectors must wear full armor. Since We turned the woros We have allowed them to eat only the flesh of men. That is what they now crave; they will not eat horse, aurochs, or any other meat. If they can't get enemies' flesh, they will try for Protectors'. We have lost quite a few keepers while training Our special weapons."

He rose, crossed to a low chest that Sumroth had overlooked before, and took out something bloody. Sumroth could not even tell for certain what it was. Could that be a man's thigh? Magi One crossed to the woro. "Remove the muzzle, keepers." They did so, warily. The Magi fed the beast the piece of flesh, which it devoured; then One casually wiped the blood off his hands on his bejeweled cloak.

"Most Fearsome Pozhar," said Two, "may these beasts enact vengeance for the loss of Our Brother Three, Our Sister Four, Our people, and Our Citadel of Flames." She and the others chanted in the Ancient Tongue for several long minutes. Then the room fell silent.

"Remove the woro," Five told the keepers; then he turned to the man standing uneasily in the back of the room. "General Sumroth, you depart on this mission the day past the morrow. Whatever you need for this expedition, you may claim.

"We expect to hear that you are successful, elsewise your precious wife, Zea, will be Our pets' next meal."

39

Emerald Lake

Tonight, all the scouts had returned to Emerald Lake Camp; Wareth soaked up the companionship and safety.

Although something Thalen had read led him to believe that horses could drink the bad water for a short period of time without falling ill, the commander insisted he still needed to know every drinkable water source in and around the Iron Valley. Guided by Skylark's hawks and owls, Wareth and the three Mellies often forayed out to scout enemy territory.

Eldo, the brother whom they had freed from captivity, turned out to be as skilled as his uncle Tel-bein had been. He was also as talkative as the sisters were silent—and with angry scar tissue instead of eyebrows, as odd-looking as his sisters were lovely. Elianna paired up with her brother, which meant that Eldie was again Wareth's companion.

This would have been fine; it would, in fact, have been wonderful if Eldie would respond to him as she had on their supply expedition to Needle Pass. During that trip they had coupled in desperate, mutual passion, as if to insist that despite death and danger all around them, they still lived. But once they met up with the Green Isles reinforcements, Eldie had insisted that their intimacy cease. Even now, when they were alone together again, she slid away from his touch. Her rejection pricked Wareth's pride and his heart. He desisted, riding behind her in what he knew to be a childish sulk.

With Tristo's help, Cook served a thin soup. Two weeks after they sacrificed Patches (partially because Cook insisted on drying strips of meat for future emergencies), rations had grown short again. Pretty soon they'd need to butcher another horse. Wareth was glad that he didn't have the responsibility for giving that order.

He seated himself as close to Eldie as he dared, which happened to place him next to Nollo. Thalen sat across the cook fire from Wareth. Thalen was the person most outwardly changed by the last wave of casualties. Nowadays, he sat with the company every evening, rather than secluding himself in his tent. True, with no raids to plan and no supplies to fetch, he had less reason to be fussing with his maps and lists, but Wareth suspected Thalen craved companionship.

We all crave camaraderie during our last days.

Tonight, Cerf sat on the commander's right and Skylark on his left. It struck Wareth that Skylark and Thalen often sat beside each other, and he wondered if that was her doing or Thalen's. Though it could be this closeness stemmed merely from Thalen needing to confer with her about the birds. Or maybe he felt sorry for her because of Adair's death. Wareth shivered, recalling the eerie night the three of them had waited for Kambey's squad to return when their chat was cut short.

But Wareth watched the way Thalen turned to listen whenever Skylark spoke; he saw in Thalen a certain eager attentiveness.

He looks at her the way I look at Eldie. Though these days I am extra-sensitive. No one has mentioned anything about those two, and gossip travels like lightning here.

Nollo noticed him gazing in their direction. "What interests you so across the fire?"

"I was watching to see how well the commander uses his arms—whether his ribs are all healed."

"Been healed a while," Nollo grunted. "My ankle healed up too."

Wareth smiled amiably. "I'm glad to hear it. What with my outings I've not been around much."

"Ever find anything to eat out there? Soup is pretty thin."

The Raiders allowed themselves to complain about only three topics: the food, the weather, and Kambey's constant drills. They said nothing about their injuries, their families in the Free States, their companions' deaths, nor their fear or despair.

This was the most Wareth had ever heard Nollo talk, even on their journey through Needle Pass with the supplies. It occurred to him that as Shyrwin had been his chum, Nollo too had recently lost someone. He wondered if Nollo had been lonely. How long had Shyrwin and Nollo ridden together? Most of the close friendships had been already forged by the time those two joined the Raiders—Nollo would now be an odd man out.

"How're you getting along?" Wareth asked.

Shyrwin's brave performance drawing the Magi's fire in that fight apparently had satisfied everyone about the two late recruits' loyalty, but Wareth doubted that his fellows had spent any sweat worrying about Nollo's grief.

"Kambey thinks if he drills me enough I might do for an extra archer. Adjusted my grip a bit. Might have made some improvement," Nollo said.

The predictability of this topic made Wareth smile to himself, but speaking of archery made him think of the Mellie girls. "Fine," he answered, his thoughts wandering.

"Do you have any kin at home?" Nollo asked.

Wareth was startled out of his reverie. "What?"

Nollo repeated his question.

"I don't know who survived."

"If I fall and you live, I have a letter to my mother in my saddle-bag. I had a scribe write it for me long ago. I've kept it for years, wrapped up, though it's gotten kind of battered. Would you try to see it delivered?"

"Aye. I vow." Wareth finished his soup, feeling hungry and depressed by the talk of dying.

He carried their bowls to the dish bucket, which brought him closer to the commander. "How about some music, 'Mander?" Wareth suggested. "We're all a little low tonight."

"I'll gladly play if Skylark will sing." Turning to her, "Do you know 'The Lay of Queen Ciella'?" Wareth noted the sound of Thalen's voice when he addressed her; it was different, somehow.

Are her eyes shining, or is that the firelight?

Oh, what business is it of mine, anyway? Leave it be.

"Aye," she responded. "But we'd need someone to sing the prince's echo."

"Nollo, we need you," Thalen called across the fire.

Wareth stood close to the musicians, toasting his backside in the cook fire, as Thalen played the fife, Skylark sang the queen's part, and Nollo sang the prince's part. Wareth was pleased to see that Nollo was included in the social circle of the group. And he did have a rich voice and perfect timing. He should have been a minstrel, singing in some royal court, not starving next to this cold, green lake.

This lay told the story of a queen of Weirandale who lost her prince to death, but found his voice again in the murmur of the

Nargis River. Wareth was caught up in a swirl of contradictory emotions. He wanted to weep yet at the same time felt so comforted by the song's romantic message that those who truly love are never parted.

As he played, Thalen gazed at Skylark with his heart nakedly visible, at least to Wareth.

When I die, Eldie, will you be brokenhearted? Or will you carry on living? Will anything remind you of me?

He was so lost in the harmonies that he did not even notice that Eldie had moved to stand by his side.

He only realized she was there when she slipped her hand into his. It was not some soft, noblewoman's hand, but dry, strong, and rough. He would not have it any other way.

Tonight, at least, they were both alive and blessed beyond words.

Skylark sang her heart out because she found it easier to stay on key when she sang with her full voice. Nollo's harmonies, as usual, chimed in perfectly, but all her attention centered on Thalen. Over the fife his eyes locked on hers; she felt as if the music was a thread of secret communion between them.

When the song ended, no one clapped or voiced approval; the circle of Raiders was so emotionally affected that dead silence was the most fitting response. No one even moved until Cook loudly blew his nose, breaking the spell.

"Ah, me!" said Cerf, stretching his arms overhead. "That just tears the heart out, don't it? I don't know if the song master who wrote that should be worshipped or just whipped."

"Nicely done." Nollo clapped her on the shoulder.

Skylark tore her glance away from Thalen's. "Couldn't have done it without you, Nollo."

Thalen stood up, but casually reached a hand down to help Skylark to her feet. Relishing the warmth, she wanted to hold on to his hand forever. She thought he kept the contact longer than strictly necessary, but then Fedak came up to him with some remark about checking his snares for small game and Thalen let go.

Skylark drifted off to get ready for another night-foraging excursion. The ferry boys, Gentain, and she planned to take a third of the horses to the mountain pasture tonight.

An hour later, in the dark field, she listened to the herd munch and switch their tails and kept half an eye on the owls. Gentain had braced his crossed arms on his bent knees; his head lolled once he fell asleep. The ferry boys, bows at the ready, watched for trouble from opposite ends of the pasture.

Skylark mused over her time with the Raiders. Adair's avid attention had intoxicated her; she'd been rushed along in the river of his charm. She could still taste his soft kisses and recall the silky softness of his long hair. She didn't regret allowing his flirtation, but she'd only known him for a few days: her infatuation had melted like snow on the first day of sunshine. He did not occupy her heart.

The commander, on the contrary, had become irreplaceable to her. From the first moment she saw him, she'd felt drawn to him. The more time she spent with him, the more she admired his leadership, his keen mind, and his character; the more she admired him, the more she craved his regard and yearned for his touch.

She was always conscious of where he was around Emerald Lake, always wondering what he was thinking, always pondering their last conversation, and always eagerly awaiting the next opportunity to interact with him. After two moons of living with the Raiders, her yearning had grown to a fog that enveloped her every moment.

During these weeks she suffered, wondering if Thalen, in fact, fancied one of the Mellie girls. Or had she ruined everything by her dalliance with Adair? Or perchance Thalen did reciprocate her love but couldn't show it because of the duties of leadership? Or maybe he had no particular feelings for her, and this was all her besotted imagination? She was new to romance; was she behaving like a love-sick milkmaid mooning after a goose boy? Did all her friends notice her infatuation and pity her?

But just when she gave up the situation as hopeless, chiding herself to concentrate on the mission, Thalen glanced or spoke to her as if he was just as smitten as she was. And tonight when he could just as easily have played some bar songs, Thalen had chosen that passionate love song.

Does he feel for me? If he doesn't, why did he hold my hand? Why does he look at me like that?

Oh, Sweet Waters. My thoughts keep obsessively treading round the same circles again and again. If only I could confide in Percie or Zillie, they would help me regain my bearings.

Skylark was self-aware enough to know that some of her yearning stemmed from the bone-deep loneliness that grew out of her life of disguise and exile. She'd never been able to show her true self to anyone. She'd lost her real mother and father, Wilim and Stahlia, Cascada and Wyndton. Often she believed that she must be the loneliest person in the world.

As if called by her forlorn emotions, Funnel trod up behind her and nibbled her hair.

Quit it, Skylark snapped, not wanting horse slobber in her hair. But she instantly regretted her impatience. *I know you're here, Funnel. It's just that a human craves one's own kind. Go find some sweet grass. We can't stay here long.*

The gelding plodded slowly off to join Cinders and Sandy.

Skylark sat up with a start. *If Thalen does care for anyone, he loves Skylark—not me. He doesn't know who I really am.*

And if he did, that secret would be dangerous for him.

If I truly love him, I must protect him—I should push him away. I must keep him from getting close to me.

Skylark gazed at the night stars, lovesick and resigned, hopeful and despairing. She felt buffeted by noble renunciation and selfish desire. No matter how she beseeched the stars for guidance, their light remained far away and cold; they provided no answers and no comfort.

40

Sutterdam

Gustie had made Umrat believe that this banquet for the high officers left behind was all his idea. He did not recognize how she had
manipulated him with little comments about how he now was responsible for morale, or how he really should show off the prowess
of his skilled chefs. The sore point of his vanity was his competitive-
ness with General Sumroth, and any comparison that would make
Umrat gain stature while Sumroth was away was catnip to his ego.
Gustie stoked this weakness with remarks about how Sumroth had
no social graces and never befriended the officers in his command.
Because Umrat had been transferred from Jutterdam to take over
Oro headquarters in Sutterdam, this was the perfect moment to es-
tablish himself as leader and win his underlings' loyalty.

She was able to manipulate him on this matter because her cam-
paign to get him to care for, confide in, and value her opinion had
been almost laughably easy. Gustie began with short expressions of
gratitude about his protection and her living circumstances, on the
order of, "I thank you, General, for the fine meal," or, "The bathing

chamber in this house is even more luxurious than the one in our last billet." A casual warning over morning tisane—"You know, in the Free States a few unscrupulous merchants have been known to rig their scales"—won her Umrat's attention and sense of obligation. As their "relationship" developed, Gustie schooled herself not to shudder when he touched her and even to make gestures that could be interpreted as reluctant caresses, as if, despite herself, she was falling for his manly attractions.

On the day of the party, Gustie fussed around the airy hall making sure that the table settings looked perfect and arranging the decorations. She inquired of the cooks about their progress. She triple-checked the sewn-in pocket in the sleeve of her fancy gown. She reminded the wine steward that the general preferred his wine chilled.

One would almost think this was my wedding.

In another life, Quinith and she used to build castles in the air about a wedding. All of Quinith's musical friends would perform, and Rector Meakey would officiate. . . . Gustie yanked her thoughts away.

When darkness arrived, the manor hall filled up with glowing lanterns and Oromondo officers, fifth-flamers and above, all sporting white-and-brown hair, red uniforms, and polished swords. A few had traveled from as far away as Jutterdam for this special event. Of course Umrat could not invite every single officer occupying the Free States, but Gustie made certain that he invited those in key positions and those most respected by their soldiers. She also saw to it that the invitation explicitly stated that comfort women be left behind. This left more seats for officers and no Free States women about whom she would need to worry.

Gustie stood with a polite smile on her face as Umrat welcomed his guests. He was a poor speaker, but at the moment he held the reins of power in these occupied territories, and the officers wanted to curry his favor. They laughed heartily at his feeble witticisms and allowed him to usher them into the banquet room, where they took their assigned seats.

Most of the waitstaff was comprised of Free States slaves, with Oro adjutants entrusted with the most important tasks, such as carving the ducks and pouring the wine. A group of Free States musicians had been released from captivity and allowed to practice for this special event. A boy was turning their pages as they played traditional Oro marches. The only Oro soldiers on duty were two ceremonial guards flanking the doors and saluting each guest.

Gustie shifted her gaze away from the lad turning the music pages. For safety's sake she knew only her own part in the evening's events. She was to wait until right before the main course, then empty her vial in the wine pitchers. She was supposed to drink along with the others, and suffer the same poisoning, in order to allay suspicion.

A handful of the officers had been delayed for some reason or another, and Gustie watched nervously as they bustled in late, full of apologies meant to show how assiduous they were about their duties, glad that she had been instructed to wait for the main course.

Gustie took the tray of opening bites from the waitstaff to serve Umrat herself. She held it before him, bending with a submissive flourish, smiling through lowered lashes. Umrat was nervous but also in high spirits tonight. He helped himself to the shrimp covered in buttered nuts and then reached inside the neck of her gown with his greasy hand to tweak her nipple. "Oh, General!" Gustie squealed, while Umrat and the officers around him roared with laughter.

Gustie took her own seat at the foot of the long table. She had thought she would not be able to eat, but she savored the delicacies and creamy seafood soup as if this were her last meal. The table sparkled with flaming candles and gleaming silver. Umrat caught

her eye and saluted her with his wineglass, indicating how pleased
he was with the way the banquet had come off. Gustie stretched her
lips into a smile. The waitstaff cleared away the soup bowls. The
platters of duck were ready to be served. With a rustle of her full silk
skirts, Gustie rose and approached the wine table to ascertain that
the white wine was perfectly chilled. While the wine steward stared
down her gown, she found it almost laughably easy to pour the vial's
contents into the three large pitchers the steward had at the ready.

Reclaiming her seat, Gustie noticed a couple of the officers were
not drinking wine. "Fifth-flamer," she teased the abstainer closest to
her, "are you afraid you might not behave properly if you partake of
the general's hospitality?" The officer a few chairs away stammered
with embarrassment. His fellows grabbed onto her suggestion and
taunted him mercilessly until he reached for his glass.

But Gustie did not know how long it would take for the poison
to incapacitate her guests, and she hoped to get the timing right. So
she tapped her spoon on the side of her own glass. The musicians
halted their playing.

Gustie called out, "Steward, be certain the glasses are full. The
brigadier has a few words to say, and then we shall drink his health."

Gustie heard not a word of Umrat's second, boring ceremonial
speech. All her attention was on the steward filling each glass. She
hated Umrat so vehemently she wished he could know this was her
doing. Her heartbeat made the blood in her ears pound loudly. She
watched until he had finished, and then she—as well as everyone at
that table—stood and drained her glass. Then she sat down to her
plate of rare duck dripping its blood onto a bed of roasted corn.

Gustie's fingers grew numb immediately. With effort she turned
her head to see if the officers on either side of her were having
the same problem. One sixth-flamer to her left was choking on a
large mouthful he could no longer chew. Down the table, someone
dropped a knife; another man clumsily knocked over his wineglass.

An officer tried to stand and pull his sword but instead tipped face-first into the currant sauce, currants splattering all over his white hair. Umrat opened his mouth as if to shout, but no noise came out.

This is when I die. Restaurà, keep me safe.

She awoke to a concerned face bending over her and some sticky liquid dripping from the corners of her mouth. She swallowed more of the liquid that pooled in her mouth; the antidote tasted foul. But her senses started to return.

Gustie recognized the woman bending over her as one of the waitstaff, darker freckles on her brown face, too homely to have been pressed into service as a comfort woman.

Gradually she took in that fighting raged between the guards in the room and the musicians, armed with weapons they had smuggled inside the extra music cases no one had thought to check. The musicians' lad was going through the pockets of the man to Umrat's right, the sixth-flamer in charge of slave labor. The boy found a large key ring and threw it out the window to a person Gustie could not see.

The waitress was pulling on her waist to get Gustie to stand up. She was able to rise, though she felt wobbly. Looking around she saw the wine steward's throat gaped—when the door guards realized the guests had been poisoned he had been the first object of their wrath. Gustie's hearing started to return, slowly.

"Come on, mam! Come on, you must move!" said the servant, tugging at her with strong arms. She pulled Gustie toward the kitchen entrance to the banquet hall. Gustie felt confused and foggy. People around her were dying. Reflexively, as she passed the table where the chefs cut up the ducks, she grabbed a carving knife.

In the kitchens: tumult. Servants were variously fleeing from the wrath of Oro guards or fighting back with tongs and fry pans. Waving her carving knife feebly, Gustie wanted to join the brawl. However, the waitress's sole job obviously was to rescue Gustie, and she was indomitable. She grabbed Gustie around her waist, half picking her up off the floor, pulled her through the kitchens and scullery and out the back door, straight into the arms of an elderly woman who stood there waiting calmly. The woman had a threadbare cloak in her arms; she swiftly draped it around Gustie's lavish attire and pulled the hood up over her fancy coiffure.

Gustie looked around to thank Freckle-Face, but she had vanished.

"Lean on me, girl," Mother Rellia said, "and walk like a crone."

"That won't be hard," whispered Gustie. "I feel as if I lost ten years off my life."

They made it down the street and turned into a dark alleyway without pursuit. Gustie felt her companion relax a fraction.

"Can you tell me what happens now?" asked Gustie.

"Any minute now the gates of the slave cellars will be unlocked. Our menfolk will find weapons at hand. There are still plenty of Oro soldiers about, but precious few officers to organize them or tell them what to do. We've been laying traps, and we'll have the advantage of numbers. The question will be how strongly our mistreated prisoners can rally. The fighting could go either way.

"You have done your own part, and that is enough. We each just do our bit. Please drop that knife, girl, before you stick yourself or me. I am taking you to a safe place."

Mother Rellia had a slow stride and wheezed with every step, yet she kept her pace steadily. Dealing with the effects of the poison, the antidote, and her terror, Gustie had to struggle to keep up. Shouts, whistles, or the clang of swords—sometimes far away, sometimes frighteningly close—broke the nighttime curfew. A church bell in the distance began clanging continuously. An Oro guard on horseback galloped past, paying no attention to two old women.

The manor house that Umrat had requisitioned in Sutterdam was on the city's northern outskirts. At their slow pace it took nearly an hour of crossing bridges, traversing alleyways and the darkest bystreets before they came closer to the center of town, ultimately arriving at a large brick building where an iron gate fronted a large courtyard. Another elderly woman stood in a shadow near the gate.

"Thank you, Mother. I've got her," said the waiting woman to the escort.

"Have me? Who are you?" said Gustie.

"Come with me, my dear. You can trust me. I am Thalen's aunt, Norling."

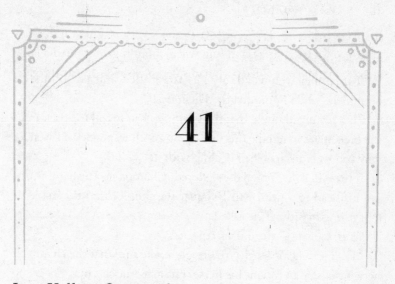

41

Iron Valley, Oromondo

Sumroth's horse plodded slowly up Iron Valley Broad Way. Swaying with the motion, Sumroth lingered over his memory of holding Zea in his arms the previous night, pressing against her body for what could be the last time.

This morning when they had gathered outside the barracks, Sumroth had recognized Champion Tulsham because the giant of a man wore a Magi cloak, and he had a great sword strapped around his waist. Sumroth approached him with his hand outstretched.

Champion Tulsham ignored Sumroth's hand. "General," he said, in an incongruously soft voice. "So we finally meet. It occurs to me I have never congratulated you on your promotions. I have often thought of them." His glance flashed to the eight flames tattooed on Sumroth's brow.

Sumroth had hoped for a comrade, maybe even a friend, on this infernal mission. Instead Tulsham's greeting smacked of envy and insolence.

"Have you?" said Sumroth. "Really, I am flattered. I have never thought of you sitting on your arse in Femturan while I conquered nations."

Tulsham glowered and sniffed. "You stuffed your face off the fat of infidels, while I guarded the Divinities."

"Interesting, though, that the Divinities had to call me back from the Free States to handle this threat," Sumroth responded. "I wonder why you were incapable of dealing with it?"

Thereafter he pointedly ignored Champion Tulsham, turning his head to a nearby fifth-flamer standing behind the man. "Is everything in order?" he asked.

"Yes, General," the officer reported.

"Let's go," he ordered. "You might make sure that the champion here has a step to mount his horse. His arse muscles may not be up to the climb."

The caravan made slow progress west on the road that ran along Gold Creek. The Free States horses that had been so healthy in Sutterdam only two moons ago had already started to succumb to the blights that plagued the Land. Sumroth swore. He should have had them checked thoroughly before setting out, although whatever their status, he wouldn't have wanted to ride on an aurochs.

The horses stumbled as if they were dizzy, and they wandered off the road unless guided by the reins, almost as if they couldn't see the path. Tulsham's horse staggered under the weight of the man, kept upright—Sumroth was certain—only by the fear of what would befall him if he tripped. Tulsham made disparaging comments about Free States horses to the soldiers nearest him.

Sumroth also worried about his men. He had chosen his sturdiest and most ferocious officers—no frightened, untrained pikemen for *this* mission. Yet his flamers had to wear all their armor to protect themselves against the invaders and the woros, and few of them were strong enough anymore to carry its weight for a day. The Oro Protectors left behind in the Land as part of the defensive army had been half-starved for so long they had given up on the required muscle-building exercises, and the men that Sumroth had brought back with him by ship from the Free States had grown soft in that rich country. Sumroth made a mental note to reinstitute strict drilling once he returned to the Free States.

Thus, the convoy moved slowly up Broad Way, a well-maintained thoroughfare cutting through the valley, with the Fire Mountains rising majestically ahead. During the first day out of Femturan, despite drinking copious amounts of water, some of the Protectors collapsed in the autumnal heat wave. On the second day, the horses struggled to walk at all carrying armored soldiers. Sumroth allowed his officers to put their helmets and backplates onto the wagon; these bits of armor were soon joined by the metal girdles from around their waists. Sumroth insisted his men keep on their metal boots, shin protectors, their chest protectors, and their gloves, but he looked the other way as other pieces dropped by the wayside. Under his thick, jeweled cloak (which was stifling), he too unfastened his shoulder plates and those protecting his thighs and sighed with relief when the rush of fresh air cooled his sweat-soaked limbs.

Tulsham kept his armor on under his red Magi cloak. As the leagues rolled on he stopped carping and lapsed into silence.

The four aurochs that pulled the wolf cart appeared impervious to the stench of their cargo or the temperature. The driver showed Sumroth that the cage was held closed by a spring mechanism. All they had to do to open the cage was cut the strings that held the latch secure. The drivers doubled as woro keepers; they were slightly less afraid of their charges than his flamers. But then they also carried long, sharp pikes to keep the beasts away from their bodies.

Sumroth's attention began to wander in the heat. He drank more water. His horse halted on its own accord; he had to whip it to get it to move. He realized that the horses would be worthless in a battle and it would behoove them to slide off and fight afoot, even though then they would be on the woros' level. And after the engagement, he very much doubted that these horses would be capable of pursuing the invaders.

"Sixth-flamer!" Sumroth shouted at a man at hand. "Ride up ahead and find us an appropriate spot to halt for the night."

"Yes, General. We'll need water for the animals. Any other particular desires?"

"No, I don't care what spot you choose. But whenever we make camp I will have specific orders about how to arrange the men for the night."

42

Emerald Lake

It was midmorning when the Lord of the Skies swooped in with tidings for Skylark. He had seen a caravan set out from Femturan, headed west in their general direction, with two Magi and a corps of mailed Oros. After she relayed this news to Thalen, he called Wareth and Kambey to consult.

"What do you think?" he asked.

"It's a trap," said Kambey. "It's gotta be a trap. They know we are out here. To send a platoon of this size means they are trying to draw us out."

Thalen nodded. "Yes, undoubtedly, it *is* a trap. Skylark, send out your birds to look for flanking regiments."

"I am intrigued by *two* Magi," Wareth said. "They might have some magic devilment up their sleeves. Could be they'll shoot fireballs at us or something-like. Could be they intend to burn up all the canyons, roast us out of hiding."

Thalen rubbed his eyes. "Anything to do with this caravan would be risky. Yet consider: we are running short of food. We can stay hidden and be marooned here, or we can take this bait. I would give my life—let me correct myself—I would give all our lives to take down two more Magi. With four eliminated, it would take years before Oromondo could threaten its neighbors again. They would call back any remaining troops they had left in the Free States."

Wareth shrugged. "'Mander, you're taking a desperate, foolish gamble. From what you've told me, exactly the kind of gamble Harthen would make."

Thalen flinched at the mention of his dead brother. "But think, Wareth. Winter will be upon us soon."

Skylark had given the change of seasons no thought, though more leaves fell every day.

"I saw snowflakes last night during second watch," Thalen said. "Maybe we could survive, most of us anyway, hunkered down, eating our horses, and breaking the ice on the lake for water. But then what? We'd live to spring only to find ourselves with no horses. And in the meantime, how many will die at home? Let us make this one last raid, strike one more blow, and then head to Needle Pass before the snows become too deep."

Kambey grunted. "Well, when you put it like that . . ."

The decision seemed to have been made. "Let me send out the hawks," Skylark said, "whilst you ready the men."

As she crossed over to the lakeside tree the hawks preferred, she overheard Kambey shouting orders to pack lightly and bring all their weapons. No one would be left behind to hold the camp. Everyone should cram portable foodstuffs into saddlebags. Full water bags. Everything else—sleeping gear, extra clothes, and cooking utensils—was to be left behind.

When she reentered the command tent, Thalen pored over his map of the Iron Valley, which lay on his desk in the patch of green-tinted light seeping through the open entryway. They leaned together over the vellum. Skylark was acutely conscious of the heat of his body; their forearms almost touched. If she moved just a tad . . .

"Eighteen against fifty," he said. "Foolhardy, don't you think?"

"Daring," she said.

"*You* won't blame me?" he asked, and for a moment his confident demeanor cracked.

"No. Besides, I'm certain you'll think of something to level the odds."

"Level the odds . . ." He tapped his quill on the map. "In this damn valley we won't have canyons to work with. Look, I've marked all the water the scouts have found. There's clean springs here and here—though I suppose if this is the final battle, it doesn't really matter if we drink their poisoned water. These are towns we must skirt. The road our quarry marches on runs along this line. By my estimate, we'll catch up to them in two days."

Thalen twirled his quill a moment. He straightened up, pulling away from proximity with her.

Skylark felt a great urgency—one or both of them would perish in this upcoming battle. This might be the last time she could be certain of being alone with him.

"So. So Thalen, we may never share ballads again?"

This might be our last moment. How can you not realize this? Won't you say something? Something that I can grab on to, rather than these hints and guesses?

She used his name, not his title, and she looked up at him expectantly, willing him to read her mind, baffled that she could share her thoughts with the least chipmunk but not with the man before her.

Won't you touch me just once? A caress to warm me against my fears and the cold of the grave?

Her desire was so fierce she could almost feel his hand on her cheek. He met her gaze. His own eyes were shaded in the tent's shadows.

He broke away from her awkwardly, looking down. He cleared his throat. His words were all business, though his tone gentle. "Raider, we have work to do. Dismissed."

"Aye, sir."

Fool! Idiot! You should have kept your mouth closed. What did you expect?

Skylark wrenched her mind back to her duties. She told Gentain to bring all the horses up to the lake to drink their fill. Then, returning to the women's camp to gather her own things from her bedroll, she considered her hair. She had run out of chamomile dye, but she did have a bottle of coal tar and bergamot. She poured a large dollop in her hands and rubbed it in her scalp and down her locks, which she kept short by sawing through them with her dagger. Then she put on Gunnit's hat to cover up her hair's transformation from yellowish to dark brown. If her companions noticed, she would fall back on the lie about a scalp disorder and a hair tonic—anything was better than blue roots growing in.

Eli-anna and Eldie came to gather their few things too. The Mellie girls linked their arms together around Skylark in such a manner that they both encircled her. She did not know what she could do to indicate her reciprocal affection and regard, so she imitated the gesture she had seen them do: she rubbed the bridges of their noses. The three women leaned their heads together for a long moment.

Her avian scouts returned with the news that the caravan followed along the same road, slowly and steadily, with no reinforcements visible in the vicinity.

The Raiders prepared to leave Emerald Lake under sunset's colors. Cook did not hold back with the rest of his supplies, preparing a strange buffet of odds and ends. Thalen went over and over and over his maps with every Raider, so everyone knew the fallback points.

The sun set behind the mountain, and the fir trees stood out as dark lines against clouds tinged red.

As they rode down FireMount, the moons rose bright as lanterns in the autumn sky. After many hours of picking their way, they reached the end of the foothills and forests. Before them stretched the wide-open Iron Valley. They rode in silence for several hours.

"Scatter and get some sleep during the daylight," came the order when dawn threatened. "We ride again at dusk."

Skylark put Cinders's saddle under the shade of a pine tree and let her filly graze. Maki came to lie near her. Tristo took the next tree over, but she didn't see where Thalen settled. She slept in snatches, shooing away the bugs that buzzed in her ears. When she sat up, annoyed and restless, she saw Pemphis, sitting alone, oiling his sword.

She thought that company might help. "Mind if I sit with you?" she asked.

"Of course not."

She watched how carefully he tended his weapon. "Funny, I hadn't figured you before as the warrior type."

"We're going into battle," Pemphis said. "We all have to be warriors. Don't tell the others, Skylark, but this will be my first time."

"Mine too. Do you worry you'll be frightened?"

He smiled. "You'll do fine, Skylark. And if you're ever in trouble, don't worry—I'll be looking out for you. Everyone will."

That night they rode hard except for two occasions when they had to stealthily skirt sizeable towns. They crossed a riverbed, bereft of water, wincing at the noise of horses' hooves striking rock. Near dawn Eldo led them to a cave out of which a small stream trickled. It flowed so sparsely that watering the horses and refilling their own water bags required patience. They ate dried horsemeat, topped off with a cache of berries Eli-anna had gathered. Again, Skylark found sleep evasive.

Once, she thought she saw Thalen gazing at her, but when she lifted her eyes to meet his, he had already turned away to talk to Wareth.

In the midafternoon she got a report from the eagle and the hawks, which gave her an excuse to approach the commander as he sat leaning against a tree. He had pulled his hat down to shade his face, but she knew he wasn't asleep, because he was shaking some pebbles in his hand.

"Excuse me, Commander."

He pushed his hat back and lifted his brows.

"They've made camp again," said Skylark. "As far as the birds can tell me, they are only a few leagues east of us, just along the road."

"Right. I'll send out Eldo and Wareth to have a look."

Skylark took her turn on watch. In a couple of hours the scouts returned and discussed their reconnaissance with the commander.

Then everyone—except Cerf, who now stood watch—circled around Thalen in the small clearing in front of the cave, breaking or bending away the fir branches that poked at them. Tristo stood next to Skylark and anxiously—maybe unknowingly—reached for her hand. She squeezed it.

Thalen tied his hair out of his face.

"We have one major advantage," Thalen said to his team. "Surprise. They may suspect we're out here, but they don't know when or where we are going to appear. We'll take advantage of this by striking right before dawn, when they're sleeping.

"We have a fast ride before us. They're camped east of this cave, on a small rise that gives them good visibility. On the north side of their camp runs the Broad Way, with Gold Creek right beside it. They've picketed their horses and aurochs on the far side of the creek. But on the south side of their rise Eldo saw a dry wash." Wareth drew the camp in the dirt and pointed out places as Thalen talked.

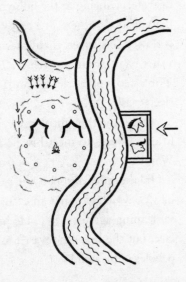

"When we get close, I'll decide on specifics, but the general plan goes like this: I'm going to divide you into four groups. The ambushers—Ooma, Wareth, and Eldo—will creep up the dry bed. You have the job of taking down as many sentries as possible without raising alarm. It's a tough job, but you'll be aided by the dark, and by the fact that the Oros don't see very well."

"*Don't see well?*" echoed Ooma. "What the fuck—how do you know that?"

"I read prayers for restoring their sight in the Fûli prayer book," said Thalen. "This also explains why they don't use archers. But never mind that now.

"Behind you ambushers will come our main strike force. Our highest priority is to get the two Magi. So the 'killers,' led by Kambey, includes all our best swordsmen." He pointed at Kran, Nollo, Fedak, and Jothile. "You will head straight for the Magi's tent. Don't get bogged down fighting other men. You want the Magi.

"Most of the rest of you will be 'diversions.' When the killers ride in, you—Gentain, Cook, Cerf, Pemphis, Tristo—will urge our spare horses to gallop around and sow confusion. Will any of our horses run down the enemy?"

"No," said Gentain. "None of our horses are vicious, except for Sukie, and all she'd do is kick or bite any bastard who annoys her. Without a rider on top, the horses will do everything they can to avoid crashing into people."

Thalen looked to Skylark. "Can you get our spare horses—how many do we have?—to knock over tents, disrupt the cooking gear, cause a lot of disruption?"

"Yes," she answered, forcing the word through a throat that had gone tight. "We have four spares. I'd suggest we keep them all saddled, in case someone loses a horse in the midst of battle."

"Maybe we should come in through the Oro herd, both for cover and to cut them loose?" Gentain suggested.

Thalen nodded. "Excellent. Gold Creek is shallow ahead; you won't have any trouble wading across. But you diversions, stay out of the killers' way. Once we've eliminated the Magi, we'll hightail it out of there as quickly as possible—we're not trying to take down the whole platoon and we don't care how many survivors we leave. Archers"—he pointed to the Mellie girls and the ferry boys—"you'll protect us and cover our retreat."

"I'm worried I might shoot one of you in the chaos," said Balogun.

Eli-anna untied her black-and-white armband and retied it around her forehead. She lifted her brows in a question.

Thalen nodded. "Good, Eli-anna, that should help distinguish friend from foe. And we'll have very bright moons tonight, though they will move toward moonset as the night passes."

"What about me?" Skylark asked.

"You stay close to me; I want to hear the reports from your owls."

Thalen motioned around him. "This cave, here, will be fallback for Cerf, Pemphis, and any wounded. A league north you'd run back into Gold Creek, which has more water for horses; Wareth's found a spot with a thicket of pines and an old, dead oak on the far bank. That will be the rendezvous point for everyone in good shape. Skylark, send the loose horses there."

"You can't miss it," Wareth chimed in. "The oak is cracked down the middle."

"Is the water safe?" asked Gentain.

"The birds tell us no," answered Thalen. "So you drink from your water bags. But at this point we need the horses well-watered more than we need to worry about future illness, so let them drink. We'll need speed to escape any pursuit.

"After tonight, after we kill two more Magi, we're *done*. We'll go home. I swear I'll find some way to get you home, stopping at safe water holes. Think of home—free of Occupation. That will hold you to this hard task.

"Any questions?"

Skylark had a million questions about death and pain and love, about how to kill someone in cold blood, and how to help a wounded comrade. But asking any of these aloud would sound impossibly green. Even here, standing on the brink of battle, pride kicked in.

"From now on, whispers only, and as few as possible. Make sure nothing jingles as you ride.

"One thing more. Raiders, it has been my honor to ride with you." Thalen turned in a circle, looking each one of them in the eyes.

"And you, sir," said Fedak, adding a crisp cavalry salute.

"Let's go gut some Oros!" Ooma added in a fierce whisper.

"I call dibs on a Magi," Kran said. "I'll take that jeweled cloak home as a trophy!"

Most of the Raiders managed a smile at Ooma's and Kran's bravado, but their smiles faded when Cook whispered, "My Maribel—I will avenge you."

Other names came pouring out, names of killed Raiders and names of lost kinfolk.

"The night runs on," Thalen interrupted. "Let's ride. Our ghosts will follow us."

The horses caught the jitters and skittered sideways when the Raiders mounted up.

Settle down, Skylark sent to the string. *You are strong and brave. Yes, we are riding you against other men, but you are trained for battle. It will be dangerous, but you have stout hearts. At all costs you must be quiet—no whinnies, no nickering.*

Then the troop was underway, galloping fast.

Skylark kept chanting to herself. *By the Grace of the Waters. Let no one suffer. Raider or horse. If death must come, make it quick and pain-free.*

By the Grace of the Waters. Let me not disgrace myself. This will be my first actual battle. Let me play the part of the soldier and not the wren. Let me prove myself indeed a queen, brave in the face of danger, as so many of my foremothers have been.

Small hills and swells broke the valley floor. A few trees stuck out of the dark landscape; most of these were stunted or dead. The fields of the farms they passed or cut through were all stubble, though whether due to harvest or blight, Skylark could not guess. Her mind focused mostly on the fact that this open landscape provided little cover.

The she-owl interrupted Skylark's repetitive prayers by soaring over her head with tidings that the enemy camp lay just over the next small swell. Skylark had chosen to ride Cinders because of the little filly's ability to dance around enemies: she found it difficult to catch up with Dishwater. Fortunately, Thalen saw her and reined in. Skylark pointed over the hill.

Thalen slipped off Dishwater, handing her his reins. He pointed to the ambushers, who also dismounted. They slipped over the ridge and disappeared into the night.

Eli-anna watched behind, and Eldie watched in front—both with bows cocked.

Skylark and the ferry boys emptied water bags and gave each horse a drink from a bucket. Maki caught up to the riders, lapped some water, and then flopped on the ground panting, cooling himself first in one spot and then shifting his body to colder ground. The big yellow moons watched the Raiders, casting their shadows on the sloping stubble, as the men and women retied their armbands around their foreheads. Kettle ambled over, lipping at Skylark's clothes, hoping for a stroke on her nose. Now that they had stopped moving, Skylark noticed the chill in the wind. She smelled woodsmoke and wondered if the enemy soldiers had enjoyed a good supper.

By the Grace of the Waters. By the Grace of the Waters.

Eldie gestured ahead at a tall shadow, Thalen, that came running toward the waiting Raiders. He pointed to the killers, who pulled their horses close and bent their heads as he gave them whispered commands. The five rode off in the direction he indicated, pulling the ambushers' three horses along behind them. Next, Thalen gathered the diversionary force and whispered last orders. The archers—the Mellie girls and the ferry boys—conferred with Thalen a moment and set off to get in position.

"Come with me on foot," Thalen said to Skylark.

"Yes, sir," whispered Skylark. "We also have Maki with us."

"Is he here? Good. You can send instructions in to the animals, but I want you to stay on the edge of the battle. *That's an order.* Do you understand?"

"Aye, sir."

"We'll crawl once we crest the hill."

Ten minutes later, from her belly in the scrubby grass she saw half a dozen campfires ahead. Man-shaped shadows occasionally walked in front of the flames. Although Skylark knew that other Raiders gathered in their appointed places in the dark, she couldn't see anyone.

Your Majesty! A strange horse spoke in her mind. *What art thou doing here? Hast thou come to help us? We be so sick, and these riders be so cruel.*

Shhh, she answered. *Don't make a sound. That's important. I will give you instructions soon.*

Skylark concentrated on the horses and listened for updates from the owls. All of a sudden Maki nipped the back of her calf.

What?

Wolves. One smells wolves.

Here? Now?

Wolves that have been . . . turned. And they are confined in wood.

Skylark couldn't figure out what Maki was saying. Wolves would never come this close to this many men. Turned into *what?* Her birds had seen nothing unusual; men, horses, tents, and supply wagons pulled by aurochs. Wagons made of wood.

The Raiders' horses had caught the scent as well. They sent her frightened messages about the disquieting smell, a jumble of questions and expressions of fear. In a few moments their disquiet would escalate into full-blown panic. Could she control them all?

Steady now. Steady now.

"Thalen," she hissed. "The Oros have brought wagons full of wolves. And they have done something to them. It's a trap. When we attack, they'll release the wolves."

Thalen stared at her, his brow furrowing as he tried to comprehend her warning. He shook his head in an attempt to clear it. "A trap, after all," he whispered.

"Thalen! Our horses will panic."

"Can you control them?"

"The wolves? I don't think so. I've failed with wolves before."

"No! Our horses!"

"Some. Most."

"Do what you can," Thalen said. "It's too late to pull back; we're already committed." Even in the dark she could see him clench his jaw. "The ambushers must be up the wash by now."

43

Iron Valley

Wareth crawled as fast as he could, but Ooma and Eldo were more spry. The three crept on their bellies in the dry creek bed, trying their best not to dislodge any stones or make noise. Ooma was the quickest, Eldo the quietest, and Wareth was certain he was the most terrified.

The firelight and the sounds of the Oro camp grew louder. Eldo tapped Wareth's leg and held up five fingers to indicate that five sentries guarded this southern flank of the camp. Wareth tried to shrink into every shadow and hollow of the wash. The rocks dug into his skin.

They heard footsteps coming nearer, alerting them that an Oro had come to the edge of the creek bed. The man stopped. Wareth held his breath, waiting for the ring of a sword leaving its scabbard or a challenge. Instead, a pace ahead of him he heard the unmistakable sound of urine splashing onto stone.

Eldo vaulted up and got his hand over the man's mouth while his knife flashed across the man's neck. Wareth pulled the dying Oro by his ankles into the shallow depression, cushioning the sound of his fall against his own body. Ahead of him in the wash, Ooma turned around at the disturbance—Wareth saw the moonlight gleam off her knife, which she held in her teeth.

They crept forward a bit farther. The thump of footsteps spoke of a man marching alongside the wash. Wareth signaled to Ooma and then threw a small stone so that it landed with a thud on the scrub behind the sentry. As the shadow twirled to investigate, Ooma's knife flew into its back. Wareth sprang up and wrapped his hands around the man's throat. Again, he pulled the body into the creek bed, trying to keep it from making too much noise. Ooma retrieved her knife.

They wiggled some paces onward until they ventured near to the center of the camp. Eldo tapped his ear and urgently pointed back the way they had come; he'd heard the approach of the killing unit. They had to hurry and clear the way.

Wareth leapt out of the creek bed and hugged the scrub. He spied a sentry outlined against the firelight who already had his sword out. The man's posture bespoke wariness; he scanned every direction. Wareth held his hand against his side to keep his scabbard from rattling and inched forward.

Spread out by several body lengths, Ooma and Eldo had followed Wareth's lead. Wareth picked up his head enough to see that the sentry had noticed something to the right, possibly the glint of Ooma's knife. He tucked his head down, gathered his knees under him, and sprang straight into the man, butting him so he fell on his back.

Wareth's curls somewhat cushioned the sound of his head striking the breastplate. The Oro grunted, but he didn't have time to call out before Wareth used his palm to smash the bones of his nose up into his skull. Eldo cut his throat, just to make sure.

The sentry's helmet had fallen on the grass. Wareth grabbed it, put it on, and stood up just in time to assume the dead man's place as the next sentry approached at a trot.

"What was that?" the Oro asked. His tone was loud enough that the head of the fifth sentry swiveled their way.

Wareth pointed into the creek bed, and the Oro reflexively peered in that direction. Eldo leapt up from the grass, his bow already drawn. One arrow struck the sentry nearest to Wareth and the second flew an instant later, thudding into the groin of the man beyond.

Both sentries cried out. Ooma's knives cut their warnings short, but it was too late.

"Watchman?" came a loud shout to Wareth's right.

"Enemies within the line!" came another voice from his left.

Skylark, waiting with Thalen at the perimeter of the camp, kept checking in with the owls, circling above.

"Tell me what they see!" Thalen whispered to Skylark.

"Some enemies down. The archers are in place with their bows ready. Kambey's group is a little ways behind Wareth, still walking their horses."

When a breeze brought a strong waft of wolf scent frightening the horses, she broke off to silently reassure them. *Steady now, steady now. I know there are predators nearby. But you are strong and brave.*

She relayed to Thalen what the owls communicated to her. "An Oro is walking out toward the ambushers. No, someone took him down."

Thalen let out his breath and slid his rapier out of its sheath.

"Raiders have kilt the men who guard the Oros' horses, and one of us is sneaking through that herd. Now he's cut the rope ties. Another Raider is moving amongst the teams of aurochs.

"Sir, the Oro horses are unwell."

Skylark was about to tell him more about the Oro herd when across the dark camp they heard a male shout, "What was that?" Another voice yelled out, "Watchman?" Then the entire camp was moving. Shouts and curses rent the dark, indicating that stealth was no longer possible or necessary.

A whir of arrows flew from the archers, deeper black against the dark sky. A few hit flesh with a hollow sucking noise, while others pinged off armor.

Thalen whistled for Dish, who cantered up over the hill, Cinders gamely following several lengths behind him.

Thalen mounted, stood up in his stirrups, and shouted, "For the Free States!"

From several directions, Raiders echoed the call and thundered into the Oro encampment.

Skylark ordered all the riderless horses, her own friends and the Oro mounts, *Cross the creek! Don't just stand there! Run into the midst of people. Make noise. Don't flee. Kick!*

Chaos grew before her. The knoll where the Oros camped soon swarmed with horses moving in every direction. Sparks flew up from disturbed fires, and cooking gear fell with loud clatters. The horses splashed through the creek and neighed. Aurochs stampeded in every direction in groups of two and three.

Skylark compromised on following the commander's order by nudging Cinders just to the edge of the encampment. She readied her spear. A man, perhaps an Oro sentry, rushed at her from her right, but a Mellie arrow thudded into him before she and Cinders could engage. Another Oro had seen her; he came at her from a different angle, slashing at her with a sword, but she managed to block his strike with her spear. Cinders whirled, and Skylark jabbed the Oro hard with the point, which slid off his metal breastplate but pushed him off-balance and made him slip to one knee. Maki seized the opportunity to sink his teeth into the enemy's throat.

The moons had lowered and the sky had taken on a lighter pearly gray. Skylark peered through all the frenzied movement, trying to make out how her friends were faring. Timid Walnut couldn't handle the smell of the wolves; she turned tail and fled the camp with Tristo barely able to stay in his saddle with his one arm.

Good. At least one of us will survive.

"Just die, you fucker!" Ooma's raspy voice carried through a lull in the cacophony.

Owls, what's happening? What do you see?

A horse galloped toward her, a pike held loosely in a man's right hand. Skylark readied herself, but at the last instant she recognized Pemphis as the rider, so she breathed out a sigh of relief.

"Pemphis! A Spirit send! But you needn't have left your duties to watch out for me."

"If it matters, Skylark—or whatever your real name is—I'm sorry," Pemphis said.

"What?" she asked, confused. It was too dark to see his face.

Then, to her disbelief, Pemphis steadied his pike and kicked his horse, Sandy.

"No!" she screamed, but he was so close—she didn't have time to raise her spear to block him and she wore no armor. She hunched low, and Cinders jumped and twisted in the air, so that instead of skewering her body, the pike just grazed her waist, tearing the fabric of the gambeson she wore.

Help! Help me! Skylark screamed in her mind. Cinders backed up a few paces, readying herself to dash in any direction. Sandy halted, confused by her rider's orders and Skylark's screams. Maki spoke in her mind, *What's happening?*

And on top of all the other messages, Skylark heard a horse call, *One comes!*

Pemphis yanked Sandy around in a circle, leveled his pike, and kicked his mare to make her charge again. But Sandy began fighting him, twisting her head away from the bit, moving sideways instead of forward. He used his excess reins as a whip. Sandy tried an experimental rear, but Pemphis kept his seat. She reared again, higher,

her front feet pounding the air, but he would not be dislodged. In desperation, Sandy vaulted herself up in the air and backward, so that she landed smack on her own back, with Pemphis on the ground beneath her body.

As Skylark screamed in astonishment, Sandy rolled off his form, scrambled to regain her feet, and raced away from a situation that felt all wrong. Skylark watched, frozen, expecting that Pemphis would be grievously wounded, but he cursed, moaned, and rolled over onto his hands and feet. The pike he had wielded lay on the ground not far from him—he started crawling toward it.

Thundering hooves from a heavy horse approached. Nostrils flaring and ears back, Sulky Sukie emerged from the gloom. She whirled so that her forceful hindquarters lined up with the man on the ground, then kicked with both feet like a donkey. Skylark heard the solid strike and bones—neck? back? pelvis? skull?—break. Pemphis crumpled on the first blow, but Sukie kicked again and again.

Leave off, Sukie, Skylark ordered.

Maki nosed Pemphis's form. *Dead,* the dog reported.

Skylark gazed at the ground, trying to process the horror. But she couldn't focus on Pemphis's treachery nor on the animals' actions to protect her, because in the next moment a loud metal clang rang out.

Wareth heard other Raiders take up Thalen's war cry. He started to run in the direction of the large tents on the highest plateau of the camp. He wasn't assigned to be a swordsman, but the sooner those blasted Magi were dead, the sooner they could all get off this killing field. An Oro soldier stood, openmouthed, in his way, so Wareth ran into him. He was sitting on top of this man, punching him, when Kambey's squad thundered their horses out of the dry wash. Fedak, the last rider, held Custard's and Gander's reins.

"Here!" Wareth shouted, and Fedak dropped the leads. Wareth whistled to Custard, who came to his call. Wareth vaulted into the saddle.

Oros boiled out of the two large tents, clad in full armor with swords drawn. They had not been caught sleeping; they'd been ready for this attack. They'd purposefully sacrificed their sentries to draw the Raiders in close. Horses screamed as halberds and blades bit into them. Wareth felt the knot of fear in his stomach grow larger.

Some of the Oro soldiers ran to a wagon and unlatched the back of it.

The noise of its door clanging open attracted every eye. Lithe figures with glowing red eyes leapt out of their cage.

The wolves lunged first for the closest meat, an Oro officer shouting orders Wareth couldn't hear. Other Oros kicked the beasts away with mailed boots and long pikes. Then, the red eyes locked onto the Raiders, noticing that their flesh wasn't covered by metal.

If Wareth had the option of changing Custard's trajectory once the monsters spilled out of the back of the wagon, terror might have prevailed. But like his fellow Raiders, he had built up too much momentum to turn.

Kambey, Kran, Fedak, and others had beaten him to the two Magi. From a different direction Cook and Cerf had almost gained the tents too; they were trying to hack their way through a squad of Oros that slowed their progress. The wolves circled Cook and Cerf, their eyes intense. Cook's horse began rearing in fear. Just then, an arrow aimed at the wolves struck Cook's horse by accident, and the poor beast arched sideways and foundered onto a knee. Cook slipped from his saddle with a drawn-out shriek.

A flash of firelight off a metal helmet brought Wareth's attention back to the danger right in front of him, and for the first time that night he pulled his sword. He tried to lop off a head, missed, but still connected with the meat of the owner's shoulder. Another standing Oro attacked him; they parried several strokes. This foe lacked muscle strength, and from his mounted vantage point Wareth managed to knock the sword completely out of his hand. Then Swordless and Bloody Shoulder joined forces against him, not trying to strike him, but rather to yank him off his horse to the ground. They clung to his stirrups and his leg, inside the reach of his sword. So Wareth used his pommel instead, smashing it down hard on a helmet. Swordless reeled away, concussed, allowing Wareth to aim an awkward blow straight into Bloody Shoulder's face and free himself from clutching hands.

Righting himself in his saddle, Wareth snatched a quick look around. Kran, Kambey, Jothile, and Thalen had converged on the two Magi. These two tall figures, both with great two-handed swords, stood back-to-back. They had ripped off the bejeweled cloaks to free their swings. But if they were Magi, shouldn't they have been firing fireballs or fighting them off with some other sorcery?

"Fakes!" Wareth yelled. "Fake Magi!!" He joined the others, shouting, "Fucking imposters!!!"

The two pretenders wielded their weapons with skill, managing to fend off four mounted attackers with their massive blades. One of them knocked Kran's sword out of his hand with a ringing blow. The other swung his great sword straight through the front leg of Kambey's horse. Kambey tumbled over the horse's head and onto the ground, struggling to regain his feet.

A pair of wolves leapt upon him before he could so much as raise his head.

Wareth howled with anger. Thalen and Jothile still pressed forward, one on each side of the two imposters. Jothile's sword flashed so fast the Magi could barely block it—the enemy had to tire soon from that heavy sword. Thalen kept Dish out of range of the air-splitting slashes while watching for an opening.

Wareth's Custard snorted and shook at the wolves boiling around the ground. "Up, girl!" Wareth shouted, encouraging Custard to rear up on her hind legs. Then, guiding with his knees, Wareth urged her a few steps ahead of Jothile—such that Custard's forefeet came smashing down smack on top of one of the fake Magi.

The wolves left Kambey and converged to taste this new kill. Thalen grabbed the opportunity to jump off his horse and hoist Kambey's limp figure onto Dishwater. Thalen slapped the horse's rump. "Go, Dish, run!"

The still-living "Magi" had managed to knock Jothile's sword out of his hand. Then he closed on the commander, standing before him. He was a head taller than Thalen, obviously stronger and more skilled, and his sword much longer.

Wareth shrieked, "Watch out!"

Thalen moved more quickly than Wareth had ever seen before, ducking inside a blow that would have severed his neck. The commander's sharp rapier caught the skin of the jaw of the second Magi, and blood spurted everywhere. The Magi recoiled two steps from the blow.

Suddenly, Tater—sent by Skylark?—streaked into the press, interposing her body between the Magi and Thalen. Seizing his chance, Thalen sprang into the mare's saddle.

"Raiders! Retreat!" Thalen shouted, first to Wareth and Jothile at hand, and then, standing up and waving his rapier, to everyone in the camp. "Raiders, retreat!!"

Wareth wheeled Custard, eager to escape, but at that moment a terrific *slap* shook his back shoulder. He tried to grab his reins but found that his arm would no longer obey his will. Three Oros grabbed his right leg—one had a tattoo of five flames over his left eye. Someone—Nollo?—smote one of his assailants. A cluster of arrows flew in the direction of the other enemies who had waylaid him.

Wareth's muscles went slack. As if watching from far away up in the now-brightening sky, Wareth saw himself slump forward in Custard's saddle, a dagger jutting out of his back and blood flowing thickly.

Thalen yelled something, but Wareth couldn't process the words. Custard ran from the field of carnage.

Skylark heard the same metal clang from the start of the battle ring out a second time. Everyone—Raiders, horses, and Oros—froze and looked toward the noise. Eight *more* wolves poured from the second wagon, sniffed the air, and headed in the direction of downed men lying on the ground.

Arrows whirred, a few striking the wolves. Were three down? The beasts came on so fast and low; even for talented marksmen they made near-impossible targets.

Skylark fled the periphery of the Oro camp. She passed the Mellies and the ferry boys, who formed a line with their bows to cover the fleeing Raiders. A horse briefly pulled abreast of Cinders; Nollo shouted at her, "You need a faster mount!!!"

As if to prove his point, the archers, abandoning their positions, sped past them on longer-legged horses.

"Out of bloody arrows!" Eldo shouted in explanation.

A faster horse. Skylark had chosen Cinders for her agility, not her speed. She reined in to look for another of the Raiders' string.

And when she did so, she saw five wolves racing in pursuit, their noses to the ground. She watched in horror as one of them sprang, grabbed Balogun's leg, yanked him sideways, and succeeded in spilling him to the ground.

"No!" she screamed. But even in the midst of her anguish for Balogun, Maki's thoughts broke into her mind: *The Oros saved the second set of wolves. The wolves are not for fighting but for tracking.*

In horror Skylark realized that her friends had little chance of escaping.

I am not helpless. I have Talent. By the Grace of the Waters, is it now strong enough to command wolves?

She turned back to face their pursuers. *DEMON-WOLVES. I*

COMMAND YOU TO HALT. OBEY MY COMMAND. I ORDER YOU TO HALT.

The woros faltered as they came close to her. She stared in their eyes. Two raced by Cinders as if the filly presented merely an unusual obstruction in their way, akin to a downed tree that interrupted their pursuit of a deer. They were not going to attack this strange presence, but they did not obey the princella's Talent.

Skylark sensed her Command had reached the minds of three of the beasts. The oldest wolf had the most memories of his former life before the enchantment. The red glow in his eyes dimmed.

Proximity helps. Touch strengthens my connection.

Skylark slid off Cinders, holding her spear tightly. Behind her came shouts from Nollo and Eldo. She also heard a woman screaming.

As she approached, the eldest woro lay down on his haunches. Briefly, she placed a hand on his head.

Pardon, Your Majesty. Pardon. They made one eat burning lava . . . They fed one human flesh . . .

The other two wolves that had also paused swayed in confusion. Their heads moved side to side indecisively. *What? Who? No. No. The Fires. The Fires will burn us.*

I COMMAND YOU TO HALT.

But the wolves were not close enough for her to reach and perchance too hungry to listen. They shook off her command and absorbed the aroma of her flesh. One of these woros leapt for her throat—only to be met midair by Maki. Wolfhound and wolf became a ball of growling, snapping ferocity, tumbling through the dirt.

The second wolf resumed slinking straight at her. His red eyes captured Skylark, freezing her with fear as she struggled in vain to make her Talent influence him.

STOP. NOW. I COMMAND—

She was pushed roughly to the side; she barely had the chance to break her fall by spreading her hands. She turned her head to see that Nollo had leapt off his horse in the path of the wolf's spring. The woro jumped on top of him, lunging for his throat, while Nollo struggled to block it with his left forearm. Skylark retrieved her spear from the grass. The woro growled as it worried Nollo's arm and strained for his neck.

Skylark screamed as she stabbed the creature with all her strength. She plunged her spear into its back, but the rib cage blocked the point; the beast twisted away and kept attacking. She aimed for its neck, penetrating the coat and pushing deeper. After an agonizing pause, the monster collapsed on top of Nollo, its black blood drenching the Raider.

Skylark rolled the heavy carcass to the side and bent down to Nollo. Dawn's first slanted rays illuminated his throat, which had been torn to shreds.

His lips moved without sound. "My Queen," he mouthed.

Skylark had long ago grown to trust Nollo. A man who sang the ballads as he did would do her no harm. What she had not known for sure, however, was whether he searched for the Nargis heir.

So he did know her. And he had given his life to protect her. "My first Shield," she whispered.

Even though she wore no Royal Stone, Skylark gave him the Queen's Blessing as he died.

Thalen saw a woro spring, its teeth reaching for Eldie's calf. She screamed and her horse bolted, dragging the wolf still attached to her stirrup.

He galloped after her, urging his mare for more speed. Drawing close, he leaned off Tater's side and was just about to skewer the animal with his rapier when Eli-anna, who circled round from the other side, shot her last arrow into the beast's eye. But the wolf still dangled by the stirrup, spooking Eldie's horse, Cinnamon. After a chase across two fields, Thalen and Dalogun managed to converge on the gelding, grab his bridle, and add their strength to Eldie's pull on the reins to halt its wild flight.

Thalen gave Tater's reins to Eli-anna, while Dalogun held Cinnamon steady. Thalen discovered that the wolf wore a linked collar and that the collar had gotten tangled in the stirrup. Thalen pried a link loose with his knife. Finally freed, the dead body dropped to the ground.

The horses' eyes rolled, they stamped their hind legs, and their ears were flat back; in a more controlled canter Thalen let their mounts put some distance between themselves and the red-eyed fiends, alive or dead.

When they regained the Broad Way at a spot with good visibility in all directions, he shouted, "Rein in!"

They paused, horses and riders heaving with exertion and horror. In the dawn light he could see who accompanied him: Eldie, Eli-anna, Dalogun, an unconscious Kambey, and several of the Raiders' riderless horses that had fled the battleground together in a clump.

Thalen pulled Kambey off of Dish, discovering that he bled from his neck, his sides, his arms, and his thighs. A big bite had been taken out of his rump. Blood dripped down his face from a tooth scrape on his bald head.

"Everyone, give me your neck drapes," Thalen called. He put pressure on the wounds and wrapped and tied. "Get me some sticks!" he ordered, and used these to twist the tourniquets tighter. Then he took a look at Eldie's calf, relieved to discover that her wound wasn't significant.

Dalogun decided to switch to Brandy, who was fresh, and Thalen and the Mellie women managed to hoist Kambey's unconscious form up to sit in front of the boy. Thalen hoisted himself back on Dishwater, feeling marginally more in control on his own saddle on top of his familiar companion.

"All right," said Thalen, rubbing the blood off his hands onto his trousers. "We've been heading pretty much straight west. We'll divide here. Dalogun will bring Kambey with me to the cave for the wounded. You two, take all the extra horses to Gold Creek; let them drink and guide them up through the water to the rendezvous. Cover your tracks as best you can."

"Where is—?" Dalogun began.

Thalen cut him off. "I'm sure we'll find more Raiders waiting for us at the rally points. Take heart."

Panting and shaking, Skylark looked around. She was on the rise that she and Thalen had crawled down in the beginning of the battle. She expected she would be alone with Nollo's body. Her horse and Nollo's—Cinders and Pepper—had fled from the terrible woros, leaving only churned-up earth. But farther up the incline and over to her right she spied another woro with the string notch and upper limb of a Mellie bow sticking out of its jaws. The whole rest of the bow had been jammed down its throat. Though dead, this last wolf had its eyes open and its jaw gaping, its fangs still aching to bite.

Its corpse lay on top of a person.

Skylark scuttled over on her hands and knees. By the burnt eyebrows she knew at once the man beneath must be Eldo. Alive? Injured? Dead? She put her hands in his armpits and tried to pull him out from under the creature's heavy body. At first she made no headway. But her efforts roused him from shock, and he contributed by digging his elbows into the dirt and wiggling his hips. Finally, he slipped out from under his burden; as he came free with a jerk she lost her balance and sat backward on the grass.

"Hey!" he cried. "Bird Girl! Why are you here? Why aren't you with the others?"

"Did they get away?"

Eldo glanced around them. "Looks that way, doesn't it? I was busy with my chum here. Couldn't let the wolves follow them."

"Nor I." She nodded down the hill toward Nollo and the dead wolf by his side.

Their legs trembled so that they had to cling to each other to stand. At the foot of the hill both Maki and his woro lay prone and unmoving.

"We kilt them all," Skylark said with wonder. "And the Raiders escaped!"

"What about that one?" Eldo said, pointing to the oldest woro and reaching for the dagger in his belt.

"He's not a threat."

Eldo stared at him suspiciously—the old woro averted his gaze like a polite dog, disengaging from a dominance fight—and then, pursing his lips, turned back to the giant carcass by his feet. "Pretty mangy looking. Not even worth skinning for his pelt. Maybe I'll take just the tail, as a trophy."

Their elation, however, turned out to be short-lived.

When they looked down toward the battle site they saw bodies on the field, horses swaying on their feet, and close to three dozen soldiers busily regrouping. They heard shouted commands. Then, edged by the sunrise, a group of eight Oros, well-armed, began walking inexorably up the rise to where the two Raiders stood.

After the hard ride, the battle, Pemphis's treachery, and Nollo's sacrifice, Skylark didn't have the strength to run five paces. All the Raider horses had followed orders and retreated to the water holes.

New horse friends, she addressed the Oros' mounts. *Can you help us? Can you gallop up this hill and save us?*

Most of the horses had already foundered, and others were too far gone to hear or respond.

One can't see, answered a strange voice.

Very sick, said another.

Skylark gave up on the idea of help from that quarter. At least she wasn't totally alone. Eldo's eyes had lost their sparkle and his lips their characteristic half smile, but his voice was steady and calm.

"I've been captured before and lived," he said to Skylark. "Here, take a deep drink from my water bag."

Skylark drank several gulps, then handed it back to Eldo, who did the same.

"Now, drop your knife and hold up your hands, Bird Girl."

She followed Eldo's lead.

44

Iron Valley to Femturan

Eldo should have died several times before in this miserable war, and he had cheated death time and again. If now the Stars decreed it was his time to be scythed, well, he was content. He had saved his sisters and the others and killed so many of those foul beasts. The memory of the wolf's red eyes and its wretched breath as it had opened its jaws a finger's breadth from his face made him shudder. At the last second he had shoved his bow down its throat with all his strength, rupturing its throat and additional internal organs.

Eldo was smiling to himself, unseeing, when a mailed hand struck him across the face, bringing him back to the present.

"You again!" roared General Sumroth.

Eldo picked himself up off the ground, spitting out a tooth and some blood. "I am afraid so, High Officer, sir."

"But *you* can't have been behind these attacks, because they started when you were in jail in Drintoolia! And that chit hardly looks worth a belch," said Sumroth, meaning Skylark.

"How many more of you are there?" he roared at the two of them.

They both stayed silent.

"Where is your hideout? Tell me, you Mellie cur!" When Eldo remained silent, Sumroth hit him again.

A man with five flames rested his sword point on Skylark's neck. "Speak, or I will slice her throat open."

Eldo spit more blood out of his mouth but said nothing. He'd be sorry if Skylark died, but his loyalties lay with his sisters.

The oldest wolf, who had remained stock-still on the slope where Skylark had stopped him, growled, startling everyone.

"Before anything else, we'd best secure the woros," said the Oro general. "Put on its chain."

Two men approached the wolf; it snapped at them. They retreated several paces.

The general sighed and leaned on his great sword. "Run back down to camp. Tell the keepers to secure those two"—he pointed at two wolves that were still eating near the wagons—"and then come up and help us with this one."

He addressed a different officer. "Bind the prisoners' hands."

The Protector tied Eldo's hands behind his back: an expert job without a bit of give.

They all watched from the top of the ridge as the keepers used body parts to lure the two feeding wolves back into the cart and closed the metal door. Then they waited silently while the keepers climbed the slope, carrying their prods, a muzzle, and chains.

When they tried to muzzle the old wolf, however, it kept moving its head just enough to frustrate their efforts. When they prodded it with their staffs, it grew angry. It raised its hackles and growled. Everyone instinctively backed up a few steps. In a sudden spring the wolf bowled through the circle of men and raced away at full speed toward the mountains and the forests. Eldo could not suppress another smile.

"Now that is just plain wrong!" said one of the keepers. "With all this fresh meat around? And I know the beast is starving!"

"We still have two of them. Two should be enough to track the invaders once reinforcements arrive. Bring the prisoners back to camp," ordered the general. Guards grabbed Eldo by his arms.

The remaining Protectors walked around the battlefield, cutting the throats of anyone—Oro, Raider, or horse—that was badly injured but still breathing. Eldo recognized the gentle horse master's gambeson and winced as a soldier yanked his hair back and sliced. The Oros harvested weapons, armor, and cloaks. General Sumroth examined the gear, pausing over the Raiders' headbands, and then went to look at the bodies himself.

Eldo spit at the ground, angered at the cruelty to the wounded and disrespect of the dead. He wanted to know which of the Raiders lay in the dirt, but at the same time, he could not bear to look. He had only lived with these Free Staters for two moons, and half that time he had been out scouting, but he liked them, especially that horse soldier who was so obviously smitten with Eldie. He wondered if that bloody mess sprawled near a cook fire was the woman who had been good with her daggers.

He glanced over at Skylark to see how she was taking this proximity to all her dead friends and kilt horses. She was staring down at her feet as if her world had shrunk to that patch of dirt.

Eldo looked at the ground too. Moving shadows cut the sunlight intermittently. Eldo wondered if vultures had already begun to gather, but the wings were slender. Hawks. Hawks circled above them.

"Are you all right?" he asked her.

"No talking!" said one of the guards watching them, slapping Eldo with a metal gauntlet. Jerking his head away reopened the cut on his lip. Blood trickled down his chin. Eldo would have liked to wipe it off. He tried to hold his head so it wouldn't drip on his clothes. His broken teeth throbbed, and he would have strangled anyone for another drink of water.

Noises indicated the approach of large contingents. Several

regiments of Oros converged on their location from multiple directions, marching double time. General Sumroth conferred with their officers. Skylark and Eldo stood where they had been placed, facing the wolf wagon, as the day slowly wore on. The sun burned the back of Eldo's neck.

An Oro officer wearing five flames came up to the Protectors who were watching the two Raiders.

"Put the prisoners in the cart," the officer said to the men.

"The cart" turned out to be a wooden contraption with high sides, pulled by aurochs. Soldiers threw Skylark inside and then pushed Eldo after.

With some twenty guards surrounding them and their officer leading the way, they set off at a bone-jarring pace to the east.

Eldo looked back at the battlefield. As far as he could tell, an argument raged between the officers, possibly over how to pursue their attackers. The Raiders now had a day's head start, healthy horses, and safe water. The Oros had started with sixteen wolves, and only two survived. Eldo smiled to himself again. Under such circumstances he would wager on Thalen's Raiders. He was certain that Eli-anna and Eldie could outwit such poor trackers.

Their cart and escorts did not stop for the night, and the prisoners were neither fed nor watered. With their hands tied behind them they could not brace themselves from jolts as the cart rolled over rocks or ruts. They were often tossed about or thrown together, and with the noise of the cart and the darkness, they sometimes whispered to each other.

"Why do they want us in Femturan?" Skylark asked.

"Easier to question us."

"Will the Magi do it themselves?"

"Don't know."

"Do you have a plan with your birds?" he asked when next he could.

"I sent them to help the Raiders," she whispered.

The bone-jarring hours passed by. Skylark eventually slipped down in the cart; Eldo tried to brace her with his feet so that she could snatch some hours of fitful sleep. When the ground grew smoother Eldo lay down and dozed too. As the sun rose, a full day after the Battle of Iron Valley, Eldo realized their escorts had headed straight across country, directly toward the capital, rather than following the road. The high buildings of Femturan rose on the horizon.

It took another day and night of miserable jolting, spare rations, and few stops until they could see the city ahead. It was a large metropolis, easily ten times the size of Drintoolia, the largest city Eldo had ever seen. In the center, the Magi's Octagon cast a dark shadow blocking out the dawn.

The procession halted for ten minutes. The prisoners were allowed to piss. In desperate gulps Eldo and Skylark drank the water they were offered, so parched by this point that they cared not whether it was pure or polluted.

In the late afternoon they trundled through the outskirts of the capital city. Their cart passed through a neighborhood devoted to metal refining, with furnaces perpetually smoking. Next Eldo saw a large wooden complex of buildings and parade grounds that bustled with red-coated troops.

Then the road led to a wooden drawbridge over a fetid moat. On both sides of the drawbridge a high stone wall paralleled the moat. The gate was a massive arch carved out of obsidian, decorated with flames wrought with gold.

They trundled over the bridge's wooden slats. Their officer stopped to answer the questions posed by a contingent of attentive gate guards. Then the cart moved forward again. The numerous buildings on both sides of the road were made of wood. Weathered, old, dry wood.

"What I wouldn't give for a few dozen fire arrows," Eldo muttered.

Skylark looked around thoughtfully.

The streets were paved with more black and shiny glass. Even at this early hour smiths clanged their hammers and jewel cutters' metal grinding wheels scraped. White-haired pedestrians, all with jewels in their ears, jumped out of the way of the cart and soldiers. Their captors seemed to be heading straight to the Magi's Octagon in the center of the city, a prospect that made Eldo quail, though he kept his face rigid.

The cart passed a Citadel of Flames of immense size and splendor, then a central courtyard. At the last moment, the soldiers turned away from the Octagon to follow a thin alley to the right. They pulled up at a low wooden building where the windows had iron bars. Their guardians pulled Eldo and his companion out of the cart and handed them over to a group of jailers. While the fifth-flamer conferred with a man who must be a supervisor, other men yanked the captives inside. Eldo wanted to say something comforting to Skylark, but there wasn't time and he didn't have the presence of mind. As men pulled her away he whistled two notes—a pitiful attempt at a birdcall. Jailers then hustled him into a cell so situated that he could not see or speak to his companion.

Once inside the small, enclosed room, the guard finally cut his bonds, which was a blessing, because his shoulders and wrists throbbed terribly. Exhausted, Eldo eased himself down to the straw bedding on the floor. The last thing he noticed before sleep caught his ankles was that his cell contained a barred window, too high to look out of but letting in air with a reeking, salty tang.

45

Iron Valley Cave

Thalen rode by Dalogun's side as the sun reached midday. Kambey slumped in front of the lad, never regaining consciousness.

Thalen tried to reassure himself that Skylark would be at the Gold Creek rendezvous. She would have obeyed his order to linger outside the battleground, and she would have been one of the first to retreat. He refused to ask Dalogun if he had seen Cinders ride west, because he wanted to hold on to this hope. Besides, Dalogun, who had asked Thalen ten times whether he'd seen his twin escape, had his own fears. Thalen did not have the heart to tell him he had heard Balogun cry out. It was still *possible* the boy had escaped to Gold Creek.

Dishwater's trot seemed to pound a message into Thalen's head. *Feelings don't count. Feelings don't count. That's what I conveyed to her—that our feelings don't count in comparison with the mission.*

When Thalen and Dalogun finally arrived at the cave in the midafternoon, they found Cerf alive and already at work, setting up a makeshift infirmary. He had cut down fir branches and lain cloaks on top to simulate beds, then set his patients in a row. One glance showed that Kran's arm had been shattered in multiple places, but Cerf and Thalen postponed setting it until they did what they could to halt Kambey's and Wareth's bleeding. Dalogun built up a small fire while Cerf heated his knife to cauterize their wounds.

"Will he live?" asked Thalen.

"Who? Wareth? Probably. Kambey's more dicey. He's out cold from so much blood loss. But by luck, the fiends missed all the major arteries. Chewed up a lot of muscle and skin, but then Kambey has layers and layers of muscle. Yet so many bites—if even one goes sour from their filthy mouths . . ." Cerf shook his head.

Thalen was glad that Cerf had husbanded his milk of the poppy wisely all these moons, crankily fighting off requests from Raiders whose wounds still throbbed. In this circumstance, when they needed it most, they could stave off suffering. He sat on Wareth's waist to hold him still as Cerf plunged that white-hot knife into the deep wound in his shoulder. Kambey's coma was so deep that he didn't even rouse to the pain of his own treatment.

When night fell, Cerf and Dalogun threw themselves down on their horses' blankets and saddles for a rest. Thalen, taking the first watch, was glumly listening to the water dripping inside the cave when a white owl flew in front of the cave opening.

Am I hallucinating?

In a moment Thalen heard the noise of a horse and sprang to his feet, grabbing his rapier. Two men riding double emerged from the dark.

"Who's there?" Thalen called softly.

"Commander? It's just me and Jothile," Fedak called out.

"Fedak! Thank the Spirits! Are you injured?"

"Nope, just bone-weary. Charcoal took a sword thrust, and the old boy died on me a little ways from the battle site. I tried to tramp to the Gold Creek rendezvous. Then that there owl led me to Jothile. He was just sitting—stock-still—on Skillet. He's not bleeding, but he's not right in his head, sir, so I brought him here. Can you do anything for him?"

Thalen and Fedak assisted the other cavalryman down from the horse. Jothile, who had earlier survived a sword slash across his neck and who fought the fake Magi so bravely, appeared to have been traumatized by the woro attack. He mumbled incoherently and trembled violently. Thalen wet his own shirt and wiped the sweat and dust from Jothile's face with soothing words.

The noise and activity roused Cerf from his deep sleep. He mumbled to Thalen, "There's a brandy sack in my bag," and turned over. Thalen coaxed Jothile into several long swallows. His shaking abated, but his eyes still darted around fearfully, and he kept spouting gibberish. Thalen took a swig of the brandy himself and lay down next to Jothile, trying to calm him by holding him close, as one would a child.

Morning brought them welcome light to tend their patients. Fedak and Dalogun scoured their immediate surroundings for any nearby threats and whatever food they could find, bringing in armfuls of wood sorrel, both greens and roots, to boil for a bitter tisane and scant mouthfuls of food. Kran and Wareth stirred and woke up several times, though Kambey sprawled without signs of life.

Then, in the late morning, three Raiders from the Gold Creek rendezvous—Tristo, Eli-anna, and Eldie—appeared, leading six spare mounts. One of these riderless horses was Balogun's Anise, and another was Skylark's little gray filly.

"No one else with you?" Thalen asked, horrified.

The Mellie girls couldn't look at him.

Tristo whimpered, "No one else *here* with you?"

Thalen counted the missing on his fingers. Nollo, whose baritone lifted their ballads; Cook, the heart of the troop; Balogun, so cruelly young; Eldo, the girls' wry brother; Pemphis, the new healer with gentle hands; Ooma, so fierce with her knives; Gentain, so skilled with the horses and so steadfast about avenging his daughters; and Skylark.

"Let's try to piece facts together," said Thalen. "What did you see? Who may still be alive?"

They talked through their separate experiences of the chaotic battle and matched the horses who had escaped with their missing riders. The Mellie girls had seen a wolf spring at Balogun. Adding everything together, Thalen realized that no one had witnessed Pemphis, Nollo, Eldo, or Skylark fall.

"It doesn't matter," Cerf interrupted bluntly after a few minutes. "It doesn't matter whether you saw them go down or not. It doesn't matter how far behind you others were riding. If we left them alive on the field, they're dead by now and you know it. The fact is they're all gone, or they'd be here. If they'd escaped with minor wounds, they'd have made it here by now."

"Maybe . . . maybe someone's horse bolted or died and they're on foot like Fedak was. . . ." Dalogun clutched at hope.

"I'm sorry, son. They would have tramped here by now," said Cerf with remorseless logic.

Dalogun began sobbing, and Cerf, with the familiarity of his years as a father, draped his arm over the young man's shoulder. Thalen walked to the back of the cave where the small spring tinkled down, wondering how Dalogun could cope without his twin. The thought of being sundered in two was so painful that Thalen had to brace himself against the rock to keep standing. He put his head in the stream, then held out his cupped hands to collect more water, splashed his face, and retied his hair band.

This is no time to wallow. We can grieve later. If we'd stayed at home in the Free States we might all be dead too.

"Raiders, gather round." Thalen waited until they arranged themselves in a rough circle just outside the mouth of the cave.

"Though you fought so bravely, we lost so many yesterday. I led you into a disastrous trap. I can never atone."

Cerf glared at him and spoke through clenched teeth. "We do not blame you for bewitched wolves. You're not expected to foresee every magic ruse."

Eldie had shaken Wareth awake. He was currently lying on his good side with his head cushioned on her thigh, but at least his dulled eyes were open. "What's your plan, 'Mander? Out with it."

"All right then," Thalen sighed. "We have wounded, no food but a little aurochs and horse jerky, and no way of getting supplies. My plan—such as it is—is to send you back to Needle Pass. Once you're on the other side, surely the Mellies will help; they'll see you to the harbor at Metos. Sooner or later a boat from the Green Isles will evacuate you. We have in large part accomplished our mission here. At any rate, the way things have turned out, we can fight no more."

Tristo asked, "Why'd you say, 'send *you*'?"

Wareth sighed. "Because Thalen doesn't plan to retreat with us. He's going to hunt for Skylark."

"Is that true, Commander?" Tristo asked.

Cerf compressed his lips, and his eyes sparked. "What the fuck!? You're our commander. You can't *abandon us* to go look for her body. She's dead—she must be dead."

Thalen rounded on Cerf. "She's not dead! The birds are still helping us. The owl that led Fedak here indicates—"

Eldie put her hand on Thalen's forearm, interrupting his anger by pointing to a high branch on a nearby fir tree. Two hawks perched there, looking down on the depleted force. Their yellow eyes withheld the information that Thalen longed for, but clearly they still watched out for the Raiders.

"See?" Thalen's voice came out as almost a snarl.

"All right," said Cerf, spreading his hands. "*She*'s alive. I don't know how. Maybe the Oros took her captive. But look at your responsibilities." The healer's glance included the group around them, including the three with physical injuries and Jothile, who sat to the side, rocking himself and making crooning sounds, with his arms hugging his curled-up knees.

Eli-anna spoke out loud. "My brother?"

They were all too heartsore to react to the unprecedented event of hearing her voice.

"I don't know," Thalen admitted. "There's a chance that he lives too. Maybe instead of executing captives, the Oros wish to question them about our identities and tactics."

"Nollo turned around, riding back toward Skylark and Eldo. He might . . ." Eli-anna gave her unused voice more air.

"This may be a fool's mission," Thalen said, inclining his head toward Cerf, "but I will not retreat and leave Raiders behind." The steel in his voice indicated that he would brook no argument.

"I will go with you," said Eli-anna. "Eldie can lead the wounded home."

Thalen closed his eyes a moment while relief warred with guilt. "I cannot deny that I would have a better chance with you than without you, Eli-anna. But I do not want to be responsible for any more deaths."

She folded her arms with a stubborn look on her face.

Tristo said, "I want to go with you too, Commander. I'm not much of a fighter or scout. I'm only half a man. But don't send me away."

Thalen started, "Tristo—"

The boy interrupted. "*Listen to me.* I have no home to return to. I have no craft. Ooma, my last chum, is dead. All I have is my life, and if I want to throw it away, that's my lookout, not yours!"

"You have more friends, and you know it," said Wareth. "Tristo, won't you come with us?"

The boy wouldn't look at Wareth.

"I too volun—" began Cerf.

But Thalen glared at him and cut him off. "Shut it. Not a chance. How can you even think of it? The wounded need you."

Rubbing his beard stubble, Thalen said, "All right. This is the plan. Tristo and Eli-anna *only* will come with me. Eldie is in command of the retreat. Cerf is in charge of what the wounded need. Eldie, this means you will have to talk to Cerf. I assume you will do so?"

She nodded, rather than speak out loud, and Cerf snorted through his nose.

They picked through all the horses' saddlebags and divvied up weapons (including some much-needed arrows), water bags, food, and anything else of use they could find.

"You'll need hats to cover up your brown hair," said Cerf. "What happened to your hat?"

"I don't know," said Thalen. "I didn't even realize it was gone until just now. Damn, I loved that hat. Adair had good taste, and that hat saw me all across this journey."

"Here," said Dalogun, "see if this cap of Balogun's will fit you."

When Thalen spotted Literoy's fife, he clutched it tightly and put it amongst his things. In Nollo's saddlebag they found a letter; Wareth asked for it and stuffed it inside his own coat.

"Commander, look at this!" Fedak had a small, heavy purse in his hands.

"What is it?"

Fedak turned it over into his palm. Jewels tumbled out: diamonds, rubies, emeralds, and sapphires, all intricately cut into many facets.

"Where did you get this?"

"From Sandy's saddlebag."

"Who rides Sandy? Wasn't she Vatuxen's favorite? Who's been riding her lately?"

"She showed up alone at the creek," said Tristo.

Cerf pushed closer. "Pemphis rode Sandy; she was faster than his original mount. Let's see what you've got there. Where did he get this kind of treasure? I thought he was an apothecary from the Green Isles whose family came from Jutterdam."

Thalen shrugged and poured the jewels back into the pouch. He had too much to worry about to care about dead stones. "Here, Cerf. Take these. Maybe you can locate his family someday."

As they waited until dark they tried to rest. When they couldn't sleep the Raiders cleaned, oiled, and sharpened their weapons. Thalen spoke to Eldie about the route and offered her his maps, but she indicated that she had the landscape memorized.

Eli-anna's horse was limping, so she decided to switch to Sulky Sukie. Dalogun roped together all the spare horses. Eldie's squad would take them, to switch to fresh mounts to keep the advantage of speed, or send a horse off in the wrong direction to confuse any pursuers. If starvation pressed them, they would butcher a horse for food. But Cinders, usually so docile, refused to be tied to this string. She broke away from Dalogun twice and trotted over to hide behind Dishwater, peering warily at her caregivers from under the arch of Dish's neck.

"Cinders wants to go with you, Commander," said Dalogun.

"Aye, I see that."

Tristo took the horse's part. "Let her come with us. Could be she can lead us to the captives. Or talk to the birds. She thinks she can do something useful."

"Doesn't look as if we have much say in the matter, anyway," grumbled Thalen, though secretly he felt elated, because Cinders's strange behavior was another sign that Skylark still lived.

Thalen knew that the chances he would see any of these Raiders again were slight to nil. If anyone could lead them to safety, though, Eldie could. He told her so, hoping to instill in her the assurance a leader needed. He scrawled a few words of farewell to Quinith and Hake; he gave the letter to Fedak for safekeeping.

"When you make it to Pilagos," he told them with as much confidence and pride as he could muster, "tell the story of what we did here. Tell them how two dozen Raiders brought thousands of Oros back across the sea. How we Free Staters redeemed ourselves from the Rout. How we made common cause with Melladrin and Alpetar. How we burnt down Worship Citadels, killed two Magi, and slew enchanted wolves. Keep alive the names of our fallen comrades, and speak often of their deeds and bravery. Find a song master to commemorate their deeds.

"I am privileged to have ridden with each of you. Your company has been the honor of my life."

Thalen clasped forearms in turn with each of the Raiders who would be heading north: Eldie, Cerf, Kran, Jothile, Fedak, Wareth, and Dalogun. Kambey was submerged in the shadows of poppy juice—they had tied him on his saddle—but Thalen rubbed the top of his bald head, practically the only place not bristling with black stitches. His skin felt hot to the touch—another calamity that Thalen could not forestall. Eldie and Eli-anna embraced for a long moment. Wareth grabbed Tristo in a headlock with his good arm and whispered something to him.

Sundering the Raiders caused a piercing pain in Thalen's chest.

Thalen watched Eldie guide her squad out from their temporary camp until the darkness consumed the last horse's switching tail. Then he turned to what remained of his once-formidable troop: Tristo, Eli-anna, and four mounts. Thalen retied his hair back, checked his sword belt, and whistled at the owls.

They flapped off their perch on a dead tree and angled east.

Tally: 11 + ? (Do Skylark, Eldo, Pemphis, or Nollo still live?)
Horses: 15 returned

I will keep
tallies no longer.

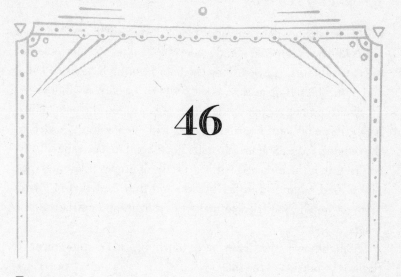

46

Femturan

Skylark lay on the straw and tried to cope with the injuries she had sustained from being interrogated earlier in the day. Her misery undermined her ability to think or to plan.

The yelling, berating Oro officer had slapped her, punched her, and kicked her when she fell down, but he did not really expect that a girl knew anything worthwhile; accordingly, after a while he grew tired and bored, and his blows became less forceful. Still, one of her eyes had swelled shut, punches marked her chest and belly with bruises, the kick that had caught her tailbone hurt like hell, and a stomp on her hand had broken her last two fingers. With each heartbeat, everything throbbed.

From what she could gather, Eldo's interrogation had been a much more serious affair. She had heard him screaming over and over. She guessed that like her, Eldo had refused to provide any information. She thought—she prayed—he was still alive. For his sake she hoped he was unconscious.

She felt so parched now she probably could not have spoken if she wanted to; her mouth had clogged with thick saliva. Her guards neither fed her nor gave her water. Her cell was a small wooden room with old straw on the floor and a bucket for waste. She forced herself to get to all fours, crawled along the floor favoring her busted hand, and pulled herself up as close as she could to the barred window.

She could not see out of the window, but unless she had hallucinated the event, some hours ago a crow had ostentatiously rustled on the window ledge. She stretched her good hand to touch the sill, discovering that the bird had left her a stalk of grapes. Eleven grapes. She stuffed a handful in her mouth, and they exploded in a rush of sweet liquid. She tried to make the remaining ones last a little longer.

A nighthawk must have been watching for her movement. It flew to the outside of the sill.

Your Majesty, the eagle sent one.

Oh, thank the Waters. Can you get me more grapes?

The crows can try to steal from the kitchen in the morning. The eagle has a message for thee: tall leader, a mate, and one-wing fledgling ride horses toward this dwelling of men.

Skylark staggered. Not that she expected to be rescued (though she could not prevent a spark of hope igniting deep within her heart that now perhaps there was a chance), but that Thalen was still alive, that he was trying, that he had not abandoned her and Eldo.

Nighthawk, do you know what paper is?

Nay.

A crow might. Will you send a crow at dawn?

The nighthawk agreed. She also agreed to check on Eldo, and reported back that the human still breathed, though with much noise.

A crow flapped onto the sill shortly after daybreak. Skylark staggered to her feet, the increased swelling from her injuries making it harder to move and the pain even worse than before. The bird looked very bright-eyed and alert, and the sun made its wings iridescent.

Can you get me more grapes?

The women who work in the kitchen put grapes on flat round things later in the day. One brought thee this instead.

It was a pear. A bruised, partially bug-infested pear. It was life itself. Skylark devoured it.

Could you get another one and give it to the man in the other cell?

Yes, that be not hard. Many have fallen from a tree in a courtyard not far from here. Your Majesty, wouldst thou like another too?

The crow started to fly away.

Wait, crow. Come back. There is something else I need.

She was able to explain to the crow that she needed a scrap of paper, one not so big as to attract attention.

She was going to add more requests when she heard a jailer on his way to check on her. The crow flapped away while Skylark threw herself into a crumpled position on the straw. Then the officer who had interrogated her came into the cell, nudged her with his boot, and turned her face up to take a look at her.

"Clean them up," he ordered two jailers. "Their Divinities might want to question them at any time. We cannot take them up there looking like this."

One tall, white-haired jailer with an ugly rash on his face came back with a water bucket and a rag, which he brought into her cell. Skylark grabbed the bucket from him and drank with greedy gulps until he yanked it away from her.

"No, ya don't. I ain't going to fetch another bucket." The jailer moved the bucket outside of her cell door, wet the rag, and threw her the wet cloth. "Wash."

Skylark wiped her face, arms, and hands. The rag came away covered with blood and grime. She threw it back to him as he stood in the doorway; he rinsed it, and she tried again, reaching down her neck and under her arms. If one jailer was supervising her, the other must be supervising something similar with Eldo; he must still be hanging on.

When the water in the bucket turned too dark to be useful, the jailer splashed it in the corner of the cell.

"You look halfway like a nanny goat now," he leered. "Though them teats are awful tiny. When the Magi are through with ya—if there's anything left—it'll be my turn. Ain't had a piece of snatch in a long time. From the back's the way I like it. Saving myself up for ya." He poked his tongue in and out obscenely a few times, then clanged the door shut, laughing.

Skylark felt better for the pear, the water, and the wash. With effort she bit and tore the hem of her shirt until she had a strip of fabric. She bound her two broken fingers to one another. But she trembled at the prospect of being questioned by the Magi. Several Magi, each accustomed to wielding more Power than she had ever touched in her life. They would know her. She would be stripped naked of all her protective disguises—her hair dye and her fictitious names would offer no protection.

Then they would kill her in some spectacularly horrible way, gloating as they ended the line of Nargis Queens. She didn't have to worry about that bastard jailer—the Magi would not even leave her body for him.

The crow returned in the early afternoon. He had another pear and a scrap of paper.

Skylark had already probed her various cuts. The one over her eyebrow was the easiest to make bleed again. She dipped a piece of straw in her blood and wrote two words upon the paper. Then she explained to the crow exactly what he was to do with the message and what he was to convey to the eagle. The crow was quite intelligent; she felt confident he understood.

She was much more worried about the Magi's timetable.

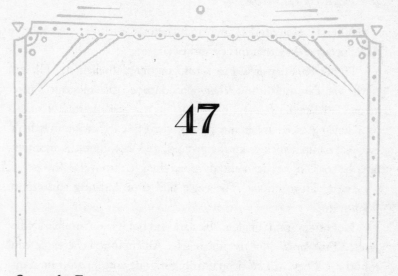

47

Outside Femturan

The birds led the three Raiders straight to the capital city without stopping at the battleground to pick up her trail or examine tracks. Obviously, they knew where Skylark was.

The closer their approach to Femturan, the more populated the countryside became. Thalen would never have made it without Eli-anna; he would have stumbled right into a group of suburbanites or soldiers. Actually, without the hawks leading them by day, and the owls at night, even a scout as skilled as she was would have been hard-pressed to weave around the settlements that surrounded the capital.

They were hiding in some scraggly sea pines on the far side of the Oro army barracks when the eagle glided down out of the sky.

Thalen bowed low. This was the first time since Emerald Lake Camp that he had seen the Lord of the Skies.

The eagle bobbed its head. It stalked a few steps toward him on its ungainly feet and dropped a crumpled piece of paper on the ground. Thalen pounced on the scrap, which contained two words:

"Fire birds."

He read it aloud to Eli-anna and Tristo.

"But what does that mean?" asked Tristo.

"Fire birds. Fire birds. Fire birds," muttered Thalen.

It was Eli-anna, the archer, who decoded the message. "Fire arrows," she said.

Thalen glanced at her and at the eagle. The eagle caught Thalen's eye, picked up a stick from the ground, and took flight. A moment later he coasted overhead and dropped the stick from the sky.

Awed, Tristo cried, "The eagle will drop burning sticks into Femturan."

"Not quite," said Thalen. "Skylark did not write, 'Fire bird.' She wrote, 'Fire *birds.*' Not *just* this eagle. All the birds the eagle can round up. They will *all* drop burning brands onto Femturan. This will create such a distraction, we will be able to slip in and free the prisoners. Oh, how brilliant!"

Thalen thought out loud. "But how do the birds carry burning sticks without the wind extinguishing the flames? And without burning their claws?

"We'll have to create some kind of perch on the arrows, like a cross-stick that the birds can hold in both feet. And the birds can carry the arrows for only a moment. We're going to need a fire source, like a brazier of burning hot coals, practically inside the gates of the city."

Thalen looked at his companions. "We need pitch, tar, oil, or anything like, to wet the end of the stick to catch and keep the flame. And hundreds of sticks or arrows. And nails. How are we going to find these things?"

"Commander, we are almost touching an enormous army base," said Tristo. "The Oros have all this stuff. All we have to do is steal what we need."

Thalen looked at Tristo openmouthed. "What? Just walk right into the barracks, find what we want, and walk out?"

"Pretty much. Sometimes all you have to do is ask. Make up a tale about how Captain Important sent you for those things requested twice already and what kind of show are they running, and they better hand them over double-quick or there'll be hell to pay."

Eli-anna wasn't listening to this exchange. She was staring at the horses. "We fix up baskets to the horses."

Thalen caught her train of thought. "Yes. Move the fire source closer, so the birds can fly short distances. But we need something like insulated metal baskets, so as not to burn our own mounts."

"I can't ask Commander Important for insulated metal baskets!" Tristo protested. He hit his forehead with his palm. "But every neighborhood in Yosta had a garbage dump. We need to find the Oro soldiers' garbage dump. Then you can cobble something together while I cadge the necessaries."

They circled round the barracks complex warily and found the post's garbage easily enough, discovering that it was both enormous and unguarded. Thalen and Eli-anna started combing through for things that would help them. Tristo searched for an Oro soldier's helmet and cloak. After only a few minutes they had secured a variety of supplies.

By this time it was quite dim, though the large full moons provided the light they needed. Eli-anna and Thalen lugged their haul back to where the horses waited in the trees, trying not to clank any metal together. The owls kept watch.

Tristo put on his disguise with a slight shudder of reluctance, because the helmet he'd found was battered, and the cloak torn and soiled. "Wish me luck. I'll be back soon." He started to slip away.

"Wait! Tristo!" Thalen called, hitting himself in the head. "Oros gave up archery. They might be suspicious if you ask for arrows."

"Don't worry, I'll think of something," said Tristo.

Thalen and Eli-anna worked in silence, starting with their saddlebags as base structures, then using their daggers to cut and weave leather and blankets, and adding pieces of discarded armor to hold the coals. They constructed a prototype for gentle Walnut, adjusting their design as they went along. Thalen became so engrossed in the challenge of the work that he forgot to be terrified for the boy.

An hour later, the owls hooted and Tristo returned. Over both shoulders he carried large quivers of arrows. "The Oros don't shoot any longer, but they had kept some arrows in a storeroom. I had to make up a long story about a Mellie captive who had been turned," he said with a bit of an earned swagger. "But without a second arm, I can't push the wheelbarrow here. Can you help fetch it?"

Thalen thumped him on the back and hurried to where Tristo had stashed his wheelbarrow. It had a large, closed metal bucket of hot embers, two buckets of pitch, two more quivers of arrows, and a sack of nails. Thalen wheeled it to their hideout in the pines.

Eli-anna started cutting up all the fabric they had gathered and soaking the pieces in the pitch, then tying the rags around the base of the arrows, just above the fletching. Thalen used the handle of his dagger to hammer crosspiece perches. Tristo scoured the wooded area for more long sticks to add to the arrows he had stolen from the Oros and made a trip back to the garbage dump for more fabric. Thalen kept working on the horses' fire baskets, feeding the embers to keep them hot and burning. They worked through the night, occasionally taking sips from their water bags. They had nothing left to eat.

At dawn, birds started to arrive. Most were crows, but a great many hawks joined the multispecies flock. They gathered in the trees around the Raiders, filling the air with their rustlings and caws.

Thalen took the scrap of paper they had received from Skylark out of his pocket. He had ink and a quill, so he did not need to use blood.

What he wanted to write was this: *I should have said something back at the camp. Now I have a second chance. Please, give me a second chance. I will never let you go again.*

Of course, such a message was impossible in the moment's peril.

Biting the inside of his cheek, he penned on the back of the piece of crumpled paper:

Call Cinders, Dish, Sukie, and Walnut to you —T.

Thalen blew the ink dry and held the piece lightly in two fingers high above his head. A crow snatched it from his hand and flew off in the direction of the walled city.

Keeping to the trees, and moving cautiously, the three Raiders led the horses closer to the main road, which even at this early hour carried walkers and carts moving both into and out of Femturan. Keeping to a ditch, they drew closer to the drawbridge that spanned the moat and led to an ornate gate. The high stone walls loomed over them, and tall towers in the middle of the city sent slanting shadows. Their avian volunteers followed in dark waves that looked like the casual, senseless movements of flocks, but actually represented the mustering of a massive army.

When the Raiders had crept as close to the road as the lay of the land allowed, the eagle joined them. Thalen bowed down to the ground in greeting and then hoisted himself up on Dishwater, his legs angled behind the specially prepared baskets, which were uncomfortably warm but not hot enough to burn either the horse or his breeches.

Then, looking the giant bird full in the eye, Thalen grabbed one of the fire arrows at the ready in his left-hand basket. He dripped its soaked end into the basket of embers in the right-hand basket and it whooshed into flame. Thalen had meant this just as a demonstration, but a large hawk swept down and snatched it from his hand—clasping the prepared perch—before Thalen could extinguish it.

Seeing the birds' eagerness, Tristo and Eli-anna undertook the same procedure. Within a minute a dozen fire arrows had been grabbed from their hands and were soaring in all directions.

In awe, Thalen realized that the birds were not releasing them randomly: they had a definite plan, though he didn't know whether this was their own devising or they merely followed instructions from Skylark. They dropped their fire arrows first in the Oro army barracks and only afterward in the city itself. The Raiders kept igniting the arrows; the birds kept swooping down and soaring off with them.

As it was early dawn, most of the soldiers and townsfolk still slumbered. The Femturan watch was slow to respond to this unimagined threat. By the time alarms and shouts began to sound, small fires had broken out throughout the army compound and the city itself.

Then, abruptly, as if a giant string had just yanked him, Dishwater leapt forward under Thalen, barreling out of their hiding place, carrying Thalen across the wooden bridge at his fastest gallop. The other horses clattered on his heels.

Roused by the commotion, shocked guards raised their pikes, but a phalanx of crows flew into their faces, blinding and disorienting them. In an instant, Thalen and his comrades passed through the gate and around a corner. If the guards sounded an alarm, their shouts were lost in a growing rumble.

Dishwater careened into a city that, with every passing second, transformed from a sleepy metropolis into an inferno.

48

Fire from the Sky

"Magi Two has woken early from a bad dream and wants to question you scum right away. Make yourself purty, nanny goat; I will be back for you in a moment." The jailer threw Skylark a wooden comb and banged the door bar back into place. She heard the sounds of guards fetching Eldo from his cell.

Jerked out of a broken sleep by this message, Skylark was almost overcome with terror. She sat on her straw, hugging her knees and trying to stop shaking.

Mamma, help me. Waters of Life, help me now.

I should have stayed in Slagos. What have I accomplished here? Nothing, except getting myself kilt.

I will be the last of the queens of Weirandale. When I die the Fountains will stop. My country's future will falter. And my death will be at the hands of and give succor to our ancient enemy.

She took a few deep breaths to beat down her initial terror and tried to calm herself.

What would Nana say to me now?

She would counsel me how to behave: hold my head up high and conduct myself like a proper princella.

What would Gardener say?

Something wise—my death will fertilize a new spring.

And Mamma?

Her memories of her real mother were too old to provide comfort. Stahlia, however, would want her to present herself well. She picked up the comb and pulled it through her tangled mats with her good hand.

Skylark was too distracted to see the crow arrive and throw the scrap of paper down into her cell—the crow had to caw at her through the window to get her attention and tell her he had brought her a missive.

But the paper had fluttered into the darkness of the straw. Skylark crawled around on her hands and knees until she felt its texture and then lifted the scrap to the gray light sneaking through the window.

Call Cinders, Dish, Sukie, and Walnut to you –T.

The message coursed through her, bringing a surge of faith even though she did not know how far away the horses were, nor if she had the strength of will left to use her Talent. But at the very least, Thalen had gotten her message and sent her one in return.

She wiped the tears on her cheeks with the back of her hand. She took two deep breaths to steady herself.

Cinders, Dishwater, Sukie, Walnut—horses I love!—wherever you are, near or far, heed my call. Come to me. Bring Thalen to me.

"Tell Us how you got into the Land," ordered a hideous man with a tumor growing out of his scalp. His eyes glowed red and his face showed not a scrap of human sympathy. Eldo tried to turn his eyes away, but the burly guards holding him on his knees forestalled this motion.

Eldo's body barely functioned. Without a doubt the beating had damaged his insides and he was bleeding internally. The Protectors had poured liquor in his mouth to abate the pain and prod him into enough lucidity to attend to the questions. The sloshed liquid dripped down his chest, burning wherever it touched ripped skin.

He mustered the only weapon that remained to him: his insouciance.

"How did I get into your Land? Protectors dragged me in as a slave. I was sitting in Drintoolia, minding my own business, and this officer came and yanked me out of my cell—which was somewhat better than the accommodations here, let me tell you—and made me come with him into Oromondo. Oh, your mountains are kinda majestic, but don't you find them cold and cruel? Kinda like fangs. Believe me, I did not come on my own accord."

A blind woman was not amused. She hissed at him in anger. "Who assassinated Three? Who did you fight with?"

Eldo made no answer.

"WHO ARE THE INVADERS OF THE SACRED LAND?"

Eldo, on his knees before them, straightened himself as much as he could, knowing that this answer might well be his last.

"The Oros are the invaders of Melladrin, my sacred land."

Thalen had drawn his sword—actually, Quinith's grandfather's sword—but so far he had found no occasion to use it. A flock of crows flew in front of him; soldiers and citizens alike dodged to either side to get away from the birds. But the birds' ability to clear the way lessened as the streets became more crowded with desperate people fleeing from the fires.

Zea was asleep in a dormitory for women and children when the screams woke her. When she opened her eyes, nearly the entire roof was ablaze. She jumped from her bed in alarm, but she had the presence of mind to stick her feet in her shoes.

As she escaped the burning building she paused to grab a crying child under each arm.

The Lord of the Skies led the way to the Octagon. A few minutes earlier he had used his sharp beak to peck holes into glass windows on opposite sides of a lower floor. A few more pecks and the glass shattered, allowing him to lead a squadron of hawks straight through the building, each hawk depositing its fire arrow as it flew, so that when they burst out the other side, wings flapping, the entire floor had been thoroughly seeded.

The wooden floors caught fire promptly, and within seconds the central staircase created an updraft, drawing the heat and smoke ever higher, up to the ninth floor.

In the streets around Zea's dormitory, Oro soldiers sought to put out small blazes and tried to keep people from trampling one another.

Zea crushed the toddler close to her chest and gripped the hand of the older child fiercely so as not to lose him in the press. She recognized drawn, bloodless faces in the crowd—cooks, carters, priests, or coworkers. All were terrified, trying to push their way out of the city, trying to escape the multitude of fires.

Sulky Sukie was the strongest and fastest of the Raiders' horses and thus the first to bull her way through the crowds and reach the jailhouse. Eli-anna dismounted, only to find the door locked. She screamed wordlessly and pounded on the door, but to no avail. In that instant, she would have given almost anything to be able to talk to the horse as Skylark did.

But as it turned out, she needed no words and no magic means of communication. Sukie understood well enough on her own; the moment Eli-anna stepped out of her way, she reared on her hind legs and kicked her front hooves into the door. *TA-BANG. TA-BANG.* One hoof broke the wood. *TA-BANG. TA-BANG.* Eli-anna rushed to the door and levered a broken plank out of the horse's way. *TA-BANG. TA-BANG.* More planks splintered. There was room enough for Eli-anna to push her hand through and lift off the latch with her dagger.

Inside the building, she saw nothing but smoke. Part of the roof had caught fire. Eli-anna held her dagger at the ready in front of herself. She ducked her mouth down in the top of her tunic and tried not to breathe. All she could discern was that she stood in a large room and that off to the side stretched a corridor with wooden doors. Suddenly a crow flew in the gaping front entrance, hovering in front of Eli-anna, beating his wings to stir the air a little. She followed the path of clearer air. The bird led her to a cell in a far corner that had a wooden crossbar holding the door closed. Eli-anna lifted the crossbar out of its braces.

Skylark crouched on the straw floor where the air was marginally more breathable, wondering if as vengeance for calling in the fire she would suffocate or burn in her cell. When she heard the door opening she tensed her muscles, fearing it was the jailer coming to collect his prize before he fled. In this weakened state, did she have a prayer of fighting him off?

When Eli-anna appeared instead, for a second she doubted her eyes; then she vaulted out into the corridor, colliding with her rescuer. The smoky air brought on a bout of coughing; Eli-anna started to drag her down the hall; Skylark had the presence of mind to break away for a moment, to stoop down to grab Gunnit's hat from the floor of her cell.

Eli-anna led her out of the deserted jail into the chaotic streets. The air here was hot but less close. By this point the growls of the fires had grown so loud that one had to yell to be heard.

"Where is my brother? Is he alive?" shouted Eli-anna.

"He was some moments ago. He must be in there," shouted Sky-lark, pointing to the Octagon. "The Magi are questioning him."

The Octagon had changed from the first time Skylark had seen it. Now, the entire building glowed red. Skylark and Eli-anna raced to the ornate metal doors, but they had melted shut. Even coming within twelve paces, the heat the building gave off was too much to bear. Rescue was impossible; no one would be able to get in or out of that structure.

The Oros didn't stable many aurochs inside of Femturan proper; most lived in paddocks near the Forge or the commercial streets outside the wall. But they kept one small barn inside the city, handy to the Octagon. Embers had set its roof on fire. The terrified au-rochs broke through the walls and stampeded through the streets, adding to the atmosphere of panic and mayhem.

The crowd in the streets near the barn redoubled its efforts to escape, and in an abrupt surge, Tristo lost his seat on Walnut. Seeing the boy fall into the press, Thalen jumped off Dishwater and pulled him to safety in the doorway of a jeweler's shop. He'd managed to keep the boy from being trampled, but now they were both afoot.

"Hold on to me!" shouted Thalen. "We follow the horses. They'll be heading toward Skylark." Tristo laced his right hand through Thalen's belt.

Thalen looked around at the throngs with dismay. He had thought of fire arrows as a distraction; but they had set the whole city ablaze. Would all these people get to safety?

· · ·

Skylark pulled Eli-anna away from the glowing Octagon with both hands locked around her waist.

"It's no use; we have to mount up. You must save yourself. Eldo would want you to!" She managed to turn Eli-anna to make her face away from the glowing building. "I *command* you to mount up!"

Eli-anna allowed Skylark to push her against Sukie, who, fighting all her natural instincts to flee, had waited for the Raiders, pawing the ground. Eli-anna reached her arm down to pull Skylark up behind her; but Skylark shook her head. She forced her bruised and cut lips into a whistle and was answered by a neigh as Cinders materialized out of the smoke. Sparing her broken fingers, Skylark laboriously pulled herself into the saddle. Despite her pain and fear, she experienced a moment of profound rightness, being back on Cinders's saddle, and the little filly capered with joy.

We found thee! shouted Cinders in her mind.

What a good girl you are! To brave the fire for me!

Magi Two forced herself not to breathe. When the smoke had begun pouring up into the Fire Room, everyone else had started shouting at guards, choking, and coughing. By contrast, she had walked straight over to Four's cradle and lifted up the babe from the cradle's ornate confines. Then she had climbed up the last spiral staircase, the one that rose out of Pozhar's Deathless Fire. She had a few bad moments, fumbling with the latch of the trapdoor while holding the bundle, but having been sightless for many years, she had long since stopped panicking over such obstacles.

Finally, she unhooked the latch. The door hinged open, slamming backward against the floor, and she awkwardly clambered out onto the parapet level. The fresh air that the trapdoor opening allowed into the Octagon did not help her fellows; in fact, it fed the flames. She heard the interior floors collapsing, one on top of the other.

But she had one more thing to do before she herself could join the Eternal Flames. She felt the presence of Power. She muttered, "The witch's spawn. She is here. She is here."

From his camp in the Iron Valley, General Sumroth looked glumly at his troop's herd of aurochs and concluded for the fifth time that morning that it was no use changing mounts because they all had the same raised bony spines. All of a sudden, the ground beneath his feet shook. The aurochs bellowed in fear and lurched in several directions, wanting to stampede but uncertain of which direction to run.

"Look, sir," cried a first-flamer, pointing. "At the volcanoes."

Sumroth glanced west toward the mountains. They had been restless this last week, sporadically emitting puffs of dark smoke and clots of red-orange, and everyone had watched them uneasily. But all of a sudden they burst into full eruption: lava shot skyward first from FireSky, then FireThorn, and finally FireMount, viscous orange liquid boiling high above the peaks, then splattering back onto the rock and sliding down the mountainsides. The edges of the mountains' craters cracked, and rocks the size of sheep were tossed in the air by the volcanoes' force. Black-and-gray smoke roiled above the peaks. The ground beneath their feet continued to tremble.

Pulling himself out of his awe, Sumroth shouted, "Men! We'll have to evacuate civilians from the area. Fûli for certain, and mayhap Wûnum too. Where is the damn trumpeter?"

"General, sir, we're surrounded!" shouted a fifth-flamer, pointing in the opposite direction and displaying far too much panic for his rank.

Sumroth whirled around and gazed east. Black smoke billowed up into the sky, smothering the sunrise.

"Something the Magi have cooked up?" asked the officer, with a quaver in his voice. "A show of their awesome Power in answer to the eruptions?"

"No, I don't think so," said Sumroth, pursing his lips in worry. "The coast lies that direction." Reaching a decision, he said, "Fifth-flamer, you stay here with a battalion to aid civilians escaping from the lava runs. The rest of the army, we will ride to Femturan. Sound the trumpets."

After five minutes of frantic struggle against the flow of desperate city dwellers, at last Tristo and Thalen broke free of the press, which thinned as they neared the hotter city center. They saw Dishwater ahead, pacing nervously because his way was blocked by a collapsed building, but Walnut was nowhere to be seen. Beyond the rubble, Thalen gaped at an awesome sight: the metal Octagon glowing red like a furnace.

Thalen forced Tristo to mount up behind him on Dishwater, slicing a length of Dish's reins to tie the lad securely to his waist. Then they reversed course and turned down a side street. From his height, over the heads of a tightly packed, heaving crowd, Thalen spotted Eli-anna riding tall on Sukie. Scanning the areas around her, he spied another figure on a smaller horse. It had to be Skylark!

But the fleeing people milled too close together, barring Dishwater from moving closer. Eli-anna saw him, gave him a thumbs-up, and pointed toward the city wall. Thalen waved his hand that he understood.

As the crowds became more tightly packed and all progress slowed, more of the Oros noticed the horses. Whether or not they noticed their riders were interlopers was unclear, but some men tried to unhorse them. Eli-anna used her dagger. Cinders bit and kicked people who got too close.

A mother lifted up a small child to Eli-anna. "Save my girl!" she screamed. "Save my daughter!" Eli-anna grabbed the child without thinking.

Laying about him with the flat of his sword, Thalen was able to keep the Oros from seizing Dish, and gradually they made progress, leaving behind the city's blazing center and approaching Femturan's periphery.

As they picked their way forward, his mind never ceased strategizing. The drawbridge was no longer an option. It would be too tightly packed, and dark-haired, mounted Raiders would be too conspicuous. Thalen started scanning the city wall for a weak point that might have succumbed to the fire. They only needed a small gap; then the horses could jump or swim the moat.

When he looked behind he could see that Eli-anna was following his lead. So too was Skylark. Thalen felt light-headed with anxiety and with the dawning of hope that he might have been able to rescue her after all. That alone would justify this destruction.

Smithy, Pozhar's human Agent, caught Walnut's reins. He regarded the horse with suspicion, knowing that a healthy horse, running loose in the city, connoted something terribly amiss.

He felt a tug on his sleeve and turned round, recognizing General Sumroth's wife, Zea, by the number of jewels in her left ear.

She knew him slightly; at least she knew of his deafness. She mouthed the words carefully so that he could lip-read.

"Smithy, you will assist me and these children."

"Aye," he replied in his uninflected cadence. He helped her to mount, then lifted the children up to her.

He spied two more of Pozhar's children in the crowd, about to be trampled. He bulled his way through the mass, grabbed them in his strong arms, and handed them up to the general's wife. She tied the youngest to her in her shawl and gave the toddler to the older boy to hold. Smithy pointed the horse toward the bridge over the moat and gave its rump a ringing slap.

Then Smithy turned back toward the worst of the conflagrations to see if he could rescue any more children.

Abruptly the thoughts of the Lord of the Skies rang in Skylark's mind, *Art thou injured, Little Majesty?*

I am saved, thanks to you, eagle. Can you lead us out of this fire and out of this city? Away from the crowds?

One will show the commander the way. Then one must fly to cleaner air. One must get the soot off one's feathers.

He flew to Dishwater and led their procession several streets north. The crowd thinned here. Sukie and Cinders began catching up to Dishwater.

Dishwater picked his way over a pile of smoldering wooden shards and tumbled bricks. A building had collapsed and had brought down with it a section of the city's defensive wall. Ahead, Thalen saw a gap wide enough for two horses riding abreast. Threading the opening, Thalen and Dishwater perched just on the verge of the moat. When Thalen glanced left he saw hundreds, if not thousands, of citizens and soldiers clumped half a league south of his position, where the drawbridge must be.

Dishwater bobbed his head, taking the measure of the moat. The water looked dark and foul, as if all the metals that had polluted the streams and all the refuse from the city had flowed into this saltwater estuary. Here and there an oily slick on top of the water had even caught fire.

Thalen wanted to wait for Eli-anna and Skylark, but Dish had had enough of the fire and the heat; when his rider was inattentive he fought for his head and leapt the moat. Thalen needed to rein him in hard on the other side to keep him from putting more distance between himself and the blaze raging across the thin strip of water.

Eli-anna found the same gap in the wall and emerged. Sukie was an even stronger jumper than Dish and needed no urging; Eli-anna flew over in an instant. She gently set the Oro girl-child down on the ground and rode over to Thalen.

"Your brother?" he asked.

Eli-anna shook her head.

Skylark emerged from the smoke. Thalen got his first real look at her. That ragged cap, the cap she had worn when he first laid eyes on her, covered her hair. One eye had a terrible shiner. Her face was smeared with blood, bruises, and tear-tracked soot. To him, however, she had never looked lovelier. She smiled at him across the moat.

Short-legged Cinders needed a good running start to clear the barrier. Skylark turned the horse back a few paces to give her the room to gain speed.

On the parapet, which was so hot it scorched her feet, Magi Two finished her Incantation of Fire. She required some matter to change into a fireball. She had nothing else available except the babe in her arms. That she was half-changed into a Magi aided the transformation. Magi Two did not aim the fireball; she could not see. She merely ordered Power to seek Power.

. . .

The fireball came rocketing through the sky just as Cinders hovered midleap over the moat. It struck Skylark in the back. She screamed once; then she tumbled off her horse into the dark water.

Cinders lost her stride; her hooves struck the bank, the rear of her body still in the water. Eli-anna jumped off of Sukie, ran to Cinders's bridle, and, with an energy surge that doubled her strength, managed to pull the filly up the bank.

Thalen and Tristo dived in the opaque water where the knit cap floated and searched frantically for Skylark. Their stretching fingers touched nothing in the dark water. They raised their heads out of the water to look. They saw no bubbles, no sign of her. Heaving themselves out of the moat, they desperately ran along the bank, following the moat in both directions, peering into the opaque blackness.

"Cinders, where is she? Find her! Cinders, please, you must be able to sense her!" Thalen pleaded. The horse didn't respond to him; she seemed to be in shock.

Skylark was gone.

49

Moot Table

This was only the fourth time that Gardener had been transported in his sleep to Moot Table.

Though blind in his real life in Slagos, at Moot Table Gardener could see with preternatural clarity. His sleeping garb transformed into the vestment that Vertia had chosen for him—a robe of intertwined vines studded with emeralds gleaming in blazing sun—which, absent real weight or materiality, floated easily around him in the constant, gentle breeze, smelling of greenery. He feasted on the colors and shapes, as if his vision had awoken from a long and deprived slumber. He gazed up at the sky of the deepest blue and focused for a long moment on the rolling waves that lapped around their tiny island in all directions. Even the slate beneath his feet, gray and orange, was like a miracle of color.

Gardener recognized Sailor from the time before. His fellow Agent was an elderly, wizened man dressed all in sea-gray, with an odd, foam-white hat and a cape resembling a silver fishing net studded with tiny, translucent jellyfish. Sailor nodded his head in mutual acknowledgment.

Looking about him, Gardener identified the other six figures by the insignia their Spirits had chosen. Saulė's Peddler wore golden bells in his yellow hair that tinkled faintly, and a short cape of hammered gold hung from his shoulders. Ghibli, the Spirit of the Wind, termed its Agent "Hunter"—there stood a young woman dressed in brown hunter's boots and leggings, carrying a bow and quiver and wearing a triangular hunter's hat, only this one boasted a magnificent, trailing, magenta-colored feather, which Ghibli's breath made float out horizontally behind her even though it stretched as long as a rosebush was tall. 'Chamen, the Spirit of Stone, arrayed its Agent, Mason, in a charmed robe of suspended marble dust, the tiny particles shimmering as brightly as any jewels.

The previous times Gardener had attended a Moot, a shy and tall man had served as Nargis's Water Bearer; now an older woman robed in blue, with a long white sash, carried the flat golden bowl, spilling small rainbows as she moved.

Restaurà's Healer played the role of host in this dreamscape, bowing a welcome to each Agent in turn. Unlike the rest, Restaurà did not assert Power through resplendent garb; instead, this Spirit chose to display its values through robing Healer in the robust nakedness of the perfectly healthy human body. The current Healer was a woman of at least forty summers, not overtly beautiful, but sporting lustrous skin, sparkling eyes, glowing cheeks, and the shimmering lilac hair of the people of Restaurà's protectorate, Wyeland. Healer was clothed only in her long hair and a loincloth of lilac silk.

One Agent stood apart from his seven associates, who had formed a loose circle. This was the representative of Pozhar, the Fire Spirit. Smithy wore chain mail that stretched down to his ankles, forged of rings of copper, silver, gold, and platinum. He carried metal tongs. Gardener recalled that the earlier Smithy was very similar in physical type: a tall and broad man of great physical strength. And like the former Smithy, this one bore a contemptuous grimace and distanced himself—in every way—from the others. With his inner vision, Gardener understood that in his actual life in Oromondo the Smithy was as deaf as he himself was blind.

Healer said, "I bid you welcome, fellow Agents, to Moot Table. The Spirit Nargis hath summoned us this late dawn when most of us would normally already be awake and about our day's tasks. Water Bearer, will you explain the cause?"

Water Bearer looked frightened and uncertain. Gardener smiled at her encouragingly, while the others waited through the pause with neutral, respectful miens.

Water Bearer stepped into the middle of the oval flat rock, wet her lips, took a deep breath, and began to speak.

"Thank you, my illustrious lords and ladies. I am but lowborn. But I serve my beloved Nargis, Spirit of Water, who will help me speak to you."

"Water Bearer," interrupted Sailor, "you are new to these meetings. Nearly all of us are lowly in life, and certainly in comparison to those we serve—that is why our titles are so commonplace. We are not lords and ladies; the magic raiment that dazzles your eyes belongs not to us but to our Principals. So speak your brief with good cheer. Lautan has ever borne a fondness for Nargis, and we will listen with a willing heart."

This interruption, which Gardener wished he had had the presence of mind to make (for how could plants grow without sweet water?) helped steady the trembling Agent.

"I thank you, kind Sailor," said Water Bearer, straightening her back.

She began again. "As you know, the Nargis heir has lived in exile from Cascada for many years. This is not the concern nor fault of any of the Spirits, but primarily because of internal strife amongst her people. Nargis will deal with this problem in the ripeness of time."

Mason sighed. "'Chamen too has seen this sort of discord in Rortherrod in years long past. The greed of men for status, power, and riches is a festering poison not easily counterbalanced, even by Spirits.

"By the by, Water Bearer, when this business at hand is concluded, I must speak with you about a Stone of 'Chamen's that is still missing and must be returned forthwith."

"I know naught of any Stone, but Mason, sir, I will be pleased to hear of the matter," answered the Water Bearer. She bit her lip. "Where was I?"

"The ripeness of time," prompted Gardener, who perceived that the novice Agent had memorized her petition and now needed help getting back on track.

"Indeed. However, 'tis not the problems in the realm that prompted Nargis to request this Moot. No. Nargis wishes to call out another Spirit for interfering in Weirandale's line of succession—indeed, for trying to wipe out the line of Nargis Queens."

Everyone stole a glance at Smithy. He stood tall; his grimace deepened; his face darkened; he tapped the metal tongs he held in his hand against his chain mail; but he did not choose to speak at this moment.

"Pray, continue," said Healer. "This is a serious charge to make. Although Sailor has already spoken of a long-lasting alliance, some of us will weigh the case with an open mind."

Water Bearer spoke again. "Thank you, my lady. An open mind is all that Nargis desires.

"This is what has happened: the Nargis heir traveled to Oromondo to seek vengeance for the death of her mother, Queen Cressa, dearly beloved of Nargis. Vengeance she sought and vengeance she attained, through her Talent, her own strength of character, and through working with other mortal men and women. But at the moment of her triumph, Pozhar did most unjustly smite her down, seeking to destroy not only one enemy, but through this act, the nation of Weirandale, Nargis's chosen homeland."

By the time she finished this recitation, tears ran down Water

Bearer's face, though she mastered herself enough to hold in any sobs.

Gardener was stunned by this news—Kestrel? Dead?

Hunter was always unpredictable. Like her patron, the Wind, she wafted restlessly from one position to another. At this moment she set herself against Water Bearer. "Let me understand the facts of the case. The Nargis heir was inside Oromondo, Pozhar's protectorate, correct? She used her Talent to destroy Pozhar's Magi, did she not? How then, can you claim it unjust—"

"She was a sneak, a trespasser, a meddler, a murderer!" Smithy interrupted Hunter. He did not join the others' cluster, but his voice was so loud he did not need to be close for them all to feel his fury. "She used the Powers granted her by Nargis to murder all—*every single one*—of Pozhar's faithful Magi! Pozhar's revenge is justified, many times over."

Gardener broke out in a voice filled with pain. "But Kestrel was only there because the Magi had meddled in the internal politics of Weirandale. And because the Magi had used Pozhar's Powers to kill her mother and her father. The woman had just cause to take the fight to Oromondo! Besides, Pozhar replaces Magi at his whim and will. But Kestrel! She is the one and only, irreplaceable, favored by Vertia and under Vertia's protection. To smite Kestrel down is to offend not only Nargis but my Spirit as well!"

Smithy sneered at Gardener's distress. "Another Agent, another Spirit, who has fallen in love with a particular human, and who is biased against Pozhar and my Spirit's people! You are all in league against Us. This Moot is a mockery of justice and reason!"

Holding up her hands, Healer tried to intervene and calm the high emotions. "'Tis true, Gardener, that many actions have tangled causes, going back through endless years of time, and we pull on one string only to find it caught on several more. In good time we will consider all the factors. Nonetheless, we must concentrate, as much as possible, on this present circumstance."

Sailor said, "Pray excuse me, Healer. The present instance has been dealt with. Lautan the Munificent has taken steps to preserve the line of Nargis Queens. At least for the moment."

Water Bearer gave a little cry of joy. This information also made Gardener's heart leap, but infuriated Smithy, who ran into the middle of the group, roughly pushing aside Water Bearer, sending wave after wave of small rainbows overflowing her bowl and cascading around her. A crown of flames burst on Smithy's head.

"What?" he roared. "Why, you interfering, old blowfish! What right had your Principal to interfere with Pozhar's mighty wrath?" He swirled his tongs in a tremendous arc and struck Sailor a blow on the head.

Sailor fell in a crumpled heap.

Gardener stood rooted to his spot with shock, but Healer rushed to Sailor's side in an instant, murmuring an incantation. Mason helped the startled Water Bearer regain her feet. Hunter slipped an arrow in her bow, though for the moment she aimed it at the ground.

"Why, you disgraceful bully!" snapped Water Bearer, quivering so violently that rainbows spilling from her bowl piled up around her ankles.

"Stop! Stop!" ordered Peddler with authority. Gardener, for one, regarded Peddler as first among equals, but that may just have been because of how much Vertia treasured the sunshine.

"We must not have such discord here," Peddler continued. "We will reason together. Set aside thy tongs, Smithy."

Smithy did not move or speak. Hunter, her eyes locked on Smithy, broke the silence. "I will set aside my wrath, but I will take the floor now. I might have been inclined to side with Pozhar in this instance, for to Ghibli, the facts of the case do not favor the Weirs. And We—unlike others I could mention"—she scowled at Sailor and Gardener—"have no favorite alliances amongst the Spirits. We flow this way or that. Fire and Wind have often worked together to spread the healthy flames that scour overgrowth or filth, just as we work with Vertia to disperse pollen. But today We will not ally Ourselves with those filled with anger and destruction."

Through Healer's ministrations, Sailor's cloven skull had reknitted, but Gardener, whose inner vision give him a keen sense of the strength of a life force, knew that this man would soon join Lautan's kingdom under the sea.

Healer stood up beside the injured Sailor, her plump lips scowling. "What my sister Agent Hunter says goes for Restaurà as well. Smithy, you have desecrated Moot Table by *shedding blood* upon a sacred dreamscape."

As he laughed harshly, Smithy's flames grew ever higher, emitting a crackling noise. "Don't pretend, you puling hypocrites, that you would have *ever* given this case a fair hearing. You have always been in league against Us. What succor have you given to the suffering people of Oromondo, afflicted by decades of blights? All of you; aye—even you, Hunter—have worked with Pozhar only when it suits your own needs! Oh, you all want Our Flames to warm you when the cold bites or to cook your food, yet always you strive to hem in and curtail Our reach!"

Smithy twirled in a circle, pointing his tongs at each of them. "But you all serve Spirits of *weakness*; only Pozhar the Powerful truly reigns supreme. Pozhar challenges all of your Principals!"

"A Spirit of weakness, you say?" cried Mason, incredulous. "When you stand on the very stone that 'Chamen created? When 'Chamen's mountains hold your hottest volcanoes within their mighty breasts?"

"Have a care, Smithy," Hunter threatened, her tone dripping icily. "The Wind that fans flames can also blow them out."

"Do you threaten me?" yelled Smithy in disbelief, and his tongs glowed red-hot.

He continued, pointing the glowing tongs at each Agent when he named them. "Sailor, have a care, for your ships burn like kindling. Have a care, Mason, for each blow of your hammer can send a spark that lights a flame! Have a care, Gardener, for your beloved woodlands, orchards, and fields blaze up quite readily. Have a care, Healer, for your precious humans also burn, and their fat renders them delightfully crispy!"

"ENOUGH!!!" shouted Peddler, outraged. He clapped his hands, and of an instant the Moot dissolved.

A sunbeam shining straight in Gardener's eyes woke him from this nightmare, and he bolted upright on his pallet in his shed with a yelp, terrified by the horror he had witnessed—Spirits and Agents in open warfare with one another over the fate of one human.

Such a situation was unallowable. Catastrophic. No single person should be allowed to upset the natural order and the balance they sought so hard to maintain.

Better she should die than the Spirits rip apart Ennea Món over one life. He understood this to be true, but he clutched his chest in misery, because he knew Kestrel—root, branch, and bud. Would the young woman with whom he had spent many companionable days never get her chance to flower?

APPENDIX ONE

CHARACTERS AND
PLACES IN ENNEA MÓN

The Spirits

'Chamen, Spirit of Stone

    Agent "Mason," chosen realm, Rortherrod

Ghibli, Spirit of the Wind

    Agent "Hunter," chooses no country

Lautan, Spirit of the Sea

    Agent "Sailor," chosen realm, Lortherrod

Nargis, Spirit of Fresh Water

    Agent "Water Bearer" (Nana), chosen realm, Weirandale

Pozhar, Spirit of Fire

    Agent "Smithy," chosen realm, Oromondo

Restaurà, Spirit of Sleep and Health

    Agent "Healer," chosen realm, Wyeland

Saulė, Spirit of the Sun

    Agent "Peddler," chosen realm, Alpetar

Vertia, Spirit of Growth

    Agent "Gardener," chosen realm, the Green Isles

Countries and inhabitants

Weirandale

THE EIGHT WESTERN DUCHIES (WEST TO EAST)
Northvale
Prairyvale
Woodsdale
Lakevale
Maritima—includes city of Queen's Harbor
Riverine—includes Cascada
Crenovale
Vittorine

THE THREE EASTERN DUCHIES ACROSS THE BAY OF CINDA (WEST TO EAST)
Androvale—contains Gulltown (port city) and Wyndton (country village)
Patenroux
Bailiwick—Barston (major city)

THE FORMER GENERATIONS ON THE THRONE
Queen Catreena the Strategist (deceased)
    Consort: King Nithanil of Lortherrod (abdicated)
Queen Cressa the Enchanter (deceased)
    Consort: Ambrice, Lord of the Ships (deceased)
    Cerúlia, the princella

PEOPLE IN CASCADA, THE CAPITAL CITY
Lord Regent Matwyck
    Lady Tirinella, his wife

    Lordling Marcot, his son

    Heathclaw, his secretary

Besi, a cook

Hiccuth, a stableman

Nana, Water Bearer

Sewel, a royal chronicler

Whitsury, a Brother of Sorrow

LORD REGENT'S COUNCILORS

    Burgn, son of General Yurgn

    Lady Fanyah, formerly Queen Cressa's lady-in-waiting

    Duchess Latlie

    Lordling Marcot, the regent's son (after Tenny's death)

    Prigent, also treasurer of the realm

    Lady Tenny, specializes in diplomacy

    Yurgn, also general of the Armed Forces

WEIRANDALE ARISTOCRACY

    Duke and Duchess of Lakevale

    Lady Dinista, former lady-in-waiting for Queen Cressa

        Lord Retzel, her husband, son of original Lord Retzel

    Duke Favian of Maritima

        Duchess Gahoa of Maritima, his wife

        Hooper, their chamberlain

IN OR NEAR WYNDTON, A SMALL HAMLET IN THE DUCHY ANDROVALE

    Duke Naven

        Duchess Naven, his wife

        Five daughters

    Duke Burdis, duke of neighboring duchy of Bailiwick

Duchess Pattengale, duchess of neighboring duchy of Patenroux

Wilim, a peacekeeper

> Stahlia, a weaver, Wilim's wife
>
> Percia, their daughter
>
> Dewva, friend of Percia
>
> Nettie, friend of Percia
>
> Tilim, their son

Carneigh, blacksmith

Goody Gintie, a midwife

Hecht, Wilim's replacement as peacekeeper

Lemle, Rooks's nephew, Wren's friend

> Rooks, retired/injured soldier

Nellsapeta, a Sister of Sorrow

Alliance of Free States, once a unified country called "Iga," now four smaller nation-states

Fígat—contains Latham and the Scoláiríum

Jígat—contains Jutterdam

Vígat—contains Sutterdam

Wígat—contains Yosta

IN SUTTERDAM (SECOND-LARGEST CITY)

General Sumroth, occupying Oro general

Hartling, a potter and owner of a thriving pottery business

> Jerinda, his wife and business manager (deceased)
>
> Hake, their eldest son (now in Pilagos)
>
> Thalen, their middle son (now in Oromondo)
>
> Harthen, their youngest son (deceased)
>
> Norling, Hartling's older sister

Ikas, a wheelwright

Mother Rellia, an old lady in Sutterdam

JUTTERDAM

Dwinny, a healer, originally from Sutterdam

Gustie, reader from the Scoláiríum

    General Umrat, occupying Oro general who has enslaved
    Gustie

THE SCOLÁIRÍUM OF THE FREE STATES,
LOCATED IN THE TOWN OF LATHAM, REACHED BY FERRY FROM
TROUT'S LANDING

Rector Meakey

Andreata, tutor of Ancient Languages

Granilton, tutor of History

Irinia, tutor of Earth and Water

Hyllidore, porter for the Scoláiríum

Wrillier, innkeeper

    Winka, his granddaughter

THE RAIDERS
THE ORIGINAL SURVIVORS OF THE ROUT

    Commander Thalen

    Sergeant Codek

    Wareth, cavalry scout

    Tristo, Thalen's adjutant, formerly a street orphan from Yosta

YOSTA ADDITIONS

    Kambey, the weapons master

    Cerf, a healer

    Gentain, the horse master

    Adair, a scout, highwayman, and cobbler

    Britmank, cavalry

Cook/Moorvale
> Cookie/Maribel, his wife

Fedak, cavalry

Jothile, cavalry

Kran, swordsman

Latof, cavalry

Literoy, cavalry

Ooma, mother hen to street orphans in Yosta,
knife-fighter

Rowe, cavalry

Slown, archer

Vatuxen, cavalry

Weddle, quarterstaffer

Yislan, archer

MELLADRIN ADDITIONS

Eldie, an archer from Melladrin
> Eli-anna, her sister
> Eldo, their brother
> Tel-bein, their uncle

REINFORCEMENTS SENT FROM THE GREEN ISLES

Dalogun, sixteen-summers-old archer
> Balogun, Dalogun's twin

Nollo, mercenary soldier

Shyrwin, mercenary soldier, Nollo's pal

Pemphis, assistant healer

Lortherrod

CAPITAL CITY LIDDLECUP, CASTLE TIDEWATER KEEP

King Nithanil, abdicated

King Rikil, the current king

Wife and two sons

In the Green Isles

PILAGOS (*largest island and capital*)

Magistrar Destra, head of the government, originally from the Free States

Olet, owner of Olet's Olive Oil and Spicery

Hake, Thalen's brother, relocated

Quinith, reader of Music from the Scoláiríum, relocated

SLAGOS (*second-largest island*)

Gardener, Agent of Vertia

Zillie, owner of the Blue Parrot tavern

Alpetar

Peddler, Agent of Saulė

THE SWEETMEADOW REFUGEES

Gunnit, a nine-summers-old shepherd

Linnsie, his mother

Linnie, his sister (deceased)

Wimmie, his friend (deceased)

Nimmet, his friend (deceased)

Saggeta, Gunnit's neighbor

Joolyn, Dame Saggeta's wife

Addigale, an orphaned baby

Aleen, seven summers old

    Alloon, her three-summers-old brother

Sheleen, four summers old, cousin to Aleen

    Doraleen, her two-summers-old sister

Gramps Dobbely

    Ma Dobbely, suffers from dementia

Aalooka, a woman from a hamlet

Oromondo

FEMTURAN, CAPITAL CITY

The Magi, One through Eight

Smithy, Pozhar's Agent

Chumelle, Sixth-Flamer who occupies the port of Drintoolia in Melladrin

Tulsham, head of the Magi's guard, past champion of the Combats

Zea, Sumroth's wife, works for the Library of Reverence

APPENDIX TWO

NOTABLE HISTORIC QUEENS OF WEIRANDALE
IN CHRONOLOGICAL ORDER

Cayla the Foremother

Carra the Royal

Chista the Builder

Cayleethia the Artist

Carlina the Gryphling

Charmana the Fighter

Cinda the Conqueror

Chyneza the Wise

Crylinda the Fertile

Cashala the Enchanter

Catorie the Swimmer

Ciella the Patient

Cenika the Protector

Chanta the Musical

Carmena the Perseverant

Callindra the Faithful

Cymena the Proud

Chella the Kind

Crilisa the Just

ACKNOWLEDGMENTS

In the years that I worked on this series I incurred debts, large and small, to those who guided, helped, and encouraged me.

I am grateful to Vassar College, which has always valued creative pursuits on an equal plane with traditional scholarship, for travel funds and the William R. Kenan Jr. Endowed Chair.

Throughout the drafting, Lt. Colonel Sean Sculley, Academy Professor and Chief of the American History Division at West Point, generously shared his military, historical, strategic, and sailing expertise. (I drew specialized information from Angus Konstam's *Renaissance War Galley, 1470–1590* and Sean McGrail's *Ancient Boats in North-West Europe.*)

Professors Kirsten Menking and Jeff Walker of Vassar's Earth Science Department led me away from grievous errors concerning world-building.

Stefan Ekman, Professor of English at the University of Gothenburg, took the time to share his unique knowledge regarding fantasy maps.

Professor Leslie Dunn of Vassar's English Department, a Shakespeare scholar, studied my poetry with the seriousness and skill she applies to more exalted works.

Professor Darrell James, who teaches stage combat in Drama, showed me his swords and taught me about their use.

I was fortunate indeed to find Penelope Duus, Vassar '17, who was trained in cartography. She started the map of Ennea Món when she was a senior and has patiently, loyally tweaked it for years. For the final corrections I am grateful to Amy Laughlin of Vassar's Academic Computing office.

A professional editor, Linda Branham, critiqued the first fifty pages. Friends who read drafts—in whole or in part—provided comments and encouragement that kept my roots watered. Thank you for your time, Fred Chromey, Joanne Davies, Madelynn Meigs '18, and Molly Shanley. Feedback from Madeline Kozloff, Daniel Kozloff, Bobbie Lucas '16, and Dawn Freer came at particularly timely moments or was particularly influential.

I tapped Theodore Lechterman for his knowledge of the Levelers (the historical analogue of the Parity Party) and his linguistic skills. Tom Racek '18, captain of the fencing team, helped me choreograph some of the fight scenes.

Rather late in my writing process I was lucky to find a writing partner with whom I exchanged manuscripts. The fantasy author James E. Graham provided irreplaceable assistance by reading nearly all of the series and filling the margins with passionate comments.

Others were kind and patient in giving a novice advice about how to publish in a new field, including Susan Chang (Tor), Alicia Condon (Kensington), Diana Frost (Macmillan), and Eddie Gamarra (The Gotham Group). Without their guidance these manuscripts might never have been published.

My husband, Robert Lechterman, supported me in this endeavor as selflessly as he has throughout our life together. Without him, the appliances would have just stayed broken and I would have subsisted on frozen fish sticks.

Martha Millard—my original agent at Sterling Lord Literistic— knew and delighted in the fact that she was changing my life when she pursued me as a client and sold the series. She has retired and I shall miss her, but Nell Pierce of SLL has now ably filled her shoes.

At Tor my manuscripts fell into the hands of Rafal Gibek (production editor) and Deanna Hoak (copyeditor), who saved me from myself.

My editor, Jennifer Gunnels of Tor, took a leap of faith on a nontraditional debut author, a four-volume series, and a rapid publication schedule. She also found the balance between corralling me when I wandered astray and giving me freedom. "You really need to research X," she would advise, and I would obediently get busy. Other times, when I fretted over whether I should change something, she'd remind me, "It's *your* book, Sarah."

It is my book, Jen, but in a larger sense it belongs to everyone mentioned here, to a dozen others who offered a hand, not to mention the books, films, and teachers who formed me. Except the mistakes and infelicities, which pool around my feet, mewling like attention-mongering kittens—those poor things are mine own.

THE
BROKEN
QUEEN

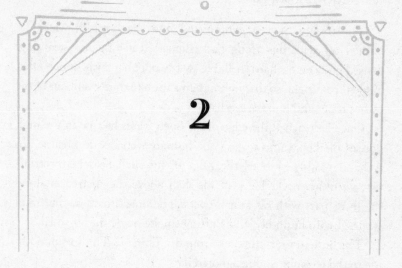

2

In the Sea

Billions of minnows lived and died without knowing anything about the Spirit of the Sea. Lautan didn't hold dominion over all sea life, just the biggest and oldest creatures in its realm, such as the few black terrapins that still lived in Femturan Estuary.

These enormous terrapins had inhabited this salt marsh for centuries, since the port of Oromondo had silted over and become worthless as a shipping harbor. Barnacles crusted their shells; their black curved claws stretched as long as human fingers. Though the mining pollution irritated their eyes and undermined their diet, they built up immunity to the metallic ores' worst effects.

The Eldest of them all, with beady eyes and a patterned shell as big and round as a carriage wheel, waited in the murky depths of the moat the morning of the Conflagration in Femturan. Of course, it was impossible that *he* could have known what was going to transpire: that Magi Two would throw a fireball at Skylark and that she would fall off her horse into the water into *this* exact spot.

A gnarled, old, ugly turtle, *he* could not foresee the future.

Nevertheless, he waited in the dirty murk.

The instant Skylark plummeted into the brackish water, he pushed off with his strong back flippers, catching her steaming, doused body on his hard shell. He swiftly bore her away underwater, hidden from sight, so that in less than a minute they swam out of the moat proper and into the salt bay.

Once he reached the edge of the open water he rose in the high grasses of the swamp to give the human a chance to breathe air. A hand weakly grabbed the ridge of his shell near his protruding, wrinkled neck. He kept his shell above the surface, making the reeds part with his four flippers. The brackish water and mud steamed with humidity, and wafting smoke made the air smell.

The human murmured one sound: "Thirsty." This meant nothing to the terrapin, and he ignored it.

After two hours the Eldest entered the ocean proper, where the sand bottom fell away and gradually cleared of plant life. This was not his territory: the cold currents and waves moved with a force that made him uncomfortable. The weight on his shell had long become burdensome. He yearned for his warm habitat. But he was old. He knew patience.

A small group of sea lions approached with their typical, noisy commotion, sending ripples through the water.

"Urt! Urt! Urt! Urt! Urt! Urt!" they hailed the Eldest. These vocalizations meant nothing to the terrapin, but he was relieved they had finally arrived.

When the terrapin submerged, the human let go. She floated loosely on the surface while a fat sea lion dove underneath and took over as the human's flotation support. His own part played, the Eldest headed back to his mud.

Sea lions prefer to swim in arches, diving and rising. To them, skimming the sea's surface—keeping their backs in the air, the Thin—feels unnatural and awkward. And their black, slippery bodies provided no purchase for the human, nothing whatsoever for her to hold on to.

She be slipping right off, blubber-puss, one juvenile female said to another. *Look out! There she goes!*

Thou gripest, thou taketh her!

Okay! One wilt take her next. See, blubber-butt? Thou gotta keep thy back flat and thou gotta kink thy head a bit, make a wrinkle round thy neck, a handhold for her strange flipper. See? She grabbed on.

Bet she wilt nay stay long.

What wilt thou wager?

Bet thee a whiting.

Agreed.

Although sea lions prefer to hover near their feeding grounds along coastlines, this group, following orders, swam deeper into the ocean, heading away from the lowering sun. The human lost strength in her fingers and slid off to the side again. This time she didn't float, but rather plunged into the colder depths. She didn't struggle, and only a tiny trickle of bubbles surfaced. The eldest female barked an alarm.

Swim beneath the creature, she ordered one of the adult females. *Lift her up to the Thin.*

The human made strange choking noises when the sea lion got her back up into the Thin.

Don't drown me, the human sent.

Not our fault, human. 'Tis bad enough to have to stay on the surface of the Thick for such a queer, misshapen thing as thee. Hey! Do nay grab at one's whiskers!

Something had scorched the human's skin, the sun had burned it further, and instead of providing relief, the night seawater scalded her again with its harsh salt and icy cold.

Burning, she sent to the sea lion.

Tell no one thy troubles. One saw two yummy octopi but one could nay dive to catch them because thou needst the Thin. One's hungry. One has already raised a pup for the year. No one asked for thee.

The stars had come out by the time the group of sea lions, with a chorus of loud exclamations of, "Urt! Urt! Urt! Urt! Urt! Urt!" rendezvoused with the school of dolphins.

"Ee! Ee! Ee!" the dolphins chattered in response.

Where hast thou been, thou stuck-up bigmouths? Didst thou get lost? Didst thou stop to chow down? Take this burden off one's backs, ordered the leading sea lion.

Your Majesty! We be here!

Never mind all the chatter. Got the burden? Good riddance to human rubbish.

The sea lions swam off, barking with relief, and then dived deep, luxuriating in their freedom.

We have thee now, cried the dolphins. *Thou art safe. Dost thou hear us? We will never let thee breathe water. We like air too. We suck it in and blow bubbles with it. Sweet sea air.*

The human made no reply, but she still had life.

Thou art injured, Your Majesty. We will take thee to help. No more fear, no more worries. We be the best. Lautan loves us the most, because we are the swiftest and the smartest.

A few times she woke enough to retch out a gob of seawater.

Well done, Majesty, said the dolphin who was carrying her.

Help me, dolphins, she sent. *I shall surely die without help.*

We know how to help thee, Little Majesty, and we are happy to do it. We apologize for the rudeness of the whiskered flat-faced ones. They have no brains. We call them "shark fodder"—though not when they are about.

What a great adventure we are having! Shall we go a bit faster? Wouldst thou like to try some leaps? Flying be the most fun.

She grabbed onto a dorsal fin for a few minutes, but then her grip went slack.

Never mind, Little Majesty. Thou canst rest. The water lies still as glass tonight. We will ferry thee over rocks and chasms, coral and seaweed, crabs and jellyfish. Some flying fish bounce beside us. We cut through the water cleanly; one's ripples barely foam. The moons hang low in the sky, watching us, making their friendly shimmer-glimmer. Perchance they smile through that little veil of clouds.

Hark! A pod of whales has joined us! They are always pleasant company. They do not compete with us for fish because they eat only krill and shrimp. Be it not rich and strange, to grow so big eating only the tiniest food? Truly, Lautan has the most magnificent creatures. We do nay often see whales. One wonders why they have come. We be better at ferrying thee—thou couldst fall off their backs and the whales wouldn't even know it. (Tell them not, but they be a wee bit stupid.)

Oh! The whales have come to sing thee a lullaby. How nice of them. They love to sing, though not all creatures can hear them. Listen carefully, now.

A dozen massive shapes surrounded the school of dolphins, swimming underwater but nigh to the surface. The females sang their baby-calf comfort songs in tandem, with long repeats.

The moonlit water reverberated with their kind intention as it washed over the human barely clinging to life.

Mother is here,
Sweet little calf.
Stay close to me,
Swim near to me.
In the gray-green deeps.
My tail is strong,
My milk is warm;
Your aunts will watch
So no harm befalls thee,
Beloved of Lautan,
Spirit of the Sea.
Beloved of Lautan.
Both thee and me.